PRAISE FOR
VIRGINIA DeBERRY AND DONNA GRANT

———

FAR FROM THE TREE

———

TURN THE PAGE FOR MORE ACCLAIM . . .

"With sassy dialogue and a suspenseful narrative, this novel whips through its prologue and 23 well-written chapters."
—*Dallas Morning News*

TRYIN' TO SLEEP IN THE BED YOU MADE

"DeBerry and Grant work well as a team, their prose is as seamless as if it were written by one hand . . . the book is a compelling, hard-to-put-down story with endearing, unforgettable characters."
—*Newark Star-Ledger*

"Artfully rendered. They break the McMillan mold, these two, blazing trails not often explored in novels about African-American women. That alone is reason to rejoice."
—*Tucson Arizona Daily Star*

"Enough plot twists and surprises for a season of soap operas . . . it eventually boils down to one affirmative, 'You go, girl' . . . this sisterhood-is-powerful first novel seems a natural for Oprah's Book Club."
—*Kirkus Reviews*

ALSO BY VIRGINIA DeBERRY
AND DONNA GRANT

Tryin' to Sleep in the Bed You Made

Far from the Tree

VIRGINIA DeBERRY
and
DONNA GRANT

St. Martin's Paperbacks

FAR FROM THE TREE

Copyright © 2000 by Virginia DeBerry and Donna Grant.
Excerpt from *Tryin' to Sleep in the Bed You Made* copyright © 1997 by Virginia DeBerry and Donna Grant.

Library of Congress Catalog Card Number: 00-031765

ISBN: 0-312-97785-9

Printed in the United States of America

St. Martin's Press hardcover edition / September 2000
St. Martin's Paperbacks edition / January 2002

10 9 8 7 6 5 4 3 2 1

To the memory of Emma Clatin Hammond, Emma Horne DeBerry, and Emma Williams Cameron, our grandmothers— the roots that nourished our tree

We Gratefully Acknowledge

Hiram L. Bell III: Thank you for lettin' me be myself again . . . and again.—D.G.

Robert L. Gore, Jr., for thirty years of friendship and encouragement, and for never letting me forget how blessed I am, and The Good Doctor, for your persistence. Without it I would have missed much.—VDB.

Lisa A. Nicholas, M.D., for assistance with our medical questions.

Anthony Cofrancesco for his help with information about the Buffalo Public Schools.

Lisa Quarles for her take on being a young, struggling performer.

Andrea Cirillo for her encouragement and advice (XOX-OXO).

Jennifer Enderlin for letting us take our time.

Always, Gloria Hammond Frye, Juanita Cameron DeBerry, and the late John L. DeBerry II for the right stuff.

Alexis, Lauren and Jordan, Brian, Christine and Arielle, the future.

And all our family members and friends whose continuous love and support is surely the grace of the Creator at work.

Prologue

*". . . dwellin' on the past won't
change nothin' now."*

TUESDAY, OCTOBER 1, 1957
PROSPER, NORTH CAROLINA

Wish I never heard of Prosper, North Carolina! Odella Womack sucked on her bottom lip and stifled the sob that rippled
just below the surface. She held a smoky blue taffeta dress in
her arms, hugged it like she hoped it would hug her back as
she tried to shake the flashes of that night in the house on Little Pond Road. The night that haunted her days and robbed
her of sleep. *Ain't nobody ever gon' make me come back to
this no-'count town!*

The floorboards creaked, and Odella shivered as she paced
the narrow space between her cot and the storeroom shelves.
A naked lightbulb hanging from the ceiling cast harsh, hot
light on the cluttered room. She could taste the thick, hot
smell of coffee, old onions, and fried everything—porgies,
chicken, pork chops, and hair—that passed for air in the
rickety, narrow building shared by Pal's Kitchen and Lucille's Beauty Parlor. But she couldn't complain. *If Hambone and Lucille hadn't let me stay here, after . . . after . . . I
don't know what I woulda done.*

Odella could still feel Henry's spit sting her face with each
bitter word he'd spewed. *"I'll get you, gal."* Her half brother
had skinned his lip back against his teeth and snarled like a
cornered, rabid dog. *"You won't know when, but I'll kill you,
and Will too, if I have to. You understand me?"*

Still clutching the dress, Odella sank to the bed and rocked
herself. *It's gon' be awright.* She buried her face in the irides-

cent fabric and caught a whiff of Lester's sweet, musky cologne. Without meaning to she started to hum her part of the harmony they had sung so well together, let the music soothe her for a minute, then suddenly she tossed the dress aside like it burned her to touch it. *What the hell am I singin' about? Lyin' son of a . . .* She turned away, determined to stomp out that fire before it flared up again. *Dreamin' ain't got me nothin' but trouble. I gotta be strong . . . like Mama was.* Odella stood, steadied her rubbery legs. *And dwellin' on the past won't change nothin' now.*

"You almost ready, Odella? Car's all packed up 'cept for your bag." It was ten till dawn, but Will sounded wide awake and raring to go. "You know we supposed to be at the justice of the peace by eight o'clock."

I gotta stop this foolishness. "In a minute!" she called. And with a sigh that said good-bye, Odella hurriedly folded the dress around her shattered feelings and dropped it in the butterscotch leather valise, beside the rag doll her mother had given her so long ago. She ran fingers over the doll's woolly black hair, almost pulled it out of the bag, but stopped. *What do I need with a toy?! I'm about to be Mrs. Odella Frazier.*

That name sounded so strange, like it couldn't possibly belong to her. Odella had never put her name with Will's before, but she'd tried on Lester's many times. It had even tickled her when Lester tacked his first name onto hers and gave her a stage name because he said all hit singers had made-up names. Now, Odella refused to look at the homemade pasteboard sign that was stuck in the pocket of the suitcase lid, but she saw it in her mind's eye anyway. "Sat'day Nite Only. Johnny DuPree. Featuring Della Lester." Those words used to make her heart fly. *We goin' all the way to the top. That's what Lester used to say.*

Odella shook her head to clear her thoughts. *And it wasn't nothin' but a bunch a mess.* "Odella—No—Della—Della Frazier. Mrs. Will Frazier." She said it aloud, as if to convince herself, because that's how it was going to be. *A new name for a new start.*

Odella didn't know how long she'd been staring into the suitcase, but she jumped when one fat teardrop plopped on the bodice of the dress, then another. *How'm I gon' marry this man? I can't even make a biscuit!* Odella wiped her face with the heel of her hand, then closed up the bag and shoved it under the cot because she wouldn't be needing the things that belonged to her old life anymore.

Will's a good man. Strong. Honest. Takes care of things . . . like Papa. Odella rolled her white cotton nightgown and put it in her battered blue suitcase, closed it up, and set it by the door. *Will saved me—twice now.* She straightened the seams of her stockings and stepped into her gray tweed skirt. She used to get up in the middle of the night to rub the silver fox collar of the jacket that went with it. The suit had been a gift from Lester, and she thought twice about wearing it to marry Will but it was the best-looking outfit she had. It made her feel grown. *Grown enough for this?*

At eighteen, Odella had seen enough to make her feel older—some days. Brown as bourbon, she was near tall as most men, with long lean legs, which she happened to think were her best feature. Nobody ever called her mannish, but pretty didn't fit either. She had a strong, square jaw and eyes that turned down at the corners, just a little, making her look sad sometimes, even if she wasn't. But her face came alive when she sang. People were startled when she opened her mouth, and a voice pure as rain and strong as a hurricane filled the room. Odella was imposing, more mountain than foothill, more river than stream; she wasn't the ribbon or the bow or the pretty wrapping paper. Odella was the whole package, she just didn't know it.

"You ain't gone and chickened out, have you?" Hambone called to her from the kitchen on the other side of the dingy flowered curtain where he was getting ready for the first morning customers at Pal's.

"I ain't studyin' you, Hambone!" She propped her hand mirror on the shelf against the red and black Luzianne coffee cans, stooped down and combed through the tight rows of hard curls Lucille had put in last night with her smallest curling iron, so they'd last. They had pretended like it was a regular hairdresser visit so neither one had to face good-bye.

For the weeks Odella had stayed in the storeroom, she'd watched Lucille and Hambone like a hawk. They seemed to be as different as day and a potato, but every spare moment they'd be huddled up together, talking, laughing, acting like they preferred each other's company to anybody else in the world. *That's just how Will and me are gon' be.* She put on her jacket, buttoned it to the top, but didn't allow herself to fondle the dense, soft fur this time.

I know me and Will gon' have a better life than the one we'd have in this town! "I'm ready!" A deep sigh escaped as Odella picked up the blue suitcase, pushed open the curtain, and walked through the doorway.

1

"You can't cut your dresses by my pattern."

"Ma?!" Ronnie leaned against the blue Formica counter and shuffled the hodgepodge of dishes in the cabinet. "Where's my mug?" Even though she'd been away for years, there was something about being in the kitchen at home that made her sound like she was nine years old. She looked over her shoulder at her mother.

Della sat at the dinette table, head in hand, staring into her lukewarm cup of coffee like she was searching for something she'd misplaced a long time ago.

Ma is really out of it. Ronnie had been torn up since she got the call about her Daddy—and getting through this long, sad day had sucked her dry. In between her own tears and grief, she wondered how her mother could act so calm. *Not that she ever goes to pieces. Ma's just strong, I guess.* Ronnie stretched to reach the top shelf and tugged at her little bit of skirt, trying to keep her butt covered. "You know the one, Ma, with the Esso tiger on it?"

Della's expression never changed.

"You mean the Exxon tiger? I haven't seen that cup since . . . maybe since before I left for college, Aunt Ronnie." Niki left the bag of garbage she was tying and opened another cabinet to look.

"There are a hundred mugs here!" Celeste backed against the swinging door and came in toting an armload of platters and serving bowls. "Use one of them!" Her tone was sharp as barbed wire. She set the stack on the counter and examined a gold-rimmed plate. "Humph! Friends call themselves helping you, but these are still greasy, Mother." She looked across the room for an acknowledgment, but Della stayed in her own world.

"Do you mind if I drink *my* tea out of the cup I want to?" Ronnie slid a foil-wrapped pound cake, a stack of paper plates, and a shrink-wrapped fruit basket out of the way and hoisted herself up on the counter. "You know that mug has been my favorite ever since . . ." Ronnie's voice caught in her throat. ". . . Ever since Daddy brought it home."

"Daddy died five days ago and you just showed up yesterday, so don't come telling me about how much some cup means to you!" Celeste rolled up her sleeves, dropped her pearls inside her blouse.

"You haven't seen your sister in a long time, Ma." Niki spoke in a hush as she stepped between her mother and her aunt. "Maybe you don't want to argue . . ."

"I do not need you to tell me what I want, Nicole. Maybe *you* could finish taking out the garbage some time tonight!"

Niki just barely turned her head before she rolled her eyes. "Right, Ma!"

"And you might sit on kitchen counters in New York, but we don't do that here!" Celeste reached in the pantry and snatched the apron.

Ronnie crossed her leg defiantly.

"Fine. Sit there. But I have work to do." Celeste turned the hot water on full force. "Of course, helping out would be of no interest to you."

"Get over yourself," Ronnie barked, then jumped down from the counter. "This has been a hard day, and I'm exhausted. . . ."

"Exhausted?!" Celeste gripped the sink with both hands to keep from throwing the plates at her sister. "You flew in here yesterday like the queen bee, acting like everybody was supposed to stop what they were doing and buzz around you."

"I did not!"

"You have no idea what we've been through this week! All

the planning, the arrangements. Funerals don't just happen!" Celeste took aim and launched a laser beam of anger. "And where were you?"

"I got here as soon as I could!" Ronnie's red-rimmed eyes filled with tears.

"Don't start that again!" Celeste snapped.

The bickering finally penetrated Della's haze. She left her long-ago memories of leaving Prosper at the bottom of her coffee cup and looked up at her daughters.

"You don't understand," Ronnie sniffled. "I didn't see him for so long, and now . . ."

"Whose fault is that? Nobody stopped you from visiting," Celeste snapped. "You barely call. We could all be dead . . ."

"Celeste!" Della fired a warning shot.

"I'm sorry, but it's the truth." Celeste planted her hands on her narrow hips.

"That's a lie," Ronnie sputtered.

"That's enough!" Della's look could have cut glass.

"I . . . I couldn't get here any sooner," Ronnie whimpered.

"Why not? Your father died! Is your so-called *acting* career more important than that?!" Celeste demanded, then sucked her teeth, turned around, and attacked a platter with a soapy sponge. "You might fool other people into thinking you're the dutiful daughter, but I know better!"

"Aw right, both of y'all." Della rubbed her thumb over the chip in her coffee cup. "Everybody's had enough today. The dishes can wait. I'm not plannin' for company tomorrow."

"It won't take me long. You never know who might stop by." Celeste put the wet platter in the dish rack and picked up a bowl.

"I said leave 'em."

"Fine." Celeste wiped her hands on her apron. "I'll go put the folding chairs away."

Della watched her first born storm out of the kitchen. *As headstrong as she ever was!*

The morning she realized she was pregnant, Della awoke to the tippy-tap of sleet against the windows. It was still dark, and the heat wasn't up good when she rolled out of bed to fix

Will's breakfast and his lunch bucket. She lit the oven, popped open a canister of ready-made biscuits. That's when she felt the tickle that started deep inside. At first she felt foolish, wanting to laugh for no good reason. And then she knew.

Will was almost done eating when she told him. He stopped, the syrup dripping from his biscuit, and gave her the biggest, silliest grin she'd ever seen on his face. There was plenty of food in the house, but that night he came in with an armload of groceries because he wanted to make sure his babies ate good.

Della stayed happy the whole nine months, and no matter what people said about carrying high or low, or whether she craved salt or sweet, she knew this was a girl, her daughter. The only thing that would have made her happier was if her own mother could have been there with her, crocheting baby blankets, telling her what it would be like.

Contrary to the horror stories about labor she'd heard from young mothers on the Michigan Avenue bus and grandmas in the Broadway Market, Celeste came into the world in a rush that was over only five hours after it started. However, the bliss ended not long after the baby came. Della was expecting a pudgy, brown cherub, but Celeste was that pinky-beige newborn shade, bald as a cue ball, and all spindly arms and legs. She was almost scared to hold her child, but when the nurse laid daughter in mother's arms, Della felt her heart swell with a new kind of love. As soon as they got home, though, the colic started. No matter what formula Della tried, Celeste puked it up. Her piercing, vibrating cries made Della feel frazzled, but the doctor assured her nothing was wrong; some babies were just fussy. So Della would walk the floor with her, bouncing, singing, whatever she thought of to make it better, but mostly Celeste cried until she fell asleep. By then Della would be exhausted, but she'd put Celeste down on the bed and lie next to her so she could feel her warmth, inhale that baby-sweet scent, play with her fingers and toes, and pray for her to grow out of this difficult stage. But colic led to teething, earaches, and colds, all of which kept Celeste cranky.

As a toddler Celeste didn't care much for cuddling. She'd

squirm out of her mother's hugs, push away from her kisses. Della craved more, and what made it even harder was that Celeste was the spitting image of Della's mother, Annie. Celeste turned out to be that red-brown that people say comes from Indian blood in the family. She had Annie's delicate build, petite, with slim, long hands and feet. Her face was wide at the forehead and cheeks, tapering to a point at her chin, and she had a slow, sweet smile that could catch you off guard when she revealed it. A sliver of brow framed deep-set, old folks' eyes. Della always thought she was too serious to be a child. She'd sit at the table, drawing, with a crayon tightly clenched in her fingers, her forehead furrowed, her mouth tense with attention. Della knew Celeste wore that same expression now.

"Grandma, did you see the hat Miz Godfrey had on at church this morning?" Niki wanted to neutralize the atmosphere. "I think some sparrow is still looking for home." She tied up the trash bag.

"I bet she got that at Dixie Hats about 1962." Della swallowed a gulp of cold coffee.

Ronnie blew her nose on a paper towel. "At least she took it off when she got here. Y'all need to tell her straw is not a fall fashion accessory." Hands still shaky, she took a cup and saucer from the cabinet and turned on the burner under the kettle.

"Katherine wears that hat to everything, weddin's, christenin's, funerals . . ." The word echoed off the sunflowered wallpaper and hung awkwardly in the air.

This time last week, nobody dreamed there'd be a funeral for Will Frazier, least of all Will. He loved to brag about his full head of hair, and he'd happily compare biceps with "knuckleheads young enough to be my *grand*kids." But Della had buried her husband over at Forest Lawn today.

Nobody could get over how awful it was, him being electrocuted, of all things, working on one of the rentals he bought and maintained so proudly for years. There were whole blocks in the Fruit Belt that still held on to their dignity because Will and Della owned houses there. Shorty Mayo, his handyman and right arm, was so broken up he cried until

Della gave in and had the funeral procession drive past the fourteen doubles Will had acquired through the years. Shorty swore Will would rest better that way.

When they got to Buffalo in the fall of 'fifty-seven, Will and Della rented the lower half of a tiny, gray frame house on Emslie Street and stepped on the first rung of the neighborhood ladder. A German family had the upper, and Della and Will had a good laugh about how in Prosper you had to go clear across town to see White people. Right away Will got a good-paying job at the steel plant, and within the year he had saved up enough to buy the house. Almost immediately the Steinbachs moved. Living in the same house was okay, but paying rent to a colored man was another story. Will shrugged it off, mentioned the vacancy at the plant, and easily found new renters. Every year he added a new property, and after three he moved the family up a step to a white clapboard single with forest green trim and a wide front porch on Chester Street in Cold Springs. Whenever he wasn't shoveling coal at the plant, Will was tinkering on one of those houses, painting, repairing, putting out folks who didn't pay or who thought that since they gave him their money order by the fifteenth, most of the time, they had the right to tear up the place.

Ten years in he finally moved his family to the house he'd been driving by to visit ever since he saw a Black family go in the front door. Hamlin Park was a solid middle-class community, home to doctors, teachers, preachers, assembly-line workers, and undertakers. Had been for years. Hard work was the price of admission. Magnificent elms, oaks, and maples lined the sidewalks and made the substantial brick and wood homes look elegant. Nobody had peeling paint or raggedy curtains at the windows. Front and back lawns were carefully mowed and weeded on Saturday mornings, rows of boxy hedges marked property lines, and driveways led to two-car garages. Will bought it from his dentist when he moved to North Buffalo. The Craftsman-style house had a mustard-colored brick front and a roof that swooped dramatically over the porch. Will used to tease the girls that he would take them up there in the winter and teach them how to ski. The mirrored basement had a wet bar, red leatherette banquettes, and a pool table, and Will swore it looked better than half the watering holes he frequented on Friday nights. Celeste and Ronnie had their own rooms and a swing set out back. There was a sewing room for Della, and Will finished the attic, added a bathroom, and made the top floor his office. And whenever he came up the walk and put his key in the door he felt proud. This was a long way from his family's rented shack in Prosper, North Carolina.

After twenty years, Will figured he'd left enough sweat by the coke oven and retired to manage his empire full-time. Even though he still worked hard, there was no time clock, no blistering heat, and nobody on his back. It had been that way for the last twenty-four years and would have continued if a faulty ground wire and a puddle on the floor hadn't changed everything.

Ronnie stopped pushing cans of cling peaches and soup around another shelf and looked at her mother. "I swear I got here as soon as I could, Ma." Celeste always knew the fastest way to make Ronnie feel like two cents' worth of nothing, even if she didn't show it. Tonight was no exception.

"I know you did. Ain't no need to talk this into the ground." Della absentmindedly flicked crumbs off the bust of the green flowered duster she'd stuck on after visitors had gone.

"Okay, Mamacita." Ronnie doused a tea bag with hot water. When she got home yesterday she was shocked by how much older her mother looked. The sprinkling of gray at Della's hairline had sprouted into a fuzzy ring around her face, and she moved slower than she used to. Ronnie piped up before the silence was too thick. "Where's the honey? Somebody told me it wouldn't collect on my hips as fast as sugar." She flipped the hair of her dark auburn human-hair fall, the one she trimmed herself so it hung straight down her back and the bangs dusted her brows à la supermodel. She wore it when she hadn't quite made it to the hairdresser to get her extensions tightened. Hands on hips, she flashed a honey-dripping smile and batted her eyelashes. "Girls my age have to work to keep it together, you know."

"Girls your age. Ain't that nothin'." Della mashed stray cracker crumbs off the table with her middle finger and sprinkled them in an empty plate.

"Sugar or honey, makes no dif. It all goes to the same place." Niki still had on the tangerine knit dress she had worn because her granddaddy liked it so much. She had worn it for her graduation from Cornell, and he said it made her stand out in the crowd, like she should. Her mother didn't see it as an appropriate tribute, and they were still only half speaking.

"I knew it sounded too good to be true." Ronnie squeezed her tea bag against the spoon, flopped it in the sink, then looked up at Niki. "And I can't believe I'm getting nutrition advice from you. Look at you. I swear you were just a little pipsqueak, but I haven't seen you in . . ."

"Four years." Della knew exactly. Ronnie had been scarce ever since she first left home right after high school, and over the last seventeen years her visits had gotten fewer and farther between.

"It can't be, can it?" Ronnie shook her head, looked off for a moment. She couldn't believe it had been that long since she'd seen her dad, and now . . . "And now you're bigger than me." She turned back to Niki. "And got the nerve to be managing a hotel restaurant. I'm scared a you."

"Assistant manager, and it's just the café, not the caviar and wine list restaurant."

"Well, I'm proud. Doin' your thing, movin' to Atlanta. I know your mother had a cow when you told her that." Ronnie continued her cabinet search.

"A cow? How 'bout the herd!" Niki set the trash bag by the back door, listened for approaching footsteps. "You should hear her." One hand on her hip, she waved the other back and forth, underscoring her words. "'Why do you want to live all the way down there? Restaurants? Any fool can work in a restaurant! You're smart, Nicole. You should apply to law school. At least get your M.B.A.' Blah, blah, blah. She won't give it a rest."

"That's my sister, Celeste the Magnificent, all-seeing, all-knowing." Ronnie plunked the remaining half of a five-pound sack of sugar on the counter and fished behind the boxes of cake mix and chocolate pudding. "You made it through the worst of it. How bad can she annoy you a thousand miles away?"

Niki pulled a new garbage bag from the box, flapped it open, and lined the can. "Yeah, but I'm afraid I've got something to tell her that's gonna fire her up again." She paused. She wasn't planning to bring this up, but now she could feel the question marks aimed at her. Besides, these seemed calmer waters to test. She sighed, dropped her voice. "I want to quit my job and go to culinary school. I want to be a chef."

"Oh shi—oot. Is that all?! What's wrong with that? It's in the same field." Ronnie opened the refrigerator and examined the bottles on the door.

"You don't get it. To my mother I'm a *manager*. At least she can tell people I'm in charge and that I'm planning to run a major international hotel conglomerate someday. A chef? I might as well tell her I'm flipping burgers."

"Move and let me find this honey before you have the whole kitchen upside down." Della planted her fists on the table, lifted herself out of the seat, and shuffled slowly across the room. Her big toe had poked through her panty hose.

Ronnie rested her hands on Niki's shoulders. "It's your life. If it makes you happy, she'll have to fix herself to deal with it."

Della could hardly keep from grinning. "Umph. Look who's givin' advice."

"They won't have to pay for it." Niki had had this conversation a hundred times in her head, knew all the arguments. "I'll work part-time and . . ."

"Don't sweat this, Nik. Celeste did what she wanted. She can't run you too. Isn't that right, Moms?"

"You can't cut your dresses by my pattern. That's how some folks used to put it." Della stopped in front of Niki, hesitated a beat. "Your great-grandma was a cook. Best for miles around."

Where did that come from? Ronnie cocked her head to one side. "How come you never told me that?"

"There's a lot you don't know."

Ronnie arched one eyebrow. "So what happened with you? The cooking gene skipped a generation?"

"Girl, move on out the way. If I got any honey, it'll be here." Della shifted jars of garlic salt, onion powder, and other seasonings on the shelf above the sink. "And if it skipped one generation, it sure skipped two."

"Mama, you have hurt my feelings."

"Wasn't the first time, and it won't be the last." Della finally found the sticky jar and handed it to Ronnie. "I don't know when I *have* used this." Most of the thick sap had crystallized.

Ronnie held it in her fingertips, draped the other arm over Della's shoulder. "No offense, but you couldn't even pass this off on a bee." They all laughed.

And in the darkened kitchen window, Della caught the reflection of three generations, all variations on a theme.

Tall like her father and the tawny gold of a lioness, Niki's microbraids shot back from the arrowhead of a widow's peak that made her slug several classmates when she was seven 'cause she got sick of them calling her Eddie Munster. To the disappointment of her mother, Niki had preferred soccer to ballet lessons. Even now, she got up at dawn most mornings and ran, just to feel herself slice through the wind, the sweat trickling down her back. It made her feel strong and free. As lively, eager, and flighty as twenty-three ought to be, what was gospel today might be history tomorrow, but Niki was ready to be baptized in life. Not a sprinkling on the forehead baptism, but full immersion, drenched with experience.

Della was amazed by how much her granddaughter had matured in the few months she'd been on her own and working. Her brown eyes seemed keener, more alive, her lips riper. It seemed only a little while ago that Niki had been sitting in the middle of the kitchen floor, playing with the pots and pans she dragged out of the cupboard. Now she was a woman. *Not as grown as she thinks, but you can't tell nobody that. Nobody could tell me. Ronnie either.*

Ronnie had always bobbed when other people weaved and somehow made it work. She came into the world two weeks late and after forty-six hours of labor, presented her butt first. She stopped wailing the moment she laid her eyes on Della and grinned, gummy and drooling, as if to say, "Now wasn't I worth it?" And Della, exhausted, sweaty, and sore, grinned back. From the time she was four, when she asked Santa for a credit card and said she'd take care of the rest, Della knew her baby girl was two steps ahead of her and everybody else. Ronnie—because by first grade she'd stopped answering to Veronica—was smart, fearless, and funny, a taxing combination from a mother's point of view, but some days Della marveled that she had given birth to such a wonder.

And when Ronnie announced that right after high school she was going to New York to be a model and an actress, she made you believe it was undisputed truth. She'd been building up to it all along. Right from her debut as an angel in the Sunday school Christmas pageant, Della knew her child was hooked on the charge that only applause gives you. Sure, Ronnie was young, but some flowers bloom in spring, and although Della couldn't tell her how to make it happen, she was sure Ronnie would find her way. And she did. Della just worried sometimes if what Ronnie found was really what she'd been looking for.

Ronnie's legs seemed to start at her armpits, so she looked long, but she was only middling tall. And just like Della, there wasn't much meat on those pins. Della said she didn't sit still long enough for the weight to catch up with her, but by the time Ronnie was thirteen she had enough curve in her sweaters and swerve in her skirts to cause men who had known her from baby booties to sneak a peek. Ronnie was the spicy brown of nutmeg with smooth, clear skin and a face that couldn't help but say what was on her mind. Her dark eyes slanted up at the corners, accentuated by the sharp angle of her cheekbones and by keen, arching brows. She had her father's square chin and his plush lips.

But she always had my tongue. Della looked away when it came to her own reflection. For the last twenty years she'd watched the face looking back in the mirror morph into someone unrecognizable to herself. Someone with creases and droopy jowls, low-slung breasts, jiggly upper arms, and too much belly. Now she felt stumpy and dumpy. *And who's lookin', anyway?*

"Mother, where are your slippers?" Celeste charged back into the room and zeroed in on her mother's stocking feet.

"I need some air." Niki grabbed the garbage and headed out the back door.

"My feet are fine. Now there's somethin' I wanna do, while it's on my mind. Both of you go on and sit down before you get into it again." Della led the way to the table. Ronnie motioned Celeste ahead with a hand flourish, which Celeste answered with sucked teeth, but she grudgingly went first. They sat on opposite sides of their mother.

Della reached in her housecoat pocket and brought out two frayed blue savings bank passbooks. She pulled off a stray thread, twirled it in her fingers, looked at her daughters. "I remember when your father opened these. You were around nine and fourteen, I guess. Just old enough to start gettin' in your own messes, he said." She chuckled to herself. "He was big on makin' sure there was money tucked aside for hard times. He wanted to make sure you had a little cushion too."

"Daddy was always lookin' out for us." There was a hitch in Ronnie's voice. She held her mug tight to steady her hands.

Celeste fingered her pearls and cast a wary eye on her sister.

"Yeah, he sure was puddin' when it came to the two of you." Della handed them each a bankbook. "Anyway, you never did get yourselves in trouble. Leastways none you told us about. You been grown for a long time now, so I figure you can hold on to your own rainy day stash, or do what you want with it."

Celeste laid hers on the table, covered it with her palms, and bit the inside of her cheek to stay composed. She'd done it so often over the past few days that it was raw.

Ronnie quickly opened the cover. It was a joint account, she and her father. She turned the pages until she found the last entry, May 23, 1984. The balance came to $10,367.54. She closed it, held it to her heart. Tears splattered her cheeks.

Della looked at her daughters. "They're both the same. I don't know what else he left you but . . ."

"How can he be gone?" Ronnie rocked back and forth in her seat, the tears coming faster.

Celeste drummed her fingers on the table. "Oh, spare me the performance! You couldn't wait two seconds to see how much was in there!"

"I never asked Daddy and Ma for a dime, and you know it!" A fringe of Ronnie's hair stuck to her wet cheek.

"She acts like she's the only one with feelings!" Celeste shot back.

"Celeste, leave it alone!" Della reached over, patted Ronnie's arm.

"Why did this have to happen?" Ronnie folded her arms on the table, laid her head on them, and bawled.

"It's all right, baby." Della wrapped her arm around Ronnie's shoulder and held her.

"I don't believe this." Celeste got up and walked to the other side of the room to keep from exploding. She paced, trying to suck down the rest of what she had to say. Through the window she saw the flash of headlights pulling into the driveway and prayed it was Everett so she could get the hell out of here before she had to listen to one more word of her sister's sniveling. Standing on her tiptoes to look out the window, she saw Niki waiting on the steps and Everett unfolding from the car. "Thank God," she said under her breath and hurried to the hall closet, where she snatched her suit jacket, pocketbook, and Niki's leather backpack to save time. All Celeste wanted was to get out of this house.

"Does Mrs. Godfrey ever stop talking?" Everett held the back door open for Niki as they came into the kitchen. "And where on earth did she find that hat?" Niki looked up at her father and stifled a giggle. You knew Everett was tall when you saw him, but it wasn't until you got up close that you realized how big he was. When they were dating, Celeste's girlfriends used to ride her about the tall men who were wasted on little bitty women. Everett was the golden brown of single malt

scotch, with a voice and a manner that were just as mellow.
By the time he met Celeste, when he was a second-year med
student at the University of Buffalo and she a college junior,
he already had the mustache and goatee. He had a serious 'fro
too, round like a mushroom; now all he had left was half a
halo. The sleeves of Everett's black mock turtleneck were
pushed up to his elbows. He and Celeste had had words about
his attire this morning. He didn't wear ties anymore, decided
they were pretentious and unnecessary. Will certainly knew
that, so Everett saw no reason to wear one to his funeral.

Celeste met them at the back door, handed Niki her bag.
"I'm ready. Let's go."

Everett saw Ronnie and Della huddled together. "Why
don't we stay for a while?" he said softly to Celeste.

She shook her head and scowled. "Be back tomorrow," she
announced.

Della looked up and nodded, and Celeste was out the door.

2

"No good-byes. Just gone."

Celeste let herself in the Volvo, which she insisted they take instead of the rattletrap four-wheel-drive monstrosity Everett couldn't seem to part with. By the time Niki and Everett came out, she had already steamed up the windows.

Everett paused a moment, looked at the night sky before he got in. "So many stars. Your dad got a nice welcome." He turned on the ignition, backed out into the street.

"My mother acts like it's just another day. For God's sake, her husband is dead. You'd think she'd show some emotion. And I am sick to death of my sister!" Arms folded and legs crossed tighter than a Scout knot, Celeste fumed. "She manages to make every situation revolve around her!"

"Sick to *death*? You have such a way with words." Niki cleared the fog from her window with her palm.

"Don't mock me, Nicole. I am in no mood."

"Aunt Ronnie expresses what she feels. What's wrong with that, Ma?"

"I *hate* it when you call me *Ma*! Don't call me anything if that's all you can say!"

"Fine!" Niki slumped against the seatback and stared out the window.

"And that skirt she had on was a disgrace. I have wider belts. This was her father's funeral, not some damn disco!" Celeste grumbled to no one in particular.

Everett glanced sidelong at his wife but decided to leave it alone. He knew there was no right answer for Celeste when she was like this. It had been a long, drawn-out day, and he had his own wounds to tend. He liked his father-in-law from the first time they met. Celeste was carrying on about Everett being a medical student. Will looked him over and said, "They let *you* practice medicine?" Everett told him yeah, and he was gonna keep practicing till he got it right. Will chuckled, handed him a beer. They watched the Bills, and they'd been buddies ever since. If he had the time, Everett still pitched in, over Celeste's objections, when Will needed an extra set of hands to work on one of his houses. Sometimes it felt good to Everett just to be the guy holding the ladder, instead of the one who was supposed to have the answers. He wished he'd been helping out the day of the accident.

They rode the rest of the way to Amherst in silence. Back when Celeste had finally convinced Everett they needed more space because of the baby, and it was time to abandon the crowded one-bedroom apartment near the hospital and buy a house, she insisted they move to the suburbs. She saw their three-bedroom cedar shingle, split-level ranch as a starter home. Problem was, twenty years later they were still in it. Even when Everett's peers joined lucrative private practices, took their long green out to the lavish new developments and built mansionettes, he wasn't interested. He thought they already had a great house, Niki liked her schools, and he preferred working at the North Star Family Clinic he had founded. His salary wasn't as big, but he found the work rewarding. It's what he always told Celeste he wanted to do when they were dating, and she'd go to his apartment and cook big pots of spaghetti and jar sauce with dry meatballs and wait up until two thirty in the morning when he finally got off duty so they could eat together. She would light the red candles she had wedged in the tops of old Mateus bottles so the wax dripped down the sides in free-form ribbons. Everett would come in all wound up about some procedure he had finally been able to use and how it had made the difference for a patient. He'd tell her that's why he was in medicine, not for the big bucks. Celeste would tell him how righteous that was, gaze at him in the twinkling light, and think she'd explode if he didn't put those big hands around her soon. Everett's goals had remained noble as the years wore on, but Celeste seemed to have forgotten how righteous she once thought they were. Between his salary and her pay as a guidance counselor they had a nice life, but somewhere along the line Celeste had started blaming him for not wanting more.

As soon as the car stopped in the driveway, Celeste made a beeline for the bottle of chardonnay in the fridge and poured herself a healthy glass by the light from inside. She had a headache that would kill a horse. She shut the door so the room was dark again, took a swig. It stung the raw place inside her cheek. *How could Daddy be gone?* She slid onto the banquette in the breakfast nook. Moonlight shone through the window, bounced off the table. At the funeral Ronnie had cried, moaned, and all but collapsed by the open coffin. She had to be helped to her seat and fanned so she wouldn't swoon. But what did Ronnie really know about their father? Did she know he still liked the peanut butter sandwich cookies and grape soda they thought was so nasty when they were kids? Or that he was considering selling most of his houses because some of the tenants were too rough for him to mess with now, and that it made him sad because he'd spent so much of his life tending to them? Or that he wished he knew how to make Della happy again? *Like anybody could make her happy.* Celeste emptied her wine glass, wasn't wasted enough, got up for a refill.

Your daddy's rich, and your ma is good-lookin'. Celeste sang the words in her head as the sound of Everett and Niki's piano playing drifted in from the living room. Niki first learned scales and "Greensleeves" sitting on her father's lap. They still played together, four hands on the piano. Celeste filled the glass to the rim this time, took a few sips so she wouldn't spill it, then sat back down, closed her eyes, propped her head against the window frame.

She hadn't gone up for a final viewing. Celeste wanted to remember her daddy her way. In the backyard, mopping barbecue sauce on a slab of ribs with one hand and sweat off his forehead with the other. During the reception he and Della gave after Celeste announced she and Everett had eloped, Will led her upstairs to her old bedroom and made sure she knew that even though she was another man's wife now, she would always be his baby. She had always felt more like his baby

than her mother's. *And he's gone and left me here with her.
What am I supposed to do now?* Tears leaked from the corners
of her eyes, down her neck. Celeste didn't know how long she
had been sitting that way, when the kitchen lights flicked on.
She squinted, shaded her eyes from the brightness.

"I didn't know you were in here. Thought you'd gone to
bed." Everett got an ice cream sandwich out of the freezer.

Celeste meant to tell him that she was on her way. That
she'd stopped off for some wine, that he and Niki sounded
good together. She meant to say that, but all that came out was
a muffled whimper, then waves of tears. Everett sat beside her,
held her until they subsided, steadied her as they walked to the
bedroom. His hands were sure as he helped her undress, get
into a nightgown, and by the time she lay down, her back
curved against his chest, Celeste felt calmer. His breathing
was always slower than hers, so she deepened her breaths to
match his. It had been a long time since they fell asleep this
way. Their schedules didn't seem to mesh anymore, especially since Niki had been gone.

Oh, they were very socially active. Celeste still loved receiving the creamy vellum envelopes that read "Dr. & Mrs.
Everett English" in lovely script. They attended openings at
the Albright-Knox Gallery, galas at the Studio Arena Theater,
and chaired fund-raisers for their local NAACP chapter. Celeste and Everett were A-list cocktail party guests because
they were such good minglers, always ready with an entertaining anecdote or an intriguing perspective on current
events. And they looked so good together. She'd been dealt a
hand full of fives and sixes in life, but with persistence and
constant attention to detail, Celeste had done all right.

So the weekends were generally inked in well in advance,
but their five-days-a-week lives didn't intersect much. Celeste
had her after-school routines. Tuesdays she stayed late to ad-
vise the prom committee. Thursdays were her standing four-
thirty hair appointment, so her precision-cropped hair looked
exactly the same at all times. She attended sorority meetings
and library board meetings. By seven or so she'd be home,
broil some sole or a chicken breast or pick at leftovers. Lately

she turned in around nine thirty, with a book and some sherry. Half the time Everett didn't get home before that. He'd get tied up checking on patients, reviewing charts, completing paperwork, or speaking to some community group about the warning signs of high blood pressure or the importance of mammograms and self-examination in breast cancer detection. Celeste didn't bother getting up when she heard his keys jingle in the door. Eventually he'd poke his head in the bedroom to talk for a minute, then he'd busy himself down the hall in his office, reading journals, or logged on the computer. Sometimes he stayed downstairs, noodling at the piano, enjoying his "live at the Blue Note" fantasy. She'd rouse a little when he'd drop his clothes in a pile by the side of the bed and get under the covers around two A.M., sometimes later. And more and more he didn't make it to bed at all. On her four A.M. bathroom run she'd shuffle down the hall and find him sprawled on the brown velour sofa across from his desk. She always felt a fist in her guts, like somebody had a handful of her intestines, but it was just that they were both so busy. They still had so much in common, what difference did it make where they slept? The next morning, the routine would start all over again.

But tonight Celeste felt calm pressed into the curve of Everett's body. She let the stress of the day pass from her and fell into a deep sleep.

At 3:12 A.M. Celeste woke up feeling too warm under the comforter. She pushed it off, reached for Everett, and shivered when she felt the empty space beside her.

Della straightened the covers on her side of the unmade bed, piled up her pillows, and sat down. Three-fifteen was a little later than she usually stayed up, but not much. Her nighttime supplies littered the crocheted coverlet on the other side: puzzle books, *Jet*, *Ebony*, *Life*, the TV remote, unread sections of Sunday's paper, a blue acrylic snack tray, her everyday pocketbook, a deck of cards, Chapstick. She slipped her legs under the sheet.

Della had stood in the doorway of Ronnie's room a long

time, watching her sleep. Ronnie slept like the dead, had since she was little. Della remembered the time the house across the street caught fire in the middle of the night. There were sirens screaming, all sorts of commotion, and Ronnie never budged. From the look of things, that hadn't changed. The whole time Della watched, the only movement was the steady rise and fall of the pink chenille bedspread. She worried about Ronnie, which was nothing new. Della worried about both her daughters, but since they'd been grown she kept her concerns to herself. They wouldn't have listened, anyway. This was a rare opportunity to worry in person for as long as she wanted.

Della wished Ronnie had seen her father more recently, not because he didn't understand that the life she had chosen didn't leave much room for stops in western New York, but because Della wasn't sure Ronnie understood that as long as she was happy, Will had been happy and proud. *Nothin' to be done about it now.*

Della reached over for the tray and settled it on her lap. She picked up the red deck of playing cards, fanned them with her thumb. She couldn't help feeling like Will was upstairs, asleep, like always. They hadn't actually shared a bed in years, ten, twelve. It wasn't planned or deliberate, not this time. Way back when the girls were teens he started showering and shaving up in his attic bathroom because there was too much commotion sharing the room with three females, and this way nobody bugged him about whisker fuzz in the sink or how he left the toilet seat. Eventually his clothes migrated up there too because he said Della didn't leave him enough space for a pair of drawers. When he retired he kept all his gadgets and whatnot up there too, and when he wasn't working he'd spend hours fooling with them, then fall asleep in the recliner with the TV set going. One day he just stopped waking up and coming downstairs. At first he used to visit Della's bed from time to time, but that had petered out a while back. She didn't think she'd ever hear herself say it, but after so many years all that bumpin' and rootin' around had stopped being a whole lot of fun. She was relieved not to hear his buzz saw snoring, or to have to wrestle for covers. Will had a mushy mattress the way he liked, and they'd meet over breakfast every morning. It was their routine. Della knew Celeste and Ronnie hadn't approved of the situation, like they had any say-so in the matter. It worked okay for the folks involved, and Della didn't see any reason to explain, especially not to her *children*. There were plenty of things she figured they didn't need to know.

Della shuffled the deck for a long time, dealt out a game of solitaire. The cool night air felt good on her bare arms. She always wore those sleeveless cotton nightgowns in pink or yellow, with the teensy ribbon tied in a bow at the yoke. She examined her up-cards, moved the ace of diamonds up top, the two of clubs on the three of diamonds, ten of clubs on the jack of hearts. Nothing in the last week had been regular, not Ronnie sleeping in her old room, not folks in and out of the house, laughing too loud or talking in whispers, or Celeste digging through Will's closet for his good navy suit. Della was tired of the phone ringing. Sick of sympathies and condolences, of folks looking at her with pity, asking how she was bearing up, what she was going to do, what she needed. She needed for all this foolishness to stop so she could get back to something like normal because now her life felt unfamiliar.

Della had been waiting for something to come over her for almost a week now. Will's death had been a big . . . well . . . shock. That last morning was the same as usual. She'd put on a pot of coffee and gotten ready for work. By the time she was ready for a cup, Will was dressed and finishing his second mug, light and sweet, with a bowl of toasted oats and skim milk because he had to watch his cholesterol. He drove her to work, like every morning since he'd retired, pecked her cheek, said he'd be back at quitting time.

Della was sorting through a stack of learner's permit applications when Everett showed up at her desk at the Department of Motor Vehicles late afternoon, looking pained. A friend of his was in the ER when they brought Will in and gave Everett a call. And that was that. No grim diagnoses, or tubes and monitors. No decisions. No warning. No good-byes. Just gone. She counted off cards in threes: four of clubs, five of

hearts, five of spades. Della thought solitaire was a lot like
life: a whole lot of shuffling, but mostly the cards don't go
your way. She put the three of clubs on the four of hearts, put
the ace of clubs up top. Snatches of the obituary Celeste had
read at the funeral drifted through Della's head. "... *leaves
behind his devoted wife of forty-four years, Della Womack
Frazier* . . ." *Forty-four years*. That was a whole lifetime, and
she'd known him longer, ever since another hasty funeral left
her world upside down. *No point dragging all that up*. As far
as Della was concerned, you couldn't change the past, so
there was no reason to look back at it. She needed to look
ahead, to what she was going to do with all those houses and
to how she was going to get back on schedule, now that a big
chunk of the last fifty years was gone.

3

". . . sleight-of-hand fame . . ."

"It's twelve noon straight up, sunny and forty-two degrees in Newark," the pilot announced as the plane smacked the runway, bounced and heaved down to land speed. *And two weeks after Daddy . . .* The pilot couldn't add that detail, and Ronnie couldn't finish the thought. She hadn't even figured out how to say it. *Died? Passed?* So she maneuvered around the exact words, just as she had maneuvered around spending any more time than absolutely required around Celeste. *Always actin' like she knows it all.* Whenever Ronnie thought of their funeral night fight it set her teeth on edge. *I'd a been home the next day if . . .* She didn't even like admitting to herself that she was stone broke and so in debt to her friends there wasn't anybody else to borrow from. She had to wait for her paycheck so she could buy a plane ticket. She certainly wasn't going to tell Celeste that.

She shifted impatiently in her seat, crossed and recrossed her legs at the ankles, and felt a corner of the check she had folded and slipped into her black suede boot. *I hope I can get this to the bank before two. The sooner it clears . . .* Ronnie looked around for a flight attendant, then jammed her empty paper cup in the seat pocket and stifled a yawn. She still could not believe this morning. It was bad enough that her period had come early again, complete with hot, pulsing cramps that kept her awake half the night, but then her mother actually came in her room at six, flashing the ceiling light off and on and barking orders like when Ronnie was in school. She hated it then. One of the best things about leaving home was no Della alarm. *Ma must be havin' flashbacks.* Ronnie could have screamed.

But she kept a lid on it and didn't bother to point out that the airport was only fifteen minutes away, or that she counted a mad dash through the terminal as exercise. Because unlike Celeste, Ronnie chose her battles carefully, and this one wasn't worth the hassle. Besides, she was ready to make her exit.

So she had downed four aspirin, thrown herself in a cold shower, stuffed her clothes in her bag, swilled three cups of Della's watery coffee because she was out of tea, and played with a bowl of oatmeal. *Only thing she didn't do was braid my hair and check my homework.* They were headed for Buffalo International by eight thirty for an eleven o'clock flight because her mother, who had no flyer miles, frequent or otherwise, thought it was a good idea. "Better safe than sorry," Della had said, then checked the window and door locks for the second time as she recounted the story of the house in the next block that had been burglarized year before last. "Cleaned them out in broad daylight." Della had a hard-luck story for every occasion, so Ronnie just nodded sympathetically and started her lift-off countdown while Della secured the perimeter.

Della had putt-putted along the highway seemingly oblivious to the rush-hour traffic that zipped by the big, gray waterbug on wheels that Will had bought because he liked his cars substantial. "Maybe this winter will be like last year. We didn't have much snow at all." Ronnie thought the city looked and smelled like it was wrapped in an old, wet wool overcoat. She had stared out the window at the ominous gray clouds to keep from screaming, "It's weather, Ma. It'll be whatever it's gonna be," but her time at home reminded her that winter weather was an endless source of conversation in western New York. Dire predictions, wise prognostications, hopeful dreams, and stories of triumph were a common denominator. Like subway stories in New York, everybody had 'em and everybody shared 'em. Snow was a safe, neutral subject, perfect for that awkward silence between people's sympathetic recollections of Will Frazier. So for nine days Ronnie heard 'em. Lake effect. The ice boom. The Snow Belt. Winter words. Words she grew up with but had long ago shoveled to the back of her mind.

Della's good-bye had come with the usual warning to be careful and a reminder to call when she got in. Ronnie had leaned across the bench seat to hug her, which usually felt good because Della was soft and cuddly. Those hugs stuck to Ronnie's ribs, but this time a wave of sadness came over her, and it was all she could do to get out of the car before she went down in the undertow. Then Della reached in the backseat, handed Ronnie a shopping bag groaning with foil packets of ham, chicken, and pound cake. They could both be spared the "You're too thin. Are you eating right?" speech. "All that food shouldn't go to waste," Della told her. "*I'll* never finish it."

Two weeks ago it would have been "we," and there and then Ronnie decided that what her mother's life would be like now was another thing she wasn't prepared to consider yet. Next week Della would go back to work and . . . *And what?* Not that her parents had been lovey-dovey. Not that she knew exactly *what* they'd been to each other. Except there. They'd always been there.

"Please keep your seats until the fasten seat belt sign has been turned off," the flight attendant's voice crackled over the loudspeaker.

"Are we taxiing to the damn George Washington Bridge?" It was out of Ronnie's mouth before she knew it. Other passengers chuckled in agreement. The whole flight only took fifty minutes. It seemed like it was taking that long to get to the gate, and Ronnie was too through. She leaned forward, clacking her heels on the floor like a flamenco dancer, waiting for the *ding* that meant she could spring for her bag. Finally, the cabin lights came up. Ronnie snatched her carry-on from the overhead and inched down the aisle with the rest of the cattle. Nine days. The longest she'd been home in seventeen years.

Ronnie slipped on her faux tortoise street-vendor diva shades, but only partially to dim the bright October sunlight that glinted through the windows. The concourse bustled with folks racing to get where they were going, but since she hadn't hit the real city, she wasn't required to up her pace yet. *Everybody looks so . . . so damn happy. Actin' like they want to be here. It's Newark Airport, for God's sake!* Still stiff from the crowded flight, she walked slowly through the terminal. *I feel like crap.* Ronnie resented coach and always cast a jaundiced eye as she passed the lucky few comfortably ensconced in the wide leather seats of first class. She'd had the privilege of the other side of the curtain only once. She'd been up for a sitcom and her then agent had somehow finagled her a first-class ticket to L.A. No one in the cabin was exempt from her profiling. For six hours she regaled them with tales of her adventures in the "business." Some of the stories were actually true, they'd just happened to someone else. The rest she had made up out of the thin air at thirty thousand feet.

Ronnie snaked through the squadron of livery-car drivers who chatted among themselves while holding signs with the name of their next fare. *Humph. One day.* By the time she reached baggage claim her aggressive edge was closer to the surface, bringing with it her need for a cigarette. She elbowed to the front of the carousel and snatched her duffel, which was now minus a strap. Disgusted, she examined the damage as the crowd scrambled around her. *They'll laugh in my face if I make a claim for this ratty old piece of shit.*

Dragging the black nylon bag by its one good handle, Ronnie made her way outside to the bus line. Until she got to the bank, that check in her boot was just a piece of paper, and she was tapped out. She thought about asking Celeste for a small loan, but it wasn't worth the lecture. From the time they were kids, Celeste kept a stash—just in case. To Ronnie, money meant a good time *now.* A candy bar. A 45 record. A movie. Because what is there besides the moment and the memory?

Ronnie fished in her purse for her smokes and started a mental list of all the good times her windfall would provide. *At least I can pay my rent on time for a change.* Before she lit up, the driver reached for her bag to stow it in the belly of the bus. "Could you put it over there?" She pointed to a corner in the front, flashed her chemically whitened smile. *So I don't have to wait two years for you to find it when we get to the city.*

"Anything for you, dearie."

"Thanks!" *Spare me.* She climbed aboard and took a seat up front next to an old man listening to headphones because he didn't look like he'd give her any lip. The tinted windows didn't let in much light, but Ronnie kept her shades on anyway.

No one knew how shaky Ronnie's life was, because Ronnie never let on. Never. She hadn't actually earned a living as a model or an actress in years. She barely earned a living, period. The folks at home thought . . . *What did they think exactly?* What she wanted them to. To her parents, their friends and neighbors, she was a star, a celebrity. After all, she'd lived in Paris and Milan and Tokyo. They didn't know that the tiny hotel rooms she shared with dozens of other wanna-bes were only a notch above hovel. They'd seen her in their Kmart circular. Not since 1988, but for them it was like yesterday. And her cigarette billboard was longer ago. For months it had guarded the Jefferson ramp onto the Kensington Expressway, but whenever she was home, no one would let her forget it.

That was back before she had an agent, when she'd been naive enough to believe the photographer when he told her that being the girl in the pink jacket, leaning on a toboggan, puffing a menthol was her ticket to stardom. He was so easygoing, so mellow. She was new; he had national magazine credits. So he taught her how to work to the camera and to the light, and she was an eager pupil. The excitement in his voice made her believe he really hadn't seen anyone in a long time who made the shot pop like she did. And no one had ever looked at Ronnie so intensely. It was as though he could see through the lens directly into her eyes and right into her soul. It had been a scorching August day, but she actually enjoyed spending hours in the un-air-conditioned studio, bundled in hot ski clothes, cavorting in fake snow, a cigarette poised jauntily between her fingers.

When his assistant and the hair and makeup guy finally left and he asked her to stay, Ronnie felt an excited tingle. So it seemed perfectly natural for her to lounge on the leather sofa while he put on some smooth tunes, turned the lights down low, poured her a glass of wine. And, oh, by the way, "Just sign the release. It's standard," he had said. Ronnie scribbled her name without thinking twice. She drank in the cabernet and his philosophy of photography, felt honored when he showed her his portfolio of art pictures even though she didn't really get the blurry black-and-white abstractions. At first it was even okay when he held her face and kissed her.

He just wouldn't stop.

She said, "No."

He said, "Come on, baby."

She said, "No!"

He said, "You know you want it," and pressed harder.

She said, "Stop!" and tried to wriggle out of his grasp.

He didn't. He held her down, covered her mouth with his, and didn't say anything else until he was finished. Then he stood up and zipped. "Later," he said.

Ronnie straightened her clothes and hair in the hallway and walked out into the anonymous Manhattan twilight feeling dazed, raw, and somehow responsible. Too stunned to cry, she concentrated on fighting back the bile that bubbled in the back of her throat, putting one foot in front of the other and re-membering how to get back to her residence hotel. She didn't tell anybody because she didn't know anybody to tell, not anybody who would care, or believe her or do anything about it. Telling her father never crossed her mind. He'd come bring her home where he could protect her. All Ronnie wanted was to put her head in her mother's lap and boohoo until she felt relief, but this wasn't a scraped knee, this was sex, and they didn't talk about that. Not in so many words, but Della had made it clear that Ronnie knew right from wrong and that was that. So if she was supposed to be grown enough to live on her own, then she should have seen the squeeze play coming.

To this day, Ronnie still hadn't said anything.

Three months after, she got a five-hundred-dollar check in the mail for what she later found out should have been a ten grand payday. She'd been screwed, any way you put it. Not to mention the nicotine jones she still had.

And then the billboard showed up that winter and taunted her from rooftops and bus shelters. Looking up at her own bright-eyed, smiling face made her want to vomit, but it made her fam-ily proud. When she went home for the holidays, her father made her pose for snapshots under the billboard. Only she could see the sadness in her eyes when she looked at the picture.

But as a result of the campaign, she got an agent to take her on, and by the time she made two appearances during the third season of *The Cosby Show,* Ronnie's star status was assured. "Damn! My baby workin' with Bill Cosby!" She could hear her daddy's pride over the phone. Will boasted to all his tenants, "My daughter, the one who's an actress in New York, yeah, she and Bill are tight." He called him Bill, as if Ronnie's brief association made *him* a friend as well. She didn't have the heart to tell him that since she didn't have any scenes with Mr. Cosby, she hadn't even met him on the set.

Even Celeste had been a little impressed. Della seemed to be too, but the only thing she said was, "Are you still havin' fun?" Ronnie had shrugged it off as some of her mother's weird gloom and doom. Since when did Della care about fun? Had she had any since 1969? Of course Ronnie was having the time of her life. It was what she dreamed about, wasn't it?

And as for men, she'd figured that out too. Never get caught off guard. Never believe they're sincere. Never show them who you really are.

These days, pretty much all that came her way was extra work on soaps and movies here and there, when they needed a Black face in the background. She couldn't even pay her SAG dues with what she earned for those shows, and even she couldn't fix her mouth to call it acting anymore. And as far as modeling, she hadn't done a print ad in five years. There was the occasional trade show at the Javits. Automobiles, computers, didn't make any difference. She'd stand in killer heels, wearing something skimpy and tight, and smile at strangers for twelve hours. She'd quit waiting tables a few years ago because that was too big a cliché, but her steadiest gig, the one that accounted for most of the income on her income taxes, was her Thursday nights and all day Saturdays and Sundays behind the Sable Shades makeup counter in Macy's. *Sable Shades, rich enough to be you.* She'd been sent on the casting for the line's debut ads a few years back. Nothing came of that, but Ronnie had figured if there was anything she'd learned from the business, it was how to beat a face, so she got herself a job as a "beauty consultant." Folks at home didn't know that, though. They still compared Ronnie stories and ate up her sleight-of-hand fame like they ate chicken wings. She'd heard it a hundred times between the wake and the funeral, from church members who remembered giving her father extra sale circulars after service, or from classmates she didn't remember who could cite chapter and verse of her career. She'd set out to become a household name, which she was, but only in the households of people she knew. People who'd restricted their dreams to fit comfortably within the limits of the world where they lived. Ronnie had become their ray of limelight, and she wanted to shine for them, so she became a master of illusion. But she was painfully aware of the trapdoors and secret compartments, and when the smoke cleared she still hadn't fulfilled the dreams she carried with her the first time she left home.

As the bus barreled along the Jersey Turnpike, Ronnie craved a cigarette. She shifted in her seat, caught the old man in the seat next to her staring at her legs. *Ain't that nothin'.* She flipped her trench coat over her knees. She wasn't glad to be back, just anxious to be away from that home and family stuff death drops on you in your hour of bereavement. The stuff that doesn't have jack to do with the dearly departed. It was her mother who seemed to float through the week like she was mildly annoyed at the inconvenience, and her darling sister who seemed to relish the respectability of mourning, that had gotten on Ronnie's reserve nerve. It was all too close, and it got harder every day to keep up the front. Questions. Too many of 'em. Three days at home was usually her max. She could make it all work for that long.

Ronnie could see a patch of light at the end of the Lincoln Tunnel. She was back to her life, such as it was. She could return to her days spent ritually traipsing to castings and auditions. She'd dress to suit the part, read the copy, and smile pretty as she exited stage right. "Thanks. We'll let you know." She heard it in her sleep. At this point hope was pretty hard to come by, but Ronnie had perfected the role of Veronica Frazier, her stage name, worked so hard trying to be who people thought she was, she had no time to think about whether it was still fun.

Ronnie was off the bus at Port Authority before the brakes had stopped squealing. "Baby, I'll carry that bag anywhere you wanna go." The man's grungy fatigues looked like they'd seen action. He quickened his steps to try and fall in beside Ronnie. She threw her hand up in a stop sign, turned her head, and never broke stride.

He stopped and let her pass. "That sorry-assed wig must be too tight." The retort smacked her in the back of the head and she felt the adrenaline surge. *Welcome home*. She needed that kick in the attitude to navigate the terminal and fend off the ersatz "door" men, eager to get her a taxi, for a small gratuity, thank you. *I should take the train*. But the thought of dragging her raggedy, one-handled suitcase down into the subway to catch the shuttle, then changing for the ride uptown was too dismal. She'd still have to lug her load another four blocks. *What could it be, ten bucks? Fifteen?* By the time her frantic waving had snared a taxi on Eighth Avenue, the sun had disappeared behind a cloud and the sky threatened rain, but Ronnie still had her shades on.

Home, Alfred. "Seventy-fifth and York." Ronnie gave the driver her cross streets. One of her first New York lessons was that only out-of-towners gave a cab driver an actual address as soon as they got in. The taxi headed east on Forty-second Street. *Home?* Although she'd lived in Manhattan a long time, Ronnie didn't really think of it as home. She'd had enough addresses and phone numbers to fill a page in the Manhattan phone book. Her current sub-sublet was just one more. All part of her glamorous, nomadic lifestyle, her parents thought. She'd overheard her father, for whom a trip to Rochester was an adventure, brag about that too. "Yeah, Ronnie has lived all over New York. Knows it like the back of her hand." When her mother asked if she didn't get tired of moving, Ronnie told her it was exciting. "I need new surroundings to stimulate me. Besides, this apartment is closer to the subway, drugstore, acting class. . . ." But what Ronnie never had was a lease or a utility bill in her own name. Della and Will never visited her, but then they'd never been invited. Celeste came once on a teachers' convention when, luckily, Ronnie was apartment sit-

ting in a high-rise on West Fifty-seventh Street. Ronnie
bought a few frames at Lamston's and put family photos on
display around the place. Celeste really bought the act, even
complimented Ronnie on her taste. A couple of years later,
Everett came to town to deliver a paper at Columbia Presbyterian and brought Niki with him. They stayed at the Plaza,
and for two days Ronnie showed them the New York they
thought she lived in. Her secret was safe. No one knew how
far her ends had to go before they'd meet.

The taxi turned up First Avenue, swerved to avoid taking
out a bike messenger. *Oh yeah, the bank.* "Make that Seventy-
ninth and First." Ronnie shouted through the Plexiglas parti-
tion, then reached down and tugged off her left boot. Years
ago, at the end of her six weeks in Tokyo, the agency paid her
in cash, nine thousand U.S. dollars. A fifteen-year-old model
from West Virginia showed her how to stuff the money in her
boots. On her customs form, Ronnie declared a hundred dollars. She had felt like a secret agent.

Inside the bank, Ronnie filled out a deposit slip so she'd
get five hundred dollars back and dragged her luggage to the
teller window. A young woman with bad skin and very long
blue and yellow striped nails examined the draft, then pushed
it back toward Ronnie with the eraser of her pencil. "You have
to get this authorized by an officer."

"I have an account here." Ronnie pulled out her miffed ex-
ecutive act. "This is a bank check made out to me."

The teller pointed the pencil toward the row of desks
across the room. "It's from out of town. Someone has to initial it."

*Yep. I'm officially back. New York City. If something is sim-
ple, they make it difficult. If it's difficult, they make it impossible.* Ronnie recalled how the branch manager at her parents'
bank addressed her mother by name, asked about her health,
and offered condolences. While they were waiting for the
check to be drawn up, the woman shared a story about how
Will recommended a good plumber and how much she and
her husband appreciated it. *But you're not in Kansas anymore, Dorothy.* Ronnie, prepared for battle, hoisted her suit-

case and scanned the suits hoping for a friendly face. *Thank God*. She spied a brother in the far corner. Brooks Brothers pin stripe, rep tie, no facial hair, no jewelry. She sauntered closer. The brass nameplate on his desk read R. Phillip Dade. *Ugh. One of those*. But Ronnie cleared her throat, focused her "sincere" smiling eyes, the look she used for young mother auditions, in his direction. On cue, R. Phillip looked up, took off his rimless glasses. Ronnie kicked up the wattage aimed in his direction.

"I'm truly sorry for the inconvenience, Ms. Frazier, but your funds should be clear in five to seven business days."

Did you have that whiny voice before they hired you, or did it come with the nameplate? "This is not acceptable." She didn't want to sound desperate. "Can't you release a portion of this?"

"This isn't a local check, you see. If you had the money in your account to cover it, we could . . ."

"If I had the money in my account we wouldn't be having this conversation, would we?" *You pompous ass*. Ronnie knew there was nothing left but to save face and retreat.

"Bank policy. I wish I could do something to help."

"Well, Mr. Dade, I need to deposit this for convenience sake, but I will be taking my business to another bank." *Right. So* they *can send me bounced check notices*. She turned on her heels and sauntered back to the teller with all the righteous indignation she could muster. And to add insult to injury, by the time she came out of the bank the sky had opened up and all the cabs that clogged the street twenty minutes ago had vanished. *It's only five blocks in the rain with a broken suitcase*. It was all getting funny now. She hoisted the bag on her head and amused herself on the walk home watching passersby try to look at her without really looking.

Ronnie stopped at the mailbox. Half was junk mail, the other half she was sure had "final notice" printed across a bill for some amount she couldn't pay yet. *What are they gonna do? Shoot me?* She trudged up the stairs and heard the voice on the answering machine as she turned the three locks and opened the door. "If you've already sent your payment, please disregard this message." *Shit!* Home. A fourth-floor walk-up studio, smaller than her bedroom in Buffalo, for which she had the privilege of paying eleven hundred ninety-five dollars a month, not including utilities. Of course, it *was* furnished, which meant there was a lumpy double bed with a Campari poster on the wall where the headboard should have been. A dark, rickety dresser that looked like somebody's grandmother must have thrown it out stood on the opposite wall. Only the top drawer had been empty, so Ronnie kept her underwear there and used her luggage to store the rest of her clothes. One of the two small closets was jammed with boxes that Ronnie guessed belonged to the leaseholder. The other had a slow leak and she wasn't sure where the water came from. There was an eat-in kitchen, which meant there was enough room to stand at the counter and eat in it. Ronnie had opened the cabinet under the sink once, heard scurrying feet, and never opened it again. The bathroom was in keeping with the rest of the decor, aged tile and rust. Truth was the place gave her the willies, which is why she spent as little time as possible there. But that's what New York was about, wasn't it? Being out and about. Besides, at least she didn't have roommates, 'cause you never knew what horror show *that* would be. She'd been here nearly a year, long enough to know the address and phone without checking her address book. The apartment belonged to a friend of a friend of someone she met on an audition. He had temporarily relocated to Brazil but wasn't ready to give up his shoe box on the Upper East Side. Ronnie never met him. The arrangements were made over the phone; the keys came FedEx.

Welcome home. Ronnie dropped her wet bag by the door, tossed her mail in the wicker basket, yanked off her soaked, squishy boots. *These are over*. She chucked them in the trash and stuck her feet in the formerly white canvas tennis sneakers she used as slippers. Her wig was matted to her head, she was wet down to her bra, the pain in her belly was back, she was tired and hungry. That's when she realized that somewhere between Buffalo and here she'd lost her care package from home. "Damn!" She knew there was only half a sesame bagel, some ketchup, and leftover split pea soup in the refrigerator, and she didn't want to know what that had turned into in her absence. "Damn! Damn! Damn!" She felt herself coming unglued, and that was more loose pieces than she wanted to deal with, so she turned on the combination radio, tape player, and three-inch TV to mask the sound of the toilet that always ran. A soothing piano melody came over the radio, and she used that little bit of calm to get herself out of her soggy clothes and wrapped in a terry cloth robe she'd swiped ages ago from a suite at the George V in Paris where she had a go-see. A few drags of menthol and she was composed enough to call Della. After all, it wouldn't do to burst out in tears and say, "My life is shit!" which was a feeling Ronnie wasn't prepared to acknowledge to herself and definitely not to her mother. "The flight was a breeze. Yeah everything is great here. Fabulous actually . . . Gotta go, Ma . . . phone calls to return, appointments to reschedule. Call ya soon!"

The DJ said it was 4:37, but Ronnie curled up on the bed and slept all night.

When she assumed her post behind the Sable Shades counter the next morning, wearing the required fashion-black above-the-knee skirt, turtleneck, opaque hose, and gold cardigan with the interlocking double *S* logo, Ronnie had rebounded. Her life was still hung together with chewing gum, paper clips, and spit, but at least this felt normal. On the M32 bus to work she had gone over next week's casting calls in *Back Stage* and *Show Business* and circled the ones that seemed right. It would only be a week till the check cleared. *The beauty shop. Rent. A new head shot and mailing. A little shopping.* She had things to look forward to. *Thank you, Daddy!*

Ronnie liked to say she worked at the Sable Shades counter to prepare for her own sitcom. The Veronica Frazier Show, *or should I use Ronnie?* She even kept notes, intended to write a TV treatment one day. Truth was she kind of liked the gig. It was a relatively new cosmetics line, and competition was stiff. Fashion Fair and Naomi Sims had a loyal following. Iman was gaining a nice toehold. Sable Shades was the new kid on the block, and Ronnie liked the team spirit and the products. She had worked for an hour, gingerly removing the sticky little tags that said "sample, not for resale" from the array of bottles, jars, and pots she'd sent to Niki last Christmas because she wanted to send her niece something nice. Who'd ever know?

In the locker room she caught up with gossip from employees and from models who had cologne sample duty. Ronnie had been booked for that job a few times, but it was a real dog. You assault innocent shoppers with perfume you know stinks, and they don't pay you enough to take the abuse. Ronnie was nervous when she signed in and saw that Marilyn Ellis, her supervisor, had scheduled a lunch meeting with her. Ronnie knew it was to chew her out for the extended absence, *blah blah blah.* But in the meantime, Ronnie's charm turned passing shoppers into prospective customers. Her skill and how-to banter as she applied foundation and powder, brushed brows into shape, or highlighted a cheekbone turned those prospects into sales. She was good. She knew it.

Fortunately, the morning was busy and profitable. She did makeovers for a bride, her mother, and her two bridesmaids, and they bought the whole package from cleanser to mascara. *Ka-ching.* But it was more than the money. Ronnie felt good because each of them looked better than when she sat down in the chair.

"Glad you're back." Marilyn perched on the chair across from Ronnie, who had been waiting, and took her menu from the waiter in the court jester's hat. Marilyn was small enough to shop in juniors, but her style was far more chignon and pumps. She used Essential Ebony, the darkest foundation in the line, but even without it her skin glowed.

Could we skip the small talk and get to the point? Ronnie had her ain't-too-proud-to-beg speech in her hip pocket because she really wanted to keep this job. "I am too. I'm sorry I was away so long. It's just that . . ."

"Unfortunately, it happens to all of us sooner or later. How's your mother handling it?"

She's being so nice. Ronnie was not prepared for this. "Uh, she's okay. My sister lives in Buffalo too, so that helps." *Helps who?* Ronnie could hear Celeste and Della at each other.

"Listen, Ronnie, let me get to the point." Marilyn laid the menu down, leaned across the table like she had a secret to share.

Here it comes.

"We want you full-time."

"Are you serious?! I knew I was history."

"Oh, no. While you were gone it became apparent that working just twenty hours a week your sales account for more dollar volume than any other Sable rep. This is a new company, so there's lots of room for growth. We're looking to expand the line into other markets across the country. You could make supervisor in less than a year. It would be a salaried position, plus commissions, which means you can really clean up. You'd have benefits, vacations."

A job? Me? "Marilyn, I don't know what to say." *This cannot be why I spent all these years bustin' my chops.* "I'm really flattered, but . . ." *Shit, I haven't had health insurance since I left home. And a vacation?* "You know I work part-time to keep my days for auditions. When the right call comes I need to be free to go." *When was the last time that happened?* "I like Sable Shades, but for me it's a paycheck, not a future."

"Don't say no. Think about it. We want you on board, Ronnie." Marilyn picked up the menu. "Let's order."

Ronnie was almost too tense to eat, but this would probably be her meal for the day, and it was a freebie.

"So I told her I'd think about it." And Ronnie had thought about it. More often than she wanted to, but right now she was happy the check had cleared, the rent was paid, and LaVonne was putting the finishing touches on her weave.

LaVonne spoke to Ronnie's reflection in the mirror. "She really thought you wanted some lousy ass full-time job at Macy's? Girlfriend better get real. See, that's what's the matter with us. The sister should be encouragin' you to follow your dreams, you know. Not temptin' you to sell out. Did you hear about Téa? She got herself a series, girl. Prime time. I think she's a cop or somethin'. Packed up and moved to Hol-

lywood. She called me looking for somebody to keep her naps
in order out there."

Téa got that show? They were the same type, and Ronnie
always ran into her at auditions, like the one for this series.
"Good for her." But Téa had been getting the callbacks.

"Ta da! Only her hairdresser knows for sure!" LaVonne
spun the chair around and handed Ronnie the mirror. It was
long, flowing, and fabulous. No one could tell it wasn't nature
made. LaVonne was the best. The wigs could go back in the
closet. Ronnie happily made out the check for eight hundred
dollars, which included her model discount.

LaVonne's was on West Fifty-seventh, across the street
from the building where Ronnie had been staying when Celeste came to visit. Ronnie looked up at the towering structure, remembered the twenty-four-hour doormen who never
failed to speak to her by name. "How's it going, Miss Frazier?" "Need a cab, Miss Frazier?" She loved it and she
wanted it again. She strolled along Fifty-seventh toward Fifth,
hair blowing in the autumn breeze. She had a really great audition this week, three scheduled for next, and a callback for a
commercial this afternoon. Her rent and most of her bills were
paid, she had money in the bank, and she was going to a party
tonight. She felt like herself again. Ronnie waited for the light
and ignored the young brother in the yellow down jacket who
stared at her and licked his lips. *But you're right. I look good!*

Who could ask for anything more? Ronnie sang to herself.
Girl Crazy. It was her first big role in a school play, a musical
with real costumes and scenery. Before the show was cast, she
made her mother buy the album. Della fussed about wasting
money, but Ronnie listened to Judy Garland belt out that song
until she had it down pat. Ronnie didn't have the best voice, as
the drama teacher pointed out at the audition, but she had the
best delivery.

From the time she was eight and sat in the audience watching Celeste in the Richmond Speaking Contest, Ronnie was
mesmerized. On the day of the citywide oratorical competition, Celeste walked onto the stage wearing her Sunday best,
navy blue Jonathan Logan double-knit dress with the brass

buttons and white stockings instead of her usual kneesocks. Ronnie, in a flowered cotton skirt Della had made, white blouse, and anklets, sat between her parents wishing that she would wake up the next day and be in eighth grade too. She thought Celeste looked so sophisticated. Celeste began, "'The Creation.'" She paused, then continued, "by James Weldon Johnson," and her voice, rich and round, filled the auditorium, and Ronnie watched with her mouth open. Celeste enunciated each syllable of the dramatic poem, and when she was finished, the audience broke into applause. All those people clapping for her sister. Ronnie was so excited she jumped to her feet cheering and waving at Celeste. Della had to yank her down in her seat. Afterward they went to Howard Johnson's for ice cream sundaes, and Ronnie tried to tell Celeste how great she was and that the judges were wrong not to pick her. Celeste just rolled her eyes and kept stirring her melting ice cream, but that didn't matter to Ronnie. She was inspired. She wanted people to clap for her too.

Then Ronnie had asked how come they spelled sundae with an *e*. Celeste said, "Boy you are really stupid!" "I'm not stupid!" Ronnie shot back. "Stupid people pretend they know everything, like you!" Will and Della stopped them before a full-fledged fight broke out, and they rode home, each wedged in a corner of the backseat, glaring at each other. Celeste went to her room, and they never talked about the contest again. Ronnie remembered it like it was yesterday.

That began Ronnie's real pursuit of stardom. She was so sure and determined that Will and Della couldn't tell her no. So she took tap at Miss Barbara's School of Dance and drama classes at the Langston Hughes Center. She learned modeling and deportment at June II. Ronnie progressed from Sunday school pageants, where every child who tried out got a role, to performing in plays at the African Cultural Center. What Ronnie lacked in talent she made up for with enthusiasm and energy, which got her as far as New York.

After high school, she convinced her father to give her the money he would have spent on her first year in college to try out Manhattan. If she made it, the money was hers, free and clear. If she couldn't take care of herself after the first year, she promised to come home, go to school, *and* get a job to pay him back. Della convinced Will it was a fair deal. Father and daughter shook on it. Celeste told them they were crazy. Ronnie took the Greyhound to the city, moved into the Martha Washington Hotel for Women, and started making the rounds. Agents, go-sees, auditions. "Too short." "Too curvy." "Too ethnic." "Would you shave your head?" "Do you have a wig?" She got a few nibbles, met some photographers. Then she lost her personal and professional cherry for that cigarette ad. After that she actually made it to Europe and back, but it had all been hit-or-miss. Her enthusiasm wasn't enough to make up for the elusive "it" she seemed to lack. The A-list girls, Iman, Beverly, Mounia, Magic, Sheila, worked all the time. The B-list girls worked when the A's weren't available. C's got the A and B leftovers, and then there was everybody else. At TV auditions the names changed to Jasmine, Janet, and Robin, but the story was the same. Ronnie was still in New York, drifting somewhere between C and everybody else. It just wasn't as easy as it used to be. Or as much fun. And she wasn't as young as she used to be, either.

But today was a good day. Ronnie turned down Fifth Avenue and slowed her pace to allow for a little window shopping. The black mink bomber trimmed in leather made her stop. The mannequin posed right next to the big red SALE sign, and for a second Ronnie's reflection in the glass made it look like she was already wearing it. It was definitely her. Not over the top and tacky like that hideous red fox number her friend Kayla had been so proud of, or uptight and pretentious like the boring little ranch mink Celeste had worn to the funeral even though it wasn't *that* cold. SALE. Ronnie looked in the window another few seconds. *If I get that commercial.*

She continued down Fifth and entered the smoked glass building for the callback. Ronnie took two spins through the revolving doors, cranking up her energy. It made the building service guys laugh. *Yes! I got the* power. She was a few minutes early for her two forty-five call time, so she paced the lobby, getting into character, focusing, transforming herself into the young entrepreneur whose business got a boost when she switched to FlexTime Long Distance Service. Ronnie wore the same black trousers, red silk twin set, and gold button earrings she'd worn to the audition and she felt like she had "it." *And my hair looks two hundred percent better.*

Ronnie always felt more confident at second readings because it meant they already liked what she could do, so she was free to do it better. At two forty she rode the elevator up, followed the sign pointing the way to the FlexTime callbacks. Before she could sign in she was greeted by the same ad exec who made her feel so comfortable before.

"We're ready for you." The woman was round and brown with short-cropped hair.

The woman's vibe was definitely large and in charge, but she was also very encouraging at the audition. Ronnie felt her confidence growing as she was ushered into the taping room. She shook hands firmly with the men seated next to the video camera, then took her place across the room, behind the white line. The copy was printed on an easel placed in her line of vision, but she knew it by heart. "FlexTime lets me do business anytime!" Ronnie's heart pumped like a runner who knew she had the race won. When she got the signal she slated her name and gave them two different readings. First she did her "mellow, unquestionably Black but not street" rendition, followed by her "so crisp and clear I could be from anywhere and nobody would know I'm Black" version. Ronnie saw them taking notes, heard whispering behind the camera. The whole thing took two minutes, but the account exec walked her to the door, gave her a wink and a thumbs-up. Ronnie was flying.

And she was still up when she arrived downtown that night for the party. She had changed clothes six times before settling on black leather pants and a skin-tight, sheer brown tank that made her look topless until you got real close. She stepped off the elevator, put on her pleasantly disinterested smile, and casually searched the cavernous space for her friend Kayla, who'd convinced Ronnie this was *the* event of the week. Kayla, whose real name was Margaret, was an in-between, like Ronnie, still struggling to make her life work out the way she planned it nearly twenty years ago. She had a high-pitched voice that she figured would make her perfect for cartoons, but the voice-over thing hadn't panned out yet. She had recently cut her hair skull-short and gotten new head shots to shake it up a little. Never one to miss an opportunity to charm the person who could turn her career around, she made it her business to know what was happening, when, and how to get in.

Ronnie was mid-makeover on Thursday night when Kayla dropped by the Sable Shades counter to give her the scoop. "The loft belongs to Michael somebody. He's some kinda investment banker or broker or something. Anyway, he made a whole heap of money in the stock market and his uncle or somebody is the mayor of . . . Atlanta, I think. I'm not sure. So this guy, the one with the loft, not the mayor, just got married to a singer who used to work with Quincy. Her brother is what's his name, you know he used to play for the Knicks, but anyway she just got a lead role in . . . *Rent*, yeah, I think that's it. And her new hubby is throwing this party to celebrate his bride's good fortune with a hundred or so of their closest friends. I heard Wesley might stop by. He's shooting a movie here, you know."

Ronnie always added an hour to whatever time Kayla said they'd meet, but even that plus the forty-five minutes it took her to find a taxi and get down here apparently wasn't enough. She adjusted her new Prada bag on her shoulder, took a glass of champagne from the passing waiter, sipped, and continued to search the sea of faces. Ronnie dug out her cigarettes, glanced around for an ashtray, then noticed no one was smoking.

"They make it really hard for us. You have to go outside or up on the roof." The nasal voice behind her was vaguely familiar. Ronnie turned. The face was familiar too. Pecan brown, bland, rimless glasses. At first she couldn't place him. Brooks Brothers pin stripe, rep tie. When Ronnie figured it out, she didn't let him know.

"I know you—Veronica Frazier." He grinned. "R. Phillip Dade. From the bank."

Ronnie feigned puzzlement for a beat to take him down a

notch. "Oh? . . . Yes . . . I remember." She only gave him her sixty-watt smile this time. "Small world."

"I'm going up for a smoke. I'd be delighted to have your company."

Ronnie looked at her watch. She didn't want to miss Kayla. "I'm meeting someone who's . . ." She was dying for a butt. "Uh . . . never mind." *Let her wait for me for a change. Besides this'll be amusing.* "Why not?"

Ronnie weaved through the crowd behind him to the bustling kitchen, which was bigger than her whole apartment, then out a steel door, up a short flight of stairs, onto the roof, into the night air. Trees and shrubs lined walkways that led off in several different directions. "Each resident has a private area," R. Phillip said. They emerged into a garden Ronnie could instantly imagine in the summertime, but right now it was really cold. She crossed her arms over her chest 'cause she knew her nips already stood at attention. A slice of moon hung over the Flatiron Building. *Wow.* But she maintained her cool, perched casually on the end of a cedar bench, and took out her pack. R. Phillip put an orange flame to the tip almost before she got the filter to her lips. Ronnie cupped her hand around his to protect the fire from the wind. His hands were soft, a little doughy, but warm.

"It's windproof." He lit his own cigarette and snapped the gold lighter closed.

"Convenient." Ronnie tried to figure out whether she meant that to sound as snide as it did. "I wouldn't have taken you for a smoker."

"I'm not. I'm a quitter!" He chuckled at his own lame humor. "About every six months, I give them up for a while. Then one day I look down and I'm holding a lit one. I never remember exactly how it happens."

"Convenient." Ronnie said again.

"Look. I'm sorry I couldn't help you at the bank. I . . ."

"Don't be. It was no big deal." *Yeah. It was no problem avoiding my bill collectors a little longer. And scrounging around in coat pockets and old purses for change and tokens.* "It's lovely up here."

"They had a great cookout last Fourth of July. Terrific for watching the fireworks." He took a drag. "So, you're friends with Mike and Felice?" He phrased it as a question, but she knew the answer was really the password. He wanted to make sure she belonged. She'd make him wait. "Mike went to Morehouse with my older brother," he offered, still waiting for Ronnie to reveal her connection. "And we're all fraternity brothers."

Ass. "Ah. Old friends. That's great. It's so hard to make new ones in this town." *Just a little longer.*

"Are you Greek?"

"No. I was never interested in pledging." *I didn't go to college either, you jerk.* "My sister did, though. I guess I'm not much of a joiner." Ronnie could hear the wheels turning, and before he could ask about her sister, she crushed her cigarette under her heel and stood to leave. "My friend must be wondering where I am by now." *Okay.* "She and Felice have the same voice coach. And they were on one of the soaps together. *All My Children* maybe?" *No names.* Ronnie had no idea where or how Kayla heard about this party. But her story sounded good. She knew R. Phillip would buy it. *Now he knows I'm a mongrel, but I have a professional connection to his crowd.* Ronnie knew the type. She wasn't really "one of them," but there were always exceptions.

"So from what I can see, I bet you're an actress as well." R. Phillip gave Ronnie a thorough, not even subtle once-over and grinned dumbly.

They were always ready to grant some sort of temporary pedigree for her. "Yes. Yes, I am." She smiled her "you'll be lucky to know me when I'm famous" smile. *How long will it take?*

"So, have I seen you in anything?"

"Maybe." She shivered against the cool breeze and hugged her arms around herself. "I've done some commercials, a few films, nothing major—yet." *Come on, Mr. Dade. Ask me out. You know you want to. You're intrigued. I'm "different from other women you know."* These guys were always good for dinner at some new, expensive, hard-to-get-into restaurant.

They spent lots of money and liked arm candy to show off, but years ago Ronnie had imposed a one-date limit. She'd use them, they'd use her, no fuss, no muss, no expectations. It worked very well. *If he starts another sentence with "so," I might strangle him right here on this roof.*

"So, I was wondering if I could call you sometime? Let me make up for what happened at the bank."

Bingo!

"There's this great new restaurant! Reservations are impossible to get, but a buddy of mine knows . . ."

Thank you very much! The streak continues! Ronnie acted surprised, then smiled pleasantly. "Um . . . ah . . . sure. You certainly have my number." *And boy do I ever have yours. And you, sir, are not my type.*

Of course Ronnie didn't know what that even meant. Over the years her type had changed almost as often as her address. She started her jock block in high school, and it lasted through her first two years in New York when she decided that while their bodies were hard, so were their heads. It was followed immediately by the deep, soul-searching, writer-actor and "by the way I have even less than you" phase. She rebounded to the TV news/sports guys but quickly tired of not being the cute one. That led to the corporately mobile, leverage my way to the top brother spate, where R. Phillip would have fit quite nicely. This moved her directly into her older men with money moment, which didn't last any longer than the "it's only angina, could you hand me my pills" date. At least one "real" boyfriend emerged from most of these periods. Ronnie would pin her hopes that this might be the one. Then she'd want too much and he'd offer too little, or she'd find somebody else's underwear, or money missing from her purse. And the same pin that held the hopes usually popped the bubble. So two years ago, fed up with the pickings and deciding her type didn't exist, Ronnie declared a moratorium. It had been a long, dry spell, but R. Phillip, while he might be useful, wasn't the one to break it.

She reached out her hand and touched his sleeve, but it was so brief and light R. Phillip almost thought he'd imagined it.

Ronnie eased away. "I'd better get back." She disappeared down the path toward the stairs and added some bounce to her step because she knew he was watching.

Kayla had been a no-show at the party, and Ronnie was on her way out the door when she called two days later. "Sorry, girl. I was on my way, then Buster called me. You know Buster. I dated him last year for a while." Ronnie played with the stack of mail by the phone while Kayla rattled on. "Anyway, he used to do the weather on Channel Five, and now he's doing sports in Miami but he still knows e-v-e-r-y-body." Ronnie didn't like mail. It was usually people asking for money she didn't have. It put her in a bad mood, so she didn't like to open it. Besides, she'd paid most of her bills. "So Buster invited me to a screening of that new Will Smith flick. *And* to the private party after. I know you know I told you I cut Buster loose 'cause he's one tired, boring motherfruther, but I had to go to this. You'll never guess who was there!"

"I can't talk, Kayla. I got another callback for that phone company gig. I'll call you later." And even though they always shared information, just in case one of them heard about a casting the other hadn't, Ronnie didn't tell her about the audition for a sitcom pilot she was going to after that.

"Thanks for coming by, Ronnie. This campaign is quite extensive. The client wanted to see you one more time." The ad exec's words echoed in Ronnie's head as she rode down in the elevator. "In order to be sure." On the corner she checked the address for her next appointment and headed up Fifth. *National ad. Major market rollout. Residuals. BIG residuals. Spokesperson! I could be the FlexTime lady. Like James Earl Jones. I could be the brand! I could be in a Super Bowl commercial!* Ronnie sailed along the street, her feet barely touching the pavement, oblivious to everything but the story in her head until she found herself smack in front of that mink bomber jacket again. Her next audition was in the same building, and the jacket was still there. *This has to mean something,* she rationalized. *It's a sign. I've never been to a call here in seventeen years.*

It fit like it was custom made for her. *Another sign.* She wrote out the check and waited while they called the bank to verify her funds. She'd have enough to tide her over. There would be a few weeks before the residuals started, but she'd have her day rate for shooting the ad right away. *Wait till I tell Ma and Da*—Ronnie stopped the thought cold. *Ma'll share the news with sister dear. I'll call Nik myself.*

Ronnie wore the jacket home. She felt so good she opened a bottle of merlot and plowed through the wicker basket of mail. Five or six pieces in, she saw the stamp and the postmark. Rio de Janeiro, Brasil. He was coming back in six weeks and wanted his apartment. *Perfect, 'cause I am tired of this shit hole. Maybe I'll use a broker this time. That's a first.* The phone rang as Ronnie counted her chickens and piled her eggs in the basket.

"Glad you left us your home number. I didn't want to leave the message on your service. I wanted you to hear it from me."

Yes! Finally! I'm the FlexTime Girl! Ronnie spooned honey into her tea.

"It was close. They really loved you . . ." Ronnie stopped stirring, her spoon suspended midair. ". . . But the client made the final decision. They got hung up on your hair being different." She didn't hear the rest.

The spoon landed on the receipt for her jacket, which sat on top of the mail on the kitchen counter. FINAL SALE. No Refunds. No Returns. No Exchanges. Drops of tea splattered onto her checkbook, which lay open next to the mail. The balance hardly covered next month's rent, let alone first and last months' security and key money for a new place. Ronnie's basket full of unhatched eggs crashed to the floor along with her cup of tea.

4

". . . running into a brick wall
only hurts you."

Here we go. Deep breath. Celeste shifted all of the plastic
grocery bags to one hand, propped the screen door open with
her foot. She dug past the date book, wallet, and coupons in
her purse, found the *F* key ring, and fumbled with the locks on
her parents' back door. Will had been dead for six months, but
she still thought of it as her parents' house. She'd taken to
stopping by a few times a week to check, because somebody
had to.

"You wouldn't need so many locks if you'd sell this place
and move out where we are. It's much safer, Mother." Celeste
fussed up the stairs and into the kitchen. "Mother!? Where are
you?" She put the bags on the counter and peeked in the living
room. It could have been a lovely room, with the fireplace and
honey oak mantel, but her mother was never more creative
than the oatmeal and gold tweed Herculon sofa and love seat
that sat on sculptured pea green carpet with the nap worn flat.
As a kid, Celeste used to be embarrassed when the neighbors
would come over because their homes looked so much more
polished. *Daddy was so ambitious. Think where they could
have gone if Mother had tried, even a little.* Celeste hung her
coat in the hall closet. "Mother!?"

"I heard you the first and second times." Della trudged up
the back steps from the basement, lugging a full laundry basket.

"Let me take that." Celeste reached for the basket.

Della shooed her away. "I wash clothes when you're not
around, you know."

Unfazed, Celeste plowed ahead. "You could have a washer

and dryer right in your apartment *and* no stairs! Wouldn't that be great?" She reached in the drawer, pulled out an apron, and shook it out in front of her. "This looks awful." Her lips tightly pinched, she examined spots and stains that no amount of washing would eliminate. "Where are the new aprons I bought you?"

"They'll end up just like that one."

"That's not the point. They'd look nice now." Celeste waited for her mother to tell her where the aprons were or go get one. But Della didn't move a muscle. Finally, Celeste slipped the scuzzy one on over her teal suit and started unpacking her bounty. "Did you see those boys hanging out on the corner by the Clifton house? Someone should call the police. This neighborhood is not what it used to be."

"No, I guess it's not." Della put the basket down by the door. "Things change." She flipped the stairway light off. "But *those* boys live in that house now. Moved in last month. I hired 'em to clean up the yard, now that the snow's finally gone." She pulled back the curtain, looked out the window, and smiled to herself. "Um-hm. Did a nice job, didn't they?"

"They might be all right, but they could be little hoodlums waiting to rob you. You can't be too careful these days." Celeste carried twenty boxes of spaghetti to the pantry.

"What the devil?"

"I was at the store this morning. . . ."

"What else is new?" Della asked sarcastically. She knew her daughter's Saturday ritual began with a seven A.M. trip to the supermarket. Whether it was Top's or Wegman's depended on the sales, which she would have carefully researched, and organized her shopping list accordingly. As a rule, by nine she had completed her shopping, picked up and dropped off dry cleaning, filled up the tank, had her car washed, and was back home putting her groceries away. Having crossed several items off her to-do list gave her a feeling of great satisfaction and, to some extent, comfort. That left the rest of her day free. Free for steering committee meetings, annoying her mother, sales at the mall, Women's Day committee meetings, annoying her mother, outlet shopping in Pennsylvania, sorority meetings, Literacy Volunteers, and annoying her mother.

"It was a great sale, Mother."

"I'm sure it was."

"Maybe I'll put this on now." She held up a huge ham.

"What am I gon' do with that? It'll take me six months to eat it! There's only one of me, you know." Della jammed her hands into the pockets of her duster.

Does she have to say the all the time? Celeste faced the counter so only the cabinets registered her annoyed expression.

"Besides, I buy my own groceries. Do I look like I'm starvin'?"

"Well, I don't think you're eating right." Celeste opened the refrigerator, moved the plastic sherbet container of fruit cocktail and the leftover half of a chicken pot pie to make room for the ham, then opened the crisper drawer. "Look at this lettuce and celery. They're turning to slime." She reached for an empty grocery bag, deposited the offending produce. "And why aren't you dressed? I ordered all those jogging suits for you to wear! Are you sick?" She gawked at Della's coffee coat.

"I dress to go to work. I don't jog, and I don't need to impress anybody around here, unlike some people." Della rolled her eyes at Celeste's suit. "I know you didn't get all done up to bring me a ham and some spaghetti." Della handed her a paper towel to wipe up the slime juice.

"I'm meeting Lydia later. We're going to select the flowers for the benefit."

"That woman won't ever be your friend, Celeste. No matter how many ways you turn yourself inside out." And Della had watched Celeste try to impress people she thought were important, had more money or higher social standing her whole life. When Celeste was young, the one or two invitations she'd receive to Doctor or Attorney So-and-so's daughter's birthday party were more exciting than Christmas. She'd go into her stash of hoarded allowance and buy a gift that was far too expensive, an angora sweater or a charm bracelet.

Other kids brought a record, or a bottle of Love's Lemon Fresh. Celeste's present never received the ooohs and aaahs she hoped for. It would stand out like a neon sign that blinked "I'm trying." The handwritten thank-you note always followed in a few days, but she never got the phone call to "come over and hang out," or "wanna go to Santora's for pizza?" that meant she was accepted. She was still trying.

"Don't be ridiculous. Of course she's my friend. We've vacationed together for years!"

Della recognized a stalemate and changed the subject. "Did your sister give you her new address and phone number?"

"Oh. She's moved again? Isn't that twice since Christmas?" Celeste replied, then changed the subject back. "You need to get out more." She opened the milk carton, took a sniff, screwed up her face, then poured the contents down the drain and added the container to her plastic bag. "You should come to church tomorrow. Reverend Walters . . ."

"I don't *feel* like going to church." Della didn't hold much with religion, hadn't since she was a teenager. Will was a staunch churchgoer, and she'd go now and then to please him. It wasn't that she wasn't a believer, quite the contrary, but Della was convinced long ago that the destiny of her soul was between her and the Lord, and she neither needed nor wanted to share her feelings with anyone else, much less a bunch of meddlesome busybodies. "And for your information, I get out of here every day. Or doesn't going to work count?" Della got the pad and pencil by the phone, copied Ronnie's new address from the Chapman Brothers Funeral Home calendar where she'd written it. "You weren't worried about how much I got out before your father passed. Why is it so important now?" She ripped the page from the spiral, handed it to Celeste. "Here. Just in case."

"I don't even copy them in my book anymore." Celeste took the paper, pinched off jagged edges as she spoke. "And it's different now. You shouldn't spend so much time by yourself. It isn't good." She took a breath, tried to sound like her plan was spur of the moment instead of carefully thought out. "Okay. Forget about tomorrow, but come to Easter service

with us next week. We're not going away. My husband says
he's too busy at the clinic." She propped an elbow on the open
refrigerator door. "I don't know how Everett can stand that
awful place. If I'm sick of it, surely he must be."

"He started it. What are the chances he's gon' leave? And
where is he? Why aren't you with him instead of annoyin'
me?"

Celeste closed the refrigerator, looked away quickly.
"He's . . . uh . . . I don't know, playing tennis or something.
I'll see him back at the house."

Della noticed the missed beat but didn't call attention to it.
She'd had a feeling something wasn't right there for a long
time. But it wasn't her place to say so.

"I made sure he's not working next Sunday." Celeste re-
covered and returned to her script. "We'll pick you up, and I
know! We'll go shopping during the week! You could really
use some new dresses. And we'll have brunch on Sunday at
Fanny's or maybe E. B. Green's. I'll make reservations."

Della sat down at the table, popped open a can of honey-
roasted peanuts, and waited for Celeste's sudden gust of wind
to blow over.

Celeste got her date book out of her purse, slipped Ronnie's
newest new address inside, then flipped to her schedule for the
week. "How's Wednesday? I'll come by your job after school
and we'll go to the Galleria. It'll be mobbed. Everyone's having Easter sales, you know, but it's the nicest mall." Celeste
penciled in the date, closed her book. "Wednesday it is."

"Did you hear me say yes?"

"But . . ."

"But I'm not goin' shoppin' this week, so you can take out
your little book and your eraser. And lunch or brunch or
whatever next Sunday would be nice, but don't do it on my
account."

"Everett and I are going anyway!"

"Okay. Thank you." Della poured a handful of nuts. "You
got any more plans for my time?"

Celeste paused. "Not exactly." She'd sidled up to this talk
before, but Della had managed to slip away. This time Celeste

was loaded for bear, and she planned to come away with an answer even if she got clawed in the process. "I hate to bring this up. . . ."

"Then don't."

Why does she give me such a hard time? Celeste took a deep breath. "Even if you won't move out of here, you have to think about selling some of those houses." She knew this had to be brief and to the point. "It's way too much for you to be bothered with."

Della cut her eyes at Celeste, returned to her peanuts.

Celeste hated it when her mother wouldn't dignify her with an answer. It made her feel four feet tall and eleven years old. "I know Mr. Shorty is looking after them, and you trust him, but he's getting old too." She furrowed her brow. "I drove past the house on Verplanck this week. One of the side windows is broken." Celeste waited for some kind of response, walked back to the refrigerator when she didn't get one. "You're only delaying the inevitable. How are you going to keep up with all that property? You haven't even gone through Daddy's clothes yet, have you? I saw that ancient plaid sport coat of his in the closet just now. Someone less fortunate can use . . ."

"Leave that jacket right where it is," Della snapped. She had planned to give the jacket away thirty years ago, until Ronnie found that note folded up in the pocket. It had hung there ever since, to remind him that she might have forgiven, but she never forgot.

"Okay. But I can go through the rest of his things, bag them up for the City Mission. I think it'll make you feel better."

"I feel fine, but go ahead since it's worryin' you."

Makes it sound like she's doin' me a favor. Celeste took out the ham again, snatched a roaster from the cabinet by the stove, struggled to keep the mad out of her voice. "Well, you went through his papers and things to file taxes, didn't you?"

Della squared her shoulders, assumed her immovable object pose. Truth was, she'd planned to tackle the attic many a Saturday morning, or Thursday night, had her hand on the knob, but she never turned it. She knew it was past time for income tax, but she'd rather take a spanking than be up there sorting through his papers and clothes that smelled of him, wading through too many yesterdays.

"You didn't, did you?! Mother! What am I going to do with you!?" Celeste's voice hit the high spike. "Why didn't you say something before now?"

"Do whatever you want, Celeste, and leave me the hell alone." Della got up, retrieved her laundry basket, and headed out of the kitchen.

Celeste's hands shook, so she steadied herself with the routine tasks of cooking. She rinsed the ham, squeezed on some syrup, shoved it in the oven, just like Della always did it. In one of her grief-counseling books she'd read about a man who kept his dead wife's false teeth in a jar on the kitchen windowsill for over a year. Used to drive his son crazy. Then one day the man just threw them away. When he was ready to let her go, he did. Until then he needed something to hang on to. Maybe that's what her mother was doing. At any rate, she'd outlasted her this time. *She'll see I'm right about this.*

After grabbing her reading glasses from her purse, Celeste walked quietly upstairs, past Della in her sewing room, which Celeste and Ronnie had dubbed Della's House of Style when they were kids. In one of their few joint efforts the girls had ganged up to persuade Della that her "original creations" made them look like rejects. Even their father helped plead their case. Della's feelings were hurt, but she turned her hand to her own wardrobe and over the years had made herself hundreds of smock tops, all pullovers since she never mastered the art of the buttonhole. And she made curtains. Every room in the house had seasonal changes of window dressing.

Celeste opened the attic door to Will's World. She and Ronnie had stopped calling it that when the name came too close to the truth. His room always smelled of Old Spice and shoe polish. It still did, a little. Right after the accident, she and Ronnie had picked up socks, stacked papers, gathered towels from the bathroom, stripped the narrow single bed that stood forlornly in the far corner. The task was too sad to stay at for long. Besides, she and Ronnie were on each other's nerves in no time. Celeste hadn't been up here more than once or twice since October. She meant to, but the holidays were busy as usual, and she had been preparing herself for the assistant principal's interview. If she could move one more notch up the pay scale, maybe she could convince Everett they could afford to buy their own summer place instead of always renting or waiting for an invite.

Celeste had expected the room to be cold. Empty, unused, and dead meant cold somehow. *It's warmer than downstairs.* She took off the apron and her jacket, draped them on the hook on the back of the door where her father's snap-brim cap used to hang. She stood in the splash of sunlight coming through the skylight, looked around. There was no Della presence up here. To Celeste it didn't seem deliberate, but gradual, the way continents that used to be joined had slowly, imperceptibly separated until there were oceans between them. Up here Della was a million miles away. *When did they start drifting away from each other?*

The room was arranged with comfort and convenience in mind. Not particularly macho, although she had flushed and fumbled when she stumbled on the stash of skin magazines under his bed. Will's entertainment center was actually a double set of deep mahogany bookshelves, built-ins he'd removed from a house on Florida Street after he noticed long, charred scars from cigarettes laid on the shelves and left to burn. They stood on either side of his megascreen television. The upper shelves held two VCRs, a couple of camcorders, a short-wave radio, an electronic weather station, and stereo components, including his latest toy, a CD player that held one hundred disks. Lower shelves were crowded with repair manuals, how-to books, and catalogs of every variety. Will loved himself some gadgets, and he believed in shopping the easy way. Celeste could hear him. "Why should I go to the store, when they'll bring what I want right to my door?"

Celeste examined the photos he had arranged on the middle shelves. Everett, arm around Celeste, who held baby Niki, giggling at the stuffed dog wrapped in her arms. Ronnie grinning five feet wide on her Expressway billboard. Celeste picked up the faded family portrait taken in the snow, in front of the house on Chester Street. Will held a shovel over his shoulder. One of Della's hands rested on her very pregnant belly, the other held hands with a decidedly grim-faced Celeste. She tried to remember that day, or who was behind the camera, but nothing came to mind. *They look so young.* She could feel tears collecting so she put it down, turned away.

The midnight blue leather sofa, ordered straight from the Penney's catalog, had a recliner at one corner and pull-out end tables. Celeste ran her hand across the rings left by countless cans of Genesee Beer, picked up the remote, clicked on the TV. *Just for a little company.* Stock car races on ESPN. *The last channel he watched.* Celeste shook off the feeling of disquiet, continued to surf until she settled on a decorating show. She figured she'd start with his papers because getting the taxes filed was the most pressing issue, so she went to her father's desk.

The thing was massive, longer and wider than the dining room table and made from heavy, dark-stained oak. It had taken him, Mr. Shorty, and the next-door neighbor all afternoon to get it up the stairs. There were carved gargoyles on the corners, and brass lion heads with bared teeth opened the drawers. Celeste remembered thinking it was the most hideous thing she'd ever seen. He'd found it at the flea market out in Clarence, and the dealer claimed it came from a castle in England. Her father didn't care whose palace it was from. He liked that it was solid and big enough to hold the paperwork, leases, receipts, deeds, mortgages, and repair estimates for all the properties he already owned, and would have plenty of space left over for those he planned to acquire.

A brand-new PC sat boldly in the middle of the huge old desk, flanked by the cordless phone and answering machine on one side and the fax machine on the other. It seemed an awkward meeting of the past and the future. Will could preach about the importance of keeping up with the times. "We don't drive horse and buggy nomore, neither," he'd say. Celeste reached across a stack of CD-ROMs and removed a fax from the machine. An estimate for a new roof for—she couldn't make out the property address. *He must have requested this before* . . . Celeste blinked back a tear, went to the cabinet by the door. On the shelf along with the boxes of Salada and Swiss Miss and a jar of store brand instant coffee sat Ronnie's faded Esso Gasoline mug. The tiger's grinning face had faded to an orange smudge. Celeste took it out, dropped in a tea bag, and filled it with water from the five-gallon cooler in the corner. She popped it in the microwave and waited. The tea would be an elixir to ward off the haints that lay in wait for her among her father's things.

An hour later, her mug was empty. She'd gone through all but two of the drawers on the right side of the desk, and the stack of paper she was currently sorting rested in her lap. Sitting in Will's oversized swivel chair, with the reading glasses she hated balanced precariously on the tip of her nose, Celeste felt like a detective, plowing through her father's history. Most of Will's files were orderly. Each property had a folder that contained the deed, bills, receipts, and records for the house. Celeste had made four neat piles on the desk in front of her. The first contained papers that pertained to their income taxes. Fortunately she found the name of Will's accountant and planned to call him Monday morning. Next came "Ask Mr. Shorty," "Ask Mother," and "File." A fifth pile contained odd bits of memorabilia she'd unearthed. Matchbooks from the Humboldt Inn, construction paper birthday cards she and Ronnie had made eons ago, a crystal teardrop earring, the receipt for the Autumn Haze mink jacket he'd bought Della one Christmas. Ronnie was barely toddling. Celeste could still see her fathers's chest poked out in his flannel robe, still hear him saying, "The whole coat is fur, not just the collar." She remembered begging her mother to let her try it on. Della draped the fur over her daughter's narrow shoulders, and the bottom dragged the floor. When Della got all dressed up and put that jacket on, Celeste used to think she looked like a movie star. *What ever happened to those days?*

The smoky-sweet aroma of the ham had worked its way upstairs, but Celeste was too deep in another world to pay attention. She dropped a January 1969 bill from Iroquois Gas into the already overflowing wastebasket, reached for another folder.

Little Pond Road? Where's that? Celeste ran Buffalo streets through her brain, but Little Pond didn't ring a bell. She flipped through the folder. The house had been painted a year ago. Will had bought a new stove and refrigerator too, but she noticed they were more expensive than the ones he usually put in the units. *And where is Gaston Appliance?* She examined the deed. *Prosper, North Carolina? Is he kidding? What kind of name is Prosper?* She thought a moment, had a vague notion that Della and Will were born there, but nobody ever brought it up. Neither one had much of an accent except on the odd word like *po*-lice or *ho*-tel so you'd forget they were born somewhere else. Their move North had pretty much been a one-way deal. There were no summertime excursions to visit relatives or even rushed car trips to bury the dead. During all the funeral preparations there was never a discussion of taking her father back home. *To Prosper, North Carolina?* Buffalo had become his home. Will's brothers and sisters had all moved away from home too. Detroit. Indianapolis. St. Louis. Camden. *Why on earth would Daddy buy property down there? And not tell me?* Celeste flipped the pages. *Deeded to: Will Frazier, Celeste Frazier English, and Veronica Frazier by Odella Womack Frazier? What the . . . ?* None of this made sense. Stapled to the back was a small manila envelope. Inside she found two keys.

"Mother!" Celeste ran down the stairs and found Della still in the sewing room, sitting on the old vinyl hassock by the window, surrounded by shelves of fabric for future projects and plastic trash bags full of yarn. She didn't knit or crochet, but she'd been "plannin' to learn" for more than twenty years, so she stocked up on skeins of yarn in every possible hue whenever she found a good sale.

"Do you know about this?" Celeste thrust the deed at her mother.

Della gave the paper a cursory glance, sucked her teeth. "Oh for cryin' out loud." She turned away. "Wish I'd a tore that mess up before your father ever saw it."

"Torn it up?! Why would you do that?!" Celeste's voice grew louder with each utterance. "Whose house was this?!"

"Don't you use that tone to me." Della shot her a look.

Celeste yielded, dropped her eyes momentarily before she spoke. "I'm sorry. I didn't mean to yell, but . . ."

"I'm a tell you this just once, so you better listen good." Della took a breath. "You listenin'?"

"Yes ma'am."

"That house and land belonged to my daddy. It came to me a couple a years back. I told Will I didn't care what he did with it, I didn't want it. When I left Prosper I said I was never goin' back and I meant it. I know he sent Shorty down to look the house over, and that's all I know. So now it belongs to you and your sister. Y'all best figure out how to sell it."

"Our grandfather's house? I don't even know his name! All you ever said is that he and your mother died when you were young." Celeste's heart was racing. "Then you married Daddy and moved here." Over the years Della's story never varied, and more probing only netted a bad attitude. Della never talked about any old days, good, bad, or indifferent, so finally Celeste had stopped asking. But this was a house, solid, substantial. *Real* estate. *She's gotta tell me something.* "Well what does it look like?"

"You heard what I said. Now I'm through with this conversation." Della picked up a skein of red yarn.

"But Mother, I . . ." Della's intense glare interrupted her. Celeste stood her ground a long moment, then realized that running into a brick wall only hurts you.

She backed out of the room, made it halfway down the stairs, then had to sit and regroup. It was like she'd won the grand prize, but nobody else seemed to want it. *I'm not gonna let her make me feel bad about inheriting a house.* Celeste leafed through the papers in her lap. They showed ownership of forty-five acres. *It's probably a swamp. That would be perfect. Whatever it is, it's one more thing for me to take care of.* The piercing bleat of the smoke alarm shocked her back to reality, and she went running to check on the long forgotten ham.

Della heard it too, but the alarm going off in her head was louder. Besides, she didn't want that ham in the first place. No more than she had wanted to go and live at Little Pond Road.

MONDAY, DECEMBER 27, 1948
CADYSVILLE, NORTH CAROLINA

"*MAMA!*" Odella's howl heaved itself against the ponderous December clouds and the pelting rain, silencing the somber, prayerful moans of the mourners.

They had been packed in the white frame church all morning, singing and praising and shouting loud enough to wake the dead. Usually Odella sang in the choir, because she had a voice that was big and rich as a grown woman's, but on this day she sat in the first pew, rocking, her hands balled up in the lap of her white cotton dress. All through the service she prayed for her sweet mama to get up out of that box, because this could not be.

Nothing had made sense since she got called out of class, how many days ago? She'd been staring studiously at the open reader in front of her because she'd already finished the story, but Ruthetta Buttons, the girl she shared the desk and book with, was still inching her finger along the page. So Odella kept her head bowed because the last time she got caught daydreaming she received a lecture about the burden of being "Aunt Haggar's chilren" and the teacher predicted her wasted future as another "no-count colored gal" who wouldn't finish fifth grade, much less go on to A&T and make something of herself. "I was puttin' my 'magination to work, like you said," Odella had answered in defense. She was rewarded by a whipping with the willow switch that always stood, a silent warning, against the slate board.

"Odella, get your things and come on up here. You're needed at home."

The teacher's voice had startled her. "Yes'm." She quickly

gathered her belongings, happy because she figured that somehow her mama had extra time off.

At twenty-six, Odella's mother, Annie, had a reputation as one of the best cooks for counties around. Annie's mother had been a good cook, but Annie had a special gift. She could fix anything, from beef Wellington and baked Alaska to fried catfish and sweet potato pie, and have people licking their lips, their fingers, and wishing they could lick the plate.

Sometimes Annie took Odella with her on small jobs, a birthday luncheon or a christening brunch if it was nearby. Odella would watch her mother take charge of the kitchen and the household help. "We'll need that silver tureen. And make sure it's polished. These string beans aren't fresh enough, try that market over on Salisbury Street." People scurried to do her bidding because they knew without her there was no party. When she was eight, Odella told her mother she wanted to be a cook just like her. Annie about bit her head off. "You'll do no such thing! I want something better than slaving over a hot stove for you!" Annie's grandmother had dropped dead in front of the stove on the plantation where she'd stayed after emancipation. Annie's mother worked as a cook six and a half days a week for thirty-seven years. Annie had come far enough to set her own workdays, but she didn't want *her* daughter in anybody's kitchen. So Annie showed her how to set a table from salad forks to fish knives and demitasse spoons, how to hold china up to the light to tell if it's really fine, and the proper way to pour tea, but never how to cook.

Between Thanksgiving and Christmas, Annie Williams's culinary services were in great demand by wealthy white families in Charlotte, and Annie made a good portion of her living in that month. She catered dinner parties and such the rest of the year, and together with the money she got from Odella's father, the two of them did just fine.

Odella liked it because her mother was home most of the time, and not grouchy and dead tired like her schoolmates' mothers who worked sharecropping, or in the mills or poultry plants. And Odella loved everything about Annie, from the way she plaited her hair in two straight rows down the back of her head to the way she sang "The Sandman's Comin'" when she tucked her in at night.

Odella still curled up with Susie, the first rag doll her mother gave her. She was a cast-off toy with wide eyes, loopy black wool hair, and a dotted Swiss dress. Annie had soaked her in tea for a week to make her brown-skinned. Odella adored the sugar cookies Annie baked shaped in the letters to spell out Odella Womack, and on her way home from school she would gather Queen Anne's lace and her mother would make them both crowns. Odella loved nothing more than to sit for hours, just the two of them, with slabs of Annie's home-made raisin bread and steaming cups of tea and milk, poring over glossy, color photos in the magazines Annie would bring from the homes where she worked. They'd drink in the unimagined possibilities life offered and plan their getaway from Cadysville to Australia or Bali or California because the pictures looked so beautiful. Even though she made Odella study her schoolwork, complete her chores, and mind her elders, Annie was fun.

So this year, like all the others, Odella and Annie had their own special Thanksgiving dinner, with roast goose and wild rice stuffing, collards from the garden, and fresh coconut cake for dessert, on the third Thursday in November instead of the fourth. Annie was feeling a little poorly, so when they'd cleaned up the kitchen she brewed some hog's hoof tea, then rubbed goose grease and camphor on her chest, which she wrapped in flannel, and got in bed under a heavy quilt to sweat it out. Despite the pungent smell and the hot, heavy quilts, Odella begged to sleep with her mother. Annie, afraid Odella would catch her cold, refused. But during the night Odella crawled under the covers to be near her and Annie didn't have the heart to put her out, so she spent the night cir- cled in her mother's arms.

The next morning Annie left for Charlotte. She wasn't due back until Christmas Eve because she flat-out refused to work Christmas Day, then she'd be gone again till the day after New Year's. Odella stayed with Miz Cora and her children during that time. It was the longest six weeks Odella could imagine, and she was just starting to get excited because there were only four days left until she'd see her mama, but now she'd come early.

Waiting outside the two-room school was not Annie but Miz Cora, rocking side to side and wringing her hands. She didn't say a word, didn't even look at Odella directly, just hurried her to the old blue Ford. Odella knew something was wrong, but she was too scared to ask what.

Pastor Malone was waiting when they got to Miz Cora's. He went all around Robin Hood's barn, clearing his throat, looking up at the ceiling for the words to tell Odella that Annie had been called to be with her heavenly Father. Odella looked at him like he had three heads, and all of them were on fire. Then she all but called him a liar and refused to listen to him or anybody else who tried to tell her some nonsense about her mother being dead.

Christmas Eve Odella sneaked out of Miz Cora's house and waited on the porch at home. Waited all night in the spindle-back rocker, bundled in the old brown Pullman blanket that stayed folded in the seat. "You are my sunshine, my only sunshine," Odella sang in a whisper through the long, lonesome night. It was the first song she learned from her mama, and they always sang it together. "Please don't take my sunshine away." So she shivered and rocked and sang, because Annie always came home on Christmas Eve.

At first light Christmas morning Miz Cora found her, shivering, fingernails blue, eyes swollen and crusty from crying. That's when Odella knew she'd never see Annie again, and she felt like she'd been sucked up by a tornado and hurled off the edge of the world. She couldn't see, or feel, or hear, not even her own earth-shattering screams. Two days after that they dressed her in white and took her to the funeral.

And now the mourners ringed Annie's grave in the small churchyard, trying as best they could to protect themselves from the relentless downpour. Odella gripped the clod of earth Miz Cora gave her to sprinkle on her mother's coffin so tightly it dribbled through her fingers. Couldn't anybody see that

Annie had taken all the air and sunshine with her and that right now all Odella wanted was to go with her too?

"Mama, don't leave me!" She flung herself on the ground and crawled in the red mud toward the gaping hole. "Mama, please!" She felt hands snatch at her, tasted the dirt on her lips. Odella kicked, squirmed, hollered, and would not be moved. Then two huge hands grabbed her by the upper arms, lifted her to her feet, held on until the struggle went out of her.

"Looka here, Odella, ain't nothing to be done." Usually Odell Womack's voice boomed, but he spoke gently to her, looked like he'd lost his last friend too. She grabbed two fistfuls of his tweed coat, buried her face in it, and cried, both her tears and the ones Odell couldn't shed. He stood there and let her, one hand resting on her shoulder, while the preacher pronounced Annie's ashes to ashes, accompanied by a weary, resigned hum from the congregation.

Odell was no stranger to his child. Three or four times a year Odella would come home after class and find him sitting at the table. Annie always cooked something extra-special those days. She wore clothes she usually saved for Sundays, and she looked even happier than she usually did. And he always brought something for Odella, whether it was a toy, a new dress, or a piece of money. She called him Papa, at least when nobody else was around, and he was the biggest man she'd ever seen, definitely bigger than anybody in Cadysville. Only thing she could think to compare him to were the hickory trees in the woods behind the house. When she was little she'd climb up his long sturdy legs and he'd stretch out his strong arms, like branches, for her to swing on. Then she'd sit on his knee, eyes wide, and listen while he told her a tale about Nat Turner or Paul Bunyan or Harriet Tubman and make it sound like he'd been right by their side. Then he'd keep company with Annie for a bit out on the porch, squeeze some folded bills into her hand, and he'd be gone. After Odella turned eight, there were no more laps or hugs. Odell kept more space between them. "You too big for all that now," he had said.

There'd been plenty of speculation around Cadysville the

last few days about what Odell should do now that Annie had passed on. People in town had always had something to say about his keeping a full-time family in Prosper and a part-time family here. Never said it to his face, though. And he didn't slink around acting like he cared about their approval. He made no bones about the fact that Odella was his child. He couldn't have denied her if he had wanted. She was strong and sturdy, a sapling to Odell's tree, not birdlike, lighter than air, like Annie.

When the preacher had stopped speaking, Odell pried his daughter's hands from his coat. Mud streaked her white dress and Annie's good black wool coat that Miz Cora had made her wear. It had caked under her nails, smudged her face. He handed Odella his handkerchief, and she barely had the strength to reach for it.

"Come on." His wide, calloused hand swallowed her small, clenched one. It was the color and texture of a razor strop and felt tough and sturdy as resoled shoes. "We goin' home."

Home.

The word terrified Odella, and she trembled from someplace deep that didn't seem to have a bottom. What home? How could it be home if she didn't know where it was or what it looked like? If there was no Annie?

Odell picked her up and carried her to his car, a new green Pontiac, parked by the side of the road. He had found a blanket in the trunk for Odella to wrap up in. She was so cold, wet, and upset when she climbed in the car that her teeth chattered almost as loud as the flip-flop of the windshield wipers. When he drove off she craned her neck to see out the window, but in a moment they were on the interstate, headed away from her familiar, everyday, toward Prosper, and what?

"I went by the house, packed up your stuff. It's in the trunk."

Odella wondered what he had brought and what she'd never see again, like the big milky green glass bowl with a chip in the rim that Annie wouldn't throw out because she liked the feel of it tucked under her arm when she mixed up a cake. Or the new white coverlet she was crocheting for

Odella's bed. "Uh . . . Did you get . . . the . . . there was some . . ."

"Spit it out, girl! You gotta speak up if you want anybody to know what's on your mind."

"There was some magazines . . ."

"Them old ones, stacked up in the corner? Naw. Wasn't no cause to take that mess."

Odella bit her lip. It was like the dreams shared over those pages got left behind too, to be thrown away with the rest of the trash. Her mother was gone, there was no going back for her, and nothing would ever be the same.

She stared at the white line in the road for miles, occasionally sneaking a glimpse of her father, but only when she was sure he wouldn't notice.

"That's cotton over there," he nodded at a field as they passed. "When I was a boy I used to pick it till my fingers bled."

"Oh," was all Odella could manage. She was having a hard enough time wrapping her mind around her father right here in the present, driving her to *his* house. She couldn't begin to imagine what he used to do.

Odell leaned to one side, wrestled a pack of Lucky Strikes and a matchbook out of his pants pocket, and struck a match with his thumbnail. Not a word passed between them for the next twenty miles, and the hypnotic, stutter-thump of the windshield wipers and the sizzle of tires on wet road put Odella in a trance. When Odell finally cleared his throat, she jumped.

"My wife, her name is Ethiopia."

"Uh . . . Yessuh."

"She knows about you, knows you're comin'." He took a hard drag on his cigarette. Hardly any smoke escaped. "You're always welcome in my house, Odella. Do you understand that?"

Odella's head bobbed up and down. She picked at the dirt under her nails.

Odell kept his eyes forward. "I can't hear you nod your head."

"Yessuh," she said, all the while trying to picture these other people Annie told her she would never meet. On one of his visits Odella had asked him why he couldn't just stay with them. That night Annie had explained that her father had a wife and son, who lived in another town. She made it sound far away, like the places in the magazines, except where they were driving now still looked about the same as Cadysville. Odella had wanted to know why he got to have two families. "He had that family before he had us," Annie said. And to nobody in particular she added, "We had love. It was just too late." Annie sounded sad for a moment, but then she hugged Odella and added, "He's a good and loyal man. I never wished for more than that. And he takes care of us, so don't you never hold that against him. You hear?" Odella had heard, but it was only words until now. She stole another quick peek. Odell had stiff, bristly hairs sticking out of his ears and a splatter of little brown moles along his jaw.

Silence for twenty more miles.

"She said you can call her mama. . . ."

"No! . . . I mean I can't . . . It's just . . ."

"It's all right. You'll figure something out. Looka here, there's some sandwiches in that paper sack on the floor."

Odella fished out two brown paper parcels, each with a slab of ham between two slices of bread. He ate and she sat with hers in her lap for forty more miles.

"See that church over there?" Odell's long leathery finger pointed past her. "Built with bricks from my yard. Got the biggest brickyard in the county. You know that, don't you?"

"Yessuh." Annie had explained what he did for a living. Odella just couldn't quite figure out how anybody *made* bricks.

"You don't have to say *yessuh* every time I speak to you, Odella. This ain't the army. I'm your father. Your brother Henry's fifteen, and I don't think he's ever said *yessuh* to me unless he was tryin' to avoid a whippin'. I don't know what to . . . say about him. He's . . . Don't let him push you around, that's all." Odell's voice trailed off, but not before Odella could hear the sadness.

The next time Odell spoke they were turning off the high-way. "House's at the end of the road. We'll be there in a minute."

The rain had stopped, and what was left of the daylight slipped quietly through the curtain of towering, longleaf pines that lined the narrow dirt road. Odella couldn't make out neighboring houses or anything else through the trees, except more trees.

Odell stopped the car. "This is it." He got out, opened the trunk, and grabbed the battered blue suitcase that had been Annie's. Odella just stared. He came around and held the door open for her. "Come on, girl, get on outta there. I'm sure Ethiopia's got supper waitin'."

The big white house loomed in front of her as they started up the brick walkway that led to the wide front porch. Odella couldn't believe how many windows there were, didn't think colored lived in places like this. The small, neat house she'd grown up in had three rooms and a little patch of yard in front and in back where Annie managed to grow vegetables and even a few flowers. It was nice by Cadysville standards, but Annie had cooked for people who lived in houses like this.

Odell caught her gawking and smiled a little. He was proud of his house, owned it and the surrounding forty-five acres free and clear. People in town thought it was funny that the brickman's house was made of wood.

"That her?" The voice was a loud whisper.

Odella looked around, but there was no one behind her.

"Guess so," another voice answered.

She fixed her eyes on the porch.

"Ain't she kinda big to be ten?"

"Look like she been rollin' in the slop pen."

"Y'all need to stop."

A dark green porch swing hung from thick chains and swayed like a ghost just got up, but there was no one there ei-ther.

"You think she even know how to read?"

"She real country, ain't she?"

Odella caught a head as it popped back around the side of the house.

"Don't pay them no mind." Odell looked toward the far side of the house. "That's Henry and them fools he hang around with." Odell put the suitcase down and squatted beside Odella. "I don't 'spect this gon' be easy for you, but this life ain't easy for none a us. I'm real sorry 'bout your mama, but this here's your home now. You gon' have to learn to stand up for yo'self 'cause I won't always be around neither." He lifted her chin. "Don't you never let nobody run you. You understand me, Odella?"

"Yessuh. I mean, yes, Papa."

"Henry! Come on 'round here, boy, and carry this bag on in the house. Lester! Will! Y'all best be gettin' home. I'm sho you done caused enough trouble for one day."

Three boys emerged from behind the huge azalea bush at the far end of the porch.

"Evenin', Mr. Womack." The boy was nearly tall as Odell and the kind of rich red-brown that made you think he might actually have been molded from Carolina clay. He tucked in his shirt and wiped his palms on his dungarees before extending it to Odell.

"Will." Odell nodded, shook his hand.

"That supper smells mighty good, Mr. Womack." The next boy shoved his hands in his pockets, hunched his shoulders, and winked at her father.

"I'm sure Henry will tell you all about it tomorrow, Lester."

"Hey. You must be Odella. Heard you was comin'." Lester grinned at her. She peeked at him from behind her father. Lester wasn't as tall as Will, and he was lean, more muscle than bulk. She thought he was the color of devil's food cake with a smooth, sweet voice.

Odella figured the smallest one was Henry. He was narrow as a band of baling wire, and he glared at Odella, his black eyes cold and hard.

Odella felt a shiver creep up her spine, but she didn't show it.

"Mind your manners, boy." Odell's words implied the threat.

Henry stared a moment longer. "Hey." His voice was as flat and empty as the gesture.

Odella, remembering her father's words, met his gaze and held it.

"You plannin' to look this bag into the house?" Odell said.

Henry snatched the suitcase and stomped down the path.

Odella wanted to run all the way back to Cadysville, and it took every ounce of determination she had left to put one foot in front of the other and follow Henry and Odell into that house.

Della hadn't moved. She still sat on the vinyl hassock in her sewing room, housecoat stuck to the backs of her thighs, damp from sitting so long on the plastic. Miles of yarn lay tangled about her feet. *And I'm not goin' back to Prosper. Not ever again.*

5

"If you don't shake up your life,
all the good stuff settles on the bottom."

"It's so sweet he left you all that property, but what in the world are you going to do with forty-five acres in the middle of nowhere?" Lydia Kendall had worked on her prep-school accent so studiously it sounded almost natural. "I looked at that outfit. It was too—I don't know—too something for me." She smiled benevolently at Celeste. "But it suits you." In her navy blazer, white shirt, and jeans, Lydia looked casually understated, and suddenly Celeste felt way overdone for a Saturday afternoon in her teal silk suit, pearls, heels, and hose.

"Thanks." *Why did I change my clothes?* "Everett and I are going to dinner," she lied. "I won't have time to change."

Lydia moved a bowl of roses aside and flipped the florist's sample book open on the counter between them. "Let's agree. No carnations. They're so—ordinary." She absentmindedly twirled the dime-sized diamond on her ring finger.

"Agreed." *As long as you agree to stop flipping that ring around.* Thornton gave it to her for their twenty-fifth anniversary and Lydia nicknamed it Plymouth Rock because she said it was proof her ancestors had finally arrived. Since then she'd taken to wearing bright red nail polish and had done everything short of learning American Sign Language to keep her hands on display. Celeste was way over it. Not that the band of diamonds surrounding her own finger was a cereal box prize. It had blown her away when Everett presented it to her after a champagne toast on their twentieth anniversary. She even muffled the tiny voice in her head that said, "It's about time." But it wasn't Plymouth Rock.

"I'm sure we can find something more interesting than carnations. The flowers they did for your friend Mimi's son's wedding were breathtaking." Celeste admired Lydia's sense of style, her flair for entertaining, and her direct connections to everybody in Buffalo who mattered. It's what Celeste aspired to, which is why she roped Lydia into the planning committee for Everett's clinic's annual fund-raiser. This was only the third year, and Celeste was determined to make it into one of the class events of the spring social season, a gathering people put on their calendar for the second Saturday in June, year after year.

"Honey, the flowers were the best thing about that wedding. The bride and her family are so—common. I know at least six girls, beautiful, smart, accomplished, I could have set him up with, but he drags this—thing home. I mean she had braids standing all over her head and had the nerve to put a headpiece on top of *that*. It looked like a swarm of snakes under that veil." Lydia pushed some stray hairs from her steel gray pageboy behind her ear with her third finger, left hand. "They'll be divorced in a year. Mark my words."

Celeste wanted to redirect the conversation. She wasn't too happy with Niki's braids either and had conveniently forgotten to mention her displeasure to Lydia, who always had an immediate, take-no-prisoners assessment of any situation. Sometimes it was exactly the kick Celeste needed to make her take action, but she wasn't interested in that kind of commentary about her baby. Celeste made it a policy never to tell Lydia anything she didn't want to hear repeated, with dramatic embellishments. She knew Lydia couldn't carry a secret across the street in a Tupperware container without spilling it. That was just Lydia.

"You know, I'm still a little flustered. Finding that deed was such a shock. Daddy left all the other property to Mother in his will, but this came out of nowhere. I mean, I don't know how, but Mother had forgotten all about it. Doesn't even know how long it's been in the family."

"Hmm. And nobody even *visited* this place?"

"Well—no." As she raced from Della's house to meet Lydia on time, Celeste had rehearsed this conversation about her inheritance. Lydia was supposed to be impressed, at least a little, but it wasn't quite working out. "Daddy was having some restoration done before he . . ."

"You can't really expect much from that. I mean it's probably a house, you know, four walls and some plumbing, maybe, but if it was so charming they would have stayed, don't you think? At least gone back to see the place once in a while."

"Well—I guess—But with so much land Ev and I could build . . ."

"Oh, what about these!" Lydia pointed to an impressive arrangement of white lilies and roses, accented with trailing ivy. "So simple. So elegant."

"And so expensive, I'm sure. This is a fund-raiser, remember. The clinic is supposed to make money." Celeste came up with the idea for an event after listening to Everett complain for the zillionth time about how tight the funding had become for low-income medical care. He was touched that she took on such a big challenge. All the planning and networking made her feel important, never mind that the pressure of wanting it to be perfect gave her sleepless nights and hives. The payoff was that it seemed to raise her profile around town. And her picture in the *Buffalo News*, presenting the board of the North Star Family Clinic with a ceremonial check, made her feel like a real philanthropist. It also meant her parents got to see her since she couldn't persuade Della to attend. They wrote a generous check, but her mother said she couldn't be bothered with all that mess.

"Just once I'd like to plan an event that didn't have to make a profit. Wouldn't it be fun to do a flawless affair instead of always planning on the cheap?" Lydia shivered with glee at the possibility.

"You'll have to wait for one of the twins to get married for that."

"Not even. Lorna will elope with some fool who calls himself an artist, because she's 'in love' and has her head stuck up in the clouds. I mean, how could you do that to your parents? Can you imagine the phone call? 'I'm fine. And by the way, I got married last week.'"

Celeste smiled tightly and offered no comment. After all, she and Everett had eloped. He wasn't into the pomp. She wanted to avoid the trying circumstances involved in planning such an important event with her mother because she was afraid the festivities would be too tacky for words.

"And Leticia never takes my advice. What a little witch she is if everything isn't exactly *her* way. She was impossible at her cotillion. Sometimes I think how lucky you were that Nicole chose not to debut." Lydia shook her head in exasperation. "We'll mark this page. Just to ask about the lilies."

Choosing to ignore the little zinger about Niki declining to be a debutante, Celeste nodded. Her eyes were directed at the sample book, but her head was still focused on the Womack Estate, which is what the property had become in her mind. "The house is on Little Pond Road so I'm hoping the name means we're by some water. I haven't had the chance to look at a map yet, but it would be fabulous if it's somewhere near the beach. Maybe Wilmington . . ."

"Thorny and I have stayed all along that coast. If it's anywhere you want to be, I should have heard of it, and believe me, I'd remember Prosper."

Celeste looked crestfallen.

Lydia's eyes brightened as the lightbulb went on in her head. "But you know, if you're lucky there'll be some development nearby, an industrial park or something. There's a lot of that going on down there. What you should do is sell the land and buy something you and Everett really want, on the Vineyard or Sag Harbor. Someplace where you can really entertain. We've been toying with the idea for years, but we just can't decide where to buy. Thorny keeps saying we have friends all over, we should just pick a place. If we get bored in a few years we can sell it. Oh, speaking of vacation homes, did you get my message about the house in Highland Beach?"

"Shoot. I forgot to mention it to Everett."

"This cottage is really special. And what a view of Chesapeake Bay! It makes me feel calm just thinking about it. It's been in my friend's family since the turn of the century when her great-great-grandfather on her mother's side had it built."

I guess that's a lot different from forty-five acres in Prosper. "Sounds perfect." Celeste turned some more pages without really looking.

"They're spending this summer with their son and daughter-in-law in Tuscany, so they won't be using it, but they won't rent to just anyone. They gave me first dibs, but if we don't scoop it up, we'll lose it."

"I'll let you know by Monday. Promise."

The Kendalls and the Englishes had been vacationing together since their kids were in fourth grade. Celeste and Lydia had accompanied the class on a trip to the Museum of Science and hit it off. Their husbands were both at the beginning of their careers, Everett as a physician, Thornton a CPA. Lydia had twin daughters, but she seemed to have it so together. Celeste learned a lot from her, things she would never dream of asking Della, like where the best families sent their kids to camp or how to tell really fine china. Thornton made partner at his firm, and the Kendalls had the goods to show for it. Celeste tried to keep up, but she usually felt like an also-ran.

"I was wondering if you two would be interested in doing a whole month this year? It's a little steep. Ten thousand dollars each couple, but they'd rather do it that way. I mean, I guess I could find another couple to take two weeks, but . . ."

"No. No, a month would be good." *It's not a rainy day, but I'm sure Daddy wouldn't mind if I used the money he left me for this.* "My husband never takes that much time because he thinks North Star would close up without him, but I could use a rest. It's been such a hard year, and in the middle of it all I'm interviewing for assistant principal in a few weeks. Then I'll be on pins and needles until I hear."

"I love ambition."

"I love the paycheck."

"Let's hear it for getting paid!" Lydia lifted a pink rose from the vase and held it like a champagne flute.

Celeste grabbed a flower too, and they toasted. *And maybe I can get Niki to join me for a week or two. Like we used to.*

After two hours of wrangling with Lydia and the florist, Celeste was pleased with the arrangements they'd worked out. There would be a bowl at the center of each table with ten separate nosegays. That way, everyone would have flowers to take home at the end of the evening. Celeste was proud she came up with the idea and that Lydia and the florist both thought it was brilliant. And the day had been productive. She'd crossed all seventeen items off her to-do list.

When Celeste drove into her block, she was usually annoyed to see Everett's heap in the driveway. She wished he at least had the decency to hide it in the garage, but today she was glad to see the outline in the evening light because it meant he was home. She hurried into the house, because despite Lydia's wet blanket, she was still excited about her discovery. Confused too. It would have been so much easier if it was the Frazier family house. She was sure there wouldn't have been all the secrecy. Repeating the details to Everett would make them feel more real.

Celeste went in and laid the yellow tulips she'd bought at the florist on the kitchen table. She heard water running and went down the hall toward the bathroom.

"Hel-lo!"

Everett cracked the door. "Hey! Be out in a few. I got something to show you."

"And I've got something to tell you." She peeked in the den, expecting the usual sprawl of newspapers and medical journals to neaten but was surprised to find he'd been rummaging through a box of old photos. The ones from back when they first met. *What prompted the trip down memory lane?* She sat in his favorite old tweedy club chair, the one from their first apartment that he wouldn't let her reupholster or throw out because it was comfortable just the way it was. She sifted through the piles of pictures in the old sneaker box sitting on the ottoman and came up with one of Everett, sitting on the hood of his prize yellow 'sixty-nine Triumph Spitfire. The one he'd still have if she hadn't convinced him there was no room for three cars with a two-car garage. Everett had one foot up on the chrome bumper, his elbow propped on his knee, and he rubbed his goatee, looking very deep. Celeste remembered taking it about three weeks after they met. It was late fall and you could tell it was windy because his gigunda 'fro and the long fringes on his brown suede jacket blew to one side. Everett looked dead at the camera, his black eyes like pools with no shallow end. The look used to give her chills. It had from the first time she saw him.

Celeste had been hanging out between classes, eating french fries and gravy and talking trash with a girlfriend down in the Rat on UB's campus. She about gave herself whiplash doing a double take when she saw him, and she couldn't take her eyes off him as he bopped across the room. He was long, lean, and confident, and Celeste thought he moved like he belonged anywhere he chose to be. By the time he plopped his tray down on the table across from them she was hot and heavy into a very raunchy fantasy that took place upstairs in one of the listening rooms where, for an hour at a time, students routinely appreciated much more than music behind locked doors in soundproof privacy. Celeste always thought it beat the hell out of a backseat because while she'd majored in education, she'd minored in men, and as she liked to tell her girlfriends, she wanted to do plenty of research for her thesis. Before she could hunch her friend, Everett had fixed her in his sights. He held her gaze for a long, slow, disarming moment before he looked down and started reading the big textbook he had with him. Celeste burned with embarrassment because she felt like he knew exactly what was on her mind, which was usually the way she liked it, but not this time.

When Celeste rose to leave, she purposely avoided looking in his direction, but she took her sweet time, hoping he'd look up from his book. She wanted to give him ample opportunity to notice her in her bell-bottom hip-hugger jeans. It was the first time she'd worn the white turtleneck that clung like a second skin and stopped just at her belly button, revealing an inch-wide ribbon of skin at her waist. She'd left the house with her jacket closed so her mother wouldn't see it. Celeste may have been old enough to vote, but Della still maintained veto power in the wardrobe department.

By the time Celeste reached for the door, his hand beat hers to the knob. "I wanted to introduce myself, since we already had a conversation back there," is what he said. Celeste had felt her skin flush hot, and she could barely babble her name. She might have fallen in love with him right there.

"Whatdya think?" Now Everett leaned against the door frame, his bath towel a sarong at his waist, arms folded across his chest like a big, brown genie.

Celeste's eyes opened like saucers. "What did you do to yourself?!"

"I was examining a little boy, seven years old, this morning. He grinned at me and said I looked just like his grandpa. And you know what? I might be as old as his grandpa, but the look had to go." Everett had shaved his receding rim, leaving a shiny dome. He grinned as he rubbed the stubble on his chin. "I'm growing the beard again too. I figure if I can't have hair on top . . ."

"You could have warned me!" She got up and stood, hands on hips, in front of him.

"Warned you? I didn't know till the razor was in my hand. Come on, Celeste. It's no big deal." Everett playfully grabbed at one of her hands. "Give it a rub. Maybe you'll get your wish."

"You think this is a joke, don't you?"

"Well, it'll look a little funny till my scalp color browns up like the rest of me, but . . ."

"You know that's not what I mean."

"If you're gonna try to run that dignified BS on me again, save it." Right after they got married Celeste went on a campaign to change Everett's hair. She carried on about how he'd look more professional, command more respect from peers and patients, if he shaved his beard and trimmed his mane down to size. It's not that she didn't like his Afro. It just wasn't dignified enough for *Dr.* English. She figured it was a wife's job to look out for her husband's interests. Her mother never seemed to do that for her dad, and Celeste vowed she would be different. After a while Everett gave in and they never spoke about it again. "If somebody's planning to give me a hard time, nothing I do with my hair will change that."

"Have it your way, Everett." She tried to slip past him, but he put his hands on her shoulders to hold her. With the distraction of hair gone, his eyes seemed even more intense.

"I got this flash a few months back." He licked his lips, looked for the right words. "Tomorrow ain't promised. If you don't shake up your life, all the good stuff settles on the bottom."

Celeste looked up at him a long moment. Moist warmth radiated from him and he smelled fresh, like a walk in the woods. There were still moments when she felt the same pull she had more than twenty years ago. Like the moon on the ocean, irresistible. Undeniable. Used to be a time they would already have been in it. They'd have found a chair to even the height. She'd straddle his lap and they would devour each other, her arms straining to meet around his wide back, his smooth, hot hands squeezing her, kneading her. "When did you add philosopher to your credentials?"

"Yeah. Cool." Everett retracted the drawbridge of his arms. "Just call me Socrates."

Celeste could feel him watch her walk back to the kitchen. It made her crazy that Everett got these ideas in his head and just *did* them without planning or advance warning. She was so pissed off she didn't even notice how he looked shaved clean. It was too big a shock, and she'd had enough of those for one day. And she had too much on her mind for a roll in the hay if that's what he was thinking one of her wishes might be.

After rummaging through the cabinet, Celeste chose a green glass vase for the yellow tulips. For the last eleven years sex for them had been more about need and convenience than passion. There were still moments. Niki's graduation weekend they shared a lusty joy that kept them all over each other, before convocation, after commencement, and any other five minutes they could steal. But for the most part, neither expected the need to be reciprocal or the convenience mutual.

The fault line in their marriage appeared eleven years ago and caused a major quake. Everett was an attending at Buffalo General when he was recruited by a group that was looking for another internist to join their private practice. Celeste never heard his doubts. Thought he was just having normal jitters when he worried that if they made an offer and he took it he'd be selling out and putting his dream of opening a clinic on hold forever. Yes, she knew he always talked about medicine as a mission, a way to help those who needed it the most, but it only made sense to her that he would take advantage of the chance to move up in his profession. Who wanted to stay at the bottom of the barrel if they could climb out?

Fresh out of the classroom and into the guidance office, Celeste was doing her part to keep them upwardly mobile. Never mind that sometimes she hated the paperwork and the administrative hassles. She missed watching ninth graders gain new insights about the world or themselves after reading *Black Boy* or *Catcher in the Rye*, but guidance counselor was a step up on the food chain. She figured Everett would see his choice the same way and do his part to assure that Dr. and Mrs. English would assume their appropriate and expected place and reap the benefits money and position offered.

Armed with visions of a luxurious home, lavish vacations, a fancy car, and quitting her job to do charity work, Celeste went into high gear, preparing him to look the part of a prosperous physician for his interview. She steamed, brushed, and fussed over his one suit, a blue double-breasted chalk stripe she had convinced him he needed. She bought him a shirt so it would be bright white, then starched and ironed it for an hour until it was a gleaming breastplate. And she picked out a new silk foulard tie for luck.

The outfit triggered the first rumbles. Everett said he was a doctor, not a corporate lawyer. He didn't see the need for such formality. Celeste told him it was an interview, not triage, but that was minor compared to the upheaval that occurred when they asked him to come on board and he turned them down.

It was like Celeste's brain seized and she had lost comprehension of her mother tongue. He couldn't possibly have said what it sounded like he said, which was no. For weeks they fought like heavyweights in a title bout, each punch intended as a knockout. They argued before Niki got up in the morning and after she went to bed at night. Once, when they were driving to the library, Niki asked Celeste if they were getting a divorce. Celeste had never actually allowed herself to say that word, not even think it. Hearing it aloud, in Niki's small voice, cut Celeste to the bone. It was unimaginable. After all, she had caught one of the good guys. The one other women told her they wanted to clone. She wasn't a big enough fool to let that walk away, so she did her best to assure Niki that her parents would never split up and what would make her say something so silly? After that, they only argued when Niki wasn't home; Celeste still felt too cheated to let it rest.

But no matter how rank the situation got at home, she maintained her composure in public. This was a private battle. No one needed to know there was trouble in Oz. It went without saying she would never tell Lydia, because this news was not for broadcast. And Celeste wasn't about to tell Della, because she had thought their marriage was a bad idea from the beginning.

Celeste and Everett had eloped on Christmas Eve and made the announcement during dessert and coffee on Christmas Day. While she and her mother were cleaning up the kitchen. Della stopped scouring the roaster and out of nowhere asked if Celeste really loved that man or whether she liked the idea of being married to a doctor. Celeste was so incensed that she got her coat right then and they left. The climate stayed chilly until Nicole was on the way.

About a month into the hostilities, Everett got an offer that he did accept. Came home one night and told Celeste he was spending six months at a medical facility in Benin, like it was around the corner and down the block. He said the hard part about being in West Africa would be not seeing Niki, but he hoped the time apart from Celeste would give them both some breathing room and a little perspective. It couldn't make things any worse than they already were.

Was he ever wrong. Celeste carried on so bad that he stayed at the hospital a few days until she could speak in something other than a screech. The drama didn't change his mind, though.

Everett left the country to stony silence. The good news was that he'd provided Celeste with a plausible excuse for his absence. They weren't separated. He was working abroad. His salary was deposited directly into their joint account. He wrote Celeste and Niki regularly and phoned home twice a month. Celeste spoke to him mostly in monosyllables and only long enough for Niki to get on the line.

For the first few months of the cooling-off period, Celeste was so angry it left a bad taste in her mouth. So mad that she felt she deserved anything that made her feel better. She bought clothes, cut her hair from a middle-of-the-road, mid-length nonstyle to a short, asymmetrical do with more pizazz. People commented on how good she looked, and all the attention kept her distracted for a while.

Toward the end of his season overseas, Celeste had to admit, at least to herself, that she was scared and lonely. She missed Everett's wisecracks, his long, square, hairy toes, his cooking, which was really much better than hers. Celeste missed the passion Everett brought to living, from his big, loud grizzly bear stretch when he first sat up in bed in the morning to deep caring for his patients and his adoration of his daughter. She missed the intensity he radiated when they held hands.

When Everett walked back through the door at the end of his stint, Celeste was planning to maintain her cool, but a force she couldn't resist pulled her up out of her chair, across the room, and into his arms.

They talked into the morning like they used to, about what he had done and seen. Everett loved her haircut. Celeste loved the way the sun had kissed his skin to a burnished brown glow. And they loved each other, wanted to try to salvage their marriage, get back to where they started. Then, in the spirit of beginning fresh, Everett confessed that shortly after he left, while he was angry and resentful, he had a fling with another doctor in the program. He explained how his transgression only showed him how much he really wanted what he already had and asked her to forgive him. Celeste cried quiet, wounded tears and let him suffer for nearly a week before she told him she was taking the high road and that she'd found it in her heart to forgive him. But she left out the part about her own extracurricular involvement with an assistant principal at her school. Everett's confession became Celeste's moral vindication, convinced her that his wrong made hers right.

The rekindled flame stayed lit for a while, but it sputtered when Everett turned down another lucrative offer in favor of opening the North Star Clinic. Celeste was proud of his accomplishments. She just wished they had a little more to show for them.

Everett, wearing baggy gray sweats and a white terry cloth sweatband around his head, dropped his gear bag on the kitchen floor and headed for the refrigerator.

"You want something to eat?" Celeste draped her jacket on a kitchen chair.

"I'll grab a snack. I'm going to the gym to scare up a racquetball game. I don't get many free Saturday evenings."

"You should have Satur*days* free too. You spend so much time at North . . ."

"This conversation is tired, Celeste. Give it a rest." The edge was sharp in Everett's voice.

"Okay. All right." Celeste retreated. "Is it hot in here?"

"I don't know. Check the thermostat." He snatched an orange and an apple from the vegetable bin.

She reached in the cupboard for a can of tomato soup, watched him a moment as he peeled the orange over the sink. "Maybe you do look younger with your head like that. I didn't mean to jump on you. I was just startled."

"Peace." He held up the two-fingered salute. "I needed a change, that's all." He popped an orange section in his mouth, put the fruit on the counter, and reached for a paper towel.

"I still haven't told you my news." Celeste got a small bowl and put Everett's orange in it, then wiped the counter.

Everett watched her and smirked.

"What?"

"Nothing. Tell me."

Celeste recounted her discovery of the deed and Della's abrupt reaction while she warmed her soup.

"Secrets in the attic, huh? That's some wild stuff. What did Ronnie have to say?"

"Humph. Ronnie? Mother told me my sister has moved yet again. I mean, what is with her? It's like she's never grown up." Celeste poured her soup into a bowl. "I'll call her when I've figured out what we need to do."

"Don't you think she should be involved in this figuring process?"

"Ronnie doesn't have a real job, she can't keep an apartment. Why would I think she'd have any clue about what to do with this property?" Celeste waved the spoon for emphasis. "For God's sake, Everett, she can hardly keep her phone turned on."

"This is her decision as much as it is yours. Both names are on that deed." Everett propped his elbows on the counter, bit into his apple.

"Whose side are you on?!" Celeste got saltines from the white metal tin that said "Crackers" in blue letters. She put a few on a bread plate.

"This has nothing to do with sides. The property is deeded to both of you." Everett roughed up the stubble on his chin.

"I'm not saying it isn't, but Ronnie has no business sense and clearly no sense of family. How could she go four years without seeing her parents? It's disgraceful! I don't think she's capable of making an informed decision about this, and as far as I'm concerned she has forfeited her say-so. She isn't responsible. Period."

"Strong words. Suit yourself, but don't forget she's a grown woman, not just your baby sister. You're gonna make this into a feud."

"I'll take my chances. We're not exactly bosom buddies as it is." She got a glass for some wine and straightened sage, one of the herb prints grouped on the wall.

"Are you gonna go see this place? School's out all next week. You could fly down."

"No time. I'm booked up here. My committee needs to finalize the menu for your clinic fund-raiser, and I've got a few more articles to read before the assistant principal interview." And Celeste wasn't ready for Prosper yet. The lifetime absence of a family history allowed her to create one that suited her notions of her ancestors, of life in the South. She had elaborate pictures of suffering and injustice, sacrifice and heroism. Besides, her father always said they left because there was nothing in the town for a Black man but hard times and old age. No telling what she'd find there now. *If Daddy had just mentioned it to me.*

Celeste headed to the pantry and got a bottle of merlot. "I thought we could drive to Prosper before our vacation this summer. Oh, I've been meaning to tell you, Lydia has access to this fabulous home in Highland Beach. . . ."

"I told you months ago I didn't want to go on vacation with

the Kendalls again. I'm not interested in another two-week dose of them. How long have we been doing this? Ten, eleven years?" He dropped his peels and cores down the garbage disposal, gave them a quick buzz. "We have to listen to them brag about their newest new car or about their fab-u-lous cruise and all the important people, in addition to themselves, who were on it. We don't do this for Nik anymore, not that she ever enjoyed it as much as you wanted her to. Can't blame her. The Kendall twins were always obnoxious."

"They weren't that bad. Besides, they don't come anymore, and this place sounds fantastic." Celeste launched into her spiel.

Everett shook his head. "I'm sick of Thornton cheating on his golf score." Everett rubbed his palms together. "And I know she's your running buddy, but frankly I could live without Lydia."

"She's helping me a lot on the clinic benefit, you know." Celeste sidestepped the issue. *This always happens. He'll be happy to go by June.*

"And North Star appreciates her efforts." Everett's eyes brightened with a sly, seductive sparkle. He sidled next to Celeste. "How about a romantic holiday for two in the south of France? We could have a little Beaujolais, a little *déjeuner,* a little matinée, oui? Or would Switzerland tickle your toes? I showed you the article about the jazz festivals in Nice and Montreux. We could explore by day, dig the tunes by night, maybe take a little side trip to Italy or Spain." He pulled her close.

"Oooh, don't put those sticky hands all over me." Celeste lifted his hand off her shoulder, plunked it on the counter.

"I remember when you used to like it." Everett picked up his gym bag.

"You'll mess up my blouse."

"Never mind. Later." And was out the door.

Celeste wrestled the rest of the weekend with what to tell Lydia. By Monday morning, when she snagged a third cup of coffee in the faculty room and headed for the guidance suite, she still hadn't made up her mind. It was such a great opportunity to meet a new group of people. *Everett was just mad because I fussed about his haircut.* She unlocked the door to her first-floor office and flipped on the light. *I gotta call maintenance again.* The fluorescent bulb hummed and flickered. She put down her insulated mug and her purse, got her agenda out of her purple and gold canvas school tote bag, and added it to today's to-do list. There were fifteen items so far. The first, "Confirm Highland Beach." *What am I going to do?*

Celeste's office was anything but picture-perfect. Battered beige file cabinets lined one wall, and piled on top of them was a jumble of papers, college and technical school brochures, catalogs, and videos. The windowsills were heaped with folders, attendance records, old aptitude test booklets, and career guides. But unlike at home, the way her office looked mattered less than what she accomplished while in it. Celeste had her own pretty awful counselling experience when she'd been in high school, one that changed her forever. Celeste's grades weren't spectacular, but they weren't awful either. She knew she had to buckle down and bring them up because she wanted to go to college and be a teacher. After her initial session in the guidance office, she was advised to forget about preparing for the SATs and to consider a nurse's aid training program upon graduation. When she got back to her homeroom she saw that every Black girl in her class had the nurse's aid brochures, while the White girls had booklets on college entrance exams and pamphlets from various universities. Celeste made up her mind she *would* be a teacher and that it would always be about the students. When she finally became a counselor she decided it was pretty much the only place in the school where the kids were dealt with as individuals, not just part of biology class or Homeroom 317. Celeste did her best with each and every one of them, and her kids did well. Whether they went on to the Ivy League or to the post office, in some way, large or small, they benefited from the time Mrs. English spent with them.

Celeste picked up the receiver.

"Do you have a minute, Mrs. English?" Joey Tsang appeared at her door.

"Sure. You're not trying to get out of your history class, are you?" She winked at him, put down the phone. Joey had spent a great part of the first grading period trying in vain to convince her that the curriculum was outmoded and that three years of history was enough for anyone who wasn't planning to be a historian or go to work for PBS.

"No. I'm goin'. I swear! I just wanted to say—uh—thanks. I know you didn't have to meet with my parents like you did, but it really made the difference."

Both of Joey's parents taught at SUNYAB, his father engineering, and his mother physics. They expected Joey to follow in their footsteps, but his true love was music. Joey wanted to be a composer, he didn't want to go to MIT. Celeste, convinced that love combined with ability made for a fulfilling and worthwhile career choice, encouraged him to follow his heart. She agreed to meet with Joey and his parents, and they'd left not fully convinced but at least able to see Joey's point of view. Joey was Celeste's first student to be accepted at Juilliard.

"Just doing my job, kiddo!"

"It was more than that. And I wanted you to know how much it meant to me."

These moments were rare, but they're what made Celeste love her job. She'd savor this on the bad days. The day she lost another fifteen-year-old to unplanned pregnancy, or the day one of the boys she thought she'd gotten through to was arrested in study hall. This was a moment she'd frame and hang on her wall.

"You're more than welcome. Now get out of here before you're late." She shooed him out the door.

Celeste still had a smile on her face as she dialed Lydia's number. "Hey, it's me." She took a deep breath, bit her lip. "Of course we're in. We wouldn't let the good times start without us."

6

"Always is over."

Spring passed in a blur of events for the Englishes. Celeste had the last-minute rush of students still trying to get admitted to college, and counseling sessions with those in danger of flunking courses. For a switch, she herself was reduced to anxiously wondering if she'd get the call that told her she'd be assigned as an assistant principal in the fall. The uncertainty reminded her of why her college-bound seniors bounced off the walls from January until April.

In May, Celeste's prom committee pulled off a lovely affair and everything was in place for North Star's event. She'd even found the perfect dress, a white sheath with a lace overslip and sleeves. Celeste wondered if it looked a little "mother of the bride," but Lydia had been with her when she picked it out and assured her it was very elegant. Celeste had put Prosper on the back burner, and she hadn't told Ronnie there was a pot on yet.

On the Friday of Memorial Day weekend, Celeste was in a great mood. The official teachers' countdown to the end of the semester had begun, and after school she stopped off at Cole's, the local faculty watering hole, to celebrate. She left the restaurant feeling mellow and strolled to her car, soaking up the warm, late-day sun. The promise of summer and two months of freedom hung sweetly in the air. *If Everett gets home at a reasonable hour, I'll throw a couple of steaks on the grill. That'll be a nice change.* Celeste looked forward to the full slate of parties and barbecues for the weekend, but she'd forgotten the last time they actually ate dinner together in the house.

Driving down Parkside past the zoo, Celeste noticed the giraffes gnawing on tree leaves in the distance. She smiled as she remembered how Niki used to wonder how long it took for their food to get all the way from their mouths to their stomachs. *I wish Niki had come up for the weekend.* Celeste had offered to send a plane ticket, but Nicole begged off, said she had to work, promised she'd come home for the North Star fund-raiser. She missed the details of Niki's life. What dress she bought, where she was going on Saturday night and who was going with her. Celeste called once a week, Tuesday morning since that was Niki's day off. It was usually a "Hi. I'm fine. I'm busy. Nothing's new. Bye." conversation that left Celeste feeling left out, wanting more. Niki hadn't been home since the funeral, not even for Christmas. That was hard. It was Celeste's first Christmas without both her father and her daughter. Della never was big on Christmas, not even when Ronnie and Celeste were little. It was Celeste's favorite time of year, but Della hung over it like a big, gloomy rain cloud over a picnic, threatening to spoil her fun at any moment. From the time Celeste was grown and on her own she celebrated with all the trimmings. So she decided to carry on with her usual traditions. She put Christmas trees in the living room and dining room and covered them with so many ornaments you could barely see the green. She decked banisters, archways, and mantels with pine garlands, red velvet bows, and twinkling white lights, and each window in the house had a glowing golden star. She and Everett had hosted their annual Christmas Eve supper, but a lot of the spirit was missing.

Celeste ditched her shoes at the back door and stepped into the white terry cloth scuffs she had waiting. She defrosted two T-bones in the microwave, put them in a bowl with Italian dressing to marinate, then collected her shoes and marched upstairs to take a shower. She figured school maintenance had sent up too much heat for such warm weather. Why else was she hot and sticky all day?

The first thing Celeste noticed in the bedroom were the blue jeans balled up on the floor on Everett's side of the bed. *He never puts things away.* She made a face and scooped them up. He'd actually made it to bed last night, although Celeste was too tired to talk or do anything else when he got under the covers. He was still a night owl like he had been since she met him. On the other hand, after Niki was born Celeste went back to being a morning bird like she had always been before she dated Everett. When he used to complain that she had vowed to love, honor, and keep company, she would bring out her iron-clad excuse: she needed her rest to keep up with the baby. Nothing had changed after the baby was grown though.

Celeste dropped the pants in the hamper and got undressed. It felt good to get out of her blue blouse and gray skirt, better to peel off her hose and her no-nonsense beige bra and panties. She had a lingerie drawer full of serious underwear. As usual she didn't look down as she slipped into her pink and white striped robe. In the bathroom she zipped past the mirror as she put on the shower cap, adjusted the water to semi-scalding, and waited until the steam drifted over the shower curtain. She stepped in and moaned as the hot water pelted her shoulders. Then she grabbed the deodorant soap and got down to business.

Bringing Nicole into the world had made Celeste feel officially grown. After all, she was old enough to be somebody's mother, but she never got over what it did to her body. She had rubbed lotions, creams, cocoa butter, and lard on her belly, but nothing got rid of the rippling stretch marks that marred what had been smooth, taut skin. Her breasts had gone from tangy apples to droopy pears. And what had been a spandex-tight love fit between her and Everett had become more like a baggy kneesock. B.C.—Before Childbirth—Celeste liked to flaunt her stuff in bikinis and clingy dresses, and tease Everett, telling him she was naked and warm under her sundress hours before he could do anything about it. A.D.—After Delivery—he used to tell her she was as hot a mama as she ever was, but she figured it was what he had to say. Besides, she didn't have time to worry about such frivolous things. Celeste was a mother.

Della had passed on lots of baby care tidbits, most of which Celeste discarded as old-fashioned, but never said two words to her daughter about the radical changes to her physique. So Celeste had been prepared for diaper changing, bottle sterilizing, and no sleep, but not to surrender her sassy shape. At twenty-three? It made her mad, but she couldn't admit it. Who could she be mad at? Certainly not her darling baby, her gift from heaven, her daughter.

Celeste was soaping her thighs and composing a mental timetable for Saturday when a knock on the door made her jump.

"How 'bout some company?" Everett came in and closed the door.

"You scared me to death! What are you doing home so . . ."

Everett pulled back the curtain. He was already undressed for the occasion. "Are those goose bumps from fear, or because I'm here?"

She smirked. "Very funny. I was about to get out."

"Then I got here just in time."

"Everett, there's no room."

"I'm sure you missed a spot." He grinned and got in. Everett closed his eyes and let the water run over his head. "Oh yeah."

Celeste shimmied past him so Everett was closest to the spray. "This is a surprise. The sun is still up and you're home." Despite her bark, Celeste's stomach flip-flopped as she watched the water gloss his body.

"You've got steaks out. You're plannin' to *cook*?" His eyes sparkled mischievously.

"Touché." They gazed at each other a long moment. A subtle vibration radiated through Celeste's body. Before she could stop herself she reached up and rubbed slow circles over his chest hair with the bar of soap until he was covered in lather from shoulders to waist and her vibrations deepened. "No meeting tonight?"

"Umm. Not one. And I played hooky most of the afternoon." Eyes closed again, he directed her hand down toward another clump of hair.

"You know I'm obligated to report this to your truant officer," Celeste purred as she kept circling.

"Can I make a plea for leniency?" He pulled her close so the shower sprayed them both.

"On what grounds?" Love in the afternoon wasn't on her list of things to do, but she was about to go with the flow for a change.

"How about that I spent the time with a travel agent and I

got a stack of brochures for places to take us on one hellafied vacation?"

Celeste's mouth suddenly felt dry as the bottom of an old shoe. More than a month had passed since she gave Lydia the okay, but she still hadn't worked their Highland Beach rental casually into conversation with her husband. Now she worked to keep her voice smooth. Head resting on his arm, she stared at the white tile. "Hmm. What did you have in mind?" *And please let it be August.*

"You, me, good food, beautiful surroundings, and a whole lotta jazz." He led her in a slow, hip-rolling dance to the music of his voice. "There are a bunch of festivals to choose from in July and I'm ready to get on the plane right now." His hands slid up and down her back.

Uh-oh. Celeste's good vibrations stopped abruptly, crushed by the lump of lead that landed in her guts. Her hips stopped swaying and Everett opened his eyes.

"What's the matter?"

"Nothing. You're gonna get my hair all wet." She edged herself away.

"Come on, Celeste."

Her body wanted to stay, but Celeste's head screamed *What am I gonna do?* so loud she had to pay attention. "I'll meet you in the bedroom. Promise."

Everett cocked his head to the side, took a deep breath. "As long as you keep on the same outfit you're wearing. I like it."

"Deal." She was still damp when she pulled on her robe and trotted down to the kitchen. She poured a glass of wine, took a slurp, topped it off, then poured a second glass and carried them back to the bedroom. Everett wasn't much of a drinker, but she hoped it would soften him up for a vacation with a slightly different beat.

Celeste found a bulging manila envelope in the middle of their bed. It seemed to throb as she sat at arm's length, looking at it and trying to think clearly. She took another swallow of wine for confidence, then picked it up, unwound the figure eight of string that held the flap closed, and let the color travel brochures fall in a heap on the bed. She swirled them with both hands, picked one at random. *What am I going to tell him?* She stared blankly at the cover.

"The travel agent stayed at that hotel, says it's a classy joint." Everett stood in front of her, still drying his hairy chest.

Celeste sipped her wine. "I brought up a glass for you."

"In a minute. Right now I see something I'd rather have." He sat beside her, tried to pull her into an embrace. Celeste was as pliable as a two-by-four. "Come here and let me ease your mind some."

I wish you could. "Everett, I kind of already made plans for our vacation."

He sat back. "You planned a vacation and didn't *tell* me? Oh! It's a surprise right? You're gonna pick me up at the clinic with my bags packed and . . ."

"Not exactly. It kept slipping my mind." That felt lame as soon as it left her lips, but Celeste had no choice but to plow on. "It was a great opportunity—so I accepted the rental in Highland. . . ."

"No you didn't." Everett shot to the other side of the room. Hands on hips, he stared at the floor. The smooth contours of his face turned to granite and Celeste felt static in the air, like right before a storm. They hadn't argued in a long time, but Celeste braced herself as he banged open a dresser drawer, grabbed some briefs, and put them on. "Please tell me you didn't do that, Celeste." He opened the closet, snatched some chinos off a hanger.

"It was getting late, and we hadn't made any plans. I didn't want us to get caught without anything."

Everett stopped in his tracks, glanced up at Celeste, then let out a big, whooping belly laugh.

"What's so funny?" Everett's laugh unnerved her.

He had to catch his breath to talk. "So you booked the one place I specifically said I *didn't* want to go! That's good. That's really good, Celeste." Everett's eyes stayed locked on her as he stepped into his pants.

Celeste wasn't sure if they were fighting or making up, but the laughter stung. "I know what you said, Everett, but we always take a rental with . . ."

"Always is over," he snapped. "And you should have listened to me, because I'm not going."

"Oh come on, Ev. I can't go alone. Lydia and Thornton would have a field day with that."

"If you had paid even a little attention to what I said, you would know I don't give a shit what they think."

"You're overreacting. It's not the last vacation we'll take. We can go to your little jazz thing or whatever next year." Celeste felt her world wobble.

Everett stared at her like he'd never seen her before, then he grinned, shook his head. "My 'little jazz thing.' That about sums it up. You obviously don't care what I have to say."

"That's not true . . ." She gripped the side of the bed to keep her balance.

"I'm not even gonna argue with you, Celeste, because if I give you enough time, you'll make this whole thing my fault." He hurriedly pulled on a denim shirt, buttoned it lopsided. "I've tried everything I know how to do—Half the time I feel like some kinda show dog. You parade me around and collect points, or ribbons, whatever you get for a good performance." He shoved his feet into sneakers, knelt to lace them.

Celeste stood up, hoping to regain her footing. She picked up his towel from the bed, folded it, and held it to her chest. "We can always cancel. It's late for them to find another couple, but . . ."

"It's not just the vacation! It's the way our marriage has been for years. You go along your merry way making plans that suit some idea you have of the perfect life. You don't give me or anybody else credit for having sense, and how fortunate we poor fools are to have you to show us the way."

"I never said . . ."

"You're right. You never came out and said I was a disappointment to you, but your message is loud and clear. Well, I can't do this anymore." He stood and looked her square in the eyes. "I'm outta here, Celeste."

"Fine. When you get back we can . . ."

"I don't mean for a walk around the block. I mean I want a divorce."

All Celeste could hear was her heart pounding. It felt like a long time before she could make her lips move. "You don't mean that."

Everett got his wallet off the dresser, shoved it in his pocket. "Do you even hear yourself? This would be funny, if it wasn't. I almost walked many times before, but something always stopped me. Niki, or the way I remembered you, back in the day. I don't know who you are anymore." He moved toward the door, then stopped. "The last time I had my bags packed, your father died. I couldn't go then. Wouldn't. We're family. It was a crisis. After that I decided to give us one more chance, but I'm through with it. I see life and death regularly as part of my job description, but when your father died, that was a personal reminder that life can be over faster than you can scratch your ear. Any time. Any day. It's too short not to enjoy every moment, and I've just been going through the motions here. This may be enough for you, but it's not enough for me."

"Who is it this time?" Celeste hissed, grasping wildly at anything to keep her balance.

"Bingo! I've been waiting for your ace in the hole. It's been more than a damn decade, but you can make it feel like yesterday. I hate to disappoint you, but it's not about anybody else. It's about what we're not anymore." Everett sounded hollow, tired. "Maybe we never were."

"What kind of example is this for Niki?"

"It's time for you to stop hiding behind Niki. In case you hadn't noticed, she's a woman. And believe me, this won't come as a surprise to her. She lived here, remember? We can tell her when she's home in a couple of weeks. I won't mention it to anyone until then."

"Tell her what!? This is crazy, Everett. Are you having a breakdown or something?"

Everett closed his eyes, shook his head, then turned and left the room.

Celeste stood, paralyzed, her hands balled into fists, her body quaking. She heard the back door close, heard Everett start the car and drive off. *He can't leave me.* The voice in her head started small, but it swelled, sending her into a frenzy. She flung the towel in her arms and knocked her empty glass off the nightstand. It was like the sound of shattered glass flipped a switch in her head. She drank down the wine she brought for Everett, then smashed the glass against the closet door. *He can't leave me!* Celeste ripped covers off the bed, tossing travel brochures like confetti. Twirling in the tangle of sheets and blankets, she knocked down the clothes valet she bought but he never used, upended a brass floor lamp. Its frosted glass globe exploded when it hit the wall, splintered into a million shards. "He can't leave me!" She didn't realize she was yelling. Celeste whirled like a cyclone, touching down at random, leaving destruction in her wake, until she got tangled in the drapes and fell, yanking the rod down with a crash. Celeste landed in a heap, wet with sweat like she'd just come out of the shower. She curled up in a ball and sobbed until she feel asleep.

It was dark when Celeste woke up, feeling like freeze-dried hell. Only the mayhem around her kept her from writing off the afternoon as a bad dream. She got to her feet, found the light switch, shuddered at the wreckage. She stayed up half the night, methodically cleaning up the mess, feeling soothed as she restored order.

The next morning Celeste jammed last night's uncooked steaks down the garbage disposal and made an extra-strong pot of coffee. She was on her second cup when Everett came down from his study and into the kitchen, still wearing his clothes from the day before.

"Are you feeling better?" Celeste's sarcasm was thick as peach nectar.

"I feel fine. As a matter of fact, better than I have in a long time." Everett poured a cup of coffee.

"The Hills' cookout starts at three." Celeste planned to treat the disturbance as only a test of the emergency broadcast system. No need to prepare for fallout. She was going back to her schedule.

"Have a good time." Everett spooned sugar in his coffee.

"If you still want to talk about this nonsense, we can. I'm willing to forget what happened. . . ."

"I'm not. I meant everything I said. And this nonsense is my life. It's about time I got on with it." He disappeared down the hall.

"This'll blow over, Everett!"

Everett kept walking.

Celeste did go to the barbecue. She extended Everett's apologies, said he had an emergency at the clinic. The next two weeks went by pretty much like normal; she went her way, he went his. Celeste filled every waking moment with busywork: rearranging closets, handling last-minute details for the banquet, getting Niki's room ready for her visit, buying her mother groceries and cleaning products Della said she didn't need. She couldn't stay around her mother too long. For some reason Della kept asking Celeste if everything was okay. She'd find some drawer to search through or shelf to dust so she didn't have to look her mother in the eye while she said, "I'm fine. It's just been so busy." Then she'd ask Della for the sixteenth time if she'd reconsider going to the North Star fund-raiser, so Della could say no again.

In the midst of her swirl of activities, when Celeste had a few unscheduled minutes, her heart would pound like a drum, but it would pass. She was not going to let Everett's tantrum get to her. She figured two weeks was enough time for whatever little midlife crisis he was having to pass, and if nothing else, Niki's arrival would snap him out of it.

Niki chattered the whole way home from the airport. Celeste had planned that they would go out for lunch, but Niki insisted on cooking. After a short detour to the grocery store, she whipped up smoked salmon and Gruyère omelets with asparagus vinaigrette, garnished beautifully with cherry tomatoes and cilantro. Everett raved, and Celeste was just about to breathe a sigh of relief when Niki put down her fork.

"I'm leaving Atlanta. This job was fine for right out of school, in fact it's been great. It's given me the chance to really be on the inside of the restaurant business and helped me to know what I want. I'm going back to school."

"Grad school?! How wonderful! Isn't that wonderful, Ev?"

Celeste moved forward in her chair, bubbling with excitement. "Where have you been accepted? Oh, I hope it's somewhere nearby. Atlanta is fine, but it's so far away from us."

Everett shot Celeste a look.

"It's upstate New York, not far from the City—but it's not exactly graduate school." Nicole took one last deep breath before spilling all her beans. "I've enrolled in the CIA." She caught her mother's quizzical look. "The Culinary Institute of America. I'm going to be a chef."

"You're what?!" Celeste's hand went up to her chest to hold her heart in place.

"I love food. I love cooking and I'm good at it. Every spare moment I had at the restaurant, I'd hang out in the kitchen, dying to take off my suit, roll up my sleeves, and grab a sauté pan. I learned the business side of running a restaurant, which is good. It'll be very helpful when I have my own place, but . . ."

"We didn't spend all that money on an education so you could become a cook!" Celeste nearly lunged across the table.

"I didn't say a cook, I said a chef." Niki held her ground.

"Don't insult me, Nicole! How dare you think that you can waste your time and your life that way? Are you insane?" Celeste screeched.

"Cut the hysterics, Celeste. Nicole has found what she loves to do in life. Some people never do. She's lucky." He turned to his daughter. "And I know you'll be the best chef in the world!"

"How can you sit there like nothing is wrong?" Celeste jumped up, waving her arms like a traffic cop. "Your daughter is throwing her life away! And you're telling her it's all right! Has everyone in this house lost their grip except me?!"

"It's my life, Ma. It's the only one I have. If I don't do this, I know I'll regret it. I may be only twenty-three, but I've figured out that I only want to regret the things I do. Not the things I never tried." She looked at her father. "You always told me I could do anything, be anything. This is what I want to be."

"I won't listen to this anymore! I'm going upstairs to get ready for tonight." Celeste started out of the kitchen.

"We have something to tell you too, Nik."

She froze. "Surely you're kidding, Everett!?"

"Sit back down, Celeste, or do you want me to do this alone?"

Celeste didn't move a muscle.

"Do what?" Niki looked back and forth between her father and her mother's back.

Everett waited a few seconds, reached for Niki's hand.

Celeste prayed that Everett wouldn't say what she knew was coming.

"There's no good or easy way to say this, baby." Everett looked at Celeste, then back at Nicole. "You know your mother and I have been—well, it hasn't been good for a long time. We've talked about it and decided we need to be apart."

"So you're getting divorced, huh?" Niki looked as though she'd been waiting for that shoe to drop for years.

"We haven't gotten that far." He spoke to Niki but he watched Celeste. "We've just agreed that what we have isn't healthy, and it hasn't been a good example for you, either. We apologize for that. We love you, both of us. And we've always wanted only what's best for you. You're grown now. A woman with a mind and life of her own." He dropped his eyes to the floor, then looked at Niki. "Now it's time to do what's best for us."

Celeste wanted to spit. This was best for him, not for her. Until now Everett's words were like a bad dream, disturbing but easily forgotten. But hearing him say it out loud, to their child, that was too real, and she wanted to make it go away. "Nothing is final, Niki. Your father is just upset right now so you don't have to feel . . ."

"Stop telling me what to feel, Ma!" Niki's eyes blazed. "You're always tryin' to tell somebody what to think, what to do, where to go! Then you don't understand why nobody can *live* with you."

The words splattered over Celeste like shrapnel. Staring straight ahead, it was all she could do to put one foot in front of the other and leave the room.

The third annual North Star benefit was a huge success and raised more money than ever, but Celeste barely remembered the evening. She spent it smiling too brightly, talking too cheerfully, and staying on the opposite side of the room from Everett. Lydia's antenna was up too. She kept shooting Celeste sideways glances and asking if everything was all right, but Celeste managed to evade her—barely. It was the hardest act Celeste ever put on.

The three of them drove home in silence. Niki and Everett retired to their rooms. Celeste brought the wine bottle and a glass up to bed because this had all been too painful and she wanted to forget it ever happened, but no matter how hard she drank, she couldn't sleep. She knew that now, since he had told Nicole, Everett would be ready for the next step, and she had to stop it. At least long enough to figure out what to do next. She tossed and turned and sweated. The semester was over in two weeks. She should be leaving for Maryland, but that was out of the question. She didn't know what she was going to tell Lydia and Thornton yet; she'd have to make up some lie. But she needed a place to go where she could be alone and think this through. Some way to stop Everett from surveying the real estate pages for an apartment.

Morning edged around the window shades before she thought of Prosper.

By the time Celeste dragged herself downstairs, Niki had already left for the airport to change her ticket and catch the next thing flying back to Atlanta, which Celeste blamed on Everett. And for the rest of the weekend Celeste stewed and steamed alternately at Everett for being irrational and at Niki for being a stubborn, ungrateful brat. Celeste didn't even go to church, and she never missed the Sunday after the North Star benefit. She'd show up early and stay long after service, smiling like a bride and basking in compliments from church members on what a beautiful affair it had been. But she didn't have the heart to put up a front. What energy she did have was devoted to finding a way to get her husband and her daughter to come to their senses before their decisions became public. Before Lydia found out, which was in essence the same thing.

By first period on Monday, Celeste was just plain evil and she stayed that way all week. Co-workers and students blamed her foul mood on end of the year pressures and stayed out of her path.

At home the week was no better. She wouldn't go downstairs in the morning until Everett left for the clinic, and although she was always wide awake when he returned each night, she'd pretend to be asleep. She quickly checked the "will not attend" box on the invitations that appeared in the mail and made hasty excuses for those that arrived via telephone. Most of the time she let the machine pick up, but she stood by, ready to snatch the receiver in case it was Niki, calling to say she had changed her mind. But Niki didn't call.

By the time Friday dawned, Celeste had made up her mind. Before she left for work she had made plane reservations for North Carolina, leaving as soon as school was over. Now she had to tell her mother.

For a hot second Celeste considered hiding her little excursion to Prosper from Della, but she'd never even gone on a long weekend without leaving her mother a detailed itinerary. Not that Della had once used the "in case of emergency" phone numbers. Of course, she still hadn't told Ronnie about their little inheritance, either, but that was a simple phone call. If Ronnie's phone wasn't disconnected again, that is. But after their one and only conversation on the subject, Celeste knew her mother would be a tough customer.

"Mother?!" Celeste trotted up the back steps, trying to keep the grease that had soaked through the pizza box from getting on her blouse. "I brought a surprise!" She'd stayed in her office late, buried under paperwork, but when the custodian had stopped by her office a third time, mop in hand, she knew she couldn't delay her visit to Della any longer. *Dreading a thing is worse than doing it. That's what Daddy used to say.* She pulled an old cookie sheet from the cabinet, put three slices on it, and slipped the pan into the oven.

Della shuffled into the kitchen. "You'd a sure been surprised if I hadn't been here." She spied the telltale half box from Bocce's. "And I *might* have already eaten," she said, knowing full well her plate of cheese and saltines sitting upstairs on a snack table didn't compare.

"You're right." Celeste didn't want the fight to start this soon. "I should've called first, but it was Friday and I just felt like some pizza. Everett is working late, as usual, and I know how much you like this."

Della examined the box. "Humph! Bet you didn't go . . ."

"Yes I did. All the way down to Clinton Street." Celeste had counted on getting extra points for going out of her way to the original pizzeria instead of one of the branches. Della swore she could tell the difference, and if pizza the way her mother liked it would make some inroads on this Prosper business, it was worth the inconvenience. "It'll be hot in a couple of minutes." Celeste grabbed two plates from the shelf.

"I don't know the last time I had some Bocce's." Della took two pale yellow paper napkins from the holder on the table and folded them in half. "Might not have been since Will passed," she said more to herself than to Celeste.

Friday night pizza used to be a Frazier family tradition. A couple of years after Will started at the steel plant, he decided to try this concoction his co-workers raved about. Until then the only "Eye-talian" food Will and Della knew from Prosper was spaghetti. So he stopped by the place they'd recommended and brought home a pepperoni pizza pie. It was love at first bite. Della even pinched off small pieces of the tomato-y crust and fed them to baby Celeste, who was teething. From then on, Will brought home pizza on Friday night.

"This sure hit the spot." Della bit into her second slice.

"Glad you like it." Celeste watched her mother dab at the corner of her mouth with the napkin. "And I'm so glad the school year is over next week. It's been a hard one." She put down the sliver of pepperoni she had squeezed between her thumb and index finger and wiped her hands. "I—uh—I've been thinking about getting away for a few days or so."

"Y'all usually take a trip. I thought you were goin' somewhere with your *friend* Lydia and her husband."

"Later. This would be a little getaway just for me. I could really use some time to myself. You know, recharge the old batteries. You want the other slice?"

"Uh-huh." Della took another bite.

Celeste got up and went to the oven. "I thought it made sense to go down to Prosper and take a look at the house."

Celeste's back was to her mother, but she felt the frosty stare, the chill that fell over the kitchen like a new Ice Age, suspending everything in one terrible, final moment. She stood frozen in place. "I'll let Ronnie know I'm going," Celeste ventured weakly. She half expected to see wispy clouds of breath as she spoke. "When I get back we can decide what to do with it."

Della shoved her plate away and pushed herself up from the table. "Humph! I shoulda known you were up to somethin'. Comin' in here with somethin' I *actually like* instead of somethin' you think I should want." Infused with an energy she didn't usually feel this time of day, Della nearly sprinted from the kitchen.

"How can you say that?" Celeste was quick on her mother's heels. "Anybody else would be glad her child wanted to see where she came from."

Della whirled around so fast that Celeste nearly tripped over her own feet trying to stop. "Didn't you hear what I said when you found that deed?!" Della's low growl made Celeste take a step backward. "Or did you just decide to go 'head and do what *you* want like usual?"

"It's what Daddy would have wanted me to do, and you know it!"

Della turned back around and proceeded down the hall. "I don't know no such thing! What I do know is that you are bound and determined to stick your nose where it don't belong!"

"Then tell me what's so bad about this place, why I shouldn't go," Celeste shouted as Della started up the stairs.

On the sixth step Della stood stock-still. She spoke without turning around. "Celeste Anne, don't let your age make you forget I'm your mother. I don't *have* to tell you a damn thing!"

7

"One last shot."

"Save your sorry-assed reasons, Celeste!" Ronnie spat into the cordless phone. She had to convey the venom without the volume because she wasn't sure who was home, and there was no reason for her roommates to know her business. "You didn't tell me about the house because *you* decided *you* know best! . . . No! You're wrong! Period!" Smoke from Ronnie's cigarette curled around her head like storm clouds. Her stomach had been churning and griping before the phone call. Most of the night, in fact. Since before dawn she'd shuffled back and forth between the bathroom and the bed. Several megadoses of Advil later, her cramps had finally quieted to a dull roar. She was just drifting off for a nap when the phone rang, and Celeste got her riled up again. "You make this sound like you found a pencil I lost! . . . And what have *you* done about it in the last three months? Not a damn thing!" The strident *beep-beep-beep* of a truck in reverse, seven stories below, drifted through the open window and underscored Ronnie's argument.

Ronnie puffed furiously and countered Celeste's version of events. "Maybe *you* didn't have the time to go down there until now, but did it ever occur to you that I might?" Anger made sitting impossible, so Ronnie climbed up out of the broken-down sofa, stuck her feet in her sneakers, because she never put a bare toe on the grimy, worn industrial tile floors in the loft, and stalked into the kitchen. "Nobody asked you to decide what my schedule would allow! We could have listed with a broker by phone. Might even have a buyer by now." Ronnie ground her cigarette out in the already full Altoids tin–cum–ashtray sitting on the fifties-era red Formica dinette table. She bent to empty the tin into the trash, but there wasn't space for another butt, and she had sworn she wasn't taking out the garbage again before somebody else did. "Cut the sentimental crap! Since when are you so interested in our family history?! And what do you expect to find in Proper, South Carolina, that Mama and Daddy . . . Fine. *Prosper, North* Carolina. Whatever. If there was anything important there, don't you think they would have got it by now?! . . . What do you mean Ma won't talk about it? . . . That's crazy! . . . Maybe she won't talk to you . . ." Ronnie grabbed a plastic stirrer from a coffee-stained white paper bag abandoned on the kitchen counter. She perched on one of the rickety, orange vinyl chairs and folded and refolded the small plastic stick into jagged peaks.

"So now I'm supposed to be grateful that you're gonna go straighten it all out!?" The little straw sprang free from Ronnie's hand and flew across the room. "You wouldn't even be telling me now except you might need my signature for something." Ronnie tromped out of the kitchen, plopped back down on the sofa, then jumped up again and went to close the window against the wail of sirens from the street. "Thank God Daddy put my name on the deed. But then, he had your number." She balanced precariously on the narrow sill. "You figure out what it means, Celeste, I'm through talkin' . . . Oh yes I *can* hang up!" Ronnie clicked off, then tossed the phone across the room onto the sofa. *Ma's father's house? My whole family is whacked.* She felt a twinge in her belly again, like somebody pinched her hard from the inside. She looked at her watch. It wasn't time for more pills yet.

What kind of idiot does she think I am? Ronnie didn't know if she was madder at Celeste for not telling her or at herself because Celeste was probably right. *I can barely handle me.*

After that big commercial fell through last fall and Ronnie had to vacate the Seventy-fifth Street apartment for the returning caballero, every part of her life seemed in a race straight down the tubes. She was back to bill-paying roulette, where only the lucky few were chosen each month. Her agent disappeared owing her for two bookings, no forwarding phone or address. She hadn't found a new one willing to take her on yet and hadn't been on a decent audition in months. *It's my own damn fault. I blew ten thousand dollars like the candles on a birthday cake.*

The one good thing about the latest dump she called an address was that most of the time nobody was around. She'd been on West Twenty-fifth Street four months. It was a share: living room, pass-through kitchen, two bedrooms, one bathroom. Four people more or less, depending on who stayed elsewhere and who dragged someone home with them. It was in one of those uniquely Manhattan buildings, zoned commercial/residential, which meant that no tenant could whine because the fourth floor was running a catering business from her apartment, or because the occupant on ten lived in his graphic arts studio. The upshot was you could do pretty much whatever you wanted within your four walls as long as you paid the rent.

Ronnie had met the guy who held the lease, a self-styled fashion designer who went by the name Rake, while she was hanging out at a photo studio with Kayla. The photographer was one in an endless series of Kayla's exes, but they had at least stayed friendly enough that he did her new head shot for free when she agreed to pose for some artful nudes. Ronnie and Kayla were weeding through chromes at the light box while Rake, a six-foot-four-inch exclamation point with platinum locks and sixteen visible piercings, attempted to convince the guy to shoot some of his designs for just the cost of film and processing. In a warp-speed harangue, Rake predicted the photographer would be able to ride his coattails to the cover of *WWD* and *Vogue,* fame and fortune. Ronnie and Kayla had been knocking themselves out laughing on the QT but they pulled on their straight faces when he approached. Somehow, in the midst of his raving, Rake had overheard Ronnie bitching about having her bags packed with nowhere to move. He said he'd just lost a roomie, and she could have the spot if she was interested. Ronnie turned the idea over for about two seconds. He looked a little orbital, but she'd definitely seen worse. The location was convenient. The rent was reasonable. And the photographer knew him, right? This was Ronnie's best offer. Actually, her only offer. He was a fashion designer after all, how bad could it be?

The apartment did have a view of sorts. The living room window looked out on a double-decker outdoor garage, but if you leaned out you could see the Empire State Building. Rake had the larger bedroom, at least that's what Ronnie had heard; she'd never seen it. He kept the door locked, and he had no visitors. The other was shared by Melise and Lucy, two girls Ronnie swore didn't look old enough to be out of high school. They were both five-foot-dust, brown-skinned with hair shaved down to scalp, and helium voices. If they weren't sharing a wardrobe, they had very similar tastes in skin-tight clothes, and they had each mastered a look of perpetual boredom. Together Ronnie spoke about six words to them a week, and so far, neither had been home on the same night. When Ronnie first moved in, she wondered what would happen if they mixed up their schedules and showed up at the same time, but she didn't give it much thought. She never paid enough attention to remember which was who; she thought of them as Mel-Lucy.

As the latecomer, Ronnie slept in the living room on a sofa bed. The arms and back of the powder blue monstrosity had been shredded by some long-ago cat and it smelled permanently of Chinese food. The first few nights she fell asleep and dreamed about moo shu and egg rolls. Ronnie kept her stuff in a big suitcase and one of those flowered cardboard chests of drawers in the front closet. She didn't kid herself; the place was a pit, but it was only temporary. Just until she got on her feet again.

Ronnie had calculated that from what they all paid in rent, Rake lived for free, which allowed him to buy the sheets of latex and rolls of plastic, from which he created the "Rake Down Chic" look. His creations, basics for the astral epoch he called them, looked like Deep Space Nine meets dominatrix. Ronnie found out firsthand how much they felt like instruments of torture when she bartered down her rent by modeling in a show he held at midnight on a Wednesday in May, behind a warehouse just off the West Side Highway.

Even her social life sucked. She'd gone out with R. Phillip a few times, enough to cajole him, after several glasses of wine, to reveal that the *R* stood for Rudolph. It was all she could do to keep from making reindeer jokes. He always took Ronnie to fabulous places, and she always had a boring time, but once he realized that all he was getting for the price of dinner was her company, the phone calls dropped off sharply. She decided he'd found a suitably attractive somebody, with better credentials and a more open admissions policy, to show off to his pretentious friends. No big loss. They had left it friendly enough. When she moved and changed bank branches, yet again, he even made a phone call to somebody he knew and arranged for her to handle Ronnie right away, no lines, no waiting, like she had more than $1.37 to deposit. Ronnie decided he liked hooking people up. It made him feel like a junior wheeler-dealer. And they still went out once in a while, last minute, like his prime candidate must have canceled. He had called Sunday to invite her to some museum reception on Tuesday. She gave him a hard time, just for practice, but she accepted because, hey, it was better than sitting around the apartment.

Ronnie still had her usual quotient of wine and hors d'oeuvres evenings. She did her fair share of talking trash, but the truth was she figured she'd heard every line and could answer them back like a champ. Nobody got over on Ronnie, not anymore. She had decided the sampler pack of male companions suited her needs; there was lots to choose from, no main course to get bored with, and there were no leftovers. But for all her bravado, she didn't part with her digits very often. She had too much important stuff to get straight and no time to be chasing after some man like she watched Kayla do. It just wasn't a priority.

She still had a few steady clients, trade shows, showroom gigs, and photographers who booked her directly because she charged them half the going rate, but she had to stand on her head to collect. If it weren't for Sable Shades, she couldn't have made it this far. Twice, she screwed up her courage to ask Marilyn Ellis if the job offer with the company was still open, but although she swung some extra hours on Monday night, she couldn't bring herself to ask for full-time. What would people say? You remember Ronnie? Ronnie Frazier? She's selling cosmetics now. Ronnie couldn't bear the ordinariness of it. She was supposed to be somebody. She couldn't give up, although it was hard some days to remember exactly what she would be losing.

Ronnie stood and opened the window again. *How come Ma never told us about this house?* Summer was only a week old, but the heat already had that thick, oily feel she had come to know in the city. Except for Rake's room, the apartment had no air conditioning. Ronnie gathered her hair off her neck. She was overdue for a visit to LaVonne, but it wasn't in the budget this week. She poked her head out the window, hoping to catch a breeze. *Prosper? That's a sick joke!* She squatted, rested her arms on the sill, and watched the midday traffic clog Twenty-sixth Street. *It's like Daddy's givin' me another chance. And this time I absolutely, positively will not screw up.* She watched a bike messenger dart between two trucks, zip past a startled pedestrian. *That much land ought to be worth something. Enough to get me settled in L.A. maybe? I can pay for some acting classes. I haven't studied in so long—too long. Celeste can build a monument on her half if she wants to. I'm gonna finance myself a fresh start. One last shot.* She pulled her head back in the apartment, got up, and brushed the soot off her hands.

I need a map. She glanced around, then laughed out loud. *Like I could just go to the bookshelf and grab an atlas. The only thing to read around here is a takeout menu.* Ronnie popped two more Advil, washed them down with a swig of diet iced tea, and made a mental note to pick up more. *Damn, that was a 250-pill bottle. Didn't I just buy it?* Then she snatched her white shirt from the back of the sofa and threw it on over her leggings and tank top because she didn't feel like listening to the nonsense she'd hear on the street otherwise.

She grabbed her purse. If she left now she'd have time to browse in the big bookstore on Sixth Avenue before she needed to come back and get dressed for work. *A first step toward my future success.*

Ronnie got on the elevator and joined a black-haired girl who wore a black leather vest, black lipstick, two safety pins in her right eyebrow, and a bright yellow Walkman. She rocked to her tunes, eyes closed, and appeared oblivious to Ronnie's presence. Ronnie waited a few seconds, but none of the buttons were lit, so she pushed *G* and the doors finally closed. *Airhead.* She dug around in her bag for the roll of antacids to help quiet her stomach. *I hate this building.* The car stopped two floors down, and an elderly man carrying a white toy poodle got on. He huddled in a corner and whispered in an unintelligible stream to his little red-eyed dog. Ronnie jammed her shades on and rolled her eyes. *Please don't let another fool get in here.* When the gears ground to a halt at the ground floor and the doors clanged open, she made a dash for the door. Through the glass she saw mystery roommate number one. Or was it two? *Melise? Lucy?* She got out of a white panel van with a rheumy looking guy wearing spattered painter's pants and a denim shirt with the sleeves cut out. He slammed the door and the van drove off. *Glad I'm leavin'.* Ronnie nodded, flipped the door open wide enough for them to catch if they wanted to, and was on her way.

In five minutes she was in the air-conditioned cool of the bookstore. *No wonder people hang out here. Tables, chairs, sofas?* She didn't remember the last time she'd been in a bookstore, certainly not since they started looking like dens. Ronnie inhaled the scent of cinnamon and chocolate, surveyed the seemingly endless rows of books. *I need a damn compass.* She got directions at the information desk and followed the instructions to the travel section with a growing sense of excitement. After collecting an armload of books that had something about North Carolina in the title, she parked herself in an empty chair and dug in.

Tar Heel State, Blue Ridge Mountains, population 7,000,000. In the whole state!? My block has more people than that. She thumbed through the volumes, scanned maps. No Prosper. She got to a book sealed in cellophane and could feel a fold-out map in back. She looked around, checked for clerks on the prowl, then punctured the wrapping with her thumbnail, opened out the map. In the index she got the coordinates, then scanned and squinted. *There it is.* Prosper was printed in the tiniest, lightest type. It was surrounded by towns with names like Peedee and Peachland. *Are they serious?* The nearest "real" city was Charlotte. Remembering her fourth-grade geography, Ronnie checked the legend, measured the distance between Prosper and Charlotte between her thumb and forefinger. *That's more than an hour away!* She checked the rest of her books for Prosper highlights, but unlike Duck, Cullowhee, and Swan City, all of which had enough going for them to warrant inclusion in one book or another, Prosper appeared to be completely unremarkable. *Great. It's probably right up there with Mayberry.* Ronnie left her books on the table. *What if I go down there too? To look after my interests, get this process moving? Celeste might not like it, but she couldn't stop me—if I wanted to go.*

By the time she turned on her block, she'd decided to call and check the airfare when she got off work. *And I bet I can get Ma to tell me more about this place than she told Celeste.* Ronnie had a little space left before she maxed out her charge card, and this seemed like a good investment. She started composing her speech to ask Marilyn for the time off. Fortunately, her ride up in the elevator was solitary. She'd have just enough time to shower and change into her Sable Shades getup.

"What the . . ." The prickly feeling started at the top of Ronnie's head and snaked down her spine. She stood in the open doorway, trying to comprehend the damage. Cans and broken jars from the kitchen cabinets spilled onto the counter, littered the floor. A sack of flour had burst and dusted the mess with a layer of white. All the drawers had been yanked out and ditched in a corner.

Fear made her want to run, but she was rooted in place. Then she caught sight of Rake, splayed on the couch, holding his head like it would fall off.

"Are you all right?" She hurried inside.

"Aw man—they cleaned me out," he wailed.

Broken glass crunched under Ronnie's feet as she walked through the kitchen. It was hot in the loft, but she was suddenly cold, about to shiver. "What the hell happened?!" She stepped over the medicine chest, which had been ripped out and abandoned in the middle of the floor. A lot had happened to her since she left home, but she'd never had a break-in.

When she got up close, Rake didn't look hurt, but the rest of the apartment had been worked over. Tables and chairs overturned, lamps broken, the heavy metal fire door to Rake's room hung precariously from one hinge. Ronnie sank down on the sofa next to him. She couldn't raise her voice above a whisper. "What the hell happened?"

"Somebody broke in." His voice was flat.

"Did you walk in on 'em?"

"Naw. I wish I had. There would have been bloodshed."

"Save it, Rake. How long have you been waiting for the cops? You didn't touch anything, did you?" Ronnie's eyes darted around the room. "Thank God I wasn't here!"

Rake just stared at the ceiling.

Ronnie noticed that the TV and VCR were still there. *Probably too old to fence.* "What did they take?" She did a mental inventory. She had on her real jewelry, her watch, a pair of gold hoop earrings, and a matching gold ring and bracelet she'd ordered off cable in the middle of the night. She didn't have anything else in the apartment but clothes, and no self-respecting burglar would waste his time on . . . *Shit! My jacket!* She'd meant to put it in storage, looked up a few places, even called for prices, but she put it off, left it wrapped in tissue paper in one of her suitcases. She stared down the hall, saw the closet door ajar, and she knew. She couldn't feel her legs as she got up to check. The clothes that had been in the bag were dumped on the floor and the empty suitcase propped the door open. She kicked it, then dropped to her knees, deflated. "My mink jacket's gone!"

"I'm sorry. I didn't check anywhere but my . . . I didn't know . . ."

"I'm callin' the cops again." Ronnie jumped up and dug the portable out from between the couch cushions where she'd thrown it. "I'll say I think they're still . . ."

"Don't!" Rake sounded panicked.

"It's the middle of the damn day! They should be here by now." She started to punch in the numbers, but Rake grabbed Ronnie's wrist and snatched the phone. "Ow! Get your hands off . . ."

"No cops, Ronnie."

"We've been ripped off! What do you expect me to . . ."

"No cops. I can't tell what they stole."

"You got so much crap in there you can't figure out what's missing?" Ronnie headed toward Rake's gaping door. She was surprised by the plush ambiance. The faux marble walls were covered with sketches and clippings from fashion magazines, secured by clear pushpins. A huge oval gilt mirror hung over the maple dresser, which matched his king-size headboard. Aside from the obvious looting, the room looked as traditional as Rake did not. The green plaid bedspread hung askew on his bed, pillows and shams tossed aside. *This boy even has drapes!* Two towering bookshelves lay toppled and splintered, the trophies, plaques, bolts of fabric, sample cards, and actual books strewn across the room. She walked farther in, drawn by the contradiction. The TV, VCR, DVD player and stereo, all state-of-the-art, had not been touched. His dressmaker's dummy lay on its side, but his work table and industrial sewing machine were intact too. Ronnie noticed that the door to what she assumed was a closet, as well as all the molding around the jamb, were splintered, like they'd been chewed up. "What the . . ." She found a room, at least the size of the other bedroom, with walls lined with aluminum foil and track lights and spots crisscrossing the ceiling. Wooden planks elevated the floor, and some kind of water tank and hose system occupied a corner. Shelves like bleachers were lined with big, plastic flowerpots, some of them overturned, all of them empty. There wasn't a leaf in sight.

He came in behind her. "You shouldn't be in here."

Ronnie whirled around. "You're growin' weed in here?!"

She shook with anger. "Oh my God, I'm livin' with a damn drug dealer! You coulda gotten me arrested—or killed, Rake! Are you crazy?!"

Rake backed away from her tirade, stumbled on the bed, and plopped down. "Naw, Ron, it wasn't like that. I swear." He talked to the floor. "I used to just grow for myself—and a couple of friends—once in a while—I was gonna finance my own show."

"Is that how you found out?" She pointed to the alarm pad by the door. *I've been sharing an apartment with a guy who alarms his room?!*

"I had to get it. My roommate situation is so . . . there's a lot of traffic through here. Anyway, the security company beeped me."

"See how much good that did!" She shoved his shoulder, hard. *How could I be so stupid? Again!*

"For all I know, *you* had something to do with it." He sat up and stared hard.

"You're not gonna blame this on me!" *Why wouldn't he? He doesn't know any more about me than I know about him. Not a damn thing.* "Talk to your little friends Melise and Lucy."

"They're not my friends. I met 'em at a club."

Great. "One of them was coming in with some skeevy guy when I left."

"Look, I don't give a shit, all right! Get the hell outta my room, and if you tell anybody . . ."

"What?!" Ronnie stood up to him, but suddenly she was aware how much she didn't want to know what. She didn't know Rake had a marijuana truck farm in his room, and she didn't know what else he'd do either. She just wanted to leave, but where did she have to go besides the Sable Shades counter? "Damn! I gotta go to work."

The tears were streaming by the time she got to the bathroom. She put the lid down, sat on the toilet, and sobbed. *What am I gonna do?* Ronnie didn't have much time to wallow in it. She pulled herself together, did her face from memory since the mirror was gone, all except eyeliner because her hands weren't steady enough, and she was behind the Sable Shades counter only twenty minutes late. Fortunately she had no makeovers, so she concentrated on ringing up the merchandise and bagging it without bursting into tears. The time weighed heavily because she knew that after the store closed she had nowhere to go except back to the loft, and for the first time in her life she was afraid to go home. So when she got out onto Thirty-fourth Street, she started walking. Nowhere in particular, just one foot, then the other, crossing wherever the light was in her favor, trying to shape some coherent plan out of ashes.

Kayla told Ronnie that if she needed a squat she was always welcome. "You know Mama won't mind. She likes you," Kayla had said.

Ronnie was afraid of what Kayla's mother was like if she *didn't* like somebody. To Ronnie, Kayla's situation was nearly as bad as her own. She still lived in Brooklyn with her mother, grandmother, and two younger sisters and their five kids. Or, as Ronnie thought of them, the witch, grand wizard, two harpies, and their evil spawn. A few years back, after a party in Fort Green, Ronnie had been too wasted to go home, and Kayla insisted she spend the night. Ronnie had been appalled at the way they spoke to each other, cursing as soon as not, children included. It made her and Celeste look like sweet and sweeter. She had no idea how Kayla put up with the anger and chaos.

Besides, this was not a story she planned to share with her flighty friend just yet. Repeating it aloud would amplify the nightmare, and the volume was already deafening. And Kayla was still in the Hamptons for a long weekend, anyway; some friend had a share and she considered the island fertile hunting ground.

By the time Ronnie got to Thirty-eighth Street, the "what if" game had taken over. *What if they do come back? What if the police find out about Rake's enterprise and think I'm part of it? What am I gonna do?* She stopped at Bryant Park. Nestled in this valley between skyscrapers, a crowd had gathered, enjoying the balmy night; people lounged on the lawn in folding chairs, stretched out on blankets with gourmet munchies and wine, or balanced on squares of folded newspaper watching *Some Like It Hot* al fresco, projected on a huge screen. That's the kind of thing she had always loved about the city, the thrill of moonlit movies, the sense that all things are possible if you just find the right corner to turn.

Ronnie sank to a bench, just vacated by two men and a woman conversing in animated German. She couldn't see stars; they were rare on a clear night. Even the moon was reduced to a bright glow showing through the haze. The park walkways still bustled with briefcase-toting yuppies, tourists out to soak up as much of the city as they could in six days and seven nights, and rollerbladers jockeying with skateboarders for sidewalk space. Ronnie marveled at a limber redhaired girl who twisted and spun with the same agility and fearless abandon as the boys around her. The girl came to a dead stop, flipped her board up into her hand, and tucked it under her arm in a motion so slick Ronnie wasn't sure she'd actually seen it. *She's got a whole life ahead of her. When will she stop enjoying it?*

Ronnie hadn't walked far, but she was exhausted. She hadn't intended to walk in the opposite direction from her apartment, but then she really didn't know what she intended to do. About anything. The weight of her day, of her life was pressing down on her. Her shoulders slumped from the load. And the soles of her feet burned. *Stupid sandals!* They were cheap and meant to be cute, not walking shoes. She wiggled her toes, hoping a little air would help cool the fire. A burst of laughter erupted from the audience and was swallowed by the night. She thought it was funny that this little bit of green encircled by concrete and granite was referred to as a park. Back in Buffalo they'd probably call it a square. It definitely wasn't a real park like Ellicott Creek or Chestnut Ridge, with hills, streams, birds, and room to run. A fragment of a memory darted across Ronnie's mind. She was seven or eight, running full out through the park with a water balloon, laughing wildly. One of her braids had come undone and she had on brand-new Keds. They were so white. Celeste was chasing her. Then it was gone, quick as it came. Ronnie closed her eyes a second, tried to get it back, but when she opened them again, tears had replaced the memory. Blinking, she looked away, brushed her cheeks with her hand. Fortunately no one was paying attention to her, because only nut jobs and losers sat on park benches crying. She tilted her head back to stem the tide and tuned in to the buzz of streetlights, traffic, and so many people with so much energy rushing by one another with conviction, purpose. The heartbeat of New York. *I'm so tired.* The charge, the excitement of being in the greatest city in the world, used to fuel her days. Anything could happen here. The possibilities were as vast as her hopes and dreams. The city used to get her up, keep her going, and put her to bed so she could do it all over again. But now that all felt like a story that happened to someone else a long, long time ago. She had tried, kept her end of what had always been a one-sided deal. New York had become another broken promise. *Maybe I'm losing my edge. Or maybe I've just lost my grip!* The rustle of a newspaper and a grunt snatched her back to park view. He sat on the bench opposite hers, the *Post* open across his lap, right hand moving up and down like a piston, his game of pocket pool well under way.

   I gotta get outta here.

8

". . . a few square miles of raggedy road and broken dreams . . ."

"Now this limited power of attorney, it means you can sign the papers for me, but only for this one closing, is that right, uh, Mr. Dawkins?" Even though Arthur Jr. had taken over the practice from his father more than ten years ago, Della still had trouble calling him anything but Chunk, which is what the senior Dawkins had nicknamed him when he was little. First time Della saw him he was a five-year-old chunk of chocolate, working diligently at stapling the papers and licking the envelopes Arthur Sr.'s secretary would hand him to keep him occupied. That was back when she and Will bought their very first house, and through the years, all of their legal affairs had been handled by father or son. Della saw no reason to change that.

"Uh, yes. That's exactly right." Even in the simplest situations Arthur chose his words carefully, like he had deliberated over six other words before choosing the most precisely correct one. "Then I can execute all the necessary documents. You won't even have to be present for the closing. I will, of course, forward you the check immediately."

The house on Minnesota was the tenth one Will had bought and the first she'd arranged to sell. Della wasn't keen on watching the change of hands. It was for a good cause, though. She wanted to make sure Niki had whatever money she needed to go to chef school.

"As for giving money to your granddaughter, you're allowed to make a gift of up to ten thousand dollars a year to a family member without any tax repercussions. If that works out for the both of you, I'd suggest handling it that way. We can make some stipulation in your will that this be continued, but I don't see the need to set up a trust."

"Once we get this house squared away, I'll come in to talk about my will." *My Will. That used to mean something completely different.* Della knew Celeste was right about getting rid of the houses. She just wanted to do it in her own time and in her own way, without Celeste any further in her business than she already was.

"This'll only take a second."

Della watched as he turned to his computer and input some information. She thought Arthur Jr. had grown into a fine man, but she always had a feeling he would. And he'd done a fine job of growing the business. He took it from a solo practice working out of a storefront to a suite in a small office building he encouraged his father to buy. Chunk supervised the renovations, then he beat the bushes for new business. Now he had five attorneys working for him.

And Arthur Jr. had his own family now. On the wall behind his desk, among the framed degrees and citations, hung a smiling portrait of his wife and their three sons. But back when he and Celeste were teens, Della had picked him as the perfect match for her oldest daughter. She thought they were a lot alike: both serious, persistent, levelheaded. He knew he wanted to be a lawyer early on, and even back in the days of ripped bell-bottom blue jeans, platforms, and love beads, he dressed more sensibly, like a professional man. Della thought they'd complement each other, and every once in a while she couldn't help but imagine a church wedding and beautiful grandbabies, not that it was any of her business. At one point she sensed ol' Chunk was sweet on Celeste too. At least that's what it seemed like to her. If he was around the office when his father had papers for Will, Arthur Jr. would volunteer to deliver them in person. Della would do everything short of fixing lemonade and cookies and sitting the two of them out on the porch swing to encourage them together. Arthur didn't help his own case much. He was slow to make a move. Celeste dismissed him as way too boring. The more Della talked him up, the harder Celeste shot him down, until finally Della gave up. It's not that there was anything wrong with

Everett. Della loved him to death; she was just never convinced he could make Celeste happy.

Not that Della cared at this moment if Celeste or Ronnie was happy. Right now she was furious at both of them.

Arthur reached behind his desk, plucked the document from the laser printer, tucked it in an envelope, and handed it to Della. "Take these home and read them over. Call me if you have any questions. Otherwise, sign both copies, send them back, and we'll be all set."

Della took the envelope without looking at it. "One more thing—It's about some land down South that was left to me." She hated to be like this, but as far as she was concerned Celeste and Ronnie had driven her to it. She didn't begrudge them the money. They could sell the property, split the proceeds, and that would be the end of it. But now they were both heading to Prosper to poke their noses where they didn't belong, and neither one seemed to care that it was against Della's wishes. So she made up her mind that she didn't care what she had to do to stop them. Della began to explain the situation, which jogged Arthur's memory. He brought her files up on the computer, read for a moment.

"The difficulty is that legally, it's not your land anymore." Arthur took off his glasses, threw them on his desk, squeezed his forehead in his hand. "I mean, I take it you grew up there, and you must feel some—attachment. But once you signed it over to Mr. Frazier, it was legally his to dispose of, and he certainly did that in a lawful way."

Della's eyes glazed with hurt and anger. She zipped and unzipped her pocketbook as she thought. "What if I buy it back from them?"

"That would be fine, as long as you three can agree on terms."

"And if they won't sell it to me, I can take them out of my will, can't I?"

"Mrs. Frazier, I—this is rather drastic."

"That doesn't answer my question."

"Well, technically, yes, you could disinherit one or both of your children. It usually creates quite a problem. You'd give them grounds to challenge the will. They'll end up with other attorneys involved, it usually drags on, stirs up bad feeling. Nobody really wins. I don't know what, uh, situation, brought this about, but if you give it some time, I'm sure . . ."

"I ain't got time." She stood and left the office.

Della ran the rest of her errands wearing a sour puss. She chewed out a grocery clerk because they were out of the sale ice cream, and when the checkout line tried her patience she pushed her whole cart of food to one side and left the store.

At the beauty shop she didn't have two words to add to the round of gossip. Della was too aggravated to work her word puzzles, so she closed the magazine on her lap, sat under the dryer, and steamed at Will for starting this whole mess. And what gave her children the right to dig around in her life without an invitation? *Goin' a thousand miles out of the way to kick a sleeping dog. Then question me about why I'm upset!*

With a flowered head scarf tied over her rows of fresh, hard curls, Della left the shop and carried her bad attitude home with her. She wandered through the house for a time, too fidgety to sit in one place for long. It was dinnertime, but talking to a lawyer about her own children had taken her appetite. *If my mother had ever asked me not to do something . . .* Della stood at the kitchen counter, ripping open mail. Half of it was junk, still addressed to Will.

Hesitantly, Della stepped into the rays of amber evening sun that flooded the living room. She stood in front of the piano, lost in thought. As far as she was concerned, Prosper was a few square miles of raggedy road and broken dreams. *Lord only knows what it's like now.* She pulled out the bench, sat down, and flipped the lid. Tentatively, she ran the back of her index finger over the keys, playing a quiet glissando that stopped at middle C, where her hands fell naturally into place. The simple melody flowed from her effortlessly, like it had waited a long time to be released. Della's whole body seemed to carry the music, swell with it, glide on it. As she continued to play, she embellished the tune, hummed the harmony. Finally she opened her mouth to sing. Her voice cracked and stopped her cold.

SUNDAY, APRIL 23, 1950
PROSPER, NORTH CAROLINA

"So your father tells me you sing, Odella. Is that true?" Mrs. Garland clasped her hands and rested them on her enormous blue and white flowered bosom.

Odella looked over at her father, who nodded. "I guess so, ma'am."

"You were in the choir over in Cadysville?" Mrs. Garland spoke in the same thin, warbly soprano as she sang. "What part did you sing?" She turned her mouth down, tucked her chin in, and her face melted into the thick fleshy rolls around her neck.

"Ma'am?" Odella folded and unfolded her church bulletin. Mrs. Garland made her nervous. She had a mustache and a mole that moved when she talked, and Odella was usually so busy watching them she had a hard time paying attention to what Mrs. Garland said. Besides, she didn't want to talk about singing today. Service had been particularly long. It was nearly three o'clock, Reverend Garland had preached two hours nonstop, and she just wanted to go home, take off her dress, and go down to the pond. Once she discovered the wide, still pool, it quickly became her favorite spot. She liked to be alone and think about stuff, and the fact that Henry hated it made the location all the more appealing.

This morning, before they left for church, her father knocked on her door. He sat on the edge of the bed, adjusted the crease in his freshly pressed trousers. "It's time you joined in things a little. You been here a while now. Your mama told me what a good voice you have so I decided to speak to Mrs. Garland after church. I'm sure she'd welcome you in her choir." Odella knew it was fruitless to protest, and although she never mentioned it to anyone, she did miss her music.

Two years ago, when Odella came to Prosper, her father said he'd give her time to settle in and get adjusted to her new life. "And give these folks time to get adjusted to you." He predicted accurately that she'd be a curiosity for a while. And she had been for most of the first year. There had been a constant parade of visitors stopping by the house on some pretext or another, but all they really wanted was a good close-up look at Odell Womack's outside child. She'd hide in the woods and hear them whispering as they walked up the road on their way back to town. "Well, she look jus' like him." "How can Ethiopia stand it?" "Right in her face. Um, um um." Odella stayed to herself, did as she was told, and spoke when spoken to.

That philosophy worked with her father's square-faced wife as well. Ethiopia was always polite, but Odella felt more like a boarder than family, which was just fine with her. She had no use for Miz Ethiopia either. There was no point in her even pretending to be motherly, because the simple fact was she could never be Annie.

The only person she couldn't easily sidestep was Henry. He kept his rancor in check when others were around to the point that Odella had heard people comment on how mature it was of Henry to welcome his half-blood kin. But when they were alone he'd unleash his pent-up humiliation. Henry viewed her mere presence as an affront to his mother. And that she was named for Odell and he was not was daily kindling to Henry's smoldering rage. He'd trip her, accidentally on purpose, tear up her school assignments, track mud into the house after she'd finished mopping so she'd have to do it again, and dare her to run to Odell. "He's a damn mangy dog, just like you." Odella dealt with his pranks and name-calling, as long as he left her mother out of it. One day he started to bad-mouth Annie, and she took after him with a mop handle. He didn't do it again.

Odella looked up at the beamed ceiling and rocked back and forth on the heels of her black patent leather Mary Janes. She wished she was somewhere else. Twelve, going on thirteen, as she told folks when they asked her age, was such an awkward stage between girl and woman. She was neither and both. Odella felt like she grew taller while she slept, and dungarees that had fit a few days ago seemed to have shrunk overnight. It was like her whole body had a secret pact she wasn't privy to. Blouses that she wore to school didn't button anymore, thanks to newly sprouted breasts. Her skirts suddenly became too loose in the waist and too tight across her hips. She hunched her shoulders in an effort to conceal her chest and appear

shorter until Odell made her stop. A few days later she came
home from school and discovered a pile of new clothes on her
bed. At the bottom of the pile, under the dresses, sweaters, and
skirts, were two brassieres, two girdles, a box of sanitary napkins, and a pamphlet entitled "Your New Body." Miz Ethiopia,
as she called her father's wife, when she had no choice but to
use a name, asked her if she found everything. Odella nodded
and that was that. But none of that helped how she felt about
growing up and out, so Odella wished for Annie and tried to
figure out what to do with herself.

"Stop fidgeting, child, and answer my question." Genevieve
Garland huffed and puffed, her mammoth breasts rolled like
the mighty Jordan. She was a formidable woman, at least twice
the size of her husband, but they were quite suited to each
other. Samuel and Genevieve took everything about life seri-
ously, and Faith Chapel Colored Methodist Episcopal Church
was their life.

"I sang whatever they needed me to, ma'am." Odella didn't
like either one of them. They may have been good, but they
weren't nice, especially to her. She longed for her church back
home.

"Come now. You have to be a soprano or an alto. Maybe
your old choir didn't make such distinctions." She looked down
her nose and over her glasses at Odella. "But in this choir we
do. Most of our members read music too." Her intent was clear.

"Odella." She could hear the warning in her father's voice.
"Answer Miz Garland."

"I guess I do both, ma'am."

"Humph." Mrs. Garland moved her considerable bulk over
to the piano and plopped down on the stool, which disappeared beneath the overhang. "We'll just see about that. Come
on over here."

Reluctantly, Odella went to stand beside her. As she did
every Sunday, before every song, Genevieve Garland made an
elaborate show of limbering her fingers before she began to
play. She started and nodded at Odella, who followed her
scales note for note. Mrs. Garland moved up an octave then
down one. She changed keys, and Odella sang, almost intuit-

ing where the music would go next. Mrs. Garland finished and glared at Odella over her glasses.

A few folks who were still milling about outside the small white building, complimenting the pastor on his sermon, catching up on news, and getting their weekly dose of gossip, poked their heads back in the door.

"Maybe it would be better if I sang a whole song, ma'am." Odella found comfort in the sound of her own voice. She hadn't sung in so long she'd forgotten how good it felt. "Ma'am?" Odella nodded slightly toward the piano. It took Mrs. Garland a moment to realize that Odella wanted her to get up, that she would play for herself. The rickety upright in the corner of the sanctuary groaned as Mrs. Garland leaned on it and hoisted herself off the stool. She stepped away, folded her arms across her expansive chest, and waited.

Odella sat gingerly on the stool, looked at Mrs. Garland, then over at Odell who was having a hard time hiding his smile. Odella put her hands on the keys, closed her eyes, and opened her mouth. "Precious Lord, take my hand. Lead me on . . ." Odella lit up the rafters with her body full of voice, and anybody who was still outside drifted back in. Will and Lester dragged Henry inside and stood in the rear of the church. Others, including Odell, Ethiopia, and Reverend Garland, took seats in the pews. By the time Odella got to the last stanza, she was accompanied by a chorus of "Amen," "Lord ha' mercy," and "Thank you, Jesus."

"We hold choir practice on Saturday afternoon," Mrs. Garland said matter-of-factly and dabbed at the trickle of sweat at her temple with a tiny blue hankie.

"Yes, ma'am." Odella got up and looked at her father, who beamed and nodded his head approvingly.

Lester left Will and Henry standing in the doorway and headed up the aisle to meet Odella. A long and lean sixteen, Lester moved with the lazy lope of a trotter. "How come you didn't tell nobody you could sing like that, Odee?" He stopped in front of her.

Although Henry remained as hateful as he was the day they met, she eventually got on well with Will and Lester,

which only made Henry more unpleasant. Will was protective
and always stood up for her, and she and Lester quickly became sparring partners, trading wisecracks and insults. Odella
spent a lot of her time at the pond wishing they were her
brothers instead of Henry.

"'Cause nobody didn't ask, and don't call me Odee," Odella
shot back.

"You got a smart answer for everything, don't you, Odee?"

Odella caught herself short of sticking out her tongue. They
were, after all, still in church, and she didn't want to know
what kind of sin Reverend and Mrs. Garland would call that.

"Well answer me this. You wanna do a duet sometime?
We'd sound pretty good together."

Lester Wilson was the best baritone for miles around. Even
though he had just turned sixteen, he sang most of the male
leads and solos in the Faith Chapel choir. Sometimes he'd
even sing at other churches, and they'd take up a special collection and give him the money.

"I sound pretty good by myself—" Odella couldn't let him
know how tickled she was that he was asking her to sing with
him. "—But I'll think about it." She flashed him a big fake
smile, walked outside, and found herself surrounded by church
members waiting to pat her on the back. Lester went past her
and rejoined Henry and Will. The three of them made it a habit
to walk home from church. Odella gave Lester another cheesy
grin and climbed in the backseat of her father's car.

"Didn't know you played the piano too," Odell said as they
pulled away from the church. Her father's wife said nothing.
"Were you taking lessons back in Cadysville?"

"No, Papa. I just play what I hear."

"Well, we'll look into some lessons."

Two weeks later and right before her lessons began, Odella
came home and found a shiny, black spinet piano in the living
room. Her stepmother asked if she'd seen it. Odella nodded,
and that was that.

If her piano lessons were magical, learning to connect
what she heard with a written note was alchemy. Turning the
sounds in her head into music on a page came as naturally as

breathing. She loved going to Mrs. Yarbrough's house for her lessons. She didn't have to be told to practice, although sometimes she had to be asked to stop. Wednesday afternoons were her favorite. Miz Ethiopia and her Sunshine Ladies from church visited the sick and shut-in. And Henry almost never came straight home from school, so Odella would run all the way, knowing she had at least two hours when she could play anything she wanted, any way she wanted. That's when she'd sound out the songs she listened to on the radio instead of hymns and waltzes.

Eyes closed, she was thumping out the melody to "Is You Is or Is You Ain't My Baby" with her right hand when she felt the pain shoot up her arm. She hollered, looked down at her throbbing fingers mashed between the lid and the keys, then up into Henry's face. "You don't play no nasty music in *my* mother's house," he snarled.

When Odell came home, saw her swollen hand, and asked her what happened, she watched Henry's eyes narrow malevolently and said simply that the lid fell. Her father put a latch on the piano to ensure the accident wouldn't repeat itself. Odella couldn't play the piano for weeks.

When did it get dark? The street lamp in front of the house had come on. Della rubbed her right hand absently, then she slammed down the piano lid. A dissonant burst of notes lingered on the air.

Della didn't want to know how time had passed in Prosper, but one way or another, it looked like she was about to find out.

9

"My life. My rules. Right?"

"Of course, Mrs. English. I'll let Ms. English know you're here." The young man behind the ornate Regency-style desk at the entrance to Les Fleurs stashed a stack of thickly bound, gold-tasseled menus in their wall rack, picked up the phone, and punched in an extension. After a murmured conversation he hung up.

"She's in a meeting with a new purveyor, but she said she'll be with you as soon as she can." He gestured toward a brocade settee by a towering palm tree. "Can I get you anything while you wait?"

"No. Thank you." *Ms. English is in a meeting with a purveyor. I hope her penmanship has improved. She'll never be able to read her notes.* Celeste sat gingerly on the edge, trying to avoid getting wet circles on her clothes. Her blouse was soaked under her linen jacket. The silk felt clammy against her back. Late June in Atlanta was much hotter than she was used to. On the ride from the airport, Celeste was sweating like a pig while her taxi driver seemed perfectly comfortable with the window only open a crack. It wasn't quite noon when they pulled in front of the hotel, but she was ready for another shower. *How can Niki stand this heat?*

Celeste shifted slightly to her left, directly in the path of an air-conditioning vent. The cool blast refreshed her. Most of the restaurant tables were still empty. Paintings of lavish floral arrangements and formal gardens decorated the walls. Servers busied themselves checking the contents of salt and pepper shakers, examining flatware, and refolding napkins. *This is casual dining? Nicole never said it was so elaborate.*

A nattily dressed elderly couple stopped at the display case outside the restaurant to look over the lunch menu. They held hands and whispered to each other before moving on. *They're so sweet. I always thought Everett and I . . .*

Celeste forced her brain to make a U-turn. She took out her agenda, crossed "take cab to airport 6 A.M.," "switch flight," and "get plane at 7:45" off her to-do list. She had managed to convince herself that she decided last night, while she wrestled in bed, unable to sleep, to reroute her flight through Atlanta. That it was a spontaneous decision just to spend a day with her daughter, not a detour that had been on her mind for weeks. Otherwise she'd have to admit this visit was one of the many land mines in her life and that she was running out of safe places to step. That she didn't tell Niki sooner because she was afraid she'd find some excuse to keep her mother away. And that the whole Prosper episode felt like one big booby trap, with a hair trigger.

Down to the last Della refused to speak on the subject, and she grew more evil about it the closer Celeste got to departure. *I wish Daddy had sold the place and left me out of it.* She tried not to hope too hard that she could convince Nicole to go with her to North Carolina, even for a day or two. Somehow Celeste imagined the house was in the boonies, down a dirt road, with no phone, and Niki's company always made her feel better. And she'd have another shot at talking some sense into her child, at making Niki see that stirring pots in somebody's kitchen was not a step on the path to a successful career. Celeste and Niki had struggled through a few fast phone conversations after her short visit. When they spoke they avoided two subjects completely, Niki's decision and Everett's impending departure. Celeste hadn't even told her daughter about her great-grandfather's house until last week.

Celeste added "call NC hotel and change arrival" to her list. She had tied herself in square knots during the last few weeks, trying to keep her life together. Once she realized that Everett thought he was serious about leaving, her first challenge had been to convince him not to go before school was out. She appealed to his sympathetic, understanding nature. "You know it's the busiest time of the year for me. I can't handle all the pressure at school and this at the same time. You owe me at least that much." His answer still rang in her ears. "I'll hang out a little longer because you asked, but don't run it into the ground. Right now I owe myself more than I owe you."

By the end of June, Celeste pleaded for another extension and asked him not to move out until she got back from Prosper. "I authorized work on the new roof Daddy got bids on. I have to go check on it."

At the last possible moment, when she'd given up hope of changing Everett's mind, Celeste called the Thorntons to postpone their arrival in Highland Beach. She told Lydia that she had to go to Prosper right away because Ronnie was pressuring her about the house. Lydia said she understood completely. "Family can get so ugly when it comes to money. But I hope you can get here for some part of the month. It would be a shame to waste ten thousand dollars." Celeste could have kicked herself for blowing all that money, but it wouldn't matter if she could stall Everett long enough for him to come to his senses and put this divorce business behind them.

Celeste watched Niki approach, carrying a maroon leather binder under her arm. Her braids, bundled into a chignon, and the creamy sheath, gold choker, and black patent pumps clearly said "I'm in charge here." *She looks so grown up.* Niki glanced down as she passed a table set for four, then whispered to a passing waiter, who immediately cleared the service plates. She waved at Celeste, then stopped a moment to examine the enormous floral arrangement in the center of the room. At the desk she conferred briefly with the young maître d' before continuing on to her mother.

"You look so professional!" Celeste stood, held out her hands, and offered Niki her cheek.

"Hi." Nicole obliged, gave her mother a quick kiss. "Sorry to keep you waiting." The older couple Celeste had seen earlier entered the restaurant. Niki instantly diverted her gaze from Celeste to the guests. "Welcome to Les Fleurs. Eric will be . . ."

"Right here, Ms. English." The maître d' appeared, menus in hand.

"Enjoy your meal," Niki said as he escorted the early lunchers to a table.

Celeste felt almost teary-eyed, watching her baby take charge.

Niki returned her attention to her mother. "Are you okay? Is something wrong?"

"Everything is fine."

Niki searched her mother's face. "This visit is really unexpected." *And you're not a spur-of-the-moment kinda babe.* Her mother's call caught Niki as she was brushing her teeth and trying to get out the door. All morning she'd been bracing for the approaching storm.

"And I know I'm barging in on your life, but it's only for a day. I leave tomorrow for Charlotte. I thought we might . . ."

"Just a sec, Ma."

Celeste cringed at the "Ma," looked to see if anyone had heard. When she turned back, Niki had gone to speak to a small, distinguished man in a tan suit. He was shorter than Niki by several inches, and Celeste was amused when he took a step back so he didn't have to lift his head to talk to her. Celeste knew that trick. She used it herself. Niki opened the notebook she carried, flipped through several sheets of paper before handing one to the man.

Niki crossed the room to Celeste in three long strides. "Ma, I can't talk now. That's the hotel manager, and I have to meet with him about—never mind what it's about. I'll see you back at my place around six thirty." *So I can find out exactly why you're here.* Nicole reached in the pocket of her dress. "Here. It's my spare." She handed her mother a key. "You have the address?"

"Uh-huh." Celeste was surprised by the thoroughness of Niki's caretaking.

"It's not far. I'll have them get you a cab. Where's your luggage?"

"I checked it with the bellman. I was hoping you could get away for a little shopping. That's a great mall across the street!"

"Not today. I'm swamped. Make yourself at home." Niki

looped her arm through her mother's and started toward the door of the restaurant. *Damn! I didn't make my bed. I wasn't expecting the inspector general. But it's my house.*

To make or not to make had been a struggle between mother and daughter since five-year-old Niki asked why she had to make her bed if she was just going to mess it up all over again. Celeste told her that nice little girls wanted their beds to look pretty. Without hesitation Niki said, "I guess I'm not that nice," but she was forced to comply anyway.

When she turned twelve, Niki started keeping her bedroom door closed and her bed unmade. Celeste had a fit, accused her of being defiant and disobedient, and grounded her. Everett came to the rescue, cautioning Celeste to give Niki some slack because considering what some of their friends were going through with their children, this was minor. Celeste grudgingly gave in, but when Everett took off for Benin, she reneged and the battle raged again. When Everett called home, Niki told on her mother, but Everett, already on the outs with Celeste and emotionally overwhelmed by the work he was doing, didn't have the will or strength to fight Celeste from the other side of the world. He told Niki to try and get along with her mother. Niki started making her bed again, but she still kept the door closed.

"I'll call the bell captain. Your bags and a taxi will be waiting when you get to the door." Niki pecked her mother on the cheek and picked up the phone. *She's gonna freak when she gets there.*

Celeste set her suitcase by the front door. *I wish she hadn't taken a first-floor unit. It's so easy to break in.* She had to admit it was a lovely, well-manicured complex, ten minutes from the hotel. *But you never know.*

Celeste sighed at the mound of shoes abandoned in the foyer. *How can she leave these lying around. It's the first thing you see.* She matched them in pairs and made neat rows of shoes on the floor of the coat closet. Rays of sunlight sliced through the vertical blinds, making zebra stripes on the creamy carpet. When Everett and Celeste came down to help

Niki get settled, Celeste had offered to stay and help decorate. Her feelings got hurt by how quickly Niki said no, but except for a boom box, her electronic keyboard, and a white chaise lounge that clearly belonged on the patio, the room was empty. Then she saw the neat rows of boxes lining the hallway, and her heart skipped a beat. *She's really planning to move! I hope she hasn't given notice yet.* Celeste felt the sweat trickle down the center of her back. She took off her jacket, dropped it across her suitcase, and turned on the AC before continuing the invasion.

What on earth possessed her? A galaxy of candles in crimson glass holders dotted the floor of Niki's bedroom. Smack in the middle sat the rumpled bed, on big industrial wheels no less, enclosed by a veil of gauzy white fabric that draped from the ceiling and puddled on the floor. The same fabric framed the large window. *It's a fire hazard, for goodness' sake!* Celeste tiptoed into the room. *And it's much too—dramatic.* A mirrored room divider stood in a corner, diagonally across from the bed, and two huge posters of lush purple orchids dominated one of the walls. The whole thing made Celeste feel squirmy, so before she could give any more thought to what scene her daughter was setting, she tucked the red sheets in as best she could, fluffed the leopard print comforter, and piled the stack of red and black pillows where she thought the head of the bed should be, then took off for the kitchen in search of dishes to wash.

She was surprised to find the kitchen immaculate. There was not a spoon in the sink, the stove sparkled. Blender, mixer, toaster, microwave, knife block, a tiny television, and cookbooks for a variety of cuisines lined the countertops. She opened cupboard doors to find them well organized and fully stocked, and the cabinets below held a collection of pots and pans, like the ones Celeste had looked at a few years ago and decided were far too expensive to actually cook in. Niki's, however, were not for show. They had been seasoned.

Celeste poured a glass of iced tea from the pitcher in the refrigerator and took a seat in the dining area on one of the violet Parsons chairs surrounding the black lacquered table. She held the cool glass to her temples a moment before taking a swallow.

There was nothing in Niki's apartment that Celeste would have chosen for her. *It's like this place belongs to a stranger.* Through the sliding glass door to the patio she gazed at the dancing shadows cast by the magnolia tree on the other side of the brick. The twelve o'clock sun had slipped a bit to the west, and Celeste decided to finish her tea outside. She stretched out in the twin to the chair in the living room, put her glass on the fieldstones stacked table-high next to it, then kicked off her shoes.

Why didn't I see this coming? Celeste remembered the first dish Niki cooked from scratch. She was ten or eleven when she decided to make muffins from a recipe she found in one of Celeste's magazines. She laid out all her ingredients, measured precisely, followed the instructions exactly, and proudly set the table for Saturday breakfast. They tasted awful. "Why would they print directions for nasty food?" Niki was incensed, and for the next several weeks she tinkered with the recipe, adding ingredients, adjusting amounts, consulting Celeste's cookbooks. They ate muffins for breakfast for a month, and Niki kept a diligent record of what worked and what didn't. Eventually she came up with Nicole's Blueberry Crumb Muffins, and they were moist and delicious. She proclaimed that recipe the first one in the *Nicole English Cookbook* and she promised there would be no bad food in it. Everett bought a brown leather book with blank pages, had the name embossed in gilt letters on the front, and presented it to her.

I wonder if Nik still has that silly book? Everett should never have encouraged her that way. Okay. She's good in the kitchen, better than I am for sure, but it's hardly a reasonable career for a girl with her background! She has so many other options!

Celeste wasn't sure how long she'd been stretched out. She may even have dozed off awhile, but she was hot again and her head throbbed. She grabbed her shoes and glanced at her watch on her way to the kitchen. *Where'd the time go? Nik should be home before long.* Celeste dumped the contents of her glass in the sink and let the water run. *I'll find something for this head, then I'll take a shower. We can go to dinner—someplace really nice—maybe Niki's restaurant.* Celeste filled her glass and started the search for aspirin. She opened all the cabinets in the kitchen, and although she found several bottles of vitamins and herbal supplements, she didn't come across anything that would relieve the pounding in her head. *Nik knows we always keep aspirin in the kitchen. Why doesn't she have any in here? It's certainly more convenient.* Celeste headed to the bathroom.

She opened the medicine chest and her eyes went right to the snapshot taped inside. A man she'd never seen before stood behind Niki, his arms around her waist. He wore a chef's jacket, and his toque sat on top of dreadlocks secured back with a rubber band. "We'll make beautiful food together!" was written across the bottom of the photo. *That's where she got this ridiculous idea!* The man was definitely older than Niki, but no matter how closely she examined the picture, Celeste couldn't tell by how much. She *could* tell that her headache had gotten worse. It took a huge effort to take her eyes off the smiling couple and resume her search for painkillers. *Oh my—* Celeste snatched the box from the shelf. *Reservoir tip. Ultra thin. Like wearing nothing.* She dropped the box like it bit her, and condoms littered the sink. She didn't mean to count them, but eight were gone and her brain felt like it would spray out of her ears like a geyser. She could hear Everett saying, "In case you haven't noticed, Niki is a woman." But a well-used box of condoms, the fantasy suite bedroom, and lover boy's picture was just too damn grown for her little girl.

Celeste didn't hear Niki come in the apartment. She just looked up and her daughter was standing by her side. Celeste's mouth went dry.

"Find everything you need?" Niki laughed and turned to leave.

"I—uh—I—I certainly don't need these. And for your information, I was looking for aspirin. I have an excruciating—" *Where did it go?* "I had a headache, that's all." Celeste tightened her upper lip, jammed the foil-wrapped packets back in the box. Then she turned the hot water on full blast and washed her hands like she was scrubbing for surgery.

Niki waited for her to finish, then moved aside the first-aid cream and the box of bandages. "Here you go." She exchanged the bottle for the box, replaced it on the shelf, and closed the medicine cabinet door.

Celeste clutched the bottle so tightly she was afraid the childproof cap would pop off. "Thank you." *My head doesn't even hurt anymore.* She pushed past Niki and headed down the hall. *But I have to take them now or she'll think I was just being nosy.*

Niki joined her in the kitchen. "I thought I'd fix us dinner tonight." *Or just slit my wrists.* "Just the two of us! We haven't done that in ages." *Which is probably why we're both still breathing.* "That'll be fun."

I won't say a word. Celeste shook two tablets into her hand, tossed them back, and took a swig of water. *There. They can't hurt. An ounce of prevention . . .*

"Did you get some rest?" Niki started removing the contents of the shopping bags she'd left on the counter.

"I don't know—I mean—yes, I did. Thank you." Celeste put her glass down. "Can I do anything to help?"

"Pick out a bottle of wine and pour me a glass." Niki opened a cabinet door Celeste hadn't, revealing a full wine rack. "I'm pretty fried. My boss is a real asshole." Niki heard it as soon as it came out of her mouth. *Shit. I shouldn't have said that.*

Celeste cleared her throat but didn't remark.

For a moment Niki didn't know what to say. *Why do I feel like I did something wrong?* She'd never cursed in front of her parents. *I'm in my own kitchen. In my own home. My life. My rules. Right?* She sounded unconvincing, even to herself. She took a sauté pan from a lower cabinet and reached for the box of rice she'd brought home.

"Wouldn't it be more convenient if you kept your canned goods down there and your pots and pans by the . . ."

"I like them exactly where they are. How are we coming with the wine, Ma?"

"My goodness. This is quite a selection. I mean for one person." Celeste pulled a bottle at random.

"I don't usually drink alone." Niki took a plastic bag of shrimp to the sink.

"I can see that." She didn't mean it to slip out. It just did.

I'm not gonna bite. Niki tore into the bag. "Choose any wine you like. Fumé blanc might be nice with the . . ."

"How can you leave those—things around like that?" Celeste slammed the bottle of pinot grigio on the counter.

"Like what, Ma?" Niki dried her hands on a dishtowel, took the bottle, and yanked a corkscrew from the drawer. "In *my* bathroom? In *my* medicine cabinet?" She stabbed the point into the cork. "Tell me, would you rather I *didn't* use condoms? Now there's a really bright idea." Niki turned the screw.

"Nicole! How can you talk like that? You weren't raised that way!"

"Gimme a break." Nicole kept screwing. "Are you trying to tell me you and Dad didn't have sex until after you got married?" The cork made a self-satisfied pop as it escaped. She laid down the corkscrew and grabbed two glasses. "I read about the seventies. He probably wasn't even the first, but that's cool."

"That's none of your business! And this isn't about your father and me." *And how many times I was worried that I was pregnant.* Celeste unscrewed the cork from the end of the opener and rolled it between her fingers. "This is about—What's his name, Nicole?"

"Brian. But that doesn't really matter, does it? This is about sex. Isn't it, Mother?" Niki filled each glass halfway. "I have a job. I have my own address, my own car. I'm an adult. And I *am* having sex." *I can't believe I said that.* "With one man who happens to mean a lot to me. Is it forever? I don't know. I haven't gotten that far yet." *Okay. The gloves are off. Let's just put it all out there and see where the dust settles.* "So now you've had your questions answered. I have one for you." Niki lifted her glass to her lips, took a deep swallow. "Just why did you come, Ma? To snoop around in my life? Or to tell me I'm wrong to want what *I* want instead of what you want for me!?" Niki reached for the cutting board and a head of garlic from a basket on the counter.

Celeste could barely keep the liquid from sloshing out of her glass. "It looks like I have to come snooping, as you put it, to find out what you're doing. You're obviously moving, but I wouldn't know that . . ."

"I told you my plans in May. What do you want, a minute-by-minute account? Okay. I'm shipping my stuff next week. Then Brian and I are driving to Hyde Park. He's up there now, looking for an . . ."

"And when were you planning to tell me you'll be living with this man?!"

Not until I had to. "When I found the right time."

"This—this Brian has obviously made you forget who you are."

"No, Mother." Niki removed a knife from the rack. "Brian accepts who I am, which is more than I can say for you! You're the one who can't understand."

"I understand he's about to make you screw up your life. Is that what you want?!" As soon as she said it, Celeste heard Della so clearly she expected to turn around and see her. *"I don't care if he's God's gift to medicine! You keep hanging around with this man all hours, you'll flunk out of school, Celeste. Is that what you want?"*

"What?" Niki stopped chopping and followed her mother's eyes.

"Nothing—never mind—how old is he, Nicole?"

"You don't get it, do you? This has nothing to do with Brian!" Niki's kitchen was a good size, but it seemed to be getting smaller. "And I still don't know why you came. I know you can fly nonstop to Charlotte."

"Your father and I have worked too hard . . ."

"My father is proud of me and what I'm doing. And your grandmother had her own catering business, back in the forties. Her *own* business, Ma. That's what I want."

"What are you talking about?!"

"Grandma told me."

"Your grandmother must be losing her mind along with the rest of you. She never said anything about her mother being a cook, much less running a business."

Niki picked up the wall phone, "You wanna call her?" She held it out to Celeste. "If it makes you feel any better, Ronnie didn't know either."

Celeste knew when not to take a dare. "Besides, this is your life. Not some fabricated ancient history!"

"You're right, Ma. It is my life. It's like Ronnie said when Papa died, you did what you wanted with your life. This one is mine."

"When Papa died?! You told Ronnie back then and you didn't tell me?! How could you, Nicole? How could you embarrass me like that?"

"That's all you care about, isn't it? Well, see these!" She pointed to the knives. "The best chefs use them. Dad sent 'em! And my tuition? Grandma asked how much I needed."

"Oh, did she?" *Thank you for finding another way to go behind my back, Mother.* Celeste chewed the inside of her cheek.

"Ronnie said if I get an externship in New York, I can stay with her, rent free. . . ."

"She can't keep a roof over her own head," Celeste hissed.

"Why can't you accept that this is what *I* want? Me. Nicole Yvonne English." Niki patted her chest for emphasis. "I love food, Ma. Everything about it. The colors and textures of fresh produce in the market make me happy." She picked a bunch of frilly greens up off the counter. "This is cilantro." She stuck her nose in, took a whiff. "It smells better to me than perfume. I love the way shallots make a recipe taste different from onions or scallions. I love inventing new dishes. You know, I've been working on one, so I thought I'd make it for you tonight. And I was hoping you'd like it and we'd have a nice meal and talk, but that doesn't seem like what you had planned. I mean you act like I want to sell heroin!" Niki walked the kitchen in small circles, came to a stop. "I don't know why Dad didn't leave before now. He should've stayed in Benin. Maybe she would have made him happy!"

Celeste sunk her fingers into Niki's arm like vise grips and shook. "How dare you!? You don't know what you're talking about!"

Niki pulled free. "At first I'd put my headphones on and go in my closet because I couldn't stand to hear you two argue. Then I decided if I knew what you were fighting about, when I grew up I'd know what not to do! I heard him ask you to forgive him. It's the first time I heard Daddy cry."

Celeste met Niki's defiant gaze but said nothing.

"I kept waiting—waiting for you to tell Daddy you did the same thing." Niki didn't take her eyes off her mother. "But you didn't."

Celeste's head snapped back like she'd been slapped. She spoke in a low, slow rumble. "What are you talking about?"

"Mr. Weeks. Wasn't that his name?"

How could she know? Celeste's jaw dropped.

"From your old school."

I was so careful—"I have no idea what . . ."

"Come on, Ma. I was twelve. Not exactly the sharpest pin in the cushion, but I wasn't dumb or blind. I didn't really even know what sex was. We'd had the egg and sperm talk, but that wasn't sex. Sex was the sighs, the long looks, like in the movies. Like you and Mr. Weeks."

"That doesn't deserve an answer." *I don't have one.* Celeste put her glass on the counter before she dropped it.

Niki was way past the deep end, so she figured she'd just keep stroking. "You were working at school that summer and Mr. Weeks would come by supposedly to talk about some school stuff. I didn't think anything of it until one night. I'd already gone to bed, but I went to the kitchen to get some water. You two were on the sofa. His arm was around you. Then you kissed . . ."

"Stop it!"

Niki finished her glass of wine, poured another, took a swallow. "After that I could see it all the time. You had all the signs. Giggly, gooey and glowy. I knew what you were doing was wrong because it wasn't Daddy. But it was romantic, and I liked the way *you* were then. You didn't pick at me the way you always did. You were like—I don't know, but I wanted to feel what you were feeling. I used to wish you'd be like that with Daddy, but you weren't, and it only got worse when he came home." She folded her arms across her chest. "After that you two just fought all the time. And you—you were so mean, and spiteful—and I hated you. I asked him once if you were gonna get a divorce. He said he didn't know."

At this moment, a knife would have felt more merciful to Celeste. "He said what!?"

"It took a while, but it looks like he's finally made up his mind."

"You just wait until chef boy comes home one day and says he's quitting his job and opening a soup kitchen! Then you talk to me." Celeste was trembling. "I won't discuss this anymore."

"Have it your way. I just know that when Daddy poured his heart out, told you he'd done wrong, you kept your little secret."

Celeste stormed from the kitchen and into the living room, but there was no place to hide. No shadowy corners or soft surfaces, no cushions or drapes. There was nothing to sink into, nowhere to shelter herself in the bare room. "And since you hate me so much, I won't stay . . ."

"Don't be so hysterical, Ma. Where are you gonna go? A hotel?" Niki chuckled at the irony as she followed her mother into the living room. *I know I'm gonna pay for this. Maybe I should have just booked her a room.*

"Well, clearly you wouldn't have someone you think so little of spend the night in your house."

"Chill, Mother. I'm not gonna tell Daddy. Your secret is safe."

They never ate. Celeste spent the night tossing and turning, alone and adrift in Niki's floating bed. Niki slept on the chaise in the living room. And the next morning didn't come soon enough for either one of them.

As soon as Niki came to a stop in front of the terminal at Hartsfield, Celeste waved for a skycap. When Niki pulled off, Celeste was rummaging in her purse for the tip, so shaken she didn't know where to look for her own wallet.

The balance of power in their relationship was shifting, and Celeste couldn't get her footing.

10

"At ease, Gomer."

"Ms. Frazier?"

"Yes." Ronnie had looked right past him in the crowd at the gate. She was expecting someone cut from the same cloth as R. Phillip. *Not Gomer dressed for gym class.*

"Douglas Pryce." He extended his hand and smiled broadly, his thick brush of mustache turning up at the corners of his lips.

Ronnie cast a disapproving eye on the shorts, polo shirt, crew socks, and sneakers. She managed half a smile as she shook his outstretched hand. *This must be Rudy's little payback for not givin' him any.* After the drug bust in her apartment left her needing to escape from New York, Ronnie called R. Phillip to back out of their date. She left out the small detail about the break-in and not knowing where the hell she was going to live. Having to dispose of property she inherited was enough reason for him. True to form, he said he went to college with a guy whose family handled real estate in the Charlotte area. By the next morning Phillip had made the connection and arranged for his friend to meet Ronnie at the airport. It was a good thing too. She hadn't figured out how she was going to get from Charlotte Douglas International to Prosper.

"Call me Doug." He caught her checking his outfit. "I coach a girls' softball team. Our game ran late." His dark eyes flashed like sparklers on the Fourth of July, and Douglas Pryce had the whitest teeth she'd ever seen.

Toothpaste commercial. He certainly wasn't drool-on-yourself gorgeous, not by Ronnie's standards. Tall and rangy, his shirt fit smoothly over a body that showed he did more than paperwork. Doug's hair was close-cropped, and, like his mustache, was sprinkled with gray, although you couldn't tell by looking at him if he was twenty-two or a hundred and two. But there was something about his face. His bold features looked like they'd been chiseled from burnished walnut. They kept her gaze a moment longer than she intended. *Not my type. No edge.* But her type or not, she was planning to make Douglas her new best friend. At least until they got this property sold. "How'd you recognize me?" *Here comes the lame line. "Phillip told me you were gorgeous" or some BS. I can flirt with him a little—*

"Black clothes. You New Yorkers wear 'em like a badge." Doug didn't bite, didn't even give her a once-over before he reached out a sinewy arm and grabbed her carry-on. "This way." He touched her back just long enough to indicate the direction they were heading.

Ronnie flinched slightly. His touch caught her off guard. "Oh. Is that so?" *It beats hell out of looking like a Boy Scout.* Ronnie was prepared to deflect the advance, not defend her wardrobe. She lifted her sunglasses from the top of her head, hooked them at the neck of her oversized black silk sweater, shoved her hand in the pocket of her black jeans, and listened to the click of her black leather ankle boots on the granite floor as they walked through the airport. Doug's sneakers squeaked. His stride was long but unhurried. *Why should I worry about a man who probably couldn't dress himself right on a bet?* She couldn't imagine Doug in a hand-tailored suit, or flying first class. Not that it mattered. Not that he mattered. This was only her natural radar at work, and he was too insignificant to cause a blip on the screen.

"I mean, people down here wear black, but not like you folks." He grinned.

She didn't grin back. *Did he read that somewhere?* "It makes life simple when I travel." *Probably not a big consideration for you.*

Doug seemed not to notice her displeasure. "Do you have a bag checked?"

"This is it. My sister and I will only be here a few days. Especially since your boss—your mother, right?" *That should sting.* "She said you had a buyer already lined up. We can take care of our business and be on our way." She wanted to walk ahead to speed this up, but since she didn't know where they were headed, she had to downshift to follow his lazy zigzag through the terminal. Ronnie noticed there were lots of people coming and going, but nobody raced around, looking one step away from a breakdown.

"So it seems. I must confess I hadn't heard of Prosper until you called. I haven't been back long. But Edna Pryce keeps her finger on the real estate pulse of southwestern North Carolina. She's been at it forty years, and nobody does it better, as they say. It's through those doors." He nodded the direction. "That's enough of the commercial. Truthfully, if she says she's got a buyer, you can consider the deal done."

"Glad to hear it." The sliding doors opened to the balmy night. Ronnie was surprised by the hint of flowers in the warm, soft air. There was no trace of the tingle, the yin and yang tug of the power surge and energy drain that fired her up in the city, kept her running, no matter what. "The sooner I can get back, the better." *Because this deal is my ticket to finally getting my life together.*

"The greater Charlotte area is really booming. . . ."

"Don't know about Charlotte *or* Prosper." *Don't want to either.* "Never been down here, and frankly, I'm not planning to be back." *I don't mean to sound like a snob—Yes I do.*

"Then I'll save the Chamber of Commerce speech." He shifted the bag to his other hand. "It's not bad here. Not bad at all." Doug sounded like he was trying to convince himself. He stopped at a shiny, champagne-colored four-wheel-drive parked at the curb.

At least it's not a pickup truck. "Convenient. At La Guardia it would have been towed." She stood at his side while he dug in his pocket for keys. *He smells like—not like Dolce & Gabbana or Gaultier. What is that? Zest or Irish Spring.* "Humph." Her reaction, barely audible, slipped out. Men in

Ronnie's world smelled like they thought money should smell, not like soap.

"I'm not used to this either. Head of airport security is a cousin. I wouldn't leave it here all day, but this comes in handy when I'm cutting it close, like tonight." He opened the door.

Ronnie sighed and climbed in. *Will I have to listen to stories about his million country cousins all the way there?*

Doug tossed her bag in back, went around, and got in the other side. "I was hoping to take you by the house as soon as you got here, but your flight got in too late."

'Cause it was the cheap fare. Charlotte by way of Pittsburgh.

"You won't be able to see anything now. We made arrangements to have the power turned on, but it won't happen until tomorrow. So I'll just drop you at your hotel. Uh, I need you to buckle up."

"Why? You plannin' to run this baby off the road?"

"It's not my driving I worry about." He flipped on the headlights and waited.

It was clear he wasn't moving until she fastened her seat belt, so Ronnie reached around for the strap. The back appeared to be the storage locker for the softball team. *No wonder it smells like french fries and sweat in here.* "How long a drive do we have?" *In a stinky car.*

"Little over an hour. Do you want to grab something to eat?"

"Uh. No. I'm fine." Her cramps were still hanging around, and the last thing she wanted was food.

They headed for the airport exit. "I realize it's a little messy in here, but it was faster than stopping to get my company car."

"No problem. I appreciate the ride." Ronnie looked out the window. The night sky was inky and spangled with stars. The motorist in the right lane slowed, flashed headlights. Doug waved an acknowledgment and merged into the steady stream of traffic on Route 74. She searched her purse for her cigarettes, stuck one between her lips and examined the dash-board. "Is there a lighter in here?"

"Yes, but I have to ask you not to smoke."

"Isn't tobacco the state flower or something?" Ronnie shoved the pack down in her bag.

"This Tar Heel doesn't go near the stuff."

Great. He probably doesn't drink or swear either.

Doug concentrated on the road and drove like he planned to shave as much off of that hour as possible. *I thought sales-men liked to talk. This one doesn't have much to say unless it's required.* Ronnie was in no mood for silence. She spent the bulk of her flight chatting with her seatmate, a young actu-ary from Vancouver, excited about being flown down for an interview. He had a ton of questions about living in the States, and Ronnie was all too happy to play the expert because it kept her from thinking about what a screwed-up mess her life was at the moment.

Staying in that snake pit of an apartment for the few days before her flight took most of her strength. Before heading to the airport, she'd packed her stuff and moved it to Kayla's mother's basement, having no idea where her next oasis would be, trying hard to ignore the fear that only mirages lay ahead. This struck her as a new low. For the first time in her life she had no official address, just an answering service phone number.

And it took the rest of her strength not to call home and cry to her mother that this was too hard and she couldn't do it anymore. Those feelings might have spilled out when she called Buffalo to see what Della would tell her about Prosper, but it was not a warm and fuzzy phone call. Ronnie got a hot earful of Della's displeasure. Her mother made it clear she felt Ronnie had no business down there. "It is business, Ma. Ce-leste is going down so I need to protect my . . ." Click. Ronnie called back every fifteen minutes for the rest of the evening, but Della never picked up the phone. It was a nice little guilt trip that Ronnie packed next to her toiletry bag, and all of it jumped out and bit her if she had too much time for her own thoughts. *He doesn't even play the radio.* "What did you mean back there when you said you weren't used to having parking privileges? Did your cousin just get the job?" *Not that I really care.*

"No. He's been there for years. I moved back six months ago."

"From?"

Doug paused, like he didn't want to answer. "L.A."

Damn. I didn't ask his bank account number. "So, were you in the business?"

"Real estate? No. I . . ."

"Show business. Movies. Is there any other business out there?"

"That's right, Phillip did say you were an actress or something, right? I don't even remember the last time I went to the movies." Doug went back to the business of driving.

Ronnie had expected some comment about her occupation. Men usually wanted to know what movie they'd seen her in, or how she got into her parts. She was having trouble figuring out which of her roles to play with Douglas Pryce. *He probably likes talking about himself.* "So—what *did* you do?"

"I was a reporter. *L.A. Times.*" Doug sped up and whipped around a slow-moving sedan.

Ronnie grabbed the dashboard to steady herself. "You coulda been a cab driver."

He glanced at her and grinned. "I still forget this isn't the freeway."

"What on earth made you move back here?" Ronnie heard her snob again. "I didn't mean that the way it sounded. You're right. It doesn't look so bad—Of course it *is* dark out! Only kidding!" She chuckled, he didn't. "But why leave La La Land for this?"

He shrugged. "My mother's had a few health problems. My kids are grown and on their own. Seemed like the time."

Ronnie examined his hands on the steering wheel. *No ring.* She hated married men who didn't wear identifying jewelry. They usually had some jive excuse about how it interfered with their work, or they claimed not to wear jewelry. But in Ronnie's experience, those guys thought they had special dispensation to eat their cake, some of yours, and still have a slice laying in the cut. Like the guy she met while she was profiling at a gallery opening. He said he wasn't with his wife. It wasn't until several months down the line that Ronnie found out he and wifey-poo were still married, just not *together* at the gallery that night. And she was too through when he had the nerve to argue that technically he was telling the truth. Personally, she thought the married ones should have a brand, on their foreheads preferably, front and center where they couldn't hide it, because she had no interest in barking up somebody else's tree. "How does your wife like it here?"

"She died four years ago."

Ronnie's stomach did a queasy flip-flop. "Oh. I'm . . ."

"No harm." He never took his eyes off the road. "My mother eats and breathes real estate. If she can smell a deal, nothing will stop her. She's wanted me to join the business my whole life. And I spent my whole life resisting." He shrugged his shoulders. "Who wants to work for his mother? But her glaucoma didn't respond to treatment and she's not getting any younger. I needed a change. It seemed like this might work for both of us."

"Is it?"

"Too early to tell." He opened his window and took a deep breath. "So what made you and your sister decide to sell this property after all? I understand it's been vacant for several years, and the owner of record never responded to letters."

"We never heard of it until a few weeks ago." Ronnie explained what she knew about the place and how she and Celeste came to own it.

"I guess all families have their mysteries."

"I don't know about all that. I'm just glad we can take care of this quickly. I'm sure Celeste will be pleased."

"You haven't told her we've spoken? That we have a buyer?"

"Like I said, we only found out about this a few weeks ago. I've been crazy busy." *Trying to figure out what to do about my drug dealer landlord.* "And so has Celeste. It's hard to keep up." She had no intention of letting him know how little she and Celeste talked about this. That her sister had known for months and hadn't mentioned it. Ronnie decided to switch to another subject. "So how long have you known Rudy? Oops! Sorry. My little joke. Phillip."

"His brother John and I were in school together. Phillip started the year we graduated, and I haven't thought about him since then. I wouldn't exactly say we were best buds."

"So he called you outta nowhere?"

"John and I have stayed somewhat in touch since Morehouse, and we alums have tried to maintain a kind of network. If at all possible, requests are honored, favors granted, exceptions made. Period. No questions. If it's impossible, we do the best we can."

"That must be—I don't know—kinda reassuring? Knowing that there's all that help out there?"

"It's useful once in a while, like a fraternity but without the secret handshake. More like being from the old neighborhood. Kinda Morehouse homeboys!" His laugh was deep and robust. Genuine.

Ronnie noticed he didn't look to see if she was laughing too. It didn't matter. He enjoyed his own humor. Her father used to laugh that way, full out. Even at his own corny jokes. Okay. *This is the part where he asks for my pedigree.* Ronnie sat up straighter, squared her shoulders, and waited for him to grill her about her background.

"So your family never visited here? No summers down south with the relatives?"

"We had friends who did." *Hmm. No third degree.* "A girl I went to elementary school with used to come back full of stories about milking cows and collecting eggs with her cousins on her aunt and uncle's farm. It sounded so exotic to me. All I had was camp."

"Exotic, huh? I grew up in Charlotte, but we'd spend a lot of time in the country during the summers. My grandparents had a place. My mother thought it was a good experience for me and my sister, but they used to work us like field hands.

You know, cows can be mean if you don't have the right touch, and chickens will peck you till you're bloody unless you're careful. I used to be glad for school to start, which was probably the point." Doug reached an arm around the back of his seat, grabbed a squeeze bottle of water from the floor. "They're kinda warm, but would you like one?"

"That's quite all right."

He took a long swallow. "I drove out to look your place over yesterday. Prosper itself appears pretty typical. Small southern town full of personal history and mystery. A lot has probably changed since your family left and a lot is likely the same as forty years ago. Population hasn't fluctuated, one way or the other, more than a hundred people in over sixty years. Depending on who's counting, the racial mix is about even. There's a brand-new Winn-Dixie, and a small radio station. The house was fairly large for its time, not many that big owned by us. And you've got a good-sized piece of land. The inlet is pretty overgrown down your end. Looks more like marshlands. But it lets out into a good-sized lake. People have boats and docks on the other side." Doug turned his head and yawned.

Must be past his bedtime. Much as she couldn't admit it, Ronnie wanted to keep him talking because his voice was soothing, resonant, like a saxophone in a smoky room.

"It's pretty isolated from the town." Doug flicked the turn signal. "Otherwise the offer might be higher, but I guess it's like found money."

"It was a pleasant little surprise." Ronnie wasn't interested in discussing how crucial this "found money" was. Her half of the $193,000 offered for the house and land was more money than she had hoped for.

They pulled into the tiny parking lot of the T ee T p Motel & Inn. The two-story cinder-block box couldn't have had more than twenty rooms, half on the ground level facing the scenic parking spaces and the others upstairs off a concrete walkway with a wrought-iron railing. *No wonder the rates were so cheap.*

"I know what you're thinking."

"You can't possibly." A flash of her ransacked apartment and Rake's empty, foil-lined closet streaked through her mind. *My luck is holding. Nobody can pick a place like I can.*

"It's not bad—really. Clean. Quiet. The rooms are really—uh." He started to laugh. "There's no need my trying to make this more than it is. You can see it's not the Ritz." He stopped the car in front of the motel office, a separate structure with a log cabin facade.

"Thanks for giving me some credit." Ronnie got out. Her footsteps on the gravel seemed nearly as loud as the buzz and crackle of the neon sign, sans the *r* and *o*. Doug came around beside her. "Is this the only place to stay around here?"

"This is it. There are others closer to Charlotte, but this will make it easier to take care of your business. You and your sister will need to spend a fair amount of time disposing of the contents of the house."

"Contents?"

"Seems that everything was left to the new owner, so even though nobody ever came to claim the place or clean it out, the taxes have been paid so nothing's been moved or sold."

"Great," Ronnie mumbled. Warily, she followed Doug up the plank stairs to the office. "Listen, do you think your buyer will want the furniture and stuff too? It would save us a lot of trouble—and time." She noticed a hand-lettered sign taped to the window. "Free Cable in Every Room."

Doug held the door open. "There's never enough of it, is there? Time."

Ronnie felt like the comment was from a different conversation, but she didn't want to know who it was meant for.

"We can ask if they're interested in the contents. I might not have an answer by the time I pick you up tomorrow, but we'll get to work on it." He led the way to the desk.

While Ronnie filled out the registration form, Doug made small talk with the clerk. She offered her anemic Visa card as guarantee, but even at these rates, a week's stay would eat up what remained of available charging privileges. *But when I leave here, these days will be over, for good.* Once she was checked in, Doug walked her back to the building, handed over her bag at the bottom of the concrete stairs.

"Can we get an early start in the morning?" Ronnie knew if she wasn't ahead of the game by the time Celeste arrived, she'd never get to play.

"I have a meeting first thing, but I can be here by eight thirty. We can have breakfast on the way if you like."

He doesn't think that's early? "No problem."

Doug gave her a card. "This has the office numbers, but it's easier to reach me on the cell."

"Okay, then. Guess I'll, uh, head up to my suite." Ronnie trudged up the concrete steps. He waited downstairs until she unlocked her room and turned on the light. She gave him a little salute. *At ease, Gomer.* Then went inside.

The sweet, cool night air stayed outside. Ronnie sucked in a nose full of the hot, deodorized-sanitized air. *Have they opened a window in the last thirty-five years?* She locked the door, put the chain on, then turned around and took in the small room in a glance. *Okay. So it's not hideous. A little on the tacky side, but I've stayed in worse. Who am I kidding? I've lived in worse. Wait till Celeste gets a load of it, though.* Ronnie walked the ten feet to the other side of the room, turned the air conditioner on high, and smirked at the thought of her sister's reaction. Then the walls rumbled. *What the—?* She held her breath, stood stock-still but ready to run. It happened again. This time a groan and rumble followed by a crash. Then she heard the whine of a motor. *Ice machine. Perfect.* She thought about calling for another room, but she'd seen food and toiletry vending machines at the other end. *What's the dif?*

She kicked off her boots and flopped across the double bed, exhausted. When she reached for the remote, she discovered it was attached to a swivel and bolted to the bedside table along with a clock radio and telephone. *Who'd want to steal this crap?* Ronnie sucked her teeth and aimed at the set. Her first click brought the eleven o'clock news; so did the second and third. She zipped past golf, infomercials, music videos, and settled on an ancient episode of *Benson*. *I'll get undressed and wash my face when this is over.* Ronnie tucked both anorexic pillows under her head.

"Mom and Dad'll never know." Voices filtered in from somewhere Ronnie couldn't place. *What the—?* She awoke with a start, the TV still playing. *Where the hell am I?* Ronnie was cold, dry-mouthed, with a stiff neck and a backache. She blinked to unstick her eyes and focus. *Oh yeah. The Inn at Hicks-ville.* The clock radio by the bed read 4:37. She sat up, massaged her neck, and stared at the screen. One of the identical cousins was slathered in cold cream, pretending to be the other one. Then both girls dissolved in a fit of giggles. When she was little, Ronnie used to watch the show after school and wish that she and her sister could have fun together like Patty and Cathy. But that never happened. Celeste was older and never seemed to think of Ronnie as much more than a nuisance she was forced to put up with because of her parents' misbegotten biological urge. Ronnie shook off a twinge of sadness. *Can't miss what you never had.* She turned down the AC, peeled off her clothes. *And I bet we'll have goo-gobs of fun when she gets here.* Ronnie padded to the bathroom and was back in bed before she was awake enough to really start thinking. Eight-thirty would be here soon enough.

11

"You never know what a day will bring."

Doug Pryce called her room at 8:29.

Damn, why couldn't he be late like everybody else? Ronnie was finishing the last touches to her hair and makeup. Not that she was getting done up, just making sure that Doug or anybody else would never mistake her for a local. And after a night's sleep she felt ready to find out what made this man tick. It was a modest challenge, just to make her stay more interesting. *He should wait a few minutes.* Casual chic was the order of the day, so she wore her same black jeans, a tailored white shirt, and black low-heeled sandals. When she locked the door behind her fifteen minutes later, her no-makeup makeup was perfect, and her hair was in a low ponytail with the grown-out edges smoothed under a wide, black hair band.

He dressed up today. Doug, wearing khakis and a pink polo shirt, leaned against a dark green sedan with a gold Pryce Real Estate logo on the door. *Charlotte by way of L.A. What more should I expect?* He seemed to be talking back to his *Observer* as he read, but he closed the paper and looked up in her direction when he heard her footsteps. Ronnie slipped on her sunglasses and her smile as she walked down the stairs.

"Morning." Doug was pleasant, but he wasn't talking to her.

Ronnie looked over to see whom Doug had spoken to and swallowed her smile.

"Uh—Good morn—Ronnie, what are you doing here!?" Celeste lost her grip on the large suitcase she pulled behind her. "How did you know where I was staying?"

"It came to me in a vision." Ronnie stopped next to Doug.

"Who's he? Last night's company?" Celeste's jaw locked in her teacher-on-a-mission position, and her upper lip clamped tightly to her lower one, forming an airtight seal.

"I'll pretend you didn't say that, especially in front of someone you haven't met yet. Good morning, sister dear. How was your trip?" Ronnie tossed her purse over her shoulder, shifted her weight to one hip, slid her hand in the front pocket of her jeans, and waited. Celeste looked a little rough around the edges, more like a day-old version of her usual neat, crisp self.

"My trip?!" Celeste hissed.

The game was on. Ronnie knew the rules and had her own strategy. She could play as well as Celeste. After all, they'd had years of practice. "I thought you'd already be here when I checked in. It's the only motel in town, you know. Well, I guess this is sort of town." She waved her hand, presenting the highway, the truck stop across the road with the faded red sign that read "EAT & Hot Showers," and the crumbling building on the other side of the Tree Top Inn. "And this is Doug Pryce."

"And?" Celeste tugged the pull strap and made her suitcase heel. "You still haven't answered my question."

"I'm not sure which question you're referring to, but Doug is a real estate agent, before you embarrass yourself any more."

Celeste sputtered. "Why is he here? Who asked him to . . ."

"*I* asked his company to handle the sale for us. We have a mutual friend in New York. A banker. Isn't that the most wonderful coincidence?"

Doug followed the volley between the two sisters like the center court action at the U.S. Open. He'd had a grandmother, mother, wife, and a daughter, and through trial and error he had learned when his two cents was welcome, but this looked like one of those times it was best to keep his change in his pocket. "Listen. I'll come back a little later. You two catch up. Ms. Frazier, call when you're ready to go out to the house." He started toward his car.

Ronnie trotted to catch up. "Doug?" She took hold of his arm and walked with him. "Sorry about that. My sister is a little intense." The firmness of his arm surprised her.

"No apology necessary. Call when you need me."

"Sure." She walked backward a few steps, watching him duck in, then turned and marched back toward Celeste, who had wheeled her bag to one of the room doors and was fumbling with the key.

"You really showed your ass, didn't you?"

"What do you mean showing up like this?" Celeste snapped.

"Like what? Like I have some interest and some say-so in what happens here? Like this house and land is half mine, whether you like it or not? Maybe that's what I mean by showing up!"

"I never said it wasn't half yours." *First Everett, then Niki, and now this.* "And besides, that isn't the point!"

"What is? That you're in charge and you've already talked to another realtor?"

"No—it's not—" *Why didn't I think of looking for one before I got here?* "What if we don't want to sell it?"

"Right." Ronnie shifted her weight to the other hip and cocked her head to the side. "I got it. You and Everett are planning to relocate. He'll start a new clinic, maybe make house calls too! And you'll teach in the one-room school! Give me a break, Celeste. You barely find Buffalo sophisticated enough for you. How on earth would you manage a place like this? Wait till you see your room!" Ronnie snorted.

"This has nothing to do with Everett!!" Celeste snapped.

"Does anybody have anything to do with it besides you?" *Damn. She's really on a short one this morning.* Ronnie noticed a man wearing dungarees with a pressed crease and a woman in a lavender pants suit looking in their direction and whispering. "And you might wanna lower your voice, unless you're planning to make this a town meeting."

"This is a legacy from our grandfather," Celeste hissed.

"Oh, yeah. Trust me, Celeste, inheriting property in Podunk, North Carolina, from some long-lost grampa we never heard of won't move you one rung higher on the social ladder! I bet you're already calling it the Womack Estate!" Ronnie folded her arms across her chest like a shield.

"Social standing is irrelevant."

"Since when? This is me. Remember?"

"I'm going to put this away, and then I'm driving out to see the place." Celeste looked at the numbers on the lower doors, then started toward her room.

"And you're gonna leave me standing here? I don't think so. Okay. We won't call Doug until later, but I *am* going with you."

"The man at the car rental said to make a *right* turn onto this road and it was three or four miles to Prosper." Celeste flipped the visor down to block the sun, which appeared to be directly in their path, like it was the destination. "He said I'd have to get more specific directions once I got to town."

"We've gone at least ten miles and we haven't passed it yet." Ronnie scrutinized the map she had spread open across her lap and over the dashboard. It fluttered and rattled, blown by the air conditioner vents. She circled a spot with her stump of pencil. "Celeste, Prosper is in the other direction. You must have heard him wrong."

"I did not hear him wrong. I . . ."

"Fine. He didn't know what he was talking about. He was confused. He wanted you to get lost. Who gives a shit? The bottom line is we're going the wrong way."

Celeste pulled onto the shoulder and stopped. "Let me see that."

Ronnie cut her eyes but handed over the map without further comment. First, Celeste dug her reading glasses out of her purse. Ignoring Ronnie's markings, she traced her index finger along the route from the airport to the motel, then along the way they had just come. Ronnie drummed her fingers impatiently on the armrest and watched tiny beads of perspiration pop out on Celeste's upper lip.

"Could you not do that?" Celeste looked over her glasses at her sister.

"For cryin' out—I'll try not to breathe too loud either. Just look at the map."

Finally Celeste dragged her finger back the other direction, landed smack in the spot where Ronnie had drawn a circle around the town of Prosper. Methodically, Celeste refolded the map, tossed it on the dashboard. She tugged out of her taupe linen jacket, chucked it in the backseat, then checked her mirrors and without a word swung a U-turn. Ronnie rolled her eyes, shrugged her shoulders, and watched the same scenery go by, this time from the other side of the road. When they passed the Tree Top Inn, she chuckled to herself and Celeste humphed.

Sure enough, three miles in, just past the Mid-State Brickworks, they saw the sign: "Welcome to Prosper, the Little Town with the Big Heart. Pop. 3,800." Except for a Hardee's, a junkyard, and a radio tower, they didn't see much else for another mile or so. Then the highway became Albemarle Avenue, an oak-shaded thoroughfare that led to the center of town. A few folks ambled along a sidewalk bordered with low hedges, petunias, and marigolds. Willows and crape myrtle graced the deep green grass in front of First Baptist Church.

"Looks like a movie set, doesn't it?" Ronnie craned her neck to look back at town hall, a quaint, pillared white limestone building that sat watch directly across from a pocket-sized park, complete with a bandstand. "Smalltown, USA."

"I need a cup of coffee." It was pretty surprising to Celeste too, but she wouldn't give Ronnie the satisfaction of agreeing with her. "And we have to get directions to the house."

"If you slow down, maybe I can find a—Let's see, there's the post office, People's Hardware, Eckerd Drugs, Zion A.M.E. Church," Ronnie recited the signs along Albemarle. "Hutchinson's Copy Shop, First Presbyterian, JD's Fish Market, Bob's Photography, Lucille's Beauty Studio, Trinity Baptist. Damn! They sure have a lot of churches! And who knows what's down the side streets?"

"I could do without the travelogue."

"Okay. There's a place called Pal's over there, and Mickey

D's is across the street. You can get coffee in either one, probably directions too. Take your pick."

Celeste eased into a spot at the curb and checked for the parking regulation signs. There weren't any. They got out, Celeste grabbed her jacket from the backseat, locked the car, and looked back and forth between the two choices. The only sound was the hollow clink of the rope against the flagpole in front of the Elks Lodge.

"This is not life and death." Ronnie crossed the street toward Pal's. "Let's try the local cuisine."

Celeste would have fussed, but Ronnie was almost in the door.

"Morning." The hefty, moon-faced man greeted her with a quick nod and a hitch of his suspenders. He was the color of a just-peeled russet potato with a bristle of nappy red hair and freckles everywhere he had skin.

"Hi," Ronnie answered. The smoky smell of bacon reminded her she'd skipped dinner. "I just realized I'm starving."

"I guarantee you won't be when you leave." The man looked at Ronnie intently, like he was trying to place her. He picked up a menu, looked again. Ronnie was used to it. Sometimes she went into her actress rap, other times she just let them wonder. Before she decided, Celeste came in the door behind her.

"Two, no smoking please. We're in a bit of a hurry."

"Chill, Celeste. It's under control."

"Have a seat anywhere you like. The breakfast rush is over. How about that booth by the window? It'll give you a fine view of our little town. I can tell y'all not from 'round here." He seated them and signaled the waitress, who hurried over with a steaming coffee pot.

"Ma'am?" The young Jheri-curled girl held the pot aloft in front of Celeste.

"Please." Just the smell of the coffee made her feel better.

"Ma'am?" The waitress smiled at Ronnie.

"Tea please." Ronnie hated being called ma'am. It made her feel older than she wanted to, like she was somebody's mother. Ronnie looked closely at the teenager, realized she was easily old enough to be that girl's mother. She shivered and shook off the thought.

"Be right back."

Celeste heaped two spoonfuls of sugar into her mug. "Do you mind telling me why you decided to come? It's really not necessary. I'm sure you have something better to do with your time." She blew on the surface of the hot liquid, took a cautious sip, then a deep gulp.

"I wanted to see it for myself. You do, don't you? Why wouldn't I?"

The waitress returned with a tea bag, a small pot of hot water, and sliced lemons. "Let me know whenever you're ready to order."

"And that's why you called a real estate agent?! You never asked if I wanted to sell. You didn't even have the courtesy to tell me you were coming! You just show up!" She banged the mug down.

"Like you would've welcomed my company!" Ronnie dunked her tea bag in the pot and closed the lid. She continued in a syrupy drawl. "And if we're discussing a lack of courtesy, let's talk about how you conveniently forgot to tell me about my inheritance until it suited you." Ronnie ditched the drawl. "I'm personally sick of this conversation, so let's drop it." Ronnie picked up her menu and blocked her view of Celeste with it. She wasn't sure if she wanted more than tea and toast, but she studied the specials anyway and was tickled to find one of her father's favorites, porgies, grits, and biscuits, listed. Della had never been able to make grits that didn't look and taste like wallpaper paste, but Will could turn out a mighty fine meal if he put his mind to it. He'd come in from Reisner's Fish Market early on a Saturday morning and get out the big cast-iron frying pan, the spider, he called it. The kitchen was directly below Ronnie's bedroom, and she'd hear him through the register, humming to himself while he cleaned fish. It gave her the creeps to watch that part, but when she heard the sizzle of the first one hitting the grease she'd put on her slippers and bound down the back stairs to join him. She'd set the table, pour the orange juice, and when the platter was heaped with crispy brown fish, the grits were bubbling just right, and the biscuits were ready to come out of the oven, she'd call her mother and Celeste to breakfast.

"Remember how Daddy used to fix this?" Ronnie pointed to the menu.

"Oh, yeah. He'd smell up the whole house with those stupid things. Why is it so hot in here?" Celeste fanned herself with the menu.

"It's not. Maybe all your heat is under your collar."

"Maybe you should shut up." Celeste sounded just like she did when she was fifteen and Ronnie was ten. She took another swallow of coffee and looked over the rim of her cup, past her sister. The beefy man was standing by the cash register, talking with great animation to a woman whose head barely reached his elbow. She was black as blue and narrow as a nail, with a soft cloud of snow white hair. Her small hand rested on his meaty arm. His big, round head bobbed and nodded in their direction. Celeste sipped her coffee, pretended not to notice them.

"I'm tellin' you, Lucille. The one with the long hair—"

"Lord, Hambone, that ain't her hair."

"It's on her head. That makes it hers in my book. Just look at her."

"You haven't seen a face in the last forty-four years that didn't remind you of somebody you seen somewhere!"

"Ain't but so many combinations of noses and eyes and lips. They bound to repeat. But that's not what I'm talkin' about now. That girl sittin' over there look for all the world like . . ."

"I guess if you look real hard, she favor her some." Lucille unlooped her arm from her husband's, put her hand on her narrow waist. "But she don't disturb the air in a room the way Odella used to."

"All's I'm sayin' is . . ."

"You been talkin' since you opened your eyes at five o'clock this mornin'! Ain't you said enough?"

He leaned over and hunched her gently. "Now you know we did a little more than talk this morn . . ."

"Hush up, Hambone!" She slapped his arm playfully. "'Fore somebody hear you talkin' that mess!"

"Probably wouldn't believe it!" He winked at her.

"I'm goin' across the street. I got Marvella Peoples at ten." She stood on her tiptoes, kissed him bye, and swatted his hand away from her butt.

They have to be older than Mother and—Celeste watched Hambone walk her to the door and wait by the window while she crossed the street. When she got to the door of the beauty parlor, she turned and waved, like it was their daily ritual. *Did I ever see Mother and Daddy act like that?* A long-forgotten image of Everett patting her behind as she bent over Niki's crib washed over Celeste, thrusting her into the past. She pushed back and shoved the memory away.

"They already have a buyer."

Just as she pushed Everett away that morning. "A what?!"

"Cash money."

"That's all it comes down to for you, isn't it? Money? And I know you're always broke, I don't care what you tell them at home. What makes you think this would be any different? You'd just blow it all." Celeste conveniently forgot how her little nest egg had cracked. "Isn't that how it goes, Ron? Well, I'm not sure I want—uh—that we should sell this land."

"What the hell else are we gonna do with it?" Of course, like always, Ronnie needed the money. But she'd be damned if she'd give her sister the satisfaction of being right. "Be serious, Celeste. You know you want to sell it. You're just mad because I contacted a realtor and you didn't have anything to do with it. You should be happy. They're the biggest Black agency in North Carolina. I wasn't sneaking around trying to pull something behind your back. I *knew* you were gonna be here. I found us some help and got here first, that's all."

"We never discussed it, so from where I sit it looks exactly like you were going behind my back."

Ronnie threw up her hands. "If you'd climb down off your high horse you'd see a whole lot better!"

Celeste waved the waitress over.

"Ready to order?" She smiled slightly.

"The check please." Celeste reached for her jacket and purse. "I'm trying to find a house around here. Do you think you could help me?"

The girl giggled, but Celeste's stony look stopped her cold. "Sorry ma'am. But if you turn me 'round three times, I get lost walkin' to the door. I'll get Mr. Anderson for you." She scribbled on her pad, tore off the sheet, and put it facedown on the table in front of Celeste.

Ronnie grabbed the check, turned it over. Eighty cents and "Have a nice day" were written neatly in pencil.

"I'll take that." Hambone reached out, and the slip of paper disappeared in his massive hand. "Can't charge nice visitors like you ladies for a little mornin' coffee." He smiled and his freckles formed a different design on his wide face. "I hear you need directions."

"The house used to belong to Odell Womack," Celeste said.

"I knew it! I knew it!" He slapped his thigh. "I told Lucille. You gotta be Odella and Will's girls. Right? Am I right?" He grinned from ear to ear. "Lordy, Lordy. It's been a helluva long time, but I knowed you right away." He looked at Ronnie. "You look so much like your mother. I gotta call Lucille." He shouted across the restaurant. "Mary! Mary!" The waitress hurried in from the kitchen. "Call the beauty parlor. Right now! Tell Miz Lucille I said to get over here. Quick." He turned back to Ronnie and Celeste. "Lord. Where are my manners? Y'all don't know me from Adam." He reached for Celeste's hand. "George Anderson. Ever'body calls me Hambone!" He laughed heartily and worked her arm like a pump handle. "Just look at you! Both of you! Umph, umph, umph! I don't hardly know what to say."

Celeste was ready to scream. Even simple acts, like stopping for coffee, led to surprises, and she didn't have time to digest before the next tidbit was rammed down her throat. "Celeste English. And this is my sister."

"I can introduce myself." Ronnie stretched out her arm. "Veronica *Lucille* Frazier."

"Veronica *Lucille*? Is that right?!"

"That's right!" *I wonder if—* "But ever'body calls me Ronnie. And I'm happy to meet you, Hambone!" She grinned. She liked this man when she first walked through the door, and it made her happy to know he thought she looked like Della, even though Ronnie didn't quite see it. After all, Della was so—dowdy. *But maybe she used to be different.* "So you knew Ma and Daddy?"

"Knew 'em? Watched 'em grow up. Your mama even lived with me and Lucille for a spell. What a spitfire! She was some gal, your ma. Loved herself a good time."

Celeste and Ronnie looked at each other like they had just heard there *was* a Santa Claus.

Ma?! Ronnie toyed with the notion that her mother had been "some gal."

"We wasn't sure your daddy could hold onto her! He had more than a bit of tamin' to do. And heaven knows, she had a stubborn streak a mile wide."

Mother? You got the stubborn part right. But a good time? Celeste was sure he had confused Della with someone else.

"Didn't take no stuff from nobody. But I guess Will musta done all right! How they doin? They come with you? Your ma ain't been back since she left. Will was here in 'sixty-three or 'sixty-four." Hambone looked up to think. "Can't remember which. He come again in 'sixty-nine. That I'm sure of 'cause it was the summer we had that 'giant leap for mankind.' Couldn't nobody talk about much else. Your daddy watched 'em walk on the moon right here with us. Well, across the street. We used to be over there where Lucille's shop is now." He gestured out the window.

Celeste instantly pulled up her memory of that night in July. *And we watched in front of that old Philco portable in their bedroom. Daddy wasn't there. Mother said he had to go away for a few days—take care of some business. We ate fish sticks for dinner that night. They were burned on the outside but still icy and wet in the middle. When Daddy came back, we got a new stove. We got a color TV that summer too.*

"Daddy died in October." It was the first time Ronnie had said it out loud.

Hambone's face fell. "Oh, Lord. I am so, so sorry." Ronnie knew his sorrow was real. "Your mama?" he asked tentatively.

"Fine. She's fine," Celeste answered. "So you know where the house is? We'd really like to get out there."

"Was a time when ever'body in this county and the next could tell you where the Womack place was, but that was a long time ago. When your granddaddy was livin'." Hambone shook his head. "Umph. Umph. Umph. Time sure do slip away from you." He looked up when he heard the door open.

"What in the world is the matter with you, George?" Lucille wore a blue nylon smock. Several combs stuck out of her pocket, and hair clips dangled from her collar. A wad of waxy, yellow grease hung off the back of her hand.

"See! I told you she reminded me of Odella! These her and Will's girls!" Full of self-satisfaction, he folded his arms over his ample belly and gave Lucille a "so there" shake of his head.

"Well, well, well." Lucille wiped her hands on her top and held her arms open.

Ronnie got up first to accept Lucille's bony embrace. She wasn't in the habit of hugging strangers—she wouldn't have lasted two minutes in New York if she had been—but neither of these people seemed like a stranger.

"Lord, child, you feel just like her. She had a fire deep down in her too, burnin' her up. You couldn't see it right off if you wasn't payin' attention, but you could sho'nuff feel it." She patted Ronnie's back with her bony hand. "Some folks didn't understand that." Lucille released Ronnie from her wiry grip and beckoned to Celeste, who stood as expected. "You must be the firstborn."

"Yes, ma'am." Celeste was startled to hear herself say that.

Celeste fit a little more comfortably in the fold of Lucille's

arms. "Welcome home, child. Welcome home. Let me look at
you." Still gripping Celeste's shoulders, she moved back a
couple of steps. "Look at 'em, Hambone. Ain't this something? Lord. You never know what a day will bring. How's
your mama and daddy?"

"Will passed last fall," Hambone said solemnly.

"He calls us all when He's ready. But Della. How she
doin'?"

"She's fine, Mrs. Anderson. Still in Buffalo. Not far from
me and my husband," Celeste answered.

"I don't suppose she's plannin' to meet you two here," Lucille said.

"No—That doesn't seem likely."

"Said she wasn't never comin' back, and she's bein' true to
her word. She left somethin' with me way back then. Figured
she'd call for it when she was ready. She never did. Hmm—
Anyways, glad y'all come to see about the old homeplace. It's
time. Was a man out there a couple a years ago workin' on it,
but it's been empty a long while. Not good for a house to have
no life in it for too long a spell. It can't settle on its foundation. Settlin' don't always work out too good for people, but a
house—a house should never stop settlin'."

Ronnie smiled at the wisdom of Lucille's down-home philosophy. Ronnie seemed more comfortable than Celeste
standing on the threshold of the past. Celeste seemed awkward in the warm gush of strange familiarity.

"Yes, Lucille, they're looking for the house, and if you be
quiet long enough, I'll tell them how to get there."

"Y'all stayin' at The Tree Top? You have to come by our
house for supper. Shoot! I got two late customers tonight, but
Sunday? We'd be honored if you'd join us." She hunched her
husband. "Wouldn't we, Hambone?"

"Yes sirree. We sure would." He tugged on his suspenders
for the umpteenth time.

"If I don't get back Marvella's gon' come after me with my
own straightening comb! I can't wait to talk with y'all some
more. I 'spect a lot's happened in forty years."

* * *

Two and a half miles down Albemarle Road, as instructed, they made the right at an old barn, right again at a rusty old truck with bushes growing out of the grill.

Towering longleaf pines lined the single-lane strip.

"You sure wouldn't know this was Little Pond Road unless somebody told you." Ronnie propped her head on her arms in the open window and peered through the trees. "But I guess if you come down this road you know where you're going." She couldn't make out neighboring houses or anything else through the trees, except more trees.

Celeste looked straight ahead and eased the car tentatively over the rocks and ruts. She prayed there were no oncoming cars because there didn't appear to be room to pass. For a change, their silence seemed more anxious than testy as they waited to see what lay at the end of the road.

12

"Let's get this show on the road."

"This must be it." Celeste slowed to a stop where the deep, wild grass swallowed the single lane.

"Wow!" Ronnie felt like she'd unwrapped a wonderful surprise on Christmas morning. A grin took over her face as she stepped out of the car, too engrossed to close the door.

"I was expecting a shack from the way Mother's been carrying on." Celeste closed Ronnie's car door, then minced cautiously through the weeds and wildflowers that had overrun the elaborately patterned brick walkway. She stood next to Ronnie, dangling her purse at her side, wishing she'd changed into pants and sneakers.

The big, white clapboard house loomed in front of them, impressive in its abandoned, lifeless silence. It had refused to be engulfed by the surrounding knee-high grass or the hulking bushes that had grown unchecked and were themselves a tangle of vines, leaves, and tiny flowers. On the porch, a weathered green swing dangled from the ceiling by rusted chains, and two wicker armchairs leaned upside down against the wooden railing like they were kneeling at an altar, in prayer. The past met up with the present at the front steps, which were concrete and obviously new, like the shingled roof, the wooden banisters primed in gray but not yet painted.

A bird chattered in the nearby woods, and a gentle, cooling breeze rustled the leaves, but perspiration ran from Celeste's hairline down her neck and into her blouse. She wiped at her forehead with the back of her hand. "My, my." She inched forward but stopped, feeling like she was trespassing. Dark, wet circles had spread under her armpits and sweat trickled down the backs of her thighs. A low-level vibration started at the top of her head and traveled south to the soles of her feet. *I wish Everett was here.* A pang of loss hit her where she'd been feeling only annoyance and anger. Right now she didn't want to lash out at her husband. She wanted his hand to hold. Celeste clinched her pocketbook tightly into the curve of her waist and took another step forward.

Ronnie shaded her eyes and counted the eight windows across the front of the house looking back at them. "This is way cool! Ma really lived here when she was little, can you believe it?" She waved away a bee, then moved toward the side of the house, using her hands and her strides to cut through the tall grass. For the first time the property was more than a winning lottery ticket to her.

"Ronnie! Where are you going? You don't know what's back . . ." But she had already disappeared from view. Momentarily dismissing thoughts of snakes and Lyme disease, Celeste took tentative steps along the path that Ronnie had walked and peeked around the corner of the house. "Ronnie!"

"Right here." She had circled once around and came up behind Celeste. "You should see all this stuff. There's a porch out back too. And a shed, and some kind of big brick fireplace. Farther back there's another shed or something. Do you think it was a chicken coop? I can just see Ma with her basket, gathering eggs. . . ."

"Don't you know anything could be back there? Are you crazy?"

"What? Lions? Come on, Celeste." She doubled back toward the front door. "Are you worried about me, or is my big sister ascared to be out here by herself?" Ronnie teased Celeste in baby talk.

"Don't be ridiculous!" Celeste couldn't admit she was glad not to be alone. She trailed behind Ronnie up the front steps.

Ronnie cupped her hands beside her eyes and peered through the oval window in the door. "I looked for the lake out back, but . . ."

"There is water! I was hoping—from the street name."

"Doug says it's kind of a little cove or something, but it lets out into a bigger lake. Can you believe none of the windows are broken out?" She looked over at Celeste. "He also said all the furniture and stuff is still in here. So where's the key? Let's get this show on the road."

Celeste opened her purse and removed the small manila envelope that had been stapled to the deed.

"Maybe we'll find some things from Ma's spitfire days! Isn't that what Hambone called her? I'm dyin' to rag on Ma about that." Ronnie watched Celeste's hand tremble as she shook two keys into her palm. "Here, I'll do it." Before Celeste could object, Ronnie had grabbed one, and the door was open. She had expected it to creak and groan, like a haunted house. Instead it swung wide without a peep.

But Celeste heard a *whoosh*, like the noise from opening a vacuum-sealed coffee can, or Pandora's box. She felt it too. "Did you hear that?"

"What?"

Celeste held her breath a moment. "Nothing."

Ronnie shrugged and walked in. The house smelled of brittle paper, musty clothes, and old furniture sealed away and forgotten. "Doug said the lights would be on today. Not that we need them." Dust motes danced on rays of sunlight that streaked across the living room and into the foyer. Ronnie hesitated a moment, as if passing through the beams would set off some alarm, but curiosity made her plunge ahead. "Look at this!" To the left and right of the hall, bulky, sheet-draped hulks of furniture floated, like specters, on islands of faded rose and ivy bordered rugs. "It's like a movie!" Celeste hung back. "Don't tell me you're afraid of ghosts!" Ronnie cackled.

"No!" At least not the ones who prowled graveyards after midnight and walked through walls. Celeste feared the phantoms who had recently come to haunt her life, some dead, like the grandmother and grandfather she knew nothing about, and the father she thought she knew so well. Then there were the living, like her mother, who was proving to be a bigger mystery than Celeste had imagined, and Everett, whose spirit she seemed to have lost somewhere along the last twenty-four years. Sweat dripped down her back, and goosebumps sprouted on her arms. This was too much to swallow, too much to digest, but Celeste screamed silently and walked into the living room anyway.

"Right," Ronnie snorted and looked around. "It's weird—all this stuff still being here. And it belongs to us."

"Is that all you can think about? What you get out of the deal?"

"No! It was a thought, all right?! You're not the only one who has them! Anyway, Doug said the taxes were paid, but nobody showed up to claim anything."

"I know Daddy had work done. Maybe he was planning to clean it out later." Celeste glanced around her. "Get it ready to sell since his wife . . ."

"You mean your mother, or aren't you claiming her today?"

"Do I have a choice?" Celeste frowned. "I mean, why is she so dead-set against this place? I could see if it was a shack, but this is a nice house."

"I bet you'd be too through if it *was* a shack. That would be so beneath you."

"Don't be ridiculous! Besides, we need to get started." Celeste took out a spiral-bound pad. "We should catalog whatever we find."

"We have to *see* what's here before we do anything."

"I think . . ."

"Do what you want. I'm exploring." Ronnie snatched the sheet from a bulge by the door and revealed a chintz-covered armchair. "Voilà!" She made short work of the living room, unveiling ornate occasional tables, a burgundy brocade sofa and two matching settees, another settee, and a grouping of wood and upholstered chairs near the window, close to a glossy black spinet piano. It was a formal setting befitting finger sandwiches and tea. An old Victrola sat on top of a glass-doored bookcase. She opened it, pulled a black bound Bible from a shelf, read the front page. "Odell Womack married Ethiopia Clayton, July 5, 1933. Think they had a barbecue?"

Celeste didn't answer. She continued sweating and folding the sheets Ronnie had left in her wake into neat squares, careful not to shake loose much dust.

"Henry Leon Womack, born January 2, 1934."

"Let me see that." Celeste squinted at the names written in a halting, deliberate hand. "Where's Mother's name?"

"Don't know." Ronnie counted on her fingers. "But I do know Henry was kinda early." She grinned. "So, Grandpa was a smooth operator."

"Ronnie, grow up." Celeste shoved the book in its place.

"Just gathering a little family history. And you're grown enough for the both of us, anyway." Ronnie moved on to the dining room. "Do you think some of this is antique? You know, the real kind, like worth something?" In under an hour, they had uncovered china and curio cabinets filled with knick-knacks, pale green etched vases, and dishes decorated with delicate lilacs and ferns.

Celeste opened a cabinet and picked up a coffee cup. "How beautiful."

Ronnie held a gold-rimmed goblet up to the light and watched the cut glass prism dance a rainbow on the faded celery walls. "I asked Doug if the buyer wanted the furniture and stuff too, but maybe we should get it appraised first."

"*We* haven't decided to sell anything." Celeste put the cup away, then put hands on her hips.

"Well, *we* certainly haven't decided to keep it, either. I'm gonna open some windows."

"They're probably stuck. Besides, maybe we shouldn't."

"Why? It's ours. Anyway, these look new." Ronnie turned the lock and the vinyl double-hung glided open without effort. "Ta da! Wrong again!" Celeste stepped into the breeze and dabbed her forehead and neck with a wad of tissues that left white specks clinging to her damp skin.

Ronnie pushed open the swinging door and went into the kitchen. "Whoa!" The room felt welcoming, from the wide-plank floors to the custard yellow cabinets with glass doors that lined the walls. Everyday utensils filled the shelves, and a blue Milk of Magnesia bottle was tucked in a corner, almost out of sight. It was like the prototype for a country kitchen from a decorating magazine. The deep double sink had enamel faucets and a view of the outdoors. A round, family-sized oak pedestal table sat in a windowed alcove, but stove, refrigerator, and dishwasher gleamed brand-new, energy-efficiency tags still in place. "You gotta see this!" Ronnie wrote her initials in the dust that covered the round table.

"My goodness! It's as big as the living room." Celeste opened the refrigerator door. The store's packing slip was still taped to the top shelf. "Gaston Appliance . . . He bought all these last year."

"He who?"

"Daddy. I found the receipts."

"Why'd he do that? Maybe he and Ma were gonna move here. Lots of people do that. You know, retire to the Sun Belt."

"Well, Mother certainly wasn't coming, so of course he couldn't. He must have planned to rent it out—or—I don't know—It would be a lot easier if he'd told me something. Anything is better than this." Celeste sank into one of the ladder-back chairs at the table.

Ronnie hiked herself up on the counter, determined not to let the fun of discovery sidetrack her from her goal. "That's why we need to sell this place. Ma doesn't want anything to do with it. I don't want to be a long-distance landlord. Do you? I'm telling you, Pryce has a buyer. They're offering almost two hundred thousand dollars. We can split it and walk away with a nice piece of change!"

"We should go upstairs before it really gets hot in here." Celeste pushed back from the table.

"Fine. Act like I'm not talkin' to you." Ronnie jumped down, dusted her butt. "Let's go!" She led the way through another swinging door into the hall and headed back to the front of the house. They poked their heads in the three doors they passed: a white-tiled bathroom; a small sitting room with a drop-leaf table, a wooden stool, and a black and gold pedal sewing machine on a wrought-iron stand. And finally they came full circle. Across the front hall from the living room double doors opened into a study about the same size as the sewing room next door. A rolltop desk and an oak swivel chair sat in front of the windows. The remains of an old calendar were tacked to the wall. It read "Mid-State Brickworks" under a drawing of a brook cascading over smooth rocks in the forest.

"It looks like they walked away one day and never came back." Ronnie saw that the pages at the bottom of the calendar had been ripped off until September 1957. "This is kinda creepy when you think about it. Walking around in somebody's house like this. Except it's really Ma's house."

"As you informed me a few minutes ago, it's *our* house, Ronnie."

Ronnie stood at the bottom of the stairs looking up. "You know what I mean. People lived here. This is their stuff. Yeah. I guess it's family, but we didn't *know* them. They didn't *know* us—except for Ma."

This time, Celeste took the lead, avoiding the dusty banister. The steps squeaked in complaint as they mounted, and busted spindles left snaggletoothed gaps along the railing. At the top, four bedrooms fanned out from the stairway, three furnished with suites of dark-stained furniture, one with white. An enormous four-poster rice bed with a two-tiered step beside it dominated the largest bedroom. A bathroom, with a huge porcelain claw-foot tub, also opened onto the center hall.

"You know we have to open every closet, go through every drawer, read every piece of paper."

"That'll take forever."

"You invited yourself, remember?"

"I can only stay a couple of days. I have to . . ."

"So you thought we'd just sell the whole shebang, take the money, and run? I told Everett you didn't have one ounce of business sense!" Celeste threw up both hands. "We have to inventory all of this."

"How come he didn't come too?"

"Who?"

"Everett. Your husband, remember him?"

Celeste rubbed the back of her neck. "He, uh—couldn't get away right now. And before we can even think about selling, we have to find out what houses and land are going for around here."

"Did you see any other houses? I didn't. Besides, I happen to think they're offering quite a bit of money. And if we throw in the furniture and stuff, we can probably get over two hundred for everything. Not even you could turn your nose up at that. I should go find a phone and call Doug, let him know we're out here."

"Suit yourself, but I won't even discuss it with him, or *you*, until I know what's here."

Ronnie huffed. "Fine. You start up here. I'll go downstairs. Let's get this over with."

Celeste thought about the afternoon heat rising. "I'll take downstairs."

"You have to be contrary, don't you!" Ronnie turned on her heels and disappeared into the nearest bedroom.

Even though Ronnie had opened all the windows, by three o'clock it was sweltering, even too hot to smoke. She had untucked her shirt, knotted it below her breasts, and pulled her ponytail up off her neck. She started in one of the smaller bedrooms, where she found men's clothes and shoes. Whoever he was, wasn't very big. His steel blue gabardine shirt fit Ronnie nicely. *What was the brother's name? Henry?* Judging by the styles, he'd stopped dressing there in the midsixties. *Wonder what happened to him?*

In the bathroom there was a used block of Ivory in the daisy-shaped plastic soap dish on the sink, and she wondered who washed their hands last and how long ago it had been. Her mother had been so tight-lipped that Ronnie still wasn't sure how Della came to inherit the house. She tugged hard at the door to the medicine cabinet and almost fell when it finally opened. She'd never heard of half the stuff: Stanback Headache Powder, Lydia Pinkham's Tonic, a petrified jar of Tussy deodorant.

Across the hall in the big bedroom she thought the electric orange and green bedspread circa 1973 looked out of place surrounded by so much old, ornate furniture. On the bedside table she picked up a framed sepia portrait of a man wearing a fedora, tilted back too far on his head to be cool, and a double-breasted pin-striped suit that seemed a bit too skimpy for his robust frame. *My man knew he was clean.* He sat confidently on a bench, his ankle crossed over the other knee, in front of a backdrop bordered with tropical trees and flowers. *This has to be Ma's father. She looks just like him.* It was odd to see a face she knew so well on the person who obviously had it first. Ronnie studied the picture for a while, then laid it on the bed to take down to show Celeste and moved on to the drawer where she found an El Producto box that held stray buttons, safety pins, a triple-strand necklace of iridescent crystals and, folded carefully in a paper towel, a well-chewed set of false teeth. Judging by their size, they fit in a rather tiny mouth. *Musta belonged to Ma's mother—our grandmother—but nobody else in the family inherited that trait. All the folks I know about have big mouths.* She put the dentures back in a hurry but fastened on the beads. She fingered them around her neck as she moved to the closet.

The smell of flowery perfume and liniment met Ronnie as she opened the door. The outfits were so tightly packed there was no room to slide the hangers. The oldest clothes were medium sized; as they got more recent, they got smaller. After careful consideration she chose a navy and white polka dot shirtwaist that was big enough to pull on over her clothes, and she remembered how she loved to play in Della's closet. After she was all done up she'd poke out her little lips for Della to add the finishing touch. Lipstick. *Wonder if Ma used to play dress-up in here.* Ronnie examined all the hats in a stack of boxes she took down from the shelf. A black straw number the size of a saucer struck her fancy, so she put it on and pulled the veil down to her chin. *All I need is some pumps with the toes peeking out and I'm ready for my close-up.* Ronnie squatted down and rummaged through the shoes, which were all too small, but she came across an Enna Jetticks box filled with report cards, two separate piles, each secured with a piece of twine, tied in a bow. Henry Womack's pile went from first through twelfth grade. Odella's started in the middle of the fourth grade and stopped at the end of the eleventh, but she got better marks in every subject. *Don't tell me she dropped out. Man, if I did that I'd still be hearin' about it! Wonder*

*when Ma started calling herself Della? Not that I blame her. I
haven't even been here a whole day, and I've got so much ma-
terial to tease her about.* When Ronnie straightened up she
noticed a black patent handbag with a brass clasp hanging
from a hook. *I'd carry this now.* She put on one of the yel-
lowed cotton gloves she found inside. There were two crum-
pled dollar bills and a brittle stick of Beechnut gum in the
pocket, but it was the old church bulletin that caught her eye.
" 'How Great Thou Art' Solo by Odella Womack" was under-
lined in pencil. *Ma? Singing in church?* Ronnie gathered the
program and her other finds and went downstairs.

"Hey, look at this stuff." Ronnie started over to where Celeste sat in a chair holding a piece of sheet music, piano bench
propped open in front of her.

She looked up when she heard Ronnie. "Do you remember—Is that all you've been doing, playing? You could have
stayed home."

"No, I've been busy. I just decided to dress for the occasion." She curtsied.

Celeste didn't crack a smile. "Do you remember when we
got the piano?"

Celeste's voice had prongs so Ronnie knew her sister was
worked up about something. "Not exactly." She barely remembered there was one in the house because no one had
played it in years. For a while she and Celeste had gone to
Mrs. Horner's each Tuesday after school, where they were
drilled on scales and contorted into proper hand position. Celeste had no ear for music, was terrified by Mrs. Horner's
gruff manner, and hated every minute of her half-hour session. And although Ronnie could carry a tune, she was completely inept at the piano. She got a kick out of serenading her
parents with the few simple tunes she managed to memorize,
but the novelty wore off quickly. When the Horners moved to
Cleveland, Celeste thought her prayers had been answered,
and Ronnie was ready to go back to singing or dance lessons,
something she was good at. Their parents asked a couple of
times if they wanted a new teacher, then the subject was
dropped.

"It was that summer Mr. Anderson was talking about this morning, the moon walk summer. When Daddy came back we got lots of new stuff." Celeste stared out the window as she spoke. "A stove, color TV, and that piano."

"I remember the TV. I didn't want to go to day camp that August. I wanted to stay home and watch all the shows in color."

"I heard Mother play it once," Celeste continued.

"The piano?"

"It was before she was working at DMV, in the fall, and I came home from school early one day. It was still warm, so the windows were open, and I heard this music. It was a pretty song, like a ballad I guess. Anyway, you know how the screen door always squeaked? When I opened it, the music stopped. By the time I got to the living room, the lid was down and she was dusting the piano, if you can believe that. I asked her to play some more and she said she didn't know what I was talking about. 'I don't play no piano, Celeste. You know that.' But I always believed it was her playing. Nobody else was home."

"She sang too." Ronnie leaned against the spinet and thrust the bulletin at Celeste.

"I found some more of those in the piano bench. And I found this." Celeste handed Ronnie the blue book in her lap.

Ronnie opened it to the first page. Groups of neat, precisely drawn horizontal lines formed the staff, marked with curly treble and bass clefs, perfectly oval whole, half, and quarter notes. She flipped the pages. There were no lyrics and no titles, but the composer was the same. Inked in plump script on the upper right of each page was "melody by Odella Womack."

Ronnie held the book to her heart. "This is pretty cool."

"Why did she lie to me like that?!"

"Celeste, it wasn't . . ."

"Yes it was. She lied. She played the piano well enough to write music. Why wouldn't she tell me that?"

"Daddy must have known. He didn't say anything, either." Ronnie cocked her right foot on its heel and looked down at the dust that had collected on her sandals. "Who knows why they did anything? They sure as hell didn't discuss it with us." Ronnie noticed that the circles under Celeste's eyes had deepened since morning, like she'd been crying. "I think we've had enough for one day, and it would be better to find our way back before dark." *Can't wait to see what'll turn up next.*

"Yeah. All right." Celeste smoothed her linen skirt, but the wrinkles were set. "We can start early tomorrow, ahead of the heat." *God only knows what we'll find out then.*

"If Daddy was working on the place, I wish he had gotten to the air conditioning." Ronnie trotted up the stairs to ditch her costume, except the crystals. Somehow she felt attached to them and she kept them on. When she locked the door behind them, she stopped on the porch and added the key to the others on her pink heart-shaped key ring. Aside from keys to her mother's house in Buffalo, it was the only one that still worked.

Celeste wanted to ask for the key back, for safekeeping, but she kept quiet. She guided the car down the narrow road and squinted as the setting sun flickered through trees.

"I'm exhausted and I'm starving." Ronnie turned around and watched the house disappear from view. "If we don't go back to Pal's, where do you suggest we eat?"

"How am I supposed to know? I'm just not sure if I can take any more southern hospitality today."

"What's wrong with it? I think they're nice. And I know the food will beat the hell out of anything else around here. It's like Mama's home cookin'! If Ma could cook!"

It was the magic word. "Speaking of cooking—" Celeste cleared her throat. "I understand you encouraged my daughter to quit her job and pursue this insane notion she has of becoming a chef."

Not this! Can't we be on the same side of somethin'? "I didn't *encourage* her, as you put it. I told her it was her life, which it is. What did Ma say? 'You can't cut your dresses by somebody else's pattern.'"

"I don't want to hear that old-timey junk! And what do you know about raising a child?"

"Nothing. But Nik's not a child anymore."

"She'll always be my child. But how could you have any idea what the responsibility of motherhood is like? You can't even take care of yourself!" Celeste checked both directions before getting on the highway that would again become Albemarle Avenue.

"She'll always be your daughter, but I got news for you. She's not your child. I bet you don't think of yourself as Della's child?"

"It's not the same! Mother wasn't very—motherly."

"And you're the Queen Mum, is that it? Have you ever asked Niki how you score on the motherhood test?" Ronnie lowered the window.

"That's the stupidest thing I ever heard. And the air is on," Celeste barked.

Ronnie ignored her and dangled her arm outside. "Says you, but I personally don't think Ma did such a piss-poor job. She didn't make cookies for the bake sale, but she was always there when we needed her."

"She was there when *you* needed her."

"She came to all our stuff at school."

"Wearing those hideous smocks she made. Maybe she should have used somebody else's pattern. I used to want to disappear through the floor."

"So she wasn't a fashion plate."

"I'm not discussing Mother! I'm talking about *you*, interfering in Niki's life, minding business that isn't yours."

"Why are you so against her becoming a chef? I hear tell it might run in the family."

"If it was true, don't you think we'd have heard it before now? And I sure haven't come across any evidence of a catering business today. Sounds like some crap Mother made up to make Nik feel better."

"Maybe, maybe not. Damn, Celeste. She's been a great kid. No school trouble, no boy trouble, no drug trouble. Niki earned her degree, not you. Can't she do what she wants with it?" Ronnie looked up and saw the flag outside of the Elks Lodge approaching. "You gonna stop at Pal's or you want to eat at the truck stop across from our five-star accommodations?"

"Fine. I don't care." Celeste braked and pulled into a space in front of the restaurant behind a red Corvette convertible. "Being a cook or chef or whatever you call it—it's not . . ."

"Not what?"

"—It's not professional!"

"Oh. You mean like a lawyer or like her father the doctor?" Ronnie scratched her head like she was thinking. "Or a hooker? They say that's a profession too, right?" Ronnie knew she was pouring kerosene on hot coals. She could almost hear Celeste sizzle.

"Well now—that's pretty close to what you do, isn't it?"

"What the hell are you saying?!" Whatever peace they had approached earlier in the afternoon was going up in flames.

"How do you manage to get favors from people like your realtor friend's friend? The banker, is it?"

"He made a phone call to a friend. It wasn't *even* more than that, so you can take your little sly implications . . ."

"And while we're at it, you don't expect me to believe you support yourself from acting. Or modeling either—certainly not at your age—not that you ever did." She mumbled the last part but clearly enough for Ronnie to hear it.

"I'm gonna pretend you didn't say any of that, because it's the only way I know not to slap you." Ronnie got out, slammed the door, and by the time Celeste unfastened her seat belt, was already in Pal's.

The fried chicken and pot roast greeted Ronnie before the hostess did, and she found herself really hungry for the first time in three days, in spite of her anger. Obviously Pal's Kitchen was the place to be on Thursday nights in Prosper. It was jammed, with nearly as many White diners as Black ones. There were no strained, hushed murmurs or delicate clinks of crystal. Forks clacked, plates rattled, and voices rose and fell in crescendos of words and laughter. A steely guitar blues from a forty-five record played on the flashy old jukebox across the room.

Celeste and Ronnie managed to get seated without drawing

blood. They had barely settled themselves when Hambone burst through the kitchen doors, an enormous tray riding on his wide shoulder. He deposited two kiddie specials and a plate of smothered pork chops at the table where a plump blonde woman cooed to a baby in a high chair, held a pint-sized, towheaded boy in a lock between her knees, and carefully spooned the ice from the glass of a tearful, pigtailed little girl. Then he hustled to the counter, deposited the one plate left on his tray in front of a man reading a magazine, and exchanged a few lively words with him. Ronnie watched Hambone's belly bounce as he laughed and shook his head. Then he slipped the empty tray into a slot on the stand by the kitchen door, scurried to the register, and made change for two waitresses who stood there, dinner checks and money in hand. After he closed the cash drawer, he looked up and spotted Celeste and Ronnie. He spoke briefly to the man with the magazine before heading over.

"I'm so glad y'all decided to stop back!" Hambone hooked his thumbs under his suspenders. "Can't go wrong with the fried chicken. It's the special on Thursday. It's on the menu every day, but folks seem to have got in the habit of comin' for it on Thursdays. If you ask me, it don't taste no different from the chicken we fix on Mondays. But if they wanna think it is, I ain't complainin'!"

Celeste gritted her teeth so she could bear his rambling chicken anecdote. Ronnie thought it was cute. His greeting took her mind off wanting to strangle Celeste.

Hambone surveyed the crowd and grinned. "I hope it wasn't too bad out at the house. I don't get out that way much no more. You know, was a time I'd stop by pretty regular. Check on things and look in on Miz Ethiopia . . ."

"Now that's Ma's mother, right?" Ronnie was proud of herself for remembering what she'd read in the family Bible.

"Miz Ethiopia was her stepmama." Hambone waved to a patron who entered the restaurant. "We never did know her mama. She passed on, you know. That's when Odella first came to Prosper."

"That's what Ronnie meant. Stepmother." Celeste was

quick to smooth over their ignorance. "Mother always referred to her as Mama."

"Well, a whole lot sure has changed. When Odella was growin' up she had no use for the lady, and she'd call her nothin' at all before she called her Mama." Hambone looked down, remembering. "Anyways, didn't nobody 'spect Miz Ethiopia'd live long after Odell passed on, but she was a darn sight stronger than she appeared to be. Proved us all wrong. Was pret' near a hundred when she died. So you two gon' have the chicken?"

"Sounds like it wouldn't be a trip to Prosper without it, isn't that right, sister dear?" Ronnie smiled innocently at Celeste.

"Uh-huh. Sure." Celeste was too overloaded to care what she ate.

Across the room, the man Hambone had spoken to at the counter got up, dropped some bills on the counter, and tucked his magazine under his arm. He was a bit bowlegged and his walk had a little hitch to it, like the cowboys in black-and-white movies. He stopped by a table, chatted a moment, waved a friendly so-long, and continued in their direction. He was reed thin, which made him look much taller than he actually was, and he was dressed razor sharp. The cuffs of his smoothly pressed red and white striped shirt folded crisply over the elastic at the wrists of his scarlet silk bomber jacket. You could slice paper with the creases in his black trousers, and he wore black suede loafers, without socks. As he got closer, Ronnie could see that despite the wardrobe, the diamond in his left ear, and the copy of *Vibe* under his arm, he was older than he appeared from the other side of the room. His dark, curly hair was gray at the temples, and the lines around his eyes mapped passages of time and experience.

He nodded at Celeste and Ronnie before he spoke to Hambone.

"See you tomorrow, man. And do yourself a favor. Don't go puttin' no money against the Panthers. They're gon' go all the way this year." His voice was deep, rich, and sweet, like dessert. "But if you insist I'll be happy to take you up on your bets."

"Just make sure you left money to pay for your dinner!" Hambone teased.

Ronnie suspected that in his day, he'd been through all the skirts in town and then some. His eye lingered a moment at her necklace and she raised her hand to touch it.

"You ladies have a nice stay in Prosper." He smiled. "And when you see your mama, tell her Lester said hello." He clapped Hambone on the shoulder. "Later." And he was out the door.

"I'll be right back with your dinner." Hambone disappeared.

"We did not know Ma had a stepmother!" Ronnie leaned in toward Celeste.

"Well, you certainly don't think I'm going to let anybody else think we didn't!" Celeste hissed.

"And if she's not actually *from* here, where is she from?"

"How should I know? And right now, I don't even care! I meant to ask if they have wine."

"All I know is the more we find out, the less we know." Ronnie watched out the window as the man named Lester got in the red 'Vette and drove off. "And how does she know this dude who wears an earring and drives a sports car?"

"Obviously that was a long time ago, and I'm sure he didn't do either back then. Besides he looks like—like . . ."

"Yes? Like what?"

Celeste sucked her teeth. "You know exactly what I mean."

"Celeste, you always mean the same damn thing." Ronnie's eyes twinkled with mischief. "I wanna know what Ma has to say about ol' Lester."

13

"... waiting for the but."

By the time the clock radio alarmed at six A.M., blaring a disco beat, Ronnie felt like she'd been run over by the Lexington Avenue Express. Her backache wrapped around to her belly like a girdle. This dawn patrol Celeste had them on was not Ronnie's cup of tea in the first place. Sunrise was closer to the time she would come dragging in from the night before, but this night had been anything but a party. Ronnie's worries had taken turns haunting the night, and sleep had been snatched in agitated naps between long bouts of wakefulness, all of it accompanied by the wheeze and snore of the air conditioner. She twisted the radio volume off, then dragged herself up on her elbow and reached for the phone to check her service. Usually she called in every hour, on the off chance someone meaningful was looking for her, like an agent or casting director. It dawned on her at 2:37 A.M. that she hadn't checked it in the three days she'd been in Prosper.

Ronnie needed her whole situation to be different in a hurry. Celeste seemed content to catalog every doodad and shoestring in the house like it would change the course of history. Ronnie had played along, figuring Celeste would get tired of this game and get down to business. Besides, as much as Ronnie grumbled, and she did make sure Celeste knew they were doing a whole lot of work for nothing, Ronnie enjoyed exploring the musty trunks and boxes, making up stories about the cotton slips, silk stockings, embroidered handkerchiefs, and other relics she found. Ronnie had cleared out a drawer in the big bedroom and started a collection of things she wanted to keep because they were pretty or odd, or she

felt a strange connection to them, like the faded deck of playing cards she found stuffed in the foot of a white ankle sock.
Blue ballpoint mustaches had been drawn on all the face cards
that didn't already have them, queens included. Ronnie just
knew they were Della's. Her mother taught her to play hearts
and pinochle and rummy, and Ronnie loved to hang over her
shoulder and help her play solitaire at the kitchen table.
Sometimes Will played too, but Celeste rarely did. Said it was
boring. Ronnie hadn't shown her stash to Celeste yet, but they
still had a lot of business to discuss.

   Ronnie let the phone ring a long time before the desk clerk
grunted a sleepy greeting and gave her an outside line. She
poked at the numbers, then entered her code and listened.
*Kayla . . . Yeah, yeah. Same sad story. No love or fame connec-
tions in the Hamptons, but if there's a way, my girl will be out
there trying again next weekend.* The whole jitney and party-
hopping scene seemed a million miles away at this moment,
like maybe on Pluto. Ronnie reached across the bed for her
shoulder bag, which was under the clothes she'd dumped out of
her carry-on last night to find her pajamas, an XXL T-shirt with
a faded logo from some trade show she worked a long time ago.
Despite the crappy room, she enjoyed the luxury of a queen-
size bed with enough space for piles of magazines and clothes
on the side where she wasn't sleeping. Ronnie dumped her last
two pills in her hand and swallowed them with her own spit.
Gotta find a drugstore and get more of these bad girls. She
didn't bother to add up the hours since her last dose. If it hurt
this bad, they had obviously stopped working.

   Ronnie erased Kayla's message and went on to the next.
*R. Phillip—guess I should call to say I hooked up with his
friend. As much good as it's done, it's not worth the quarter.*
Last night she found a message from Doug slipped under the
door and wondered what took him so long. *Some salesman. He
needs to be about selling my sister so we can get this over with.
Actin' like I got all year.* Ronnie shrugged her shoulder up to
hold the phone, lit the half cigarette she had carefully tamped
out the night before. It tasted nasty, but she smoked it anyway.
Haven't heard from him since he left me in this dump. You'd

think he'd call at least to see if I'm still breathing. Then she remembered him leaning up against the car that first morning, reading his paper, waiting for her. And she recalled Celeste's curt dismissal. *Guess I did say I'd call him—but still, this is business.* The fact that he was a man and some little part of her wanted him to call first, she swept that under the rug.

Ronnie blew smoke down over her bottom lip, made a mental note to call Doug at a slightly more reasonable hour and to decide whether to call R. Phillip at all, then moved on to the next message. *Marilyn Ellis?!* Ronnie froze, as she listened to her supervisor, who sounded stiff, not chatty like usual. Covering Ronnie's shifts wasn't working out. Marilyn wanted to confirm that Ronnie was on the schedule for Thursday evening and that it was imperative she be there. *No sweat. I'll be back by Tuesday and—* She dropped the receiver into the cradle. And as soon as she touched down she would be officially without a residence. She had been pushing all thoughts about her shaky situation to the back of her mind, but they always elbowed up front and center, bigger, uglier, and louder than before. The vise that squeezed her head and her guts felt another notch tighter, and it wasn't until the ash dropped off her cigarette and onto her knee that Ronnie realized her hands were shaking. She hurriedly crushed out the butt and turned up the radio to drown out the voice that kept screaming, *What the hell am I gonna do?*

"This is Johnny DuPree, your morning MC, and if your rooster don't crow, then let me cock-a-doodle-doo ya in the morning!" Ronnie let the patter of the smooth-voiced DJ distract her. "You're listening to WDLA, and if you're old enough to remember when rock was somethin' you throw, then this record will bring back a whole lotta memories." He played another cut with a heavy dose of rhythm, and Ronnie forced herself into the groove and up on her feet. She glanced in the skimpy bathroom mirror, stuck her tongue out at herself. It was going to take some serious effort to make herself presentable, because the act was wearing thin and right now she looked as whupped and scared as she felt. She hopped into the shower, making sure to wrap her hair carefully. She didn't have the patience to deal with two feet of wet, tangled weave.

The spray of warm water loosened up Ronnie's brain, and her thoughts began to flow. By the time she dried off with the scratchy towel, she decided she needed to talk to Doug and see if his client would be interested in twenty-two and a half acres. That sounded like a whole lot of land to her, and that way Celeste could take her sweet time and Ronnie could pocket her sweet cash and be on her way.

Dressed in a short black skirt and a slightly damp, clammy cotton tank she'd hand-washed last night, Ronnie was outside, perched on the fender of the rental, by ten minutes to eight. She wanted her sister in a good mood, and the best way to assure that was to keep things moving on schedule. When Celeste came out at eight, she was surprised that Ronnie had beaten her.

Celeste's lemon yellow shorts set stood out brightly against the hazy, humid day. She wore it to help her keep putting on a happy face. "You're up early."

So you can cross that off your list of things to bitch about. "All this clean country air, it makes me feel so—alive." Ronnie sounded like a stale air freshener ad, even to herself. She noticed that her sister looked a little wilted too. "And how was your night?"

"Fine. Just fine." But the load on Celeste's mind showed in the bags under her puffy eyes.

Ronnie saw the strain, but she also recognized the "case closed" expression and didn't press the issue. She wasn't hankering for an argument before they left the parking lot.

"I made a grocery list. We can stop on the way." Celeste started the car. She needed to get busy to keep her demons in check because she'd had close encounters with her real life last night too. She reached Lydia and managed to make the situation in Prosper sound messy enough to require her attention for a few more days. Her friend sounded sympathetic, while also managing to rub in what an incredible time she and Everett were missing. "Why doesn't he come on down?" Lydia said. "You two are like family. You know we'll take good care of him, unless there's some *reason* he's not taking time off."

Celeste could tell Lydia was searching for the faintest whiff of turmoil, but Celeste was careful to keep all traces of concern out of her voice. Whatever it took to keep Lydia off the scent Celeste would do because she had no intention of showing up in Highland Beach without her husband.

And Celeste had been leaving messages for Everett, with only her own clipped voice on the answering machine as a reply. Finally, he had called last night. She was already in bed, filing her nails and working on her to-do list when she picked up the phone, expecting Ronnie with some nonsense. When she heard Everett say her name, Celeste got the high-voltage jolt that always thrilled her when they were dating, and waiting for his calls had made her ache deep inside. He sounded so relaxed and matter-of-fact that she started asking him about regular things: the weather, the mail, watering the lawn. She had leaned back into her pillows, twirling and untwirling the phone cord around her index finger as she described her adventures since she left Buffalo. So at first, when he said he had been to a lawyer and filed a legal separation, she was sure she'd misheard him. He went on to explain that the papers would be waiting for her when she got back. And he was on his way to the jazz festival in Portugal day after tomorrow. Celeste's heart began to pound so loud and fast she could no longer hear him speak. She put the receiver down on the bedside table and sat, knees pulled up to her chest, arms wrapped around them, rocking. She didn't know how long she'd been sitting like that when the knock on the door interrupted her trance. Her phone had been off the hook so long that Everett phoned and asked the night clerk to check on her.

Celeste had paced the room, stoking her anger, rehearsing her harangue. It was 3:16 in the morning when she called her house to tell him off, but when she heard his sleepy hello, the steam seeped out of her. All she could do was hang up gently and cry.

"Hey, aren't you gonna stop?" Ronnie said just in time for Celeste to swerve into the Winn-Dixie parking lot.

Ronnie tagged behind as Celeste maneuvered the cart to get more boxes of super-size, extra-thick trash bags, smaller resealable storage bags, tape, paper towels, a pound of sliced turkey from the deli, bread, an apple, and a pear. Ronnie tossed a box of tampons and a bottle of Advil into the cart and ignored the evil eye Celeste gave her when she slipped outside to the pay phones while Celeste waited on the checkout line.

Ronnie hated skirting the issue of her share of the bill; she knew Celeste kept a strict accounting. She'd never ask for the money outright. The debt would be transferred to Ronnie's already lengthy tab for use during some future fight. Ronnie's operating capital was dwindling, though. *If we can just unload this damn land.* She fished the card from her pocket and dialed.

"Mr. Pryce, this is Ms. Frazier. If you can find the time in your busy schedule, I would appreciate your stopping by my house in Prosper this afternoon. You know, the one on Little Pond you're supposed to be trying to sell. Would your buyer be interested in half the property? Let me know." Ronnie hung up, hoping she sounded snippy enough to get a rise out of him, not desperate, which was the God's honest truth. Then she helped Celeste load the groceries into the car and followed her around back of the store, where a stock boy told them they'd find a stack of flattened cardboard boxes. They took as many as the compact car would hold, then they were off for another day of discovery, each working overtime to keep her own secrets in check.

As had become the routine, Celeste perked a pot of coffee in the white enamel stove-top percolator she found in one of the cupboards. Her liberal use of pine-scented disinfectant and her decorating touches had made the kitchen feel quite homey in the short time they had been in town. She had washed two place settings of the blue willow china she thought was so pretty, as well as bamboo-handled cutlery she'd found in the drawer next to the sink. A ruby glass vase filled with wild goldenrod, cosmos, and cornflowers she had picked from near the house, not too far into the woods, sat in the center of the table. She was so deep in thought that she didn't comment when Ronnie turned on the portable radio on the counter while she waited for her tea water to boil.

Ronnie searched the dial until she recognized the lively

baritone of Johnny DuPree reading the community calendar, birthday greetings, and help wanted ads for the station. *How sweet. Do they read personal ads for cows and chickens too?* She kept surfing the dial and tried to gauge her sister's mood while Celeste got the remainder of a Danish ring out of the bread box, sized it up, sliced it in two precise halves, and put them on two plates.

"Remember how we used to fight over who got the biggest half of anything when we were kids?" Ronnie pulled two paper towels from the roll and folded them into napkins.

"You started it, making a big deal if you didn't get exactly what I got." Celeste sprinkled sugar out of a Mason jar into her coffee cup, then handed the jar to Ronnie.

"Then Daddy'd get all serious." Ronnie dropped her voice to her father's register. "'Half is half. Ain't one bigger than the other.' That's when you started bringing a ruler to the table till Ma threatened to spank you with it."

Celeste had to choke down her coffee to keep from spitting it out with her laugh. She nibbled her breakfast a moment, mashed some crumbs off the counter with her finger and sprinkled them in the sink. "I miss him all the time. He was so—I don't know, good, fair, easy to get along with."

"Are you implying your mother is not easy to get along with?" Ronnie smirked.

"Don't just give her to me," Celeste cracked. "She's your mother too." Celeste took a sip, thought a moment. "You know, going through all this stuff—it seems so regular. What's the big deal about this place? Why does she hate it so much?"

"Who knows? And I don't see her playing true confessions anytime soon." Ronnie broke off a small piece of coffee cake, crumbled it on her plate, took a deep breath. *And there's no time like the present.* "Listen, I called Doug Pryce this morning—to ask if his buyer would settle for half the property."

"Is that all you can think about, Ronnie? You're like a broken record!"

"And I'm gonna keep sayin' it until you hear me! You may have all summer to make this into some kinda archaeological dig, but I don't, and you're not gonna make me feel bad about wanting to sell this place and get out." Hand on hip, foot tapping, Ronnie waited for the next volley.

But Celeste had no stomach for a battle; her wounds from last night were too fresh. She swallowed a sip of coffee, watched the scarlet blur of a cardinal dart past the window and out of sight. "Is that really what you want to do?" she said quietly.

Ronnie was caught off guard by the sudden de-escalation. *I don't know—but I don't have a whole lotta choice!* "Yes."

Celeste poured more coffee. "All right then. Let's see what he has to say."

Hallelujah. "Thank you." The clock had stopped, with not much time to spare, and Ronnie felt like skipping upstairs, but she maintained her cool until she was discreetly out of sight. For the first time in a week she felt hopeful. She attacked Henry's room with plenty of hip in her hop, singing snatches of songs, wishing she had the radio to keep her company. And she checked her watch, wondering if Doug would show up. The odd assortment of items scattered among the run-of-the-mill clothes and underwear made her chuckle: a cocoa tin half filled with Indian-head nickels in the back of a dresser drawer, old razor blades impaled in a rusted bar of soap in the nightstand, a crowbar wrapped in a dingy pillowcase in the closet. Ronnie got a flash of someone trying to make sense of her remaining box of possessions but she had to dump that thought in a hurry.

By one-thirty there was still no Doug. She and Celeste took a brief lunch, long enough to grab a sandwich and clear the dust from their nostrils. Celeste had her morning's finds displayed in the dining room: neat stacks of tablecloths and napkins with sticky notes on top indicating the count, a graceful cut-glass pitcher, a silver compote. She would have waxed poetic about each one, amazed that their mother had grown up with such nice things, but Ronnie cut her short so she could resume her own excavation.

By the time Ronnie folded the last pair of trousers and added them to the bulging black garbage bag on the floor, the sun had burned away the early haze. She unbent herself, braced her hands on her hips, and massaged her lower back.

Then she heard the knock on the doorsill and Doug's "Hello" through the screen door.

It's about damn time. Please let him have good news. Ronnie shuffled quickly to the bathroom, rinsed her hands, smoothed her wet palms over her hair, wiped at the sweat on her face with a paper towel, then trotted casually downstairs. "At least you listen to your messages." She could see him through the screen, palm pressed against the door frame.

"And I do my best to deliver—soon as people let me know what they want." In the hand resting on his hip, Doug held a vinyl binder that was Pryce Real Estate green, the same color as today's tennis shirt. "May I?" He watched her tuck in her T-shirt.

R. Phillip had described Ronnie as a fox and provided a detailed summary of her attributes, at least the physical ones. When he first saw her come off the plane, Doug thought she looked okay, although she had enough hair for six people attached to her head, which didn't do anything for him. But right now she looked like a rumpled teenager. R. Phillip also admitted, kind of sideways, that Ronnie had been more of a challenge than he anticipated. "I mean, I took her out a bunch of times, off and on, and she never gave me a play," he had said. "Did it ever occur to you that she just doesn't dig your shit?" is what Doug told him, but frankly, he wasn't looking at her as a potential playmate. He had more female attention than he knew what to do with since he became a widower.

Doug had been unprepared when so many women he knew, including Janice's girlfriends, only gave him a two-week mourning period after she died. Then the phone calls started. Women asked him out, offered to come over and cook him dinner, left homemade meals in microwaveable containers on the porch. For a while he ignored them and focused on tasks with steps he could follow, like work, coaching softball, shooting hoops at the gym. When he was finally ready for some company, he kept running into women who wanted a lifetime commitment after brunch and a movie. There was no letup in Charlotte either, but he took it all like a nickel change; it was nice, but it didn't add up to much.

"Are you gonna tell me somethin' I wanna hear?" Ronnie crossed her arms and playfully blocked the doorway.

"If you're interested in what the buyer had to say." He chewed on his mustache, tried to figure out why he was smiling to himself as he remembered the surprised look on her face when he first said hello at the airport.

With a sweeping gesture, Ronnie opened the door. "By all means, come in."

"Ronnie, who are you talking—Oh, uh, Doug, is it?" Celeste dusted at a smudge on her shirt. "I didn't realize . . ."

"He's got news." Ronnie motioned toward the living room.

"Just a moment." Celeste disappeared toward the kitchen while Doug took a spot on the sofa and Ronnie perched on a chintz chair arm, her fingers crossed in her pockets. She was glad Celeste returned quickly. Ronnie was suddenly too nervous to make small talk, and Doug didn't have many words to spare.

Celeste sat stiffly on the edge of another chair, crossed her legs at the ankles, and opened her agenda to the back where she kept her lists.

It figures! My sister would prepare a cross-examination. "So, what's the scoop?" Ronnie clasped her hands, rubbed them together.

"First of all, who *is* this mystery buyer?" Celeste checked off question number one, leaving her pen poised to jot down the answer.

"What difference does that make?!" *And what are you up to?*

Doug consulted his binder. "DW Enterprises."

"What would a corporation want with this land?" Celeste asked.

"Why do you care, Celeste? It's their money."

"I just want to know. Do you mind?" Celeste shot Ronnie a pointed glance. "It might be worth more to them than they're offering, for one thing."

Ronnie nearly strained an eye muscle to keep from rolling them.

"And what do they plan to do with the property?"

"I can't answer that." Doug shifted back in his chair, crossed his leg. "What I can tell you is they're willing to consider your offer."

Time seemed to stop and Ronnie tensed, waiting for the but.

"They do have two stipulations."

"Uh-huh." She wanted to snatch the words out of his mouth.

"Their acreage needs to have access to the lake."

"That's doable." She balled her hands into fists.

"Their other requirement is they want the house."

Celeste closed her book. "I'm afraid that won't work. We are absolutely not ready to sell the house yet."

Ronnie's face about fell into her lap. She struggled to keep the quiver out of her voice. "Celeste, we need to discuss . . ."

"Not the house, Ronnie. Not yet."

"Can we step outside for a second?"

"We can, but it won't make any difference."

"If time in the house is an issue, I can see if they're willing to delay the closing." Doug hoped to head off the collision.

"That sounds reasonable." Ronnie followed Doug's change of direction.

"I'm sorry, but it puts us right back where we started. I am not willing to come to terms about this house until . . ."

"Why are you so determined to hold on to this place?!" Ronnie spoke through her teeth, because if she opened her mouth she'd holler.

"I don't owe you an explanation!" Celeste didn't exactly have one. *Selling this place is really the only reasonable thing to do.* But right now Prosper was her safe haven because those separation papers were waiting at home, and then Everett would be gone. "And if you had an ounce of sense . . ."

"That's it!" Ronnie stood up. *She will not embarrass me again.* "Listen, Doug, I'm sorry about all this. I'll be in touch." She ducked out of the room and banged out the screen door. She had no idea where she was heading, but she was not about to have another one of their little "family discussions" in public. *What kind of lunatics must he think we are?* She took off, following the stepping-stones that curved through the yard from the stairs to the edge of the trees. When the path ended, her agitation propelled her down the hill, zigzagging to avoid prickly bushes and low-slung tree limbs, stumbling on loose rocks that rolled underfoot. She continued until the lake appeared before her, murky green at this narrow inlet. At waterside she plunked down on a stump. The sky was a dazzling blue that doesn't come in the box of Manhattan colors. Wispy clouds floated like vapor on the air. Ronnie dropped her head in her hands. A bullfrog grunt interrupted the uneven lapping of water on the shore. With her eyes closed, the wet musk of damp moss, dead trees, and pond scum sent Ronnie back to her first summer in sleep-away camp.

Celeste, a camp veteran, had worked her way up to junior counselor for her four-week session. Before the summer began she had regaled Ronnie with endless explanations of how things were done at camp and warned her it would be hard to fit in and make friends for a while. Ronnie took the first opportunity to prove Celeste wrong. One of the older girls taunted her bunk about the legendary sea serpent that lived deep in the lake and dared one of them to go in. Without hesitation Ronnie jumped into the slick, still water that only looked like a real lake on the postcards they sent home. Now she rubbed her arm, expecting to feel the same thick slime that coated her skin and clung in green gooey clumps to her hair that day. Her bravado made the others cheer, and Ronnie became one of the camp ringleaders, the girl everyone wanted as a friend. "Let's ask Ronnie!" "Does Ronnie want to play?" "Are you coming back next summer, Ronnie?" Celeste was outdone and Ronnie loved it. Her credo became take the dare. Do it *because* you're scared. Dance on the edge of the volcano. Whatever you do, just don't be ordinary.

Except I'm tired of being brave. Ronnie grabbed a stone and hurled it as hard as she could out over the water. *I'm tired, period. I want to sell this damn house so I can stop being terrified. Stop wondering if I can get by one more month.*

"That's pretty good."

She whipped around to see Doug walking toward her.

Aw, damn, what am I gonna say to this man? "It's the only camp skill I have left. That's also the last time I sat on a tree stump." *Just act normal. You can do this.*

"No canoeing? No fire building?"

"You must be joking."

Doug came up beside her. As tough as she liked to appear, he thought she looked as though she'd lost her last friend. He bent over and picked up a rock, then threw it side arm. It skipped three times across the water before it disappeared. "I did some checking." He squatted down next to her and pointed. "Hear the fishin's pretty good beyond that bend."

"Darn. You know," Ronnie looked over at him, "I meant to pack my pole."

"You may laugh, but I've done a lot of good thinking sitting in a rowboat with a line in the water."

"The fishin' philosopher. You should have had a column."

"There's a lot I should have written about."

"You still got a pencil, don't you?" Ronnie cocked her head sideways. Somehow talking with Doug about ordinary nonsense helped her catch hold of herself for a second.

Doug smirked. "I guess I've got a nub or two in my desk drawer." He stood up. "Anyway, if you walk a little ways over, you can see houses across the way in Jessup. It's a relatively new community, but suburban Charlotte is creeping out here pretty fast. What I'm saying is, if this buyer doesn't work out for you, I'm sure I can find another one who will." He knew Edna would be beside herself if she heard him, but his reporter's instincts said this story had as many sides as a prism, and each one shed a different color light on the situation. It was going to take these women a while to agree on the same shade.

"Not before Monday," Ronnie mumbled, the truth oozing around the edges of her mask. The clock had started ticking again, loud, and she was running out of ways to stop it.

"Monday?"

"Nothing. Never mind."

"We can't wrap this up by Monday, no matter what. Now, we can handle it all long distance, but I gotta tell you, you and your sister seem pretty far apart about what needs to happen here. It would help if you could stay in neutral corners long enough to decide what you want to do."

"Excuse you!"

"Just an observation."

"So now you feature editorials too. Only thing left is gossip and the funnies." Ronnie snapped. "You got a whole lot a nerve."

"Tell you what, from now on I'll keep my comments to myself. I'm gonna go. I'll call Monday, find out where we are. Until then, you know how to find me."

Ronnie tattooed the spongy ground with her heels, watched him stride up the hill. *Thinks he knows too damn much.* As Doug got farther away, though, Ronnie realized she had won that battle, but her prize was a trip back to the house to deal with Celeste. *Damn!* She got up and paced around the stump. Even the air felt unbearably heavy, like it would crush her to the ground. Another confrontation would be pointless at the moment. She just wanted to go back to her room and lie in the dark so she could figure out her next move. But if she was going to avoid Celeste that meant hitching a ride with Doug. *Damn!* He was disappearing into the trees. *How do I get myself in these*—"Hey! Doug!" Her voice bounced off the silence. He stopped but didn't turn around. "Can you give me a ride?"

He didn't answer but waited until she caught up. *Now he's gonna act like he's doin' me some big favor.* She followed him to the house, went inside long enough to grab her purse and tell Celeste she was leaving.

On the ride back she kept her mouth shut, looked at the scenery. She'd been in town less than a week, but she found herself looking for the curly faced calf grazing on a dandelion-dotted hillside just beyond the no-name gas station, the tufts of cotton clinging to a field of grass, and other sights that had become familiar in such a short time. They rode without speaking, Doug watching the road. Ronnie feeling a little guilty for leaving Celeste up at the house alone. *But that's how she wanted it from the beginning.* She managed a "Thank you" when he stopped in front of the Tree Top. He stopped chewing the corner of his mustache long enough to manage a nod and a "Yeah, sure." Then he pulled off, leaving Ronnie alone with her misery.

After twelve hours of wrestling with the covers, Ronnie awoke feeling like bulldozed blacktop. Yesterday she'd had a half-day reprieve from her cramps, but they had returned and seemed to throb with every beat of her heart. She wanted to stay in bed, but she knew her sister would be all over her. So she pulled it together for another day at the Womack Museum.

She had debated her dilemma most of the night. She didn't know if she could face starting from scratch, clawing her way to bare bones survival so she could hang on to the edge by her fingernails a while longer, but the only solution she had hatched was to fess up, tell Celeste why she was in such a rush, how badly she needed the money, but as they passed Sunday morning not exchanging much more than terse "excuse me's" and "thank you's," Ronnie couldn't fix her lips to lose that much face. The lectures alone would be endless, delivered in triumphant "I told you so" glee that would confirm Ronnie had wasted the better part of two decades, and that was still too painful for her to admit.

Celeste engrossed herself in the details of other people's lives. She found out the house was built in 1935 and that Odell and Ethiopia Womack were the first owners. Tucked in a tin box full of wooden thread spools she found papers for the sale of Mid-State Brickworks to a South Carolina company. Each new discovery gave her more ammunition for why it was so important that she stay and continue, more important than going home to face her own paperwork.

They stopped work early to freshen up for three o'clock, after-church supper at Lucille and Hambone's. Not that either Ronnie or Celeste was in the mood for a social call today, but these were old friends of their mother, and they *had* promised to come. That, and Hambone had reminded them every day, so there was no chance they could conveniently forget.

"That's the one." Ronnie pointed at the single-story brick rectangle that looked to be modeled on a first grader's drawing of a house. "It's so small. How in the world does he fit in there?"

"It's probably a tight squeeze," Celeste said out of the corner of her mouth. As soon as the wheels hit the driveway, Hambone appeared on the steps. His red button-down shirt, matching suspenders, and white pants were a perfect complement to the tall red and white rosebushes, thick with flowers, that flanked the door.

"Y'all found us! See, I tol' you, Lucille!" He shouted and waved as he lumbered down the walk to greet them.

"Your directions were right on the money!" Ronnie waved the map he had drawn on the back of a restaurant place mat.

Lucille appeared at the door. "I 'spec so. You 'bout worried 'em to death with instructions." A ruffled pink apron protected her matching red and white ensemble. At Pal's, Hambone ruled the kitchen, but at chez Anderson, the cooking was Lucille's domain. It surprised most folks, but that's the way they'd done it for nearly fifty years. To look at her, skinny as she was, you wouldn't think she had an appetite at all, much less knew her way around a stove, but the truth was she loved to eat and could give Hambone a run for his money when it came to chowing down.

"Lord, Hambone, move outta the way and let 'em in the house!"

"I ain't stud'in' you." But he moved aside and let Celeste walk past him. She was grateful to hear the drone of the air conditioning unit at the side of the house. Ronnie put her arm through his and they strolled up the path together.

"Come on in. I just made some sweet tea. 'Sides, it's much cooler in here." She hugged them both and ushered them in where a grandfather clock that came within a hair's breadth of the ceiling filled the entryway. Around it family photos covered the wall: parents, kids, grands, and cousins, old black-and-whites and recent photo studio portraits smiled a warm reception that was continued by the sweet, buttery smells of scratch cake and homemade rolls, mingled with the scent of onion and savory spices.

"Is that Pal's famous fried chicken I smell?" Ronnie thought their invitation was sweet. There were people she'd known for years and they'd never had a meal together that didn't involve a waiter.

"Smothered chicken, but the buffalo fish is fried. And there's candied sweet potatoes, fresh tomatoes, and okra, and snap beans from the garden, and . . ."

"She's makin' like she can cook." Hambone winked conspiratorially.

"Proof is in the eatin'." Lucille motioned them toward the living room. "Make yourself to home. I'll be right back with the tea."

And then they were engulfed by decor. Every inch of space in the room was accounted for. Celeste and Ronnie shuffled along the narrow aisle, past the large round glass and brass coffee table, and moved aside mounds of throw pillows, all in shades of green, to take seats on the ample leaf-patterned sofa.

Hambone plunked down in the big matching chair near the door. "This is the first house we bought, and the last. We talked about movin' once upon a time, maybe someplace bigger, but no place else felt like home."

"It's quite—impressive." Celeste didn't know where to look first. Two end tables held cut crystal lamps and white china baskets full of nuts and candy. Brass etageres showcased porcelain figurines and hand-painted dishes. All sizes, shapes, and varieties of prints, from lounging tigers and still lifes with fruit and flowers, to frolicking brown cherubs and portraits of Dr. King, J.F.K., and Jesus filled the walls so completely it was hard to tell what color the room was painted. And a riot of plants trailed, climbed, and flowered, covering the rows of glass shelves that stretched across the wide front window.

"Your mama was still here when we bought this place. Bet she wouldn't hardly recognize it now. Hmm. Seems to me I got a picture." He raised himself up out of the chair and started searching a row of photo albums in a bookcase by the door. "Her and Will and Lester, out back—must be in one a these."

"Goodness, let 'em get some refreshment 'fore you start draggin' out those old things." Lucille appeared with a pitcher, an ice bucket, and four daisy-covered glasses on a tray. She sat on the love seat and poured while her husband kept searching. "How're y'all makin' out at the house?"

"We were wondering about real estate prices in the area. I checked the *Observer*, but I didn't see any listings for Prosper." Celeste sipped her tea and was surprised by the syrupy sweetness.

Come on. Not now. Ronnie knew she should be eager to hear the answer to this question, but she had so many other things to ask the Andersons. She settled into a corner of the sofa. "Did you ever hear Ma sing?"

"Many a time. Couldn't nobody outsing Odella! Leastways not 'round here. And boy, she and Lester sure did sound good together."

"Hambone!"

"I'm only tellin' her what she asked. Should I lie to the child?"

"No, but you could leave a few things for their mother to tell 'em."

"I woulda thought they knew."

"You mean the Lester we met in Pal's? He used to sing with Ma?" Ronnie leaned toward Hambone with anticipation.

"Yes indeedy." He hooked a thumb in his suspenders, looking for a place to start. "Truth is your mama and daddy and Lester were all friends."

Celeste knitted her brows. He sounded like he was talking about some stranger, not her mother.

Lucille pursed her lips and looked over at Hambone.

"Henry too, for a time." Hambone ignored Lucille's warning glance.

"And what happened to Uncle Henry?" Ronnie asked.

"I bet my macaroni and cheese is ready to come out the oven." Odella and what she had and hadn't told her children was territory Lucille didn't want to get into over Sunday dinner. "You two come on and help me put the food on the table. We'll sit down in a minute."

Ronnie looked toward Celeste, but she looked away. "Which way is the bathroom?" Ronnie asked.

"Come on, I'll show you." Lucille led the way, her white vinyl bedroom slippers flapping against her heels. She pointed Ronnie down the hall.

Ronnie chuckled to herself when she eased open the door. The room, a riot of rain forest colors, was small and densely packed like the rest of the house. Nothing was left uncoordinated, uncovered, or unaccessorized. The purple toilet lid and tank covers matched the U-shaped rug in front of the bowl, which coordinated with the half circle in front of the sink, the bathmat on the floor, and the one draped over the side of the tub. A plastic peacock whose colorful plumage hid an extra roll of toilet paper sat on the counter next to a fuschia swan that held tiny soap eggs. Towel bars next to the vanity held guest towels, hand towels, and fingertip towels in alternating purp-turq shades.

Ronnie tossed her purse on the counter, unbuckled her belt. *Hambone and Lucille are so nice—Ma must've missed—* Without warning, a white-hot pain, like a blowtorch flame, shot through her guts, doubled her in half, and dropped her to her knees in one fiery instant. *What the hell is happening?* She panted, quick and shallow, the air caught in a bubble between her throat and a scream she couldn't voice, then she rolled to her side. Ronnie'd had more pain then she cared to acknowledge for more than a year, but she never imagined it could turn into this.

The short fuzzy nap of the lavender rug tickled her nose, but she couldn't lift her head, couldn't move. Her agony pinned her in place. Curled in a fetal ball, fighting for the sliver of consciousness that remained, she prayed that someone would come or for the strength to make them.

The seconds felt endless as beads of sweat popped from her pores, evaporated on her fevered skin, leaving her shivering. *Celeste!* Her brain yelled. *Ma!* Ronnie's eyes darted, searching for a way to signal her distress. The door, with its crocheted knob cover, was little more than arm's length away, but Ronnie couldn't will her leg out straight to kick it. She held her breath and mustered enough energy to squirm and scoot, but she'd barely moved before she lost her breath to a gasp as the fire again seared her insides and brought with it a surge of nausea. She choked back the bitter liquid. *I won't lay here in my own puke.*

Then she spied the shelves above the toilet, crowded with jars of pastel powdered bubble bath, plastic tubs of multicolored, oil-filled beads, ceramic birds and flowers. *I can reach it if I just*—Clenching one fist tight to her belly and pressing her back against the tub for support, she strained to reach out an arm, hooked a finger around one of the support poles. She closed her eyes and pulled. The cabinet toppled into the tub.

In an instant Lucille burst into the bathroom. "Oh, my Lord!" She knelt and dabbed at the sweat on Ronnie's face and neck with her apron. "What happened? Where does it hurt you?" Jumbled fragrances perfumed the air with a sickening sweetness and a film of dusting powder blanketed the debris like early morning frost. Lucille swept away the rubble nearby until she could sit and put Ronnie's head in her lap.

Ronnie looked up at her and the tears seeped from the corners of her eyes. Help had arrived.

The crash brought Hambone right behind Lucille. "What in the—" He stopped in the doorway, not sure if he should come in, or if this was one of those "woman things" and they were going to chase him away.

"Grab one a them hand towels and run some cool water on it!" Lucille barked at her husband, then turned back to Ronnie. "Are you pregnant?"

Ronnie's eyes widened. She gasped in another wave of pain and tried to grunt no. Hambone handed Lucille the wet towel and returned to the doorway.

"It's okay, honey. It's okay." Lucille patted Ronnie's face with the damp terry cloth. "Go get her sister. And call Doc Lomax. Don't stand there, George! Go!"

Celeste arranged the chicken on a platter in the kitchen. She heard the commotion but wasn't up for another of Ronnie's performances. She'd hear the story secondhand soon enough.

"Uh—It's Ronnie." Hambone sounded shaken. "She's sick or somethin'."

"Sick?! Ronnie's not sick!" *What crap has she cooked up now?*

Hambone picked up the phone. "I gotta call the doctor."

"For goodness' sake!" Celeste stomped toward the bathroom. *Still crying wolf.* Just like when they were kids, and she was convinced, even in the face of swollen glands or a fever, that Ronnie was faking some ailment so she could stay home from school and have Della fix her milk tea and raisin toast and make a big fuss. "What is going on?" She reached the open door and saw Ronnie shivering on the floor, her skin ashen and gray, Lucille stroking her head, and she knew Ronnie wasn't faking.

Celeste felt faint and her heart started to pound. "What—" She couldn't find enough words for a sentence. "Ron—" She held on to the door. "We have to . . ."

"Calm down. You can't help her like that," Lucille warned. "Is she allergic to anything?"

Celeste shook her head.

Lucille continued to dab Ronnie's forehead and neck with the damp towel. "Did she eat something that could make her sick like this?"

Celeste shook her head again. "I—I—" Then she shrugged her shoulders. "I—uh—not that I . . ."

"Was she complainin' of anything?"

Celeste saw Ronnie at eight, trying her best to keep up with Celeste and her girlfriends who had decided to walk the six miles to All High Stadium and back one June Saturday, just because. Her parents made her take Ronnie, too. Rankled, Celeste just about wore everybody out, marching them double time. She left Main Street and paraded them the long way, up and down side streets, and while her friends complained, Ronnie never said a word in protest. She just did her little skip-hop-walk and tried to keep pace. When they got back home, Ronnie's heels were blistered, her toes raw and bleeding.

She wouldn't tell me *if something was wrong.* "No." The sadness weighed heavy and the panic rose, just as Ronnie was engulfed by another wave of nausea, one she couldn't control. Celeste watched helplessly, able to respond only to Lucille's orders to moisten another towel while she rolled up the rug, dropped it in the tub, and began to peel Ronnie's soiled clothes off.

Hambone appeared in the doorway, then backed up, allow-ing Ronnie her modesty. "Doc Lomax said take her to the hospital." He spoke from the hall. "I can do it fast as waitin' on the ambulance. She'll meet us there."

"Get me one a your shirts, a robe, anythin' to put around her! We can't take her there half-nekked. And bring a blanket too."

Ronnie's hair, wet from sweat, clung to her face. Lucille smoothed it back and cooed, "There, there, child. It's gon' be fine. You hear me? You gon' be fine." Hambone came back and thrust a red and blue striped bathrobe around the door. "Celeste, help me get her into this."

Lucille lifted Ronnie's torso and held her up long enough for Celeste to maneuver Ronnie's limp arms into the sleeves. She looked so small wrapped in Hambone's generous robe. Ronnie's eyes rolled, searching the room lethargically, until she focused on Celeste.

"Lessie, it hurts." She whispered hoarsely, then her body went rigid, racked by another spike of pain.

Nobody had called her Lessie since she went on a tirade and refused to answer to it when she started high school. Celeste was lost and terrified, and she wanted Everett.

Anson County Hospital was twenty minutes away in Wadesboro. Hambone made it, door to door, in fourteen. Celeste sat beside Hambone, repeating, "What am I gonna do?" over and over. Sitting in the backseat, Ronnie's head cradled in her lap, Lucille's soothing words were meant to calm everybody in the car. She was surprised by Celeste. She'd expected someone with that much gristle to be in complete control. Especially a doctor's wife.

Hambone carried Ronnie into the emergency entrance, where she was loaded onto a gurney and whisked away. Celeste searched Ronnie's purse for her insurance card and came up empty-handed.

She doesn't have any. To Celeste, not having health insurance was as inconceivable as going to the supermarket naked. The panic engulfed her again. "She doesn't have insurance," Celeste whispered to Lucille. "I know she doesn't. What should I do?"

"You should call your mother." Lucille sat next to Celeste in the nearly empty waiting room while Hambone paced. "And *you* should sit 'fore you wear out these people's floor."

"It's better if I keep movin'." Hambone continued his journey to nowhere.

"I—I don't know. She didn't want us to come down here in the first place. It's not like she's going to die—you don't think she's going to die, do you?"

"No, child. She's not gonna die." Lucille hoped. "But she's real sick, and that's one a her babies. She wants to know. I'd want to know if it was one of mine. Wouldn't you?"

"She's not like that—you wouldn't understand . . ."

"Understand what? She's a mother whose child is in the hospital. None of the rest of it matters. She wants to know."

Celeste sat bouncing her knees and wringing her hands. "Maybe it's nothing serious. Why worry her if there's no reason?" She didn't look at Lucille, or at Hambone.

"Are you gon' call her, or am I?" Lucille asked.

14

". . . a woman's rights and a
daughter's guilt."

"We'll be there directly." Hambone sneaked a quick glance at Della, who nodded in response, then he returned his attention to the business of driving in the rain. After so many years, small talk felt awkward and shallow, the old banter and bicker out of place. So, unlike the road to the hospital in Wadesboro, which he knew in his sleep, the road to conversation was one he and Della hadn't traveled together for so long he didn't know the dips and curves, the yield signs and stop lights. The trip was a cautious, quiet hour.

Della stared out the window, impatient with the metronome beat, beat, beat of the wipers, anxious to be there. When she touched down in Charlotte, happy to be on the ground again, even if it *was* shaky, she expected it to look unfamiliar; she had never once been to this airport. But when they left the interstate, the old road she had traveled many times was unrecognizable too. It seemed smoother and wider, and where there had been a few barns and shanties and long stretches of nothing, now there were shopping centers, gas stations, fast-food franchises, a lot like Buffalo, really. Della knew the way, nonetheless. Just like she'd known Hambone as soon as she saw him. He recognized her immediately too. Waistlines had expanded, hair had grayed, time lines had etched their faces, and their shoulders stooped a bit from the weight of responsible lives, but the years hadn't physically changed either one enough to make them strangers. Each saw who the other had once been.

Last night, when the phone rang after midnight, Della put aside her game of solitaire and muted the TV. She had a gruff hello and some choice words on the tip of her tongue for who-ever was so careless about dialing the phone so late at night, because this had to be a wrong number. No one in their right mind would call her at that hour.

"Odella?" Hearing that name, her name, it was like being grabbed by the scruff of her neck and snatched back forty years. Nobody, not even Will, had called her that since they left. "Odella, this is—" Della recognized Lucille's chickadee squeak from the first three words because some things you don't forget, even when you close the door and think you've thrown away the key.

"Odella, ain't no good way to tell you," Lucille began. "We had to take your Ronnie to the hospital." Right then it was like Della's world cleaved and she split in two; one Della dazed, in agonized disbelief, only able to watch as the other became hyper-aware, decisive, methodically doing what needed to be done.

Ronnie's in the hospital.

The only other time Ronnie was in the hospital, Della had been right there too, and she had borne the brunt of the suffer-ing. The first labor pain came while she was eating breakfast, a grilled cheese sandwich on raisin bread with a Kosher dill and orange juice. Della had been scared the first time, but now she knew what it was, so she called Will at work and made arrangements for Celeste to be picked up after school. She fin-ished her sandwich in the car with Will teasing her that this was gonna be one eating child because Della started eating the moment she found out she was pregnant and still hadn't stopped. Della looked up at the clock when she heard the first cry. It was 12:34 P.M. The doctor said it had been almost two days, and she'd lost track of how long she'd been trying to bring this baby into the world. But when her daughter, bald and squirming, grinned at her, then nestled into her chest, Della forgot all the pain. She sang softly, just for the two of them, "You are my sunshine, my only sunshine—"

Will wanted to name her Willa, or Willie Mae, since it didn't look like he was getting a son, but Della knew her name from that first meeting. Veronica. Veronica Lucille.

Della wrote the information Lucille gave her in the margins of a newspaper, struggling to keep her hand steady, to get it all down correctly. She asked if Celeste was all right and Lucille assured her she'd look after both her girls until Della could get there. A hazy fog crept in and cushioned the space around part of her, but the other part steered clear so she could think. This was a call she hadn't gotten before. For Della, it was always sudden, final. Her mother, her father, Will. No opportunity to comfort or be comforted. No farewells. This was different. Ronnie was in the hospital. The fog swirled around Della, made everything soft, but she wouldn't fall. This time it wouldn't hurt. And although she wasn't a religious woman, she knew God wouldn't offer her this chance, then wrench it away.

Ronnie will be all right.

But Della had to go. What else could she do?

Ronnie will be all right.

What else could she think? Not about her vow never to return. Not that her heart and her spirit were broken in Prosper. Not about how fervently she wished Will had dumped the place on Little Pond and saved her from this journey. And certainly not about the fact that from the moment Celeste stormed into her room waving that deed she knew no good would come from it.

So she made her first-ever plane reservations. Climbed the attic stairs to get one of the brand-new suitcases Will ordered for their retirement. He had said, "We gon' go *some*where, Della. Like you used to talk about." Della was calm as she dug in the back of the closet to find the suits and dresses, tags still attached, that Celeste had bought her over the years. She remembered the suit with the fox fur collar she had on the day she left Prosper. How she thought she looked good and that gave her confidence. It didn't matter what she wore to the DMV or to CVS, but this was different. How she looked after a forty-year absence mattered. She didn't leave to do bad. Della packed and puttered until dawn. Then she called her job, notified her neighbors, stopped the paper, set the timer for the lights, and when the taxi came, she locked the door behind her.

"We're here." Hambone slid the car between two others in the lot. The Anson County Hospital building was new, modern, and nothing like the place where they took her father, even though he was already dead. No "colored" section. No separate door.

Della picked at a speck of lint on the sleeve of her navy suit jacket. *Ronnie will be fine.* Hambone heaved himself out of the car, reached in the backseat, and grabbed an umbrella. *Open the door. Get out.* But she sat there gripping the handle. Hambone came around and opened it for her, stood a moment in the rain, not sure whether to extend his hand or wait, but Della couldn't make herself move. Then, clear as day, she felt a shove. She looked over her shoulder, but she knew no one was there. Hambone held the umbrella over her as she finally climbed out. Della looked back in the car, then up at the hospital. And just before the past and the present collided, the fog drifted in, offered its cushion once again, and she moved forward. Her steps were slow but sure. *Ronnie will be fine.* What else could she think?

"Mother." Celeste looked rumpled. Tired. Her features even more pinched than usual. She met Della and Hambone at the elevator. Celeste grabbed both of her mother's hands, and Della was surprised by how cold they were. "She's fine. They're bringing her back from recovery." Her voice wavered a bit and she spoke more to herself than to her mother. The corridor bustled around them. Della, still in Celeste's icy grip, stepped aside to make way for a technician rolling a portable EKG machine. "The operation was—it was only a cyst."

"Let's go down the hall," Hambone said, and they followed, still holding hands, to the waiting room where he, Lucille, and Celeste had camped all night.

Della eased herself into a chair. "What kinda cyst?"

Celeste perched on the edge of the chair next to her. "It had wrapped itself around her ovary. Seems it must've been there a while. But she's fine."

"I been tellin' Odella, your mama, that she was gon' be fine the whole way here." Hambone shoved his hands awkwardly in his pants pockets and looked around. "Lucille? She go down for some coffee?" He took them out again and hooked his thumbs on his suspenders.

"Oh, I'm sorry, I forgot. No. She got a ride home to shower and change. She'll be back soon. And—uh—thanks for going to get Mother," Celeste said.

"No trouble. No trouble at all." Hambone busied himself at the window.

"I called Everett, and he talked to the doctors." After they finished examining Ronnie, the doctors explained her condition and said surgery was the only option at this point. Lucille prompted Celeste to call Everett. She managed to pull herself together long enough to leave urgent, detailed messages on the machine at home and on his service, hoping he hadn't left for Portugal already. He called back within fifteen minutes, got as much information as she could offer before speaking with Dr. Lomax and the surgeon who would perform the operation. Everett told her that any kind of surgery is a serious matter, but that Ronnie's procedure was not unusual and that it sounded like she was in capable hands. He didn't think it was necessary, but he offered to fly down, even if it meant postponing his vacation. She said she'd let him know. Everett was confident, reassuring. And although talking to him made her feel better, there was no reason for him to cancel his vacation. After their last conversation, Celeste wasn't up to facing him yet under the best of circumstances. Definitely not while handling her mother and Ronnie too. Not yet.

"Ma?" Ronnie blinked, trying to focus, trying to be awake. The urge to keep her eyes closed and drift back to sleep, to that dark, quiet cocoon she had just come from, was overwhelming.

"Shh." Della kissed Ronnie's forehead and smoothed the tangled mess of hair. She could never explain how glad she was to see Ronnie, to talk to her, to feel her cool, dry skin beneath her lips, to smell her stale, sour breath. Celeste stood at the foot of the bed, holding on to Ronnie's feet through the sheet and watching a ritual she'd seen dozens of times. If she thought about it hard enough, Celeste could recall countless incidents of Della tending to Ronnie in the same exacting detail she cataloged them in. She expected the old familiar anger—and jealousy, that's what it was, but this time it wasn't there. This time Celeste was grateful as she slipped out of the room and left them alone.

"You didn't have to come." Ronnie's voice was hoarse and scratchy, her lips chapped. *How can I be glad you did and wish you hadn't at the same time?* "I know you didn't want . . ."

"Hush." Della gently patted Ronnie's arm.

Never in her life had Ronnie felt so exhausted. Her arms were weary from holding up the walls. The roof had become too heavy to balance on her head. Her feet were bogged down in the muddy foundation. Ronnie's house of illusion had crumbled. She took a breath and forced her eyes to stay open. "I'm so sorry—I didn't mean to . . ."

"You didn't get sick on purpose, did you?" Della teased and stroked her cheek.

Ronnie shook her head and started to speak. Her mouth was so dry that her lips stuck to her teeth in a grimace. The words were stuck too, but she had to tell her mother. *I can't pretend anymore.*

"Does it hurt you?" Della watched the IV drip.

Yeah. It hurts. Ronnie could see the worry on her mother's face. She tried to lick her lips. "I'm a little sore, but it's okay, they gave me a shot." Della opened a glycerine swab and rubbed it across Ronnie's lips. "Ma—I didn't mean for this to happen." *I really didn't. This isn't the way any of it's supposed to turn out.* Ronnie felt a tiny swell of nausea, the truth bubbling in her throat, and she turned her head away.

"Of course you didn't." Della cupped Ronnie's chin and turned her face back.

"But—you don't understand." Ronnie swallowed hard. "Ma—I—I can't pay for this—for anything—" *There. I said it.* "I don't have any insurance. Haven't for—ever. It's been so hard. I—don't have anything." She held her breath and waited. For so long Ronnie had believed this revelation would stop the world from spinning, but it didn't. That she would be hurled into space, alone and adrift, but she wasn't. Della was still beside her bed. Ronnie blinked again, this time she was awake, but she wanted to slow down the tears that welled up from deep inside.

"I know."

"How? How did you . . ."

"I been guessing you had your struggles for years. Didn't know about the insurance. Celeste told me when I got here. That's plain foolishness, Ronnie. Pride is one thing, actin' stupid is another."

Her mother was right. She had no defense for how stupid she'd been. "I'm so sorry, Ma."

"I'll take care of your bill, so don't lay there worryin' about that now. Or maybe I should let them keep you behind this mess."

"I'll pay you back. I promise I will." And the tears came. "I'm so sorry."

"We'll figure all that out when you're better."

In the flood, Ronnie couldn't distinguish the release from the relief. And while she cried until she couldn't anymore, Della fought back her own tears. *I knew she'd be all right. Thank you, Lord. Thank you.*

When Ronnie was asleep, Della, full of the anger she held onto until she knew Ronnie was safe, went down the hall to find Celeste. *If they had stayed where they belonged, none of this would be happenin'.* She'd give Celeste a piece of her mind first. *That girl never did understand leaving well enough alone.* Ronnie would get her piece when she was feeling better. But the same unseen hand that pushed Della out of Hambone's car, now snatched her, like a choke chain. She pulled up short next to the cart where an attendant stacked lunch trays. And before she turned the corner into the waiting room, she knew he was there. *I don't need this mess now.* She felt the deep, piercing vibration, like a tuning fork, like she hadn't felt in a long, long time. At the airport she had recognized Hambone at first glance, but she didn't have to see Lester to know he was there. She could feel him, just like she used to.

WEDNESDAY, APRIL 17, 1957
PROSPER, NORTH CAROLINA

Odella sat on the old hickory stump at the edge of the pond, hunched over her history book, deep in the throes of the Industrial Revolution. There were six weeks left until the end of the term and then only one more year until graduation. "Come on out, Lester, or whatever you're callin' yourself this week!" She never looked up from her book. Four years of singing with Lester taught her to tune in to him, where he wanted to take a song, where she should go in response. After a while, she discovered that she was pretty much always locked in to whatever frequency he was on whether she wanted to be or not. "I know you're out there. You should quit tryin' to sneak up on me 'cause you ain't never gon' do it."

Lester stepped through the bushes, one hand sagged in his pocket, the other holding a bottle of RC Cola. "I been here at least five minutes, and you didn't know squat." He'd been unable to slip through Odella's radar since the day she first honed in on him. Today was no different.

She slipped a Beechnut wrapper between the pages to mark her place, closed her book, and looked up at him. "You a liar, Lester Wilson. You know well as I do you just got here."

He couldn't figure out how she did it. This time he even took a different path down to the lake, careful not to step on a twig or snap any branches. He moved only when the breeze rustled through the trees. She couldn't have heard him.

"'Sides, I thought you had somewheres to go." She started to swing her long legs, then stopped and tugged the skirt of her plaid cotton dress over her knees. The impulse to show off waged its newly declared battle against her urge to cover herself up. Lately, Lester made her feel that way, and she didn't know why. She wished her mama was around so she could ask, because she could never fix her lips to ask Miz Ethiopia about stuff like that. *Maybe I can ask Lucille.*

"I do. Tonight. But Titus ain't that far." Lester bent down, got himself a glimpse of leg, then picked up a handful of stones.

Since he finished high school, Lester had been looking for a way to get out of Prosper. He even moved back to Charlotte for a little while but reappeared after two months with no explanation. Odella had missed him, a lot, but she'd rather die than admit it. So she just shrugged her shoulders and met him as usual before choir practice and they picked up their rehearsals for the Easter Pageant exactly where they left off.

"Well, with that ol' piece a junk you drivin' it might be farther than you think. You best be startin' early." Odella clasped her book to her chest, crossed her legs at the ankles.

Between Lester's odd jobs around town, helping out anybody who needed an extra hand, what he got from the churches where he sang for special programs and his "gigs" as he called his performances at juke joints around south central North Carolina, he'd managed to buy an old Studebaker that looked like scrap metal, but it ran pretty good.

"Least it's mine." He took a slug of RC, put the bottle on the ground.

"Nobody else fool enough to buy it."

"I worked out my own arrangement of 'Blueberry Hill.'" He ignored her last comment and plunged into the reason he'd tracked her down, because as much as they sparred, he trusted Odella's opinion and her ear. They were used to reworking songs since most of the gospel songs and spirituals they sang were arranged for quartets like the Pilgrim Travelers or the Soul Stirrers, not for duets. "I'm doin' it tonight, but I want you to hear it." He tossed a rock into the pond and it made a soft *blop*. "I'm gon' be outta here soon. Goin' all the way to the top." He punctuated every sentence with a stone's throw. "That's right. I'm gon' get me a record deal, be a star. See the places you been readin' about in them books, then come back and buy me a big piece a land, like the one your daddy got, for when I'm in between tours. You wait and see!"

"Uh-huh." But Odella believed him, believed in him. She was sure that when he left for good he was gonna keep going, like the ripples in the pond, and she wanted to go too.

"You should come with me one a these times." He sat next to her on the stump. "Do some real singin'. With a real live audience."

"I will—Soon." She hated it when Lester was this close to her. It made her tingle, like when they sang harmony, except it wouldn't stop. When they were singing, she could control it better because she had something besides him to concentrate on. But this was like sitting next to him on the front seat of his raggedy car when he gave her a ride home from choir practice. She'd pretend they were boyfriend and girlfriend, like in the movies, or even married like Lucille and Hambone, until she'd remind herself that Lester and Will were like her brothers, the ones she wished she had instead of Henry. Besides, she'd watched the women in church watching Lester. They'd start to twitch in their seats, feeling spirit before he even opened his mouth. Young ones and old alike were particularly fond of Lester's brand of cocoa. He'd gone with Eula Mae Dyson and Marvella Cox, the two prettiest girls at George Washington Carver High School, but he told Odella he wasn't looking to make some girl pregnant, ruin his big chance, and end up stuck in Prosper doing odd jobs for the rest of his life to support a bunch of snaggletooth kids. Said he wanted somebody smart, a girl who wanted more than a man to take care of her.

But Odella didn't fool herself. She had a good shape, all right. Even in her school clothes, she couldn't walk to town and back without commentary, but it wasn't enough. Pretty counted and she came up short. She knew she could make it better. Lucille had shown her how to put on lipstick and powder, but Odella stopped her when she wanted to pluck her eyebrows. She knew her stepmother wouldn't approve; she could feel Miz Ethiopia's withering gaze. She could wash her face before she went home, but she couldn't make the hair grow back, and pencil-drawn lines would only make it worse.

Odella clutched her book tighter. "But right now you know

I can't be goin' to no honky-tonks. I can't even go to Pal's no more." This wasn't a new conversation, and it always turned out the same way. She wanted to see inside of one of those places with dim lights and hip-shaking music, to see if it was as exciting as Lester made it sound. Listening to him talk made her want to sing in front of an audience that wasn't filled with old ladies wearing ugly hats. She wanted to wear a pretty dress or maybe even an evening gown that Lester helped her pick out, to hear people clap for her, to leave Prosper and not look back. But she wished her mother was alive and they still lived in Cadysville, and she knew that couldn't happen either.

Not that she didn't have a voice. Folks raved about Odella Womack's singing. Her father even told her she sounded better than most of the singers he heard on the radio. She wanted to broach the subject of singing someplace other than church with him, but he stayed so busy at the brickyard, and when he came home he mostly ate dinner and went to bed, so she hadn't found the right time. As a matter of fact, Della never saw him look happy anymore, the way he used to when he was with Annie. He never sat on the porch with his wife on his knee or held her hand like Della used to sneak and watch him and Annie do. And the longer she'd been gone, the more distant he seemed from life on Little Pond Road.

Besides, she figured Henry had pretty much put the kibosh on her chances anyway. One Sunday morning, early, when she was coming downstairs with her white choir robe, she heard him telling his mother what a shame it was about the new jukebox in Pal's. Della knew he did it to spite her, probably for getting on so well with Hambone and Lucille, and with *his* friends Will and Lester. And right on cue Miz Ethiopia started her sermon. Said it was a sin and a shame they were playing that music at Pal's. They had been such nice young people, she said. Odell had walked by and said he thought they were smart. It would be good for business. "Give colored folks in Prosper somethin' to do besides sit on the porch complainin'," he had said. But Henry reminded his mother how much time Odella spent with Lucille. Odella wanted to interrupt, but before she could, her stepmother told Odell that she thought it would be a good idea if Odella came straight home after she got her hair done from now on. No more hanging around the beauty parlor or the lunch counter because they would be attracting all kinds of lowlifes with that music. Odella could hear Miz Ethiopia giving her father one of her looks. She'd seen them often enough to know what they sounded like. Her father changed the subject, and that was that.

Odella was crushed. Lucille was only six years older than she was, but in many ways she reminded her of Annie. They didn't look alike unless you counted that neither one was bigger than a minute, but Lucille had the same way of making Odella want to be around her because that's where the fun was. Hambone obviously thought so too. He finished high school two years before Henry did and went into the army, which is where he learned to cook. Just before he was discharged, he wrote and asked her to marry him. Lucille still had the letter. Until Hambone and Lucille, Odella hadn't known any married people who were young and still had fun. And even though she argued with Hambone even more than Lester, Odella loved being around them and their new baby. But when Miz Ethiopia told her not to dawdle after she got her hair done, Odella obeyed even though she wanted to listen to Sonny Till and the Orioles and Johnny Ace on that big Wurlitzer more than anything. Lester and Will had told her that you put a nickel in the slot, and music filled up the whole restaurant and the beauty shop next door, like the Platters were actually there. But she never put herself between her father and his wife, ever. And since Henry cured her of playing the kind of music she wanted to on the piano, she'd lock her door, turn on the radio in her room real low so nobody else could hear, and dream about her and Lester having a hit record.

"Ask Mr. Womack. He knows I'll look out for you." Lester offered Della his bottle of soda.

She took a drink and handed it back to him. "When I'm ready. And *you* can't hardly look after yourself."

"You ready now, and you know you wanna come with me. All the time talkin' 'bout gettin' outta here. Where you gon' go by yourself? You and me, we could make it big." Lester ran his index finger down the length of her forearm and stopped at her wrist.

"Am I gon' hear this song or just hear *about* it?" Odella pushed him off the tree stump and hoped he didn't feel her tremble at his smooth touch.

"Hey." Will ducked under a low hickory branch and stepped into the clearing. "Sorry I ain't had a chance to get cleaned up, Odella, but I jus' now left the job." Will took off his cap, nodded, and brushed red dust from his overalls. He and Henry worked at the brickyard, although Odella suspected Will did most of the working and Henry just tried to boss people around.

"You through slavin' for today?" Lester took another swig of soda.

"Hell yeah. Shoot. I gotta get outta here. My cousin Melvin moved to Buffalo, New York. Got him a good-payin' job at the steel plant. If I'm gon' sweat, might as well be for good money." Will reached in his bib pocket and handed Odella a five-cent Butterfinger. "Here, I brought you this."

"Mmm." Della zipped off the paper, started to take a bite, then looked up at Will. "You want some?"

"No. If I did, I'd a got me one." Will jammed his hands in his overall pockets and shifted his weight from one foot to the other.

"You didn't offer me." Lester folded his arms across his chest.

"You right, I didn't." Della took a big bite and licked her lips in his direction.

"Ain't stud'n' you." Lester sucked his teeth.

"If you still goin' to Titus, I'll go with you, Lester."

"Cool," Lester said. "See! Ol' Will here wasn't goin' tonight, but looks like he changed his mind. Maybe you'll change yours. I been tryin' to get Odella to do one a these gigs with me, but she won't even ask her daddy can she."

"Odella don't need to be doin' no gig. Them kinda joints

ain't no place she should be singin', and if you had any sense
you'd know that."

"Man, you don't get it. We could be big time, me and
Odella."

"She doin' jus' fine like she is. Odella don't . . ."

"When y'all finished decidin' what I need to do with my
life—" Odella stood and put her hands on her hips. "—Maybe
you'll sing the song!" She spoke to Lester, "I ain't got all
night."

Lester cleared his throat, and Will sat on the stump Odella
vacated.

"Ladies and gentlemen, pre-senting Johnny DuPree!!"

"Who?" Odella started to giggle. This was at least the
fourth stage name he'd come up with in the last year, but he
knew for sure Lester Wilson had to go. "Move." She bonked
Will over with her hip and sat beside him on the stump. He
reached his arm around her. His hands felt rough and scratchy.
"Move your ol' heavy arm, Will." She shrugged it off.

"You heard me," he said defiantly. "I like it. Johnny
DuPree. It's the best one yet. It sounds like a star, don't it,
Will?"

"It just sound made-up to me, Lester." Will scraped mud
off his boots with a stick.

"Well, I like it," Della decided. And so it stayed.

The lunch cart was nowhere in sight when Della finally gathered herself. She stood up tall and rounded the corner. Celeste
stood at the far end of the waiting room, talking to him. His
back was to the door. He was still long and lean, like a lickin'
stick, Hambone used to say, like the last time she saw him.
He'd let his hair go back to natural. Della had never liked it
conked.

"Mother. I don't know if—"

Lester turned around.

He told me the truth and I didn't believe him. Della continued walking, trying to keep her steps in a straight line.

"—You know Mr. Wilson. Ronnie and I met him at Pal's.
He came to see if there was anything he could do."

I can do this. "Lester." Della adjusted her purse on her shoulder, then held out her hand.

"Odella." He clasped her hand but didn't shake it. "It's been a long while." Then he let go.

"Yes. It has." Della jammed the hand he released into her jacket pocket and hoped he didn't feel her tremble. His hands were still soft, like they used to be. And he still had that kinda bowlegged stance, with his shoulders leaned back just a touch so you were drawn into him. She thought he'd come pretty close to fitting in one of those narrow, royal blue suits he used to favor, back in the day, with the black shirt and skinny tie and "JD" in rhinestones on the tie tack. Della wasn't surprised by the earring in his ear. Somehow, it suited him.

"I'm glad your daughter will be all right. I was telling Celeste here that if you-all needed anything, to just call. I saw Lucille this morning. She told me what happened—she didn't say you were coming, though."

Oh, she didn't, did she? "Must have slipped her mind."

"That would be a first." Lester flashed her a smile. They both knew Lucille's forgetfulness was no accident, but both Della and Lester let the oversight pass. The situation was strained enough. "You look good, Odella. The years must have been kind to you."

"Umph." Della looked down at her hands. She knew what was in the mirror. There had been a change of seasons since she saw him thirty years ago. She was in her summer then. Ripe, bold, confident, but *wrong*, so very wrong about him. These were the short, cold days of winter. The ones that made summer a haunting memory. But she *was* glad she had worn one of those suits Celeste paid too much money for.

He looked down at his shoes, then back at her. "Uh—sorry to hear about Will."

Will. She wanted to blame him for their standing here like strangers, but that train left the station too many years ago to try and catch it now. She fidgeted with the zipper pull on her bag. "Yes. It was mighty sudden." *I can do this.* "Lester, last time we spoke I said some things . . ."

"No need, Della." He waved her off quietly. "You didn't know." He looked at her for an instant, then looked off.

Celeste scrutinized their faces, hoping for a clue to the meaning of their coded conversation, but she didn't find one.

Lester cleared his throat. He didn't know what else to say. "I better get going. And remember, if y'all need help with anything—" He nodded and left.

Della sank into a chair, tried not to watch him walk away. She'd been up all night, been on an airplane for the first time in her life, her daughter, who had no health insurance, just had an emergency operation. Talking to Lester used up what little juice Della had left.

"What was that about?" Celeste took the seat across from her mother.

"Huh?" Della said, distracted.

"You and Mr. Wilson. It looked to me like . . ."

"And give me one reason I should care what it looks like to you." Della glared at Celeste, then picked up a *Reader's Digest* from the end table next to her.

Celeste looked surprised. "That's a hideous thing to say."

Della flipped through a few pages until she found the middle was stuck together with a wad of gum. "If you hadn't started this—You just had to come down here meddlin' in stuff you don't know nothin' about." She threw the magazine back on the table.

"That's it exactly. There's a whole part of your life I don't know anything about. That you've been keeping some deep dark secret. But whatever it is, that makes it a part of my life! Ronnie's too," she added as an afterthought.

"Look what it got you!" Della knew it wasn't Celeste's fault Ronnie got sick and that it would have happened whether she was in Prosper or New York City. But Celeste, already treading on territory where she had no business, was now in knee-deep and Della had no intention of being pulled into the mire with her. "Ever since you were a little girl, you've been tryin' to fix stuff that wasn't broken. Trying to make everything better. Neater. Prettier. Straighter. And that includes me."

"Mother, your voice." Celeste didn't see this one coming, so she wasn't prepared to duck.

Della got louder. "Well I got news for you, Celeste Anne English, some things are fine the way they are. They don't need no help from you." Della paused to take a breath. "If you wanna fix somethin', try fixin' the mess you made of your marriage."

Celeste was stunned. "You have no idea what you're talking about." How could her mother know her secret? She had no right.

"Don't sit up in my face and lie to me, Celeste. Everett took me out to dinner, to make sure I knew that even if you two divorce I can always count on him like a son. Do you have any idea how I felt, sittin' up there like a simpleton? You'd think my own child would tell me . . ."

"I am not your *child*, Mother!" The words exploded out of Celeste's mouth. "I am a grown woman, and what goes on in my house is my business!" And just like a boomerang, those words came back and dropped in her ear in Ronnie's voice. She had argued with her sister then, told her she had never been a mother and that she was wrong. Of course your child is always your child, she had said, but she was reacting like a mother that day. Right now she was feeling like a daughter.

Della's expression shifted in a rainbow of emotion from outrage to hurt. Without another word, she pushed herself out of the chair, turned her back and walked away, leaving Celeste stranded, between a woman's rights and a daughter's guilt.

15

"... the fan was on, they just weren't
sure when the shit would hit."

On the ride back to the Tree Top after visiting hours, Celeste
and Della chitchatted with Hambone as necessary but didn't
say a word to each other. He had arranged for one of his
kitchen crew to deliver Celeste's rental car back to the motel.
When he asked if they wanted to stop at Pal's for dinner, Celeste said they were too tired.

"Y'all must be hungry." Hambone patted his belly in sym-
pathy. "Least we can stop for some takeout."

"Ah—Sure. Thanks." It suited Celeste fine because her jaw
was too set to actually chew in public.

"Uh-huh. That's fine." Della had had enough of everybody
for one day.

As they entered Prosper proper, the rain that had welcomed
Della home earlier in the day started up again, and she
dropped out of the conversation. Through the misty drizzle,
she eyed the town she hadn't seen in a lifetime. Some that was
old remained, like the town hall and the square, but she found
herself superimposing the old upon the new. She didn't realize how jarring it all was until Hambone parked and she
looked out at the cool blue neon Pal's sign.

"You used to be ..."

"Yep. 'Cross, over there." He pointed. "Lucille still is. The
whole street got renovated in the seventies. They built this
side new, so we took advantage and did some expandin'.
Whatchu want?"

"Somethin' good, Hambone. Somethin' good." Della
gazed across the street. All the storefronts were modern, with

plate-glass windows and professional signs. "You still make barbecue sandwiches?"

"With my sweet and sassy sauce that's so good it makes you lick your fingers and shiver?" Hambone did a little shimmy behind the wheel. "It's one of our specialties. Still make the sauce myself. Should I make that two?"

Celeste nodded.

Della hadn't thought about those sandwiches, piled high with tender shreds of pork shoulder, since she stopped thinking about Prosper. While Hambone went inside, Della looked across shiny wet asphalt at the storefront where the restaurant used to be. Above the new facade was a black awning that read "Lucille's Beauty Studio" in gold script. But what she recalled was the big board that Lucille had carefully lettered PAL'S in green paint with black trim around it that used to decorate the old window. And in the bottom left-hand corner of that window had been a little sign: "Shampoo, Press & Curl, $2.00." The patter of rain on the car even sounded the way it used to on Pal's corrugated tin roof.

SATURDAY, OCTOBER 6, 1956
PROSPER, NORTH CAROLINA

"So where you say you singin' tomorrow afternoon?" Lucille dabbed at the yellow grease on the back of her hand, smoothed a fingerful onto a section of Odella's hair.

"Mount Calvary. Over in Titus. You and Hambone should come. It ain't but about an hour away."

"I just might do that, but you know I have a hard enough time gettin' that man to one church service, much less two!" Lucille pulled the curling iron from the stove, clanked it open and closed a few times, then tested the temperature on the burn-stained white towel folded on the counter.

"Why they like that? Even Papa's that way. Miz Ethiopia makes him go to church. She don't never say nothin' about it in front of me. Well, she don't have much to say to me no way 'less it's to bawl me out, but I know she's the only reason he goes. I mean he likes my singin' and all, but most Sundays I watch him with his head down, sound asleep when Reverend Garland's preachin'." Odella twisted her head slightly and tried to sneak a peek at what Lucille was doing.

"Hold still 'fore I burn you. I'm almos' finished. Then you can look all you want."

"Okay." Odella slumped back in her chair. The cloudy, secondhand glass propped up on the counter didn't offer a clear image under the best conditions. On a rainy, dreary afternoon like this one, the most she would get was an idea of what she looked like.

Lucille clamped the hot iron onto a hunk of Odella's hair. The grease sizzled and tendrils of smoke drifted toward the ceiling. "You'd probably sleep durin' them sermons too, exceptin' you're sittin' up there in the choir where everybody can see you!" She set the iron back beside the burner. "That should do it. I can comb you out, but with all this rain, you might wanna do it yourself tomorrow."

"You can go ahead and style it." Lester was coming by this evening so they could rehearse one more time. "It'll be all right."

Lucille pulled a rat-tailed comb through Odella's hair and began to arrange the curls. "You got a rain scarf?"

"No. I got a new umbrella, though. One of them fancy ones with the ruffles around the outside."

"That's mighty nice, but ain't nothin' like a good rain scarf. Wind'll blow water right under that umbrella." Lucille unfastened the plastic cape around Odella's shoulders, and her tone became very professional. "I always recommend them to my customers."

"That's 'cause you sellin' 'em." Odella couldn't miss the cardboard display leaning against the mirror with the small plastic envelopes stapled to it. "Lucille, you ain't even slick." Odella examined her hairdo. The way Lucille styled it, with a wave in the front that kind of dipped down over one eye, it looked grown up. Just like she wanted it to. She reached in her pocketbook for her change purse and the three dollar bills her father had given her. "But I will take one, just in case."

"Always better to be safe than sorry." Lucille tugged one of the packets free, handed it to Odella, then counted out eighty-five cents change from the metal box on the counter.

"See you tomorrow." Odella thought about putting the scarf on, but she decided it wasn't raining *that* hard and she didn't want to mash her hair down, so she tucked it and her change into her purse, grabbed her umbrella from the corner by the door, and left.

Strolling up Albemarle Avenue, Odella twirled her umbrella like a parasol and wondered if Lester would say her hair looked nice. Lost in a daydream about the two of them singing on a gospel radio show some day, she sailed along toward home.

"Wait up!"

Odella heard him, but she didn't turn around.

"Hey! You hear me! Wait up!"

Henry was the only person in all of Prosper who never, ever called her by name. He just said what he had to *at* her.

Odella quickened her pace. She didn't want any trouble with Henry. She just wanted to get to the house. She took a deep breath when she heard his heavy footfalls splash behind her.

"You can't be hoggin' that whole umbrella for yourself." He poked his head under the rim. "I'll be soaked through 'fore I get home."

Jammed up next to her in his dungaree jacket and overalls, Henry smelled musty, like old cigarettes and not enough soap. She knew he'd been at the brickyard for at least half the day. Where he was coming from now she couldn't say. He didn't hang with Will and Lester much anymore, so they weren't likely to be around to bail her out. "There ain't room under here for two people, Henry!" Odella protested.

"Then it won't be me gettin' wet." Henry grabbed the handle and pulled the umbrella in his direction.

"Stop!" She jerked it back. "I just got my hair done!"

"Like that's gon' make you pretty?" He snatched the umbrella and ran ahead.

"Gimme that back!" Odella caught up and lunged for him,

but he danced out of reach. "Come on, Henry!" She held her purse over her head as she chased him, but she could feel her hair starting to melt, her wave drooping down over her eye.

"You want it so bad—" He skipped backward, holding the umbrella out, then yanking it away when she reached for it. "Beg me."

Mad tears washed Odella's face. She was just glad he couldn't see them in the rain. "Hell with you!" She stopped running and hunted in her purse for the rain scarf.

"Then I guess you'll be a nappy-headed jigaboo singin' in church tomorrow! Let's see how Lester likes that." Henry laughed as he trotted ahead, tossing the umbrella in the air and catching it.

Odella fumbled with the accordion pleats of the plastic scarf, feeling like it was already too late. She covered her head but pulled the ties so tight that one popped off, so she walked the rest of the way home holding it together under her chin, the rain dripping down her sleeve and blowing around her.

When she got to Little Pond she saw that Henry had abandoned the umbrella, opened upside down, under the azalea bush. One of the spokes poked through the fabric. She grabbed it and shuffled up the porch steps, trying to smooth it closed, trying not to make any noise. As mad as she was, she just wanted to get upstairs to her room and assess the damage before crossing Miz Ethiopia's path.

Odella eased open the hall door. The house smelled like burnt fish. Her father's wife never seasoned anything enough and she cooked it to death. Two steps in, Odella squeezed the door shut.

"Is that you, Odella?" Miz Ethiopia called from the kitchen in her prickly voice. "It's about time you got home."

Odella could hear her approaching. She wanted to hide, but the floor didn't open up and swallow her in time.

"It doesn't take that long to get—What in the world?!" Miz Ethiopia's withering look cut Odella to the quick.

Water trickled from Odella's hair and ran down her neck and her temples. Her clothes were wet down to her bra and panties. She knew it was pointless to mount a defense. It was

Saturday evening, which meant her father had already been home, cleaned up, had supper, and was on his way. He wouldn't be back until well past her bedtime, and he was her only prayer of being heard. Henry could do no wrong as far as his mother was concerned. Now, it was simpler to keep quiet and hope this was over soon.

"I don't know why your father wastes his money trying to make you look like something." Miz Ethiopia took Odella by the chin, swiveled her head from side to side, examining her hair. "You had precious little to start with, and you don't have sense enough not to call attention to yourself." She never raised her voice, but her words sliced clean and deep as a switchblade. "And what happened to your umbrella?"

Odella saw Henry sniggling over the upstairs railing, and she knew there was no point broaching that subject. "It got broke."

"It got broke? All by itself? Jumped up and got broke?" Everything about Miz Ethiopia was just so: her shiny black hair cascading over her shoulders, her clothes tailored to fit her trim figure precisely, her wide dark eyes framed by thick lashes and arched brows, her modulated voice and exactly chosen words. Odella would have thought she was pretty if she had been somebody else, and always wondered how her father could have loved a woman as full of life as Annie but stayed with someone as cold and spiteful as his wife. "First of all, the word is *broken,* and secondly *it* didn't break anything, but you obviously did. I guess it was too much to expect you to take care of something nice. . . ."

"All righty. We're ready to roll."

Della was startled when Hambone opened the back door and deposited a small brown shopping bag on the seat, but in the dark she could hide her distress. And right now she could do without any more random recollections, intrusions from the past. On the way to the motel Celeste asked him to stop at the package store too, because she definitely needed some wine. Before Hambone carried Della's suitcase up to Ronnie's room, Celeste handed her mother the key and snorted "'Night." And while she should have been sleeping, Celeste fumed at Everett for daring to think she'd confide their problems to her mother, of all people. She sipped wine from the plastic-wrapped plastic cup in the bathroom and licked her wounds, because she felt like all of them, her mother, her husband, her sister, and her daughter, all of them were in cahoots, determined to chip away at her armor until she sent up the white flag. She just didn't understand what she'd done to deserve this, and it made her resentful and just plain mad. So most of the night the screws continued to turn. By dawn, she had lockjaw.

"What's the matter with you two?" Ronnie was sitting up in bed, a vision in blue striped front and back hospital gowns, when Celeste and Della dragged in the next morning. She'd done her best to smooth her hair with her IV-free hand, but it still looked like week-old roadkill. "Have you been up all night sucking lemons, or am I actually dying and they didn't tell me yet?" She half smiled, hoping she really was only making a joke.

"You're going to be fine. Not that you have sense enough to take care of yourself anyway. Isn't that why you're here?"

"That's enough," Della interrupted. She passed a rugged night as well. Oh, she wasn't bothered about upsetting Celeste. That was routine even when she wasn't trying, but this time Della knew exactly what she was doing. She wanted to rattle Celeste, make her look at herself and what she was about to lose. What kept Della tossing and turning was how the past she had fought so long to keep at bay just jumped up, sank its teeth into her, and apparently had no intentions of letting go. She wasn't a person to go digging up what was done. Della had no interest in history, hers or anybody else's. She buried it and moved on. She thought she had put the last of her yesterdays in the ground last October when Will died. It wasn't that she had the rest of her tomorrows laid out all bright and shiny, but she stopped counting on blue skies a long, long time ago. Truth was, last night, as tired as she was, Della found it hard to sleep in a room full of ghosts, even though she'd brought them along on the trip herself.

"You know, maybe I'll stay over here in the neutral corner. Let you two heavyweights duke it out." Ronnie dropped her head back on the pillow, feeling tired and bruised, as much from the collapse of her world around her ears as from the physical breakdown. It had taken a lot of energy to keep pretending to herself there was nothing wrong when she'd been living on painkillers like they were a food group. She hadn't had time to process the doctor's explanation yet; it involved an ovary, a blocked fallopian tube, and something called a torqued chocolate cyst. Ronnie was just relieved it wasn't as life-threatening as it was painful.

"No. I believe you are the main event, as usual." Celeste re-tucked the hospital corners at the foot of the bed. "And if your mouth is any indication, you must be feeling better."

Ronnie actually looked better too, thanks to some pain-free sleep. Neither Della nor Celeste had seen a scrub-faced Ronnie in recent memory, but without her paint and the "seen it all–done it all" attitude that went with it, she looked surprisingly young. She made Della think of the days before Ronnie started taking her allowance downtown to the cosmetics aisles of W. T. Grant's. Celeste was just plain envious of Ronnie's smooth, unlined skin.

"Since you mentioned it, I'm not exactly ready to run a marathon." Ronnie scooted her hips forward, trying to find a comfortable position in the rigid hospital bed. "But I'll take the way I feel this morning over the last two days anytime. The doctor said I might get out of here tomorrow. I can't do much of anything for a couple of weeks, but at least . . ." Then Ronnie's eyes clouded over and her lip began to quiver. She grabbed a handful of sheet in her fist. This was good news. It was supposed to make her happy. *What a joke*. She looked from her mother to her sister and knew she had no choice but to tell them all of it. That she had nowhere to go when they let her out. And when she didn't show up at the Sable Shades counter Thursday, she most likely wouldn't have a job either.

Maybe it would make Celeste see why it was so important to go through with selling the place, even if it was only her half. Ronnie took a deep breath and decided that if the world didn't end yesterday, it probably wouldn't today either.

"I—I have to tell you the rest."

"Rest of what?" Della asked.

Ronnie laid out the unadulterated truth, no filler, no by-products. She told them about Rake, about her series of slap-dash living arrangements, about how little work she had had over the last several years. On one side of the bed, Celeste listened with a smug "I knew it" expression. On the other, Della's concern changed to a frown, and by the time Ronnie delivered an accounting of the now defunct $10,000 rainy-day fund, Della wore a full-fledged scowl.

"It's a good thing you're layin' in that bed 'cause it's the only thing that keeps me from smackin' you right into tomorrow!" Now Della was mad. "How long have you been livin' like this?" She moved the hospital gown Ronnie used as a robe when the aide got her up to walk this morning and plopped down in the chair next to her bed. Since the other bed in the room was still empty, Celeste hopped up there, primed to watch the fireworks. She knew her dollars and cents were ticking away too but wasn't about to say so.

Ronnie felt like she did when she was ten and got caught trying to change a C to a B on her report card, only a whole lot worse. She cast her eyes down and played with the edge of the waffly yellow blanket. "A while," she said softly.

"Well, that's just plain stupid. I told your father it wasn't as easy or as good as you made it out, but I had no idea you were livin' hand-to-mouth! Why didn't you say somethin' before now!?"

"Ma, it wasn't exactly hand-to-mouth. You make it sound like I was livin' on the street." Ronnie still averted her eyes. She knew she was cornered.

"Close to it," Celeste interjected.

For once Ronnie didn't have a defense or an act prepared. She knew all along her parents would have helped her, if they knew she needed it. She just never wanted them to know, al-

ways planned to pull it off in the final reel, make them proud
as the credits rolled.

"Well, you can come on back home with me. When you're
feelin' better you can find somethin' to do. At least you'll have
a decent roof over your head." Della was so upset she could
hardly talk. She rubbed two tears back up into her temples
with her middle fingers. "They're hiring folks out at UB, all
kinds of jobs. My new neighbor—" now she turned to Celeste, "—the one your sister thinks is raising hoodlums—"
she turned back to Ronnie and continued, "—works on the
Amherst Campus. We can talk to her."

"I don't . . ."

"Sittin' up, are we?" Lucille's squeak interrupted them.
"Mornin', everybody!" She stood in the doorway holding a
bunch of daisies.

I can't go home. But Ronnie smiled at Lucille. "Hi!" *Shit.*
Ronnie knew this conversation with her mother wasn't over,
and she wanted to finish it. She was certainly happy to see Lucille, and grateful to her. Ronnie didn't know how she would
have survived her attack without Lucille's calm, reassuring
presence. But this was family business, as Della would say,
and you don't put family business in the street. All his life,
Will had tried to impress upon Ronnie that dreading a thing
was worse than doing it. Of course, it wasn't a philosophy
Ronnie embraced. Procrastination was her MO. "Never do today what you can put off until it goes away." But she had
found the fatal flaw in that logic. And it was actually feeling
good to tell the truth.

"You look a darn sight better than you did when I saw you
last, Miss Ronnie!" Lucille chirped from where she stood and
looked at Della like she was waiting to be invited in.

"Lucille." It was a statement of identification and recogni-
tion more than a greeting. Della's gesture, not quite a smile,
not quite a nod, was slight enough to be missed if, like Ronnie
and Celeste, you weren't paying attention.

Lucille walked into the room and stood near the foot of
Ronnie's bed. Celeste took the flowers and went to the nurses'
station to get something to put them in.

Della got up. "Thank you for . . ."

"Don't be thankin' me for nothin'. You'd a done the same thing if need be. I'm glad we could help, such as it was." Lucille turned to Della. Her eyes spoke a million things she'd wanted to say through the years. "Umph. Umph. Umph. It's been a long time."

"Yes. It has." Della moved a little closer to Lucille.

Just as she recognized Hambone, and knew Lucille's voice over the phone, Della would have known Lucille anywhere, white hair and all. With Hambone, Della saw who they had been. But now she saw very clearly who she and Lucille had become. If looking at Hambone was a flashback, being face to face with Lucille was like looking in the mirror, and Della knew Lucille saw it too. The years were there. Every one of them, and the problems, joys, fears, solutions, disappointments, questions, triumphs, and answers lined up and marched through the split second that passed between them. They didn't know each other well anymore, but womanhood was a common denominator. What was above the line might be different, but you could always reduce what was below the line to the same number.

"I'm just so sorry it took this to bring you back."

Della didn't know what to say because she was sorry to be back at all, so she just nodded.

They were stuck for words, so they stood awkwardly next to each other, Della's gray head towering above Lucille's white one.

"This is all they had." Celeste returned holding a blue plastic pitcher. She disappeared into the bathroom to fill her makeshift vase.

Lucille took the opportunity to move on. "Now, Miss Ronnie, that hair of yours looks like it's been through the spin cycle." Ronnie had to crack a smile. "Why don't you let me take that mess out?"

"You don't have to do that," Ronnie said.

"Don't you have customers waitin' on you?" Della asked.

"I've come a long way since the old days. I got three other girls in the shop. Course most of the steady clients are mine.

And most of 'em want their hair just like they been wearin' it for the last hundred years." Lucille winked at Della. "Ain't them the same tight curls I put in your head the last time I saw you?" Della humphed and patted her neat, boring gray spirals. Then Lucille turned back to Ronnie. "I guarantee you'll feel a whole lot better." She opened the tote bag she had with her. Lucille had come prepared.

"Uh," Ronnie hesitated. Even when it was looking rough because she couldn't afford to have it done, she hadn't been without a weave or a wig since disco was in diapers. But she had found the mirror under the lid of her tray table this morning. There was no use holding on since the rest of the charade was over. She sighed, "Okay."

Celeste emerged from the bathroom and put the flowers on the windowsill. "Won't that take hours?"

"Maybe a couple," Lucille said. "Why don't y'all go get a bite to eat or do some shoppin'? There's a mall not too far from here. I bet Miss Ronnie would like a real nightgown, wouldn't you? And she won't be wearin' them tight jeans when they let her outta here. Pick her up a few things that are loose—and cool," she added as an afterthought. "And think about what you'll need in the house for a week or so."

"The house?" Celeste realized Lucille was talking about Little Pond. "Oh, no. We're not planning to stay there." She watched her mother to gauge her reaction, but Della's expression didn't change. They had been too busy feuding to discuss what they would do after Ronnie's release from the hospital. Della had been so enraged about Prosper and the house that Celeste wasn't sure she'd come, even if Ronnie *was* sick. It never occurred to Celeste to suggest they stay there, even for a little while.

Ronnie wanted to tell them not to go through all this trouble. She could take care of herself, but nobody was buying that story anymore, not even her. So she counted ceiling tiles above her bed, wishing one of them would open and she could float out of the room.

"Well, she surely don't want to be gettin' on no airplane right away. She's gon' need a few days to recuperate, at least.

Y'all are perfectly welcome to stay with Hambone and me if there's somethin' wrong with the place out there. It'll be tight, but we can manage."

"We can stay right at the Tree Top." But even as Celeste spoke, she realized how difficult it would be caring for Ronnie in that place. And Celeste was fed up with the lumpy bed, the paper-thin walls, the antiseptic smell. She had already made Little Pond feel homey. There were sheets, towels, and new appliances waiting to be used. It wouldn't take much to get the place ready for houseguests, but still—

Lucille shrugged and turned her attention to raising the head of Ronnie's bed to a sitting position. By the time Della and Celeste left, she'd already covered Ronnie and her bed in black plastic capes and laid out her combs and scissors. She unraveled the loose braid Celeste had made in an attempt to control the thicket of hair. "Any longer and somethin' would be burrowin' in here." She opened a plastic garbage bag for the discards.

"That bad, huh?" *Even a ten-year-old can take care of her hair, but I screwed that up too.* She clasped her hands tightly in her lap and held her breath to keep from crying. She had done quite enough of that in the last two days, and she decided it was time to suck it up and move on.

"It's gon' be all right. When I'm finished you'll be lookin' so smart you won't know why you didn't do this a long time ago."

Lucille's touch was gentle as she made sections and secured them with pink clips. Even when she pulled no punches, Ronnie found talking to her comforting too. "Did you used to do Ma's hair?"

"Yeah. I worked on that hard head many a day."

Ronnie snickered. "It was already hard, huh?"

"Yes ma'am. But I suspect more times than not, she was the one hurt by it. Seems to kinda run in the family." Lucille winked.

"Lucille's right, you know. It would be easier and more pleasant to stay at the house." Celeste tested the waters as they wandered around the lingerie department at Belk's. "I've been straightening up some since we've been here. It wouldn't take much more . . ."

"Medium should fit her all right, don't you think?" Della kept sifting through a mound of nighties, purposely sidestepping Celeste's remark.

"That's what I buy for Niki." Celeste held up a white eyelet gown. "How about this?"

"Ronnie is recuperatin', not gettin' married." Della headed off toward three racks marked "Take 40% off." "That's what we should get." She pointed to a display of jelly bean–colored jumbo cotton T-shirts.

"But they're so loud."

"They're bright and cheery."

It was the usual point, counterpoint.

"You know she won't be in any shape to buckle a seat belt around her belly for at least a week." Celeste decided to try another approach. "And as you know, that motel is dismal."

Della knew she was going to have to address the issue sooner or later, but her plate was brimming, her mouth was full, and going to the house was more than she could swallow at the moment. She watched Celeste run her hand over a lacy black number with spaghetti straps. "Are you seein' another man?"

"What!?"

"Well that's sure not for your sister, and if Everett is leavin' you, why else would you want a fancy nightgown?"

"For goodness' sakes!" Celeste dropped the nightgown.

"You wouldn't be the first woman who thought the grass was greener . . ."

"I was just *looking*, Mother."

Della wanted to ask more questions, to understand what was going on. She was truly shocked when Everett told her about the breakup. Celeste wasn't the easiest person to get on with, but they seemed to have had that figured out. Except Celeste was acting like it wasn't a big deal. Della had seen her child more upset about picking up the wrong brand of detergent than she appeared to be about the demise of her mar-

riage, but there wasn't anything more to say about it. Della
knew Celeste was as stubborn as they come, and she was
likely to cut her tongue out before she admitted there was
something wrong that she couldn't handle. So Della sucked
her teeth and went in search of cotton drawers, because she
had seen those silly thong things Ronnie wore, and for the life
of her she didn't know how they could be comfortable any
time. She knew they wouldn't be now. She glanced up from
the display, caught Celeste's reflection in the mirror on the
other side of the department. *She looks more like her now than
she ever did.* But Celeste was nothing like Annie, not the way
Della remembered her. Since she'd come back to Prosper,
some old memory or "what if?" seemed to leap out at every
corner she turned. She watched Celeste, unnoticed, a little
while longer and thought about the women on her job who
sounded devastated when they talked about getting older and
finding they looked like their mothers, frown lines and all. It
seemed like a privilege to Della. She could still see her father
in her face, especially when she was tired, but she could never
mistake herself for Annie, not even in a fun house mirror.
Annie hadn't lived long enough to look old, to be a yardstick
for Della to measure herself by, but here was Celeste, looking
like her grandmother might have looked if—like someone
Della never brought herself to mention to her. She knew it was
wrong, but she held those memories close, afraid there wasn't
enough to share.

Finally Celeste felt Della's stare. "You can ignore me if
you want to," she said when she joined her mother. "You can
change the subject. You can walk away. But it doesn't change
the fact we have to go somewhere when Ronnie gets out of the
hospital."

"Yes, I guess we do," Della replied. She carried her armful
of panties and nightshirts to the cash register and didn't say
any more about it.

They picked up some baggy shorts and two cotton sun-
dresses in sportswear, and grabbed canvas sneakers from the
shoe department on their way out. When they arrived back at
the hospital, shopping bags in hand, Ronnie was sitting up in

bed, dozing. Her store-bought mane was gone. Her own, close-cropped hair, au naturel, remained. The after was so different from the before that Celeste gasped.

Ronnie's eyes fluttered open. She reached her hand up to her head, and although she didn't say a word, her tentative expression said, "What do you think?"

"This sure is a lot better than that other." Della dropped her packages on the empty bed. "All that hair hanging down to your behind . . ."

"Which nobody thought was yours, anyway. And I know it cost a fortune." Celeste added her load to her mother's.

"Will somebody tell me if I need to put a bag over my head?!"

Della leaned back and gave Ronnie a good once-over. *Looks like my bald-headed baby.* She brushed hair clippings off her cheek. "You look right cute. Lucille did a real nice job, but she always did have the gift."

Celeste turned her attention to the cut glass vase of freesia and irises on Ronnie's bedside table. "Where did all these flowers come from?" She lightly lifted the fall of one of the deep purple irises.

"Not bad, huh?" Ronnie smiled coyly.

Celeste parked her hand on her hip and waited for an answer.

"They're from Everett."

"And those?" Celeste pointed to the wicker basket of miniature roses on the windowsill next to Lucille's daisies.

"From Doug Pryce."

"He must really want to make this sale." Celeste went over to the window and tapped the rim of the wicker basket that held the roses. "How in the world did he find out?"

Ronnie shrugged.

"A bed full of shoppin' bags and a room full of flowers." Della paused a second. "Not bad at all, for a girl with dust in her pockets, and no pot to . . ."

"Thank you, Ma." Ronnie knew she wasn't just teasing. "So what's in the bags?"

Della only half watched the fashion show. Her mind was on Little Pond.

"I didn't know they still made bloomers." Ronnie held up a pair of sensible panties.

"Did the nurse say for sure you'd be released tomorrow?"

Ronnie sobered up before the next exhale. She knew they hadn't finished their conversation about her unsettled future. "As long as my incision passes inspection and I don't have a fever."

"Celeste, what do we need to do so we can stay out at the house?" You could tell by the gruff edge in Della's voice that this was a bitter pill, but she was choking it down.

What brought this on? "Not much. There are sheets and towels there. I'd run them through the wash, just to freshen them up, but I can do that tonight—or tomorrow." Celeste said it as matter-of-factly as she could.

"Then that's where we'll stay."

Ronnie and Celeste exchanged a glance that said the fan was on, they just weren't sure when the shit would hit.

16

"There were no good old
days, only now."

"You're drivin' too fast," Della complained as Celeste passed
one slow-moving car, then another.

Celeste checked the speedometer. "I'm actually five miles
below the speed limit, Mother."

"Well, you're goin' faster than those cars back there." And
Della was in no hurry to arrive.

"They obviously have nothing but time, but we need to get
there before the phone company or we'll have to reschedule."
Hambone had taken care of having the phone service con-
nected on a temporary basis.

"It doesn't feel too fast to me." Ronnie pressed a pillow
against her belly to keep it steady from the road dips and
bumps. She didn't usually feel compelled to stick up for Celeste, but Della had been steady on both of their cases all
morning. At the hospital she groused at Ronnie for not being
packed when they got there. Ronnie had had a rough night.
Her incision throbbed, she didn't sleep because she couldn't
find a comfortable position, but she wouldn't complain or ask
for medication, afraid that if she did, they might keep her another day, which would only add to her bill, which she
couldn't pay anyway. Fighting back tears as Della lit into her,
she tried to explain that it had taken her two hours to get
showered and dressed and that she couldn't move any faster,
but it didn't get her any slack.

"Was I talkin' to you?" Della barked.

No, you were biting my head off. Ronnie flipped the radio
on to distract her from the barrage.

"And I'm not payin' for no speedin' ticket." Della paused a

moment, and Ronnie and Celeste both prayed they had heard the end of her diatribe. "Used to put you in jail for that down here, if you were colored."

"I've been driving since I was sixteen and I've never had a ticket."

"There's always a first." Della hugged herself and exaggerated a shiver. "Are you trying to freeze us to death?" It was only middling cold in the car, and she knew she was being impossible, but she couldn't help it and she didn't care. This was the last place on earth she wanted to be, and the closer they got to Little Pond, the more she felt trapped and lashed out. It was their fault she was here, and they were getting Will's share too. This wasn't easy for her, and it wasn't going to be for them, either. "The rest of us don't wanna have icicles just 'cause you're havin' hot flashes."

"I'm having no such thing."

"Don't you think I've seen you sweatin' like a steelworker when it's two degrees outside? If I had a nickel for every time in the last year I heard you say, 'Is it hot in here?' I'd be a rich woman. I went through the change too, you know."

"That's ridiculous." They hadn't had one of these talks since the day Celeste's sixth-grade class witnessed the arrival of her womanhood. Della was called to pick Celeste up from the nurse's office where she had cried until she made herself sick because she had no idea what was going on. By the time Della stumbled through her rendition of the facts of life, Celeste was mortified. She felt just about that embarrassed now. "I'm not old enough."

"I was there when you were born. I know how old you are," Della jabbed from the backseat.

I cannot be old enough . . . This was not a topic Celeste cared to debate, so she turned the AC down and kept her eyes on the road.

"*This is Johnny DuPree, and even when ya don't know I'm lookin', I got my eye on ya.*" The DJ's rap filled the moment of silence.

"Turn that mess off! I can't hear myself think!" *And I can't listen to no Johnny DuPree right now!*

Celeste beat Ronnie to the off button. Right now her mother was more annoying than fingernails on a chalkboard.

"Aren't you gonna stop for groceries?" Della asked.

"We have some. I'll go out later for more. We can't afford to miss the phone company."

"You act like you're expectin' a call," Della said pointedly. "Who would that be from?"

"I won't discuss this, Mother," Celeste hissed.

"Don't forget the drugstore. We have those prescriptions to fill," Della snapped.

Great. Something else I can't pay for. Ronnie squirmed in her seat, screwed up her mouth, but she stayed quiet, grateful that, for the moment, nobody was picking on her.

"I haven't forgotten. There's a pharmacy in Prosper. I'll go after we get her settled."

And mercifully, as the highway turned into Albemarle Road, Della settled down too. Or at least she got quiet. She closed her eyes and swallowed hard to keep down the memories of her first reluctant car ride to Prosper. She wasn't prepared yet to see anybody else she might know or who might remember her. There was no point in wasting energy on minor haints when she knew the big ones were waiting.

The slow crunch of gravel signaled their arrival, but Della's eyes stayed closed. She'd spent a good part of the time since Lucille's phone call trying to knit herself back together, but once again she was on the verge of splitting in two. The sad little girl who arrived at this house so long ago joined with the scared, confused young woman who left and swore she'd never come back, both begging Della to stay in the car. But the mother of two grown women, grandmother of another, that side pushed her to do what had to be done.

"I think she's asleep," Celeste whispered.

"I'm not sleepin'." *One, two . . .* Della opened her eyes. She'd seen the house many times in her mind's eye, but in the dappled sunlight it wasn't nearly as oppressive as she recalled. The house looked older, a little run-down, not as imposing as it used to be. *Like me, I guess.*

Della pushed open the car door. *Smells the same.* The

twang of the red earth beneath her feet, the dank, mossy musk of the lake on the other side of the woods, they were still familiar perfume. *Just keep it together.* She heard a low grunt overhead, looked up and saw the big dark bird circling way above them. "Snakebirds," she muttered to herself. "*They got long, skinny necks and they look like snakes when they in the water, but they ain't no such a thing as a bird that turn into snakes,*" Will had told her.

"*You smart and Henry's a liar,*" Lester had added. "*He's jus' sayin' that to scare you.*" That was the day they became her friends, and Henry never forgave her for that.

"You say something, Mother?" Celeste asked.

"Never mind." Della shook free of the memory. "Come on, Ron. If you scoot over you can grab onto our arms and pull yourself up when you're ready," Della instructed.

"I can't wait to get this over with." Ronnie held her pillow tight as Celeste helped ease her legs out of the car. She took a breath and slowly inched over until her butt was perched on the edge of the seat. *If it hurt this bad gettin' out of the car, I'll be wrecked by the time I get upstairs.* But she managed to pull onto her feet.

"Does it hurt?" Della asked. She'd never had an operation. Only been in the hospital when Celeste and Ronnie were born, and that hurt, but when it was over it was gone. She didn't know what a six-inch slice across the bottom of your belly felt like.

"You can do it. Just take one step at a time," Celeste encouraged.

One step at a time. It's just a house. Della held her arm straight and strong for Ronnie. Her upper lip she kept stiff for herself. Before they got to the steps, Hambone's big, blue Caddy pulled up the drive, kicking up a rusty dusty cloud.

Celeste, Ronnie, and Della's one, two, three stairstep heads turned when they heard the car. Hambone hustled over to them.

"Lucille was out here earlier and left y'all some food. But I thought you could use a hand gettin' Ronnie in the house. She ain't supposed to be takin' no stairs for a while. I had my gallbladder out, couple a years back," Hambone said, verifying his knowledge of approved post-surgical activities. "I'll have her upstairs in no time flat." Before anybody could object, he scooped Ronnie into his arms and carried her up the walk to the front door. Celeste scurried to open it for them, then headed back to the car.

"I'd like a minute down here before we go up, if that's okay."

"Whatever you want, little lady." He deposited her on the settee by the window. "This good?"

Ronnie nodded.

Hambone found Della outside on a wicker porch chair. "Looks pretty near the same, don't it?"

"I guess it does. It's been an awful long time, Hambone." Although Della could still picture every nook of that house.

"I know what you mean. The phone people been here?" he asked.

"You got here same time we did, so how would I know?" Della rolled her eyes at him.

"Now that sounds like the Odella Womack I used to know." Hambone grinned and hooked his thumbs around his suspenders.

Celeste stumbled up the steps, three purses on her shoulder and lugging Ronnie's duffel bag. "If it wasn't so damn hot—" She caught herself before she finished, but not before Della looked at her and nodded.

"You shouldn't be totin' that." He grabbed the suitcase from her. "Let me get the rest of 'em, while your sister's taking a rest."

"You an old man, Hambone. How you gon' manage the suitcases *and* have the strength to carry Ronnie?"

"Yep. Soundin' more and more like ol' Odella every minute." Hambone laughed. "And for your information, I carry fifty-pound sacks of potatoes and flour better than them young boys who work for me, so my mind tells me I can carry Ronnie just fine."

"And if you were half as smart as you are fat, your mind would tell you somethin' worth knowin'."

"Didn't I always say you should never trust a skinny cook?" Hambone stood in profile, showing off his girth.

"All right. Be my guest. Carry all you want. Just don't be complainin' to Lucille about your aches and pains tomorrow."

Hambone waved away her warning and helped Celeste unload the car, then followed her inside for iced tea.

Della knew she couldn't stay on the porch forever. She braced her hands on the chair arms. *One, two, three . . .* stood and walked inside.

It really did look like her father would stride out of his study any minute. Like Miz Ethiopia would call out from the kitchen, "Odella? That you?" Like Henry would come sneaking up on her from some unsuspected corner. But they were all dead now. And never in a million years did Della think Miz Ethiopia would leave this house to her. Della ran her hand over the mahogany hall table, listened to Hambone joshing with Celeste and Ronnie in the living room.

Della walked to the back of the house, into the kitchen. The appliances were new, but the cabinets were the ones she remembered. She stood at the window, her eyes locked on what was left of the chicken coop.

THURSDAY, MAY 9, 1957
PROSPER, NORTH CAROLINA

"Don't you peck me, you mean ol' biddy," Odella warned as she sidled up to the brooding pen, her water bucket still in hand. She'd already seen to the other chickens outside, so the frenetic chatter and wing flapping had simmered down. Only thing left was to check on this hen who'd been sitting inside on her clutch of eggs for weeks. Then she could head down to the pond to study. And to see if Lester or Will showed up.

"Let me see if you got any peeps yet and I'll leave you alone." Cautiously she slid her hand along the side of the nest. "Just let me—Ow!!" The hen squawked and went for her arm. "Stupid bird! Look what you did!" She examined the damage.

"Whatchu doin' in there?!" Henry straddled the doorway, a silhouette against the bright sun at his back.

Odella jumped and overturned the bucket, splashing water on her legs and feet. "See what you made me do!" She wiped at her legs with the tail of her dress. "Don't sneak up on me that way!" The henhouse was a place she didn't expect to run into Henry. The only point Odella had in her favor with him was that since her arrival in Prosper, he didn't have to tend the chickens anymore. Only thing he still did was wring their necks when his mother needed one for dinner. It had taken Odella a long time to get used to the ornery birds and their stinky droppings, but once she got the hang of it she could finish her job by rote. So she'd scatter feed and replay her old *Life* magazine daydreams of beautiful, far-off places. Or conjure up something about Lester, like how giddy she felt the day he let her take the first sip out of his bottle of RC. "And any fool can see what I'm doin'!"

"Who you callin' fool?"

"It's just a sayin'." Odella was sure Henry was the most annoying person who ever drew breath. "Why are you here?"

"This is my house. I can be any damn where I want!" Henry was moody in general, and the worse his grades got the harder his father rode him. Last night Odell reamed him out all through dinner, called him a dunce. Odella was certain she had turned her head before she smirked.

"You must be talkin' about this chicken coop 'cause everythin' else is Papa's." Normally she avoided confrontations with Henry. She didn't even like him to look at her because she never knew which of his two faces would be showing, and any little thing could set him off, but right now her feet were squishing in her shoes, her arm was bleeding, and she was going to have to clean up the wet straw and put down fresh before she headed for the pond.

"You shut up! Ain't none of it yours and it never will be!" Henry bellowed.

"I don't want it no way!" Odella bent down to pick up her bucket, and Henry was on her before she could straighten up.

"Think you better than me, don't you?!" He grabbed her arm and flung her into the back wall. "Callin' me a fool!"

The impact shook the narrow shed and knocked the breath out of her. "Stop it . . ."

Before she could move he grabbed her shoulders and slammed her into the wall again. "You thought it was funny last night, what Pa said!" Henry hurled himself against her, full force. He was smaller than Odella, but rage amplified his power.

"No!" Too terrified to feel the pain, Odella pushed and squirmed, trying to get free. He'd shoved her around before, but never like this.

"I saw you grinnin'!" Sweat ran down his temples. "Like I'm some kinda joke!" He snatched her wrists, crushed them against her chest. "I'll tell you what's funny! Him sayin' I should be more like you! I should be like his damn bastard!"

"Let go a me, Henry! That's not what he meant!" She wriggled against him, stomping, kicking.

"Didn't give me his name, but you got it!"

"Mama named me! I swear!"

Then Henry got still and his eyes flashed cold. "Your mama?! You stand here and talk to me about your mama?! I'm a show you what he did to your mama!" He grasped both her wrists in one hand and started pawing at her skirt.

"Stop it!" Odella exploded in a panicked fury. She slid herself down the wall, felt splinters in her back from the rough wood. When she got near his shoulder she bit down as hard as she could, but her mouth flew open when he punched her in the gut.

"Bite me, you bitch!" Henry hurled her facedown in the wet hay and chicken shit, twisted her arms behind her back, straddled her legs.

"Don't, Henry! Please!" Odella screamed as he pulled her white cotton panties down to her knees and stretched out on her back, fumbling with his pants, grunting and wheezing.

Odella bucked and rolled to throw him off her, but she couldn't. "Henry, no!" The scream scraped her throat.

He planted his knee between her thighs to pry them apart.

"Nigga, I'll kill you!" In one motion Will lifted Henry and heaved him through the doorway. The chickens fluttered and cackled wildly. Henry tried to scramble to his feet and run, but Will tackled him and started to pound him with leaden fists.

Odella got to her feet, fixed her clothes as best she could, and ran outside. Henry was limp, unable to fight back. She could see blood running from his nose and mouth. Will's face was like stone as he whaled away on him. "Don't kill him, Will!" She grabbed at his arms. "Please don't kill him!"

"Look what he did to you!" Will's voice cracked.

Odella stood before him, trembling, coated in filth. "I'm all right! He didn't do nothin'! You stopped him, Will!" She started to cry. "Please, Will! I don't want you to get in trouble."

"Awright, Odella." Will stood, dug in his pocket for his handkerchief, and handed it to her, keeping his eyes averted. He couldn't look at her that way. "Awright."

Henry got up off the ground, staggered toward the house.

Odella wiped at her tears. "And please don't tell Papa! I gotta live here. It'll only make things worse." She looked in his eyes. "Promise."

"Awright," Will sighed.

Della hurried out of the kitchen, toward the voices in the living room, but she hung back in the hall a moment to collect herself. She didn't notice Ronnie stretched out on a settee by the window.

Ronnie watched as Della folded her arms across her chest, rubbed her shoulders as if to give herself a hug. She tried to place the look on her mother's face. Ronnie had seen anger before, and she was familiar with that sadness that shaded Della's face without warning or explanation, but this was different. Della looked shaken.

What's it like for Ma, being here? Ronnie never knew her mother to relive the past. Della's philosophy had always been there were no good old days, only now. She'd been so angry about the house, but here she was walking around in it, in her past. All of a sudden Ronnie found herself trying to imagine

Della sitting on the bench with her blue composition book, writing her music, and she wondered what on earth had made her leave it all behind. Ronnie liked the feeling of singing, whether it was to herself under the covers or to a crowd. The thought of walking away from something you love made her sad for her mother, and for herself because that looked exactly like the corner she'd painted herself into.

"You 'bout ready to head upstairs, Missy?"

Hambone snatched Della out of her reverie. She felt flustered when she caught Ronnie's eye and realized she'd been watching, but Hambone was there to defuse the moment. "Look a here, George Anderson . . ."

"Ooohwee, using my whole name, like I'm in trouble or somethin'."

"I'm tryin' to keep your sorry self outta trouble. You don't have to carry her . . ."

"Woman, hush and move out my way."

Hambone lifted Ronnie and walked toward the stairs. Celeste was two steps ahead, leading the way. "We can put her in the master bedroom. It's the biggest one," Celeste said over her shoulder.

Della looked up the stairs after them, her eyes purposefully avoiding the railing and the missing spindles.

"I told them if y'all need anythin' to call me." Hambone, wiping his brow with a big white handkerchief, trudged back down the steps. "You awright?"

Della leaned against the front door, looking out into the yard, still catching her breath. "Yeah—I'm fine. I should be askin' you that." Della jugged with Hambone awhile, and before he left he promised to stop by to check on them.

Finally Della stoked up a head of steam big enough to carry her upstairs and into the bedroom that Odell and his wife had shared. This room had no strong memories. She was rarely in it. When she got there, Ronnie was propped against the pillows in the four-poster while Celeste busied herself unpacking. Della thought Ronnie still looked slightly gray against her fuchsia sleep shirt and the white sheets.

"Celeste, you need to go fill those prescriptions now,

'cause it'll be time for Ronnie to take 'em. And if you wait much longer you'll be complainin' about how hot it is."

"I'll go in a minute. I want to get these things organized." Celeste hung a sundress in the closet.

"Well then, gimme the keys and I'll go!" Della paced at the foot of the bed.

"I said I'd go as soon as I'm finished, Mother! Will you give me a chance to breathe?!"

They picked at each other, back and forth, every subject a cause for disagreement. Ronnie tried to ignore them, but she felt their bickering land like body blows, wearing her down, punishing her for causing this mess in the first place. Finally she couldn't take another word.

"I'm sorry, okay!" Celeste and Della whirled around to face her. The yelling hurt, so Ronnie pressed down with her pillow, but she had to say this. "You're both mad. I know it's my fault! But believe me, I wish this never happened!" Tears streamed down her cheeks. "Ma, I'm sorry you had to come back to Prosper. I know you don't want to be here. I don't know why, and you won't tell anybody, but I'm grateful you came. I said I'm gonna pay you back, and it may take a while, but I swear I will!" She swallowed some air, wiped her nose with the back of her hand. Celeste handed her a tissue. "And I know that as far as you're concerned, sister dear, I've always been a pain in the behind, and you're just dying to say, 'See! I told you she wasn't ever going to be an actress.' So say it!" Ronnie blew her nose and looked at Celeste for a comment.

Celeste gave her another tissue. "Ronnie, I never . . ."

"Yes you did. And I know you're enjoying this! And yes, as you've already figured out, I've been hassling you to sell this place because I need the money—again. Man, have I done some stupid stuff in my life! Big time! So I can't say jack. I'm probably getting more than I deserve, but I screwed up enough to know I have to do better." She flopped her head back on the pillow and closed her eyes. "I wish we could be in the same room together for more than two minutes without somebody fighting. You do the same thing with Niki, Celeste. You never give anybody a break!" Ronnie gulped for a breath.

"When we were little, I used to try so hard to be good enough to be your little sister. You did everything right—you were so neat and tiny—and perfect. I wanted to be like you, but I couldn't ever be that—together, no matter how hard I tried. I couldn't even get you to like me." Ronnie talked and cried. Della and Celeste stood there not knowing what to say. "And I always wished I could make you happy, Ma." Ronnie's voice got quieter. "At least get you to say you were proud of me. Daddy did, but I couldn't get it out of you, not even when I had that stupid billboard and everybody you knew talked about it. I heard you brag to other people, but you never said a word to me." By now she was talking mostly to herself. "Guess proud is not gonna happen right now." She trailed off. Limp. Spent.

In a few minutes Ronnie was asleep, leaving Celeste and Della wounded and on their own.

17

"The footprints are always behind you."

"You want some lemonade?" Celeste called from the bottom of the stairs.

"Yeah. Thanks. That would be great." Ronnie sat in the rocking chair by the window, still hugging her pillow and gazing out over the backyard to where she knew the lake was. *Wish I could see past the trees.* She'd only been up an hour, but already she wanted to get back in bed. *Is this ever gonna stop?* Sitting, standing, walking to the bathroom, all things she had taken for granted a week ago, now involved planning, and once she executed them her energy was sapped.

Two days after the Event, as Ronnie called it, mother and daughters spoke only to exchange necessary pleasantries. It was like she'd tossed a rotten egg into the room. The odor was rank and thick, and it lingered, but they cleaned it up quickly and went out of their way to act like they didn't smell it. They tiptoed around the remaining eggshells scattered throughout the house, afraid to shatter the fragile peace. She wondered if they actually thought she was a little wacko after her outburst, but she didn't care. For a little while Ronnie had enjoyed the dubious truce.

Celeste stayed busy, somehow managing to fill her to-do list. She ran errands, like getting oscillating fans for the bedrooms and a box window fan for the kitchen. She washed and ironed all the tablecloths and napkins from her neat piles, polished furniture and washed floors, like she was planning to take up residence, and she prepared meals, such as they were, mostly sandwiches, broiled chicken, salads, and vats of lemonade, something she rarely made at home. At scheduled intervals she'd peek in Ronnie's room from the hallway to ask, in an unnaturally cheerful voice, if she was hungry or needed anything.

Della was in charge of dispensing pills and rebandaging Ronnie's incision. Ronnie felt kind of strange, lifting up her dress, rolling down her panties, and letting her mother tend to her wound. It was harder than letting a complete stranger mess around down there. She had grilled the nurse about how prominent her scar would be and whether she'd always have the belly pooch that hung over it now, but the hands-on intimacy with her mother made her squeamish. Never mind they were both women with the same equipment package. Della certainly hadn't been in that region since Ronnie had grown short and curlies, so they carefully avoided each other's eyes and got through it as quickly as possible. And aside from her nursing duties Della mostly stayed in the kitchen, a room where she hadn't spent much time back then. She had asked Miz Ethiopia a few times if she needed help with the cooking, but the answer was always no. After a while Della didn't bring it up anymore; she stayed out of her father's wife's kitchen. Now it was her sanctuary, the place where she drank her coffee, worked her puzzles, played solitaire, and watched her TV shows right on schedule. If she didn't look too far to the left or right, she could pretend she was still at home in Buffalo, and maybe she could get away before the place had a chance to settle on her clothes, seep into her pores.

Ronnie rocked forward, rested her hands on the windowsill, and pushed herself out of the chair. She reached behind her, grabbed the pillow, and clutched it to her abdomen as she shuffled across the room. She knew the cease-fire couldn't last, but for the first time since she was a teenager they were stuck at close range, under the same roof. They'd be there at least another week, and Will wasn't around to keep them civil. Right now the most important thing to Ronnie was that the fussing was on hiatus, because she had finally lost the game of procrastination she'd been playing, big time, and she had to get her head together. For once in her life she wasn't looking for distractions.

When Celeste had asked, ever so nicely, if Ronnie would

like the one TV in the house brought up to her room, she surprised herself by saying no. TV was in your face, and after seventeen years in New York, she'd had quite enough daily assaults. She was surprised by how soothing she found the birdsong that wakened her before first light. This was definitely a calmer start to her day than the growl and grind of the 4:00 A.M. garbage trucks that had become her routine. Instead of the constant thunder of traffic, howling horns, wailing sirens, and exhaust fumes with taste and texture, now trees rustled outside her window and softly scented the room with pine. There was no urgency to these sounds and smells. They played backup to her thoughts, although at a much slower tempo than the driving beat she'd gotten used to. When she wanted entertainment, she played the radio, alternating between an oldies station out of Charlotte and WDLA. They provided a rhythm for the blues that came and went as she dealt endless hands of solitaire and pondered her future.

It wasn't that she was that sad. In fact, physically Ronnie felt better than she had in a long time. Fear had kept her from checking out the nagging, intermittent pain in her belly for more than a year. Fear that it was something terrible. Fear that even if it wasn't fatal, she didn't have insurance and couldn't pay for whatever it was.

This morning she'd been thinking about patching things up with her mother and Celeste. She'd had no idea she was about to burst at the emotional seams until the tirade started and she couldn't stop. Living on a financial precipice had kept the pressure on, but she was used to that. The first thread had popped with the Rake episode. The house in Prosper seemed to be the stitch in time, but Celeste's refusal to sell started the seam splitting again. Ronnie barely managed to hold on, hoping her sister was just being difficult and would eventually change her mind. By the time she found herself writhing on Lucille and Hambone's bathroom floor, it had all started to unravel, and listening to her mother and sister fight had finally torn her to shreds. The Event provided a release she didn't know she needed, but at this point, she didn't have the strength to keep up appearances. *My stuff is pretty much out there any ol' way,* so *"let's pretend" is over.* She needed it real if she was ever going to find her way out of the mess she'd made. *And I guess the first step is getting them to speak to me again.*

Ronnie heard Celeste rattling ice trays in the kitchen. She raised her foot to the first step of the little stool beside the bed and rested. *That's after I get myself in this bed so my sister doesn't think I'm completely— Listen to me. "Let's pretend" is over except I'm scared to let my own sister see that I might need help—again.* She held the pillow more tightly as she took step two. *Ain't that nothin'.* Ronnie turned around and sat on the thick, soft mattress.

"Here you go." When Celeste bustled into the room and handed her a frosty glass, Ronnie was sitting up in bed like she'd been there all along. "Would you like anything else?" She had already turned to go.

"Some company." Somebody had to go first, so Ronnie took the chance.

"Pardon?" Celeste didn't know what to say.

"Don't go." Ronnie took a sip. "Listen, I'm sorry about the other day—I was kinda—rough."

"Kinda?" Celeste had the whole speech committed to memory.

"I didn't mean for it to come out like that."

Celeste brushed her hair away from her face. "But did you mean it?"

Damn. Here we go. "Well—uh—" *Keep it real.* "Yeah."

Celeste leaned against a bedpost. "I've called you some choice names in the last few days too."

"I bet. You can run 'em past me if you want. I deserve it." Ronnie laughed, hoping Celeste would too. "That hurts." She grabbed her pillow.

Celeste cracked a grin. "I know. They told you to hold on when you cough or sneeze, but nobody mentioned laughing." She looked down at her hands, rolled her wedding band around her finger. "And yeah, you do deserve it. You haven't exactly made any of this easy."

Ronnie felt a comeback land on her tongue, but she kept her lips sealed and braced for whatever Celeste had to dish out.

Celeste wandered over to the dresser and straightened the tray that held a matching tortoiseshell dresser set. She had re-played a lot of conversations in the last few days, with Niki, with Everett, with her mother. Somehow she always came off as the villain. "Am I really that bad?" she looked at Ronnie.

Ronnie sipped her lemonade. "What do you mean bad?"

"Don't tell me you're hedging. There's no point getting shy now." She picked up the hairbrush, rubbed her thumb across the boar bristles. "Come on. Give it to me straight."

Ronnie looked at her big sister over the rim of her glass, trying to figure out what was on her mind. "Okay." She took a gulp, then smiled. "Yeah. You can be a pill. You never give anybody any slack and . . ."

"Okay. I haven't forgotten. You made yourself very clear already." Celeste sat on the foot of the bed, still playing with the brush. "I get it. I just don't know what to do about it."

"I hear that." Ronnie rubbed the back of her hand, which was still tender from the IV. "We're not in such different places, you and me—I take that back. At least you have a job and an address. Oh yeah, and let's not forget you're married to the greatest guy in the world. A true prince among men." She bowed her head and held up the sheet beside her as if to curtsy.

"I guess." Celeste wasn't expecting Everett to come up. *I should tell her.* But it was hard to admit being left by the prince. She wasn't prepared to trade confidences, especially when she ran the risk of being the heavy again. Celeste stood up. She needed a break from this topic. "I really like your hair. I know I didn't say it before, but it's pretty hot."

"Hot? My sister using the word *hot* to describe something other than coffee?"

"I work in a high school, you know. I can only be so lame. Want me to brush it for you?"

Do what? "Uh—I—sure." Ronnie sat up and edged to the side of the bed. "If you can find enough to brush."

Celeste climbed up and kneeled beside her. Ronnie hadn't used much more than a washcloth on her hair since Lucille cut it, but the bristles felt good against her scalp, and Celeste's touch was surprisingly gentle.

"I used to do this when you were a baby. You were too little to remember."

"I guess I was." Ronnie closed her eyes to enjoy the feeling.

"When they brought you home you were bald as a cue ball and I was afraid you were going to stay that way. I asked Mother and Daddy to take you back and get one with hair."

"So you thought I was defective from the beginning."

Celeste ignored the comment. "They assured me your hair was coming, and after a while the fuzz appeared. As soon as there was enough to do anything with, Mother handed me this tiny brush with bristles soft as cotton." Celeste's voice floated with the memory. "And it was my job to brush your hair. It was so soft—and I'd make this one big fat curl on the top of your head."

"You had me lookin' like a cartoon, didn't you?"

Celeste smirked. "A little."

"Uh-huh. See, I knew you never liked me."

Celeste stopped brushing and sat next to Ronnie. "You really think that, don't you?"

They were sitting so close it was hard for her to say yes. "The thought crossed my mind once or twice."

"I do like you, Ronnie. I may not always understand you—" She tapped Ronnie's leg with the brush. "And I'm *not* glad things haven't worked out the way you wanted. Really I'm not."

"For real?" Unbelieving and hopeful, for a moment Ronnie sounded like a kid.

"Cross my heart." And Celeste did.

"You know, we've never done this."

"What?"

"Sit on the bed and talk, like sisters." Ronnie elbowed Celeste in the side. "It's not too painful, huh?"

"Ask me tomorrow. It always hurts worse the next day."

"If there are no side effects, you think maybe we could do this again? Sometime?" Ronnie asked.

"—Sure—I guess so." Celeste needed to find a place for all this sisterly affection. "But if I don't get downstairs, Mother will think you chewed me up and swallowed me instead of spitting me out, like you did last time." She got up and put the brush back on the dresser. "And Ron, we'll work this house thing out. I promise."

"Speaking of the house, did Ma give up any information about livin' here? Playin' the piano? Somethin'?"

"If I heard it, you did."

They both stopped at the sound of Della's footsteps on the stairs. She poked her head in Ronnie's room. "There's a man downstairs named Doug Pryce. . . ."

"Doug? Here?" Automatically Ronnie reached up and smoothed her head, where there used to be hair.

"I didn't know you were here long enough to be keepin' company. . . ."

"He's a real estate agent, Ma."

"Whoever he is, he wants to know if he can come up." Della spoke from the safety of the doorway.

"I don't know. What does he want?"

"Said he stopped by to see how you're feelin'. People down here are either neighborly or nosy, but I don't know him so I don't know which he is."

"He's not from here. Well I guess he is, but he moved to L.A. years ago. They don't drop in on people out there."

"He surely isn't here to pressure us about this sale?" Celeste put her hands on her hips. "That's not even decent."

"No, but he used to be a reporter and now he sells real estate. Could anybody be pushier?" Ronnie and Celeste laughed. Della didn't seem to think it was funny.

"Gimme a couple of minutes, then you can send him up."

"What am I supposed to do with him until you're ready?"

"Talk to him, Ma. This'll only take a minute."

Della grumbled and disappeared back down the stairs.

"Celeste, would you get me one of those dresses?" Ronnie eased over to the side of the bed. "Whatever he wants, I cannot have a conversation with this man in my pajamas." She pulled her lime green sleep shirt over her head.

"This one?" Celeste held a black and white polka dot sundress out of the closet.

"Uh. No." *Why does it matter?* "Give me the other one."

"Really? When I picked it out, Mother told me you'd never wear it." While Ronnie sat on the side of the bed, Celeste helped her slip the pink sundress over her head.

"I don't know. It's somethin' different from my usual black, brown, or navy. Does it look okay with my new hot hair?"

"Yeah. Want your makeup?"

Ronnie thought about it, but she wasn't even in the mood to paint on her five-minute quickie face. "Just hand me a lipstick." In two swipes and a blot her lips were coppery red. "Should I stay here or move over there?"

Celeste looked from bed to chair. "I'll help you." She eased Ronnie down and got her settled in the bedside chair. Then Celeste smirked. "I think you were wearing more clothes before."

Ronnie looked down at the neckline and the glimpse of cleavage it revealed. She tugged the bodice up, but it slipped back down. "You picked this?" Not that Ronnie was modest, but she wasn't trying to get Doug's attention, at least not that way. She was already feeling exposed, vulnerable, and the dress only added to it. She tugged at the front again, then with a shrug gave up and hid behind her hugging pillow. "Ready."

"You want me to stay?"

"Nah. Send him up." She crossed her legs primly at the ankles. *Let her rip.*

Doug tapped on the wall by the door before stepping into view. "Hey."

"Welcome to the recovery room," Ronnie said. *Why is this making me nervous?*

Doug came in. "Wow. That's some surgery they did. What do they call it, a hairodectomy?"

"Radical hairodectomy. It was the only way." The twinkle in his eyes was like sunlight, warm and welcoming, and Ronnie's face brightened with a smile.

"You look—"

"Shorn?" Her hand shot to her head.

"No. No. No. Nothing sheepish about it." He stroked the corners of his mustache with his thumb and forefinger. "It's pretty bold." He tilted his head to the side for another angle. "Very becoming."

"Becoming what is the question." She rubbed her bare neck. "Kidding. I think it's okay too, but it'll take me a while to get used to it—Glad it's not winter. I'd freeze to death."

"Yep. It's definitely all right." He nodded his approval.

"Thanks," Ronnie said shyly. She didn't know why she was self-conscious. *Not sheepish, remember!* "Speakin' of lookin' different—" Doug appeared cool and crisp in his tan suit, pale blue shirt, and tie. She looked at his loafers and was surprised at the multihued blue swirls on his socks. *Pretty sharp! The boy cleans up good.* "You get dressed to visit me?"

"This?" He smoothed his tie down into his jacket. "No."

Guess he pricked my bubble.

"I've got a bank meeting later. And look at you. I didn't think pink was an approved New York color."

"When in Prosper . . ." *Did I just say that?*

"In any case I'm happy you're doing better. It must be rough getting sick away from home, without your own doctor."

"I'm not sure it would have been easier in New York. I'm just glad it's over." She had no intention of giving Doug the scoop on her dicey circumstances. "And maybe one day I'll even let this out of my sight." She patted the pillow. "But right now, I don't make a move without it!"

"I remember that from when Janice had surgery."

Ronnie didn't know what to say on the subject of his late wife's operation. *Either their thing was really deep, or he's a little weird.* "Have a seat." So she plowed past it.

"No. This is just a quick stop. I brought you something."

"I haven't thanked you for the flowers yet. They're beautiful." Ronnie pointed to the basket of roses on the windowsill, feeling stupid again. *Bold!* "How'd you find out I was in the hospital, anyway?"

"A man has his methods."

What conversation are we having? "So I've heard." If there was flirting involved, Ronnie was usually three steps ahead, but she was never completely sure if the entendre was really double with Doug or if he was just being straightforward.

"You're asking me to reveal my sources. That's serious business."

"Just this once."

Doug folded his arms, arched an eyebrow. "Prosper's still small enough that word of most things gets around."

"That's unique." Ronnie figured she could walk down Broadway wearing peacock feathers and singing hip-hop and nobody she knew would have heard about it. She thought out loud a second. "Must be somebody Hambone told . . ."

"Hambone?"

"Old family friend I just met. But first things first, what did you bring? If it's the contract, we're . . ."

"No, but I do have some news on that front. But before we get to that." He reached back into the hall and produced a fishing rod and reel.

"You are outta your mind!" Ronnie held herself and laughed. "A gen-u-wine fishin' pole?"

"You bet. Worms not included."

"You know, I was sittin' by the window a little while ago, wishin' I could see the water. But somehow fishin' never came up!"

"I'm telling you, it's good for what ails you. I don't know if you'll get to use it before you leave, but it'll be a souvenir. Put it in a corner in your apartment. Hang your hat on it. It's sure to be a conversation piece in your part of the world." Doug leaned the pole against the wall. "But I guess you won't need a reminder of this trip."

"Hardly. But I can definitely tell you no one's ever given me one of those before."

"Are you guys all right up there?"

"Fine, Celeste!" Ronnie dropped her voice. "My sister is dying to know what's goin' on."

"I'm sure. She gave me a pretty strange look when she saw me with the pole. Anyway, the official reason I came out was to let you know the buyer understands that things this trip haven't gone exactly the way you anticipated."

"You mean you don't think I had all this planned when I called you? What was it?" Ronnie puzzled a second. "Was it really only two weeks ago?"

"Time flies . . ."

"I'm not having fun yet, Doug."

"Well, my client said you and your sister can take your time. The offer stands, and when you're ready, I hope we can find a solution that'll make everybody happy."

"Why are they being so nice? They don't know us."

"Gotta have a reason to be nice, huh?"

"You know what I mean."

"Nice, patient, whatever you call it, it's for real. You can trust me on that, even if I can't convince you about fishing." He saluted. "I'm outta here. Gotta see a man about a house." He chuckled. "Real estate humor's pretty lame, isn't it?"

Ronnie smiled and nodded.

"Call me when you guys figure out what you want to do, or before you head home. Whichever comes first."

The word *home* made her queasy. "Will do. And thanks for everything. I guess we've been a real pain in the . . ."

"Assets are our business, our only business—I warned you about the jokes." Doug headed for the door but turned around just before he walked out. "Let me know if you ever use it." He tapped the rod and disappeared. Ronnie listened to his footfalls double time down the stairs, quickly followed by Celeste's dainty shuffle coming up.

"Why in the world did he bring you that thing?"

"Wouldn't you like to know!"

The rest of the day and the next passed uneventfully, with Ronnie upstairs, Della downstairs, and Celeste shuttling between. Sunday's adventure was Ronnie's first trip downstairs, which was slow but uneventful. Celeste had fixed her a spot in the living room, but although she was more mobile, she wasn't any more energetic and napped intermittently. Lucille stopped by late in the afternoon with a pecan pie. Friday and Saturday were her busiest days in the shop, so this was her first trip out to the house since the Frazier family had set up temporary residence. But Della had been expecting the visit and she knew Lucille had more on her mind than how Ronnie was doing.

"She looks good, Odella."

Della looked up from her word puzzle when Lucille

walked out to the porch. Unread sections of the Sunday paper lay in a pile at Della's feet. "Pays to be young." She leaned to the side to get a paper towel out of her pants pocket, lifted her sweating glass of ice water, and mopped up the ring on the rusting wrought-iron table between the two chairs. Della had hoped to avoid this conversation, but deep down she knew that wouldn't happen, couldn't happen. After all, she'd tried to get away without coming back to Prosper too, hadn't she?

"I can't hardly believe it was just a week ago." Lucille eased into the other wicker chair. Her denim shirtdress fell open around her legs, and she massaged her knees like she was used to them aching. "Umph, umph." She shook her head in disbelief. "It was just about this time too. We were gettin' ready to eat."

Della folded the damp towel into quarters and put it away. "I'm sorry they came down here with this mess, disruptin' your life. You and Hambone are too busy for all this foolishness."

"Never too busy for family." Lucille paused to let her words settle over Della. "Odella—I mean Della. That's how you call it now."

"Call me what you want, Lucille."

"Awright then, Odella, you know you became family to us not long after you got to Prosper. So your children—well, they're family too." She sat on the edge of the big chair because if she slid all the way back, her feet wouldn't touch the floor. "I'm gon' say this 'cause I promised myself I would—if I ever got the chance." She waited for Della to look her in the eye. "It was wrong what you did. Not one word in forty-some years. Not one. You don't treat folks like that." Della looked down at her sneakers. She would rather have had a toothache; it would have been less painful than hearing this. Lucille was the last person she intended to hurt, but this talk was about the effect of her disappearance, not the cause. "Not folks that care about you." Lucille's normally chirpy voice was sad and solemn. "I understand why you left. Nobody would fault you for that. But you never answered one letter. Not even a Christmas card. Hambone told me it was the best way you knew to carry your load. Took me a long time, but I finally made my peace with it."

Della pried her eyes off the ground and peeped at Lucille again. "And with you, in case you're interested. I ain't mad. I know you been dreadin' my comin' out here. 'Fraid I was gon' plow up a perfectly nice field. When I saw you at the hospital it was written 'cross your face, plain as day."

Della cleared her throat. She wanted to explain herself, but the time for that had passed. She averted her eyes from Lucille's X-ray gaze and paused at the azalea bush beside the house. *I wonder what it looks like when it's in bloom.* It was almost as tall as the porch roof now. *I wish this was over.* Della had given many a lecture, but she hadn't been on the receiving end in years. Neither Celeste nor Ronnie would have believed their mother could listen this long without comment. In a few seconds she faced back around to finish taking her licking because she knew Lucille had no intention of stopping until she had said her piece. She also knew Lucille was right.

"Everybody got pain. Some worse than others, but it's a part of life. I know what you wanted and I know you didn't get it, except that don't excuse you from considerin' anybody but yourself. You not the girl who came here with her heart in a sling, or the young woman who left with it that way, but she's still in you. We are our past, Odella. You can't get away from it no matter how long and hard you try. Actin' like a part of your life didn't happen don't wash it away!" Lucille tapped her long, narrow feet against the floorboards. "Miz Ethiopia had a long life to think about what she done. She knew Henry wasn't no good, but she didn't do nothin' about it. I guess she tried to make amends for what he did and what she didn't do by leavin' you this place. In the end both she and Henry had a whole lot to answer for." Lucille paused.

Della nodded her head. She didn't know if Lucille was taking a breath or giving her a chance to ask about Henry, but mending this old friendship was more important. *I just hope Henry got whatever he deserved. No more, no less.* Right now, she didn't need to know. "You want some ice water or some lemonade?"

"Thank you, no. I got to get goin' in a minute." Lucille looked at Della another few seconds. "It looks to me like you been stumblin' around, trippin' over your own big feet, tryin' to walk away from here, 'cept I got news for you, Odella. The footprints are always behind you."

Eyes filled, Della bobbed her head slowly and swallowed back her tears. "Lucille—I didn't mean to . . ."

"Don't." Lucille held up her hand. "I don't need no 'I'm sorry.' I tol' you, I'm through with all that old stuff. I still care about you, always have, guess I always will." She stood to go. "But Celeste and Ronnie, they need to know a whole lot more'n they do." She smoothed the front of her dress. "Come on, walk with me. I got something for you in my car."

The wicker creaked as Della got up and followed Lucille off the porch.

She pushed a button on her key ring, and the trunk of her car popped open before they got there. "I done had this a whole lot longer than I expected." Lucille nodded at the inside of her trunk. "Just like you left it."

Della stared at the butterscotch leather valise. She used to think about this bag all the time at the beginning, but as time passed, she stopped wondering. It never occurred to her that Lucille still had it. *Why'd she keep it?* "Why'd you keep it?"

"You asked me to." She patted Della's arm. "Go on, take it."

Della reached out tentatively, the way you approach an unknown dog, even when you've been assured he won't bite. She hesitated, her hand hovering above the leather handle, but finally, she fastened her fingers around it and hauled the suitcase out into the afternoon sunshine.

"How much longer y'all gon' be here?" Lucille got behind the wheel.

"Mostly depends on Ronnie. And Celeste ain't in no hurry to get back either." Della's thoughts drifted off. When she saw Lucille's quizzical look, she added, "It's a long story."

"Uh-huh, always is. Especially with our children." Lucille started the engine. "And I thought it was hard when they were little, but it got worse when they called themselves grown."

"Yes, indeedy!" Della said.

"Worse on us and on them too I 'spect. Umph. You should see Jessie, Dianne, and George Jr. And we got four grands!

Can you believe it? I don't feel old enough to be this old!" Lucille recognized the troubled look on Della's face. It wasn't much different now than it was then. "You know, me and my kids, we had us some battles, 'specially Dianne. Lord, my girl enlisted in the army, and first I knew she had bags packed and was walkin' out the door. Umph. This took me a while, but I figured out that the more I let my kids see who I was when I was young, mistakes and all, the more they let me see who they were grown. Now, I'm still Mama, and we don't have to share *everythin'*, but it's kinda comfortable now."

Lucille patted the steering wheel, then reached for the gearshift. "Come on by one morning and we'll swap stories. You don't need an invitation." She put the car in drive, then stopped again. "Ronnie told me her middle name. Thanks." And she drove off, leaving Della to ponder in her wake.

"What's that suitcase doing on the porch?" Celeste asked when she got back from Winn-Dixie with a car full of groceries.

"Is it botherin' you?" Della snapped as she helped Celeste carry the bulging paper bags into the kitchen.

"No. It's just that—"

"Is it bothering anybody else?" Della grumbled as she started unpacking food. "You plannin' on stayin' through the winter?"

"Forget I asked, Mother. However long we're here, we needed some things. There was no sense in making a thousand little trips to the store when I could make one."

But Della had walked out of the kitchen by then, and Celeste left the suitcase alone. Just another straw on the camel's back.

18

". . . we could be so good together."

Maybe it's time. Della sat on the side of the white iron bed, listening for sounds of nocturnal wakefulness. All she heard was the beating of her own heart and the insistent cricket chorus. That twittering accompanied Buffalo nights too, but it didn't fill the house, echo off the ceiling, dance through the halls like it did here. Like she remembered from her nights in this room. It was twice the size of her room at home in Cadysville, and she recalled her first nights in it when she would lie awake counting the nosegays on the wallpaper or the slats in the wainscoting. The nights she pretended it was Annie down the hall sleeping in the room with her father. The nights she prayed to wake up in the morning and be in her old bed in her old room. As weeks turned into months, and she resigned herself to her new life, sleep claimed her nights again.

And when she went up to bed her first night back in this house, Della walked into her old room and wondered what the nights would have in store for her now. The furniture was the same, and when she removed the lowest drawer of the painted white dresser, the OW she had carved on the bottom with a penny nail was still there too. Nothing here had changed, but maybe she had. It was only a room in the same way she was discovering Little Pond was only a house. So she counted slats, thirteen until the one that was cracked, twenty-six more to the window, just like always. After that, the nights were hers, and Della played solitaire, read magazines, and worked her puzzles like always, then drifted off for her usual four or five hours of shut-eye. But tonight she couldn't get that bag waiting for her on the porch out of her mind. When she crept downstairs, careful to avoid the squeaky one, she was sure Ronnie and Celeste were fast asleep. They had walked around the suitcase for two days, acting like it wasn't there, and Della hadn't missed the looks her daughters threw in her direction every time they passed it, but they gave it and her a wide berth. She wasn't ready to address it until now.

Bag in hand, she returned upstairs with the same stealth as she had descended. Della padded silently down the hall and closed her door. She placed it on her bed and unfastened the straps that held it closed. It had never been locked. Slowly she raised the lid. Before it was open all the way, she reached in and pulled out the blue taffeta dress.

FRIDAY, AUGUST 23, 1957
TITUS, NORTH CAROLINA

"Come on outta there, Odee. We on in five minutes." Lester whispered loud so she could hear him through the bathroom door, above the raucous music in Tremayne's Klub Kozy. "O-dee?!"

Odella stared in the motley, cracked mirror in the ladies' room, a lean-to beside the club. It looked more like an out-house, but at least it had four walls and a lightbulb jury-rigged from the main power line. The men had to take care of their business in the narrow strip of woods out back. *I can't do this.* School had just started, and Della hadn't heard a word her teachers said all day. Her liver quivered imagining tonight, her real, professional singing debut. She and Lester had been sneaking to practice for weeks, down by the pond, blending songs he already used with new duets and solos for her. They picked big hits from the radio, and he talked about the rhythm of a set, how you had to arrange the music from fast to slow, from ballads to blues to guide the audience along with you. During rehearsals Will was their only audience and critic, al-though his main comment was, "Odella don't need to be doin' this." He even tried to talk her out of it, but she wouldn't lis-ten. "I gotta get out of Prosper, Will," she'd told him. In secret, Odella had worked out the piano arrangements, and now she rolled the sheets of music like a funnel in her hands. *I can't do this*. Tonight she and Lester would split twenty dollars plus tips and two shots of booze apiece if they wanted it. She took a final look in the mirror and hardly recognized the person looking back. It certainly wasn't Odella Womack from Cadysville, North Carolina. Before Lester had picked her up, Lucille had greased and pressed her hair till it looked like a patent leather bouffant. Her eyebrows were drawn in a dramatic arch, and Odella didn't know whose Orange Flip lips those were on her face, but her mouth was dry as old shoe leather. Lucille had made her buff the dry patches on her heels with a pumice stone and slather Vaseline on her arms and legs so her skin gleamed. Della's toe knuckles were jammed so tight into Lucille's clear plastic ankle-strap heels that her feet were already numb, but when she complained about the rigors of her wardrobe, Lucille pooh-poohed and assured her, "Glamour is painful but worth it." Della pressed on the spit curls Lucille had glued to her temples. *It's just singin'. I can do it!* She pushed the weathered boards nailed together and attached to the wall with a rusty spring hinge, and the door creaked open. She looked at Lester with a dazed expression. "I can't do this." Odella's arms crossed high on her chest, covering the décolletage of her dress. There was nothing she could do to hide the way the taffeta outlined her hips, tapered down past her knees so she had to walk in mincing steps. She looked down into her very voluptuous cleavage, which was highlighted by a triple strand of crystal beads she'd managed to sneak out of Miz Ethiopia's drawer. "It wasn't supposed to be so—so—"

"Ain't nothin' wrong with that dress. You look exactly like you supposed to. Like a singer!"

The makeshift walls of the Kozy, red and gold Moroccan patterned linoleum tacked directly to furring strips, vibrated with the rhythm of the wailing jukebox and barely contained the Friday night crowd, primed with mean payday green and ready to shake off the workweek blues. The music clung to the thick August night and battled with laughter, sweet talk, and cussing to be heard. Tremayne's was on Lester's regular circuit, and after more than a year he had finally convinced Odella to work it with him.

Della jumped when she heard a woman's squeal, followed by raunchy laughter. "Lester Malachi Wilson, this was a mistake."

"You gon' be smokin', Odee. Trust me." The headlights of a wheezing pickup truck pulling onto the crunchy brown grass cast them in long shadows. Lester gently pried her arms down, and she let them hang at her sides. "How else we gon' make it to the top?" He raised her chin with his forefinger, looked in her eyes, and she could feel his raw energy shoot through her and give her a boost.

"What if somebody knows me?" Odella didn't really suspect that would happen. They were far from Prosper, and nobody she knew went to places like this, but right now she was looking for any excuse not to go through with it. Her father and Miz Ethiopia thought she was baby-sitting little Jessie while Hambone and Lucille were in Rocky Mount overnight. That in itself had been a hard sell. Miz Ethiopia started her harangue about the jukebox, but this time her father held his ground, stilled her comments, and said he thought it would be fine. Della would be at the house, not at Pal's after all. And that was that.

Of course her father's trust only made Odella feel more guilty about lying. But she was seventeen and dying to do something grown up, something that would get her away from that house and from Henry. Lester's plan was the best she'd heard, and she loved to sing, so she had put her guilt in her pocket and stuffed the dress she had made in secret on Wednesday afternoons in a paper sack under some magazines and a change of underwear and headed to Lucille's after school for her rendezvous with Johnny DuPree. She was put out with Will for not coming, but he was acting kind of funny anyway, so she decided it was best he stayed home.

"Ain't nobody from Prosper even heard a this place. I been here five or six times already. Ain't no reason for folks to come way over here when they got perfectly good juke joints close by." Della knew he was right. "They're gon' love us, Odee. I'm tellin' you, baby, tonight is just the beginning." He grabbed both her hands in one and pulled her toward the door. "You wait and see." With his free hand, he straightened his skinny tie, patted his hair, and adjusted the pocket square she made him to match her dress. His narrow blue suit emphasized his wide shoulders and his trim, muscled build. They waited outside, holding hands, until the music stopped and they heard Tremayne's honking voice, then Lester guided her just inside. Sultry air greeted them at the door. He buffed the toes of his pointy shoes on the backs of his trouser legs.

"Hey! Lissen up!" Tremayne, who was four foot and change with sandy yellow hair, skin to match, and a patch over his left eye, stepped onto the stage, an old hay wagon turned upside down. The crowd continued to rumble and roar so he banged on a dented soup pot with a big metal ladle for order. "Was y'all raised in a barn?!" Three young men at a three-legged table down front answered with farmyard noises. "Hit the nail on the head, huh!" Tremayne spanked his pot until the crowd settled down enough to hear him. "We got a real treat for y'all."

Odella squeezed Lester's hand tight as a vise. Christmas lights in red, green, blue, and gold outlined the room, and silvery tinsel hung shaggy from the ceiling. She'd never seen so many people jammed this tight together. She took a deep breath to steady herself, and her lungs filled with a heady mix of Chesterfields, Old Spice, Pabst Blue Ribbon, Dixie Peach, Wild Turkey, My Sin, fried catfish, barbecue, and sweat.

"Now, y'all open yo' ears, shut yo' moufs. Put yo' hands together and give a warm Klub Kozy welcome to one a yo' favorites. Mr. Smooth—Mr. Cool—Mr. Johnny DuPree! And tonight, as a extra added attraction, he's brung with him the lovely and talented Miss Della Lester!"

Odella about yanked his arm out of the socket. "Della Lester?!"

"Odella Womack is just plain country."

Whoops, whistles, and hollers rose from the audience. Johnny DuPree headed through the maze of mismatched tables and chairs, dragging the new Della Lester behind him. He jumped up on the stage, spun around on one foot to face the audience, did a split, and sprang back up like his legs were rubber with a spring attached, then he reached down and lifted Della up next to him. She didn't know he could do splits or that he was so strong. Her eyes darted around, scanning the crowd. All the faces looking back, none of them wearing ugly hats, made her giddy. A little voice in her head told her to smile, so she locked her lips in a frozen grin. Johnny yanked the sheet music from her hand and gave it to the old man at the ancient upright. Odella felt like she barely knew how to talk, let alone sing. *I can't do this!*

As the piano man pounded out the intro, Lester winked, grabbed her around the waist, and squeezed the music out of her like an accordion.

"*Hey everybody, let's have some fun. You only live once and when you're dead you're done, so let the good times roll. . . .*"

The crowd was with them from the git-go and swayed, clapped, and sang along. They were at the center of a sho 'nuff party, and by the second verse the rhythm took over and Odella forgot to be scared. It was just like always when they sang, in church or down by the lake. The song, and their blended voices, his deep and tangy, hers sharp and sassy, carried them along. Johnny preened and strutted, and Della matched him step for step in a way she didn't know she could.

Johnny jumped down and stood by the piano when it was time for Odella's first solo. She almost panicked, standing up there alone, but she sang directly to Johnny for the first few bars, then she was strong enough to look into the audience, at least long enough to hook them. After that she closed her eyes to conjure up the emotion of the lyrics. Emotions she hadn't yet felt. "*If you don't think, you'll be home soon, I guess I'll drown in my own tears.*" Her voice swooped and soared, touching her and everybody else in the room deep down at the root.

It felt to Odella like they had just begun when the set was over. She looked at Johnny, who beamed back at her, then grabbed her hand. They took their bows, dashed off stage, and made their way out the way they'd come in, but this time there was applause, enthusiastic shouts, and hand grabs to escort them.

"See, I *told* you there wasn't nothin' to be scared of! Didn't I!?" Once they got out beside the building, Johnny did his spin, then grabbed Odella by the shoulders and shook her playfully. "You did it, baby! Tomorrow them folks will be tellin' their friends, 'Whoo, now that Della Lester, she can *sang*!'" Sweat ran down both sides of his face, met at the point of his chin, and dripped to the ground.

"Della Lester, huh! And did you *ask* me if you could change my name?!" Della fanned herself with her hands, trying to cool down, but it felt like she was trying to stir a vat of thick, hot soup.

"No, but it sounds good, don't it?!"

She tried to make like she was mad, but she couldn't stifle the grin. "Yeah!" *Della Lester*. It sounded high-class. Della Lester could go places and do things Odella Womack only dreamed about. *And* it was part of his name. She wiped the sweat off her brow and flung the pellets off her hand.

"See, I told you I'd look out for you." Lester took a fresh handkerchief from his inside pocket and gently dabbed the water from Odella's forehead. She stood stock-still, but inside it was like she stuck her toe in an electric socket, except it was kind of good. When he was done, he dried off his face and neck.

"Della Lester sounds like somebody who wears diamonds and furs, drives a Cadillac, and has a fancy apartment in New York City." Hot rivulets trickled down her back and her belly. Their time on stage had gone by in a blur, and she was still not sure it wasn't a dream, but she was intoxicated with the night and the possibilities.

"Now you're talkin'! We can do this all over the state, and then—" He churned his arms like the axles on a locomotive and chugged around her, building up speed. "Next stop— Memphis—Chicago—Cleveland—Baltimore and New York City! All aboard!" He blew the train whistle and Della laughed. "All it takes is for the right person to hear us, and bam! We'll be whipping out hit records, and the folks back in Prosper will be listenin' to us on the radio and talkin' about 'Remember them when'! I'm tellin' you, Odee, this is just the beginning. I can feel it!" He stopped, and the look in his eyes was one Odella had never seen before. At first she looked away, but slowly, drawn by a force she couldn't resist, she answered his gaze. Johnny moved closer, and before she knew what happened she was in his arms.

The air that moments ago had been too thick was suddenly too thin for Della to breathe. *This is Lester!* They were pressed body to body, so close she couldn't tell if it was her heart pounding or his. Somehow her arms found a place wrapped around his neck, and then she was squeezing him too. *This is crazy.* She tried to pull away, but he wasn't letting her go. Hands flat against her back, he drew her closer, his cheek prickly next to hers, and she felt a slow tingle way down low in a spot that hadn't awakened until now. Odella closed her eyes. Just to think. Just for a second, but then she was surrounded by the smell of him, crisp and fresh like soap, spicy like the lavender and licorice of Sen-Sen. And when he nestled his face in the crook of her neck, kneaded her back, the blood rushed to Odella's head and she felt like it would explode.

"Odee, we could be so good together."

The tickle of his lips, his breath, soft against her ear made Odella shiver. She could always feel his presence, but this close was overwhelming. She always told herself she was foolish to daydream about Lester Wilson. Now here she was in his arms, and she wanted to believe him, but daydreams don't come true. *Do they?*

Lester took her face in his hands. "You're somethin' else, you know that," he said hoarsely. Lester had been drawn to her from the first time he saw her, in that muddy white dress, standing by her father's car. Crazy as that was. He couldn't explain it then, and he wasn't sure he could explain it now. Odella wasn't exactly beautiful, but the prettiest girls didn't have what she had, a presence he couldn't call by name, but he felt it strong and knew she did too.

Odella's knees turned to mush, and she thought she would faint dead away, so she just held on. And not a moment too soon. He felt her weight shift, sink into him. The velvety softness of his lips brushed her own, and she didn't know what to do in response so she stopped breathing through her mouth. Odella pushed back with her lips and held the air in her lungs until she got dizzy, then panted in short, staccato wheezes through her nose. When she felt his tongue pry her mouth open, she panicked and clenched her teeth against the invasion. But that didn't last long. Lester's hands slipped down to her waist, made their way around to her back again, and when they came to rest in the curve above her butt, she relaxed her jaw and let him in. Lester was a flavor she'd not tasted before, salty and mysterious. He tantalized her appetite, and suddenly Odella was hungry and she knew what to do. She let her tongue wander, exploring his mouth like his hands explored her body. She rubbed the back of his neck, felt the bristly hairs left by the razor the barber used to neaten up his hairline.

Arms locked around each other, they swayed to a song they wrote as they went along. Then sweaty and hearts racing, they heard voices, opened their eyes, and saw they had company. He took her hand and led her to the car.

"I should change my dress before we go. I don't want to get caught."

"Keep it on. I like it. I like the way it sounds." He ran the tip of his fingernail down her side, and the shiny fabric hummed. "Won't nobody see you before I take you by Lucille's."

"But—"

"I promised nobody you know would be here, didn't I?" He smiled, reached past her to open the car door but stopped for a kiss on the way.

Odella brushed him away. "So you did!" She got in the car, thinking about how many times she sat right there, next to Lester, wishing what happened tonight would happen, and she wondered if he knew.

He climbed in and started the engine. "What you doin' way over there?" Lester stretched his arm across the back of the seat and waited. She slid into place, happy in a way she never knew existed.

They had been driving about an hour when he pulled off the road onto the edge of a tobacco field, cut the engine, and turned off the headlights. He pulled her closer and traced the low neckline of her dress with his finger. His touch was light and sure, and Odella felt the panic and the hunger rise again. She knew that kissing wasn't all there was to it, but she didn't exactly know how everything else happened. Logically and physically it didn't make sense, but she had heard that it was supposed to be magic. She just didn't know if she was ready.

Lester kissed her neck, the swell of her breasts. "Odee?"

She heard the rustle of the taffeta, felt his hand work its way under her skirt, and her insides liquified. "Huh?" she managed.

He massaged her knee, and his hand moved slowly up her thigh. When he reached the top of her stocking and slipped his finger under her garter, he felt her resist, stiffen. He took his hand away. "We ain't gon' do nothin' you don't wanna do." He lifted her chin. "I want you to be my girl."

"Its not that—I—" She had a flash of lying facedown on the floor in the chicken coop, Henry pressed against her back. She hadn't told Lester about that day, didn't want him to know. And as much as she didn't want to be thinking about that now, it hung over her.

"It's okay. You and me, we gon' make it, Odee." He kissed her gently. "You'll tell me when you're ready. You won't have to say a word. 'Cause even when you don't know I'm lookin', I got my eye on you. Always have."

Della clutched the dress tight. It was musty, but the icy hot blue never faded. *And I made you promise not to tell anybody we were going together. We fooled most folks, at least for a while, but Will knew. I think he knew from the beginning.*

19

"Ain't nothin' hurts worse than a lie."

Ronnie shuffled into the kitchen, her hugging pillow tucked under her arm. She poked her head out the back door to get her lungs full of early morning air, feeling pretty chipper and pleased with herself for getting showered, dressed, and downstairs before nine with no help. And when she dug around in her purse looking for her wallet and checkbook to tally up the actual sad state of her finances, she came across a pack of cigarettes and realized she hadn't touched one since before the surgery. Ronnie had made a career of quitting, but right now she just didn't have the urge, and that felt good. She spied Della at the table in her housecoat and spongy pink curlers, finishing a toaster waffle. The slack non-expression on her face, the slump to her shoulders struck Ronnie. *Ma's not that old. Why does she look like that?* "Hey, Mamacita."

"We should be plannin' to go home soon." Della had been up all night with nothing to chew on but her own thoughts and memories. She was sick of that taste and ready to sink her teeth into something else. "I know you don't *want* to move back to Buffalo, but I can't see much else for you to do." She folded her hands in front of her, like it was a done deal.

Ronnie recognized the no-nonsense voice and realized she'd walked smack into an ambush. *Oh, shit. Ma's on a mission.* She still hadn't come up with a concrete bail-out plan, but she knew it had to be radical; there wasn't much left of her old life to salvage. And the game clock was ticking down to double zero. The one thing she was sure about was that moving home now would make her feel like a total failure. "I can't have a life there."

"Looks to me like you ain't had much a one in New York neither." Della swallowed some coffee. "You want eggs for breakfast?"

Food wasn't a priority, but it would give Ronnie a moment to collect her thoughts. "I can't keep eating like that. I'll be big as a house!"

"You have to get your strength back." Della got up and turned the heat on under the iron skillet and the kettle.

"Isn't there any yogurt or fruit?" Ronnie examined her choices in the refrigerator.

Della came up behind her, reached in, and took two eggs from the door. "You eat that when you're sick, not when you're tryin' to get well." She broke them over a bowl and whipped them into a frenzied froth.

"Fine! I think I'll have eggs." *I can't live like this.* Ronnie plunked down on a kitchen chair, and in no time Della set a plate of pebbly scrambled eggs and slightly burned toast slathered in butter in front of her. "Ma, it's been a long time since we lived under the same roof. We're . . ."

"You won't have to live with me after you're on your feet." Della sat down with a cup of tea for Ronnie and more coffee for herself. "Lord knows I ain't lookin' for a room-mate. When you're up and around, you could move into one of the houses if you want to. There's plenty of addresses to choose from. You might even want to help Shorty manage the rentals. Maybe that way I wouldn't sell all of 'em. Keep it a family business." She heaped sugar in her cup and stirred. "Although I do have to sell another one since your hospital stay used up the money I was gon' give Niki for school." Della sipped again to give her pointed reminder of how little choice Ronnie really had a chance to sink in. "I don't know what you gon' do, but I know you got to do somethin'." It didn't look to Della like either of her children was in any hurry to leave Prosper, so she decided it was time to move things along. "We can't stay here forever. Your sister's layin' in supplies like she's expectin' a blizzard and . . ."

"I wasn't plannin' to stay forever!" Ronnie pushed her plate away. "Ma, give me *some* credit. Until now I've always taken care of myself. And it may look to you like I loafed around wastin' time, but I hustled every day, tryin' to get the next gig, tryin' to get noticed by the right people. And let me tell you, there are worse actors than me makin' a livin' at it. I just couldn't seem to catch a break." Ronnie crumbled the crust off her toast. "All I'm askin' is for a little more time to figure some things out."

"You had seventeen years. How much more time do you need?" Della was unmoved.

"That's not fair!" Ronnie knew it sounded juvenile, but she was scrambling.

"Did somebody finally steal that suitcase off the porch?" Celeste, brow furrowed, headed for the coffeepot.

"No," Della snapped.

"Well, what happened to it?"

"It's *my* business what happened to it. Just like it's *your* business why Everett is divorcin' you."

"What?!" Ronnie jerked around so fast she almost toppled her teacup. She was feeling good because she thought the wall between her and Celeste had come down some in the last few days, but there were obviously still enough bricks left to block the way. "You didn't say one word."

"Now, I don't see you bendin' over backward explainin' to nobody what happened to your marriage." Della plowed over Ronnie's comment and headed straight for Celeste. "So don't you keep worryin' me about my bag."

The unexpected blow dazed Celeste, but she still had enough wits about her to duck out of the way. "I don't have to take this!" She hurried from the room, snatched her purse from the chair in the hall.

Della was hot on her tail. "You need to go home and tend to your own mess instead of hiding out down . . ."

Celeste slammed the door so hard the house shook and windowpanes rattled. Della was rattled too, down to the bone. But it wasn't Celeste that got to her; it was the violent crash, still echoing in her ears. She grabbed hold of the banister and sank to the steps.

TUESDAY, SEPTEMBER 10, 1957
PROSPER, NORTH CAROLINA

"I knew it soon as she set foot in this house!"

The front door slammed like a gunshot and rattled the house to its foundation. Odella jumped in her bedroom chair. She knew Henry meant her, and she knew he meant to stir up trouble.

"She ain't nothin' but a ho. Just like her mama!"

Odella's hands sank to her lap, and the sweat on her skin turned icy. She'd been sitting by the window, mending a nylon slip, trying to get some air on this muggy evening and repeating every word Lester said when he called her, long-distance, from Cleveland. Then all hell broke loose.

"You must be drunk, boy! And you better get out my house till you're sober!" Odell, still wearing a T-shirt and blue work pants, bellowed from the landing.

"Ain't hardly drunk!" Henry stomped up the steps, and when Odella peeked out of her door he and Odell were standing toe to toe in the hall. Father was still a head taller and half again wider than son, but Henry was swelled with defiance. "I was by the barbershop today. Man in the next chair tol' me my sister sure could sing, and I know he ain't been to nobody's church. Said he saw her in some gin shack over in Titus. Seems she and Lester been gallivantin' 'round, call themselves singers. And who knows what else they do?" Henry's hollering rang through the house. "She ain't been baby-sittin' on the weekends for Lucille and Hambone no more than I have!"

Odella had hoped she and Lester would be bags packed, headed out of town with no looking back by the time anybody found out. Will and Lucille were the only ones who knew she was planning to go, and she made them swear not to tell. Will looked hangdog, but he knew why she had to get away. What could he say? Lucille didn't know what Henry had tried to do to her and did her best to convince Odella to wait, at least till she finished high school. But when Lucille realized there was no changing her friend's mind, she slipped Odella advice on taking care of herself and an old tan leather suitcase that looked better than the ratty blue one she had brought with her from Cadysville. Odella had already stashed some of her best clothes in it because the time was coming. Lester was already out on the road, setting things up. He had begged her to come with him, even surprised her with a tweed suit with a real silver fox collar that he bought in Charlotte. Said it would be her traveling clothes, "'Cause homemade won't make it for you no more." The suit was the most beautiful thing she'd ever seen, and at night she'd pull it out from the back of the closet, rub her face in the smooth, soft fur, and dream about being famous and making records. Della Lester and Johnny DuPree. It sounded so far-fetched, but Lester believed, and that was enough for her. Being with Lester was all she really needed. She had planned to tell her father, right as they were leaving Prosper, thought maybe he'd understand. Odella decided she owed him at least that. She hadn't figured out how to put it yet, but it looked like time had run out. She was going to have to say something right now.

"If you believe everythin' you hear in a barbershop, then I raised a fool." Odell poked his son's shoulder with a corner of the newspaper in his hand.

Henry smacked the paper aside, and the pages skittered across the floor. "You quick to make me the fool! You do it at the brickyard. You do it here!"

"You don't like the way I run my business or my house, you know what you can do." Odell's low rumble threatened, like he was on the verge of erupting.

"You would throw *me* out and have *her* sittin' up in here like—like she somethin' special!" Henry hollered. "The garbage goes outside!"

Odell snatched Henry by the front of his shirt. "Don't you ever talk to me like that, boy. . . ."

"Ain't none a your damn boy!" Henry squirmed out of his father's grasp. "And what you gonna do about her and her damn lies?! You brought her up in here like you proud of her. Even gave her your damn name! And what am I supposed to do? Huh? What about your wife?!" He jabbed an irate finger in the air.

Odella knew this pot had been bubbling for years and now it had boiled over. She felt like she had to go out there. She was scared, but this was her battle, and she had to fight it. She just wished Lester was in town.

"Papa?" Odella opened the door before she chickened out and walked to the head of the stairs where her father and Henry had squared off. "Me and Lester—we *have* been singin' around some." Eyes cast down, she caught sight of Miz Ethiopia's sour face peering up from the dining room. "But I swear that's all we . . ."

"Now you see!" Henry poked her. "She the one been lyin'."

"Watch yo'self, boy!" Odell warned.

When Odella got up the nerve to look at her father, his disappointed expression made her feel two feet tall. "I—I wanted to tell you—" She stumbled over her own guilt. "I was gonna, but . . ."

"*Now* who you gon' put outta your house?" Henry glared at Odella. "You can look all innocent here in your proper little high-collar dress, but that's not what you wear to them joints, is it?! Way I heard it, your singing wasn't the only thing you was featurin'." Henry yanked at her skirt.

"Don't!" Odella pulled away.

"Leave her be!" In one motion Odell spun Henry by the arm and slammed him up against the wall. "This ain't your concern." Odell's wide hands covered most of Henry's chest as he pinned him against the delicate floral patterned wallpaper.

"I'm sick a you tellin' me what to do!" Henry ranted in an uncontrollable squeal. His eyes burned with hate as he swung his fists wildly, his arms too short to reach their target.

"Stop it, y'all!" Odella tugged on her father's arm, stumbled on the newspaper underfoot. "Please stop!" She despised Henry, but she didn't want her father to beat him. At least not for this. It would give her brother another reason to make her life miserable.

Odell shook off his daughter's grasp, then grabbed the front of Henry's shirt again and hoisted him off his feet.

"Papa, please—This is my fault." One of Henry's fists bashed her temple, and she clutched at the railing to keep from going down.

Odell dangled Henry until all the struggle went out of him. "Now, go on 'bout your business." He abruptly let go, and Henry landed in a heap on the floor and scrambled to his room. Then Odell turned heavy eyes on Odella. "Ain't nothin' hurts worse than a lie." His gaze left her nowhere to hide.

Odella shriveled with shame. "Papa—I—" She couldn't find any cooling words to soothe his wound. "I—I didn't mean—" Then, out of the corner of her eye, she saw Henry charge, quick as a mad dog, toward Odell, wielding a crowbar high over his head. "Papa! Look out!" Odella's yell scraped her throat, but to her ears it was like a distant, fading echo. The action played out in front of her faster than the sound could catch. Faster than she could stop.

Odell pivoted just in time to intercept the iron bar mid-swing. He and Henry scuffled on the landing, like mortal enemies until Odell slid on the fallen newspaper, and the force of Henry's fury sent him tumbling.

"Papa!" Odella lunged, grabbed the tail of her father's shirt. The momentum of his fall ripped it from her hand, tore loose two of her fingernails, but she never felt her own pain. "No-o-o!" Odella's thick, hoarse scream saturated the air, but she never heard it. She felt the house quake, watched helplessly as he rolled head over heels over head down the stairs, his head bouncing on the steps, his arm crashing through a section of spindles. There was deathly silence when he came to rest at the bottom. When she saw him splayed out on the floor, Odella felt a massive hand crush her heart and squeeze the air from her lungs.

"Papa—" She felt her lips move, but her whisper was thin and parched. Slowly she edged down the steps, her back pressed to the wall. "Papa." Odella held back a sickening wave as she stepped over the bulk of his torso and dropped to her knees beside her father. His head arched back at an impossible angle, his mouth agape, his stare empty.

Before she could reach out her hand to touch him, Henry pounced and pinned her to the floor, the crowbar pressed across her throat. Her tongue waved, but she couldn't swallow her own spit.

"It's a damned shame he fell. Ain't no more to it. Ain't that right?" Henry's face was contorted into a grotesque mask, and his hot spit showered her with every word he spoke. The veins in Odella's head felt like they would burst, and the room grew dim, but she could see Miz Ethiopia looking on, not moving a muscle to help her. But she hadn't moved a muscle to help her husband, either.

"If you ever breathe a word about this—or what happened in the chicken coop, I'll get you, gal. You won't know when, but I'll kill you, and Will too if I have to." Henry squeezed harder. "You understand me?"

Before she passed out, Odella nodded yes.

"Ma? Are you all right?" Ronnie was unnerved to find her mother slumped on the steps, head in hand.

Still dazed, Della looked up at Ronnie, trying to shift her focus from the past back to the present.

"Should I call for help?"

"I don't need help! I need for the two of you to start acting like you got some sense so we can get on outta here!"

20

"... it's okay to say 'when.'"

Gravel sprayed from beneath Celeste's tires like buckshot as she sped away from the house. It didn't matter where she went as long as it was away from her mother. *I hate her! I just hate her!* Celeste stopped in the middle of the road, no longer able to see through her tears. *Nothing I do is right, not for her, or Niki, or Everett, or my sister. None of them!* Her hands trembled on the steering wheel. She leaned back against the headrest and bawled like a child. Right then, the thing she wanted most in the world she couldn't have. She wanted her daddy. She wanted to confide in him, like she always had, since she was a little girl and she'd come home with her feelings hurt, boohooing. She could see him standing in the basement, wearing faded khaki work pants and dusty shoes, holding a hammer or a wrench. He'd stop whatever he was doing, get his hankie out of his hip pocket, squat down, and wipe her eyes. Her daddy would talk to her. And he'd listen as she told him how she'd done everything exactly right, tried to show the other kids how to do it right, and it still hadn't worked out. She wanted to tell him now.

Celeste fished a tissue out of her purse, dabbed at her eyes, blew her nose. And what would he say? As soon as she asked the question, she heard Will. "It did work out, sugar. Just not the way you planned it, that's all." She could feel the calluses on his hand as he cupped her chin. "Sometimes you got to be willin' to change up your direction, Lessie, or whatever it is will sideswipe you and leave you layin' by the side of the road wonderin' what hit you." *Wonderin' what hit you.* Celeste had composed herself enough to ease up to the road.

Without knowing exactly how she got there, Celeste parked in front of Pal's. She was too upset to eat, but she had to be somewhere, so she checked the mirror on the sun visor, put on shades to cover her red, froggy eyes, and went inside. The restaurant bustled like a beehive and smelled like bacon and good coffee.

"Morning! You by yourself?" Hambone had flounced out of the kitchen with half a cantaloupe and cottage cheese with a cherry on top. "Come for a little carryout to take on back?"

"Uh—No. Breakfast for one."

"Well, happy to see ya. It'll be a minute 'fore we have a table."

"I can sit right there." She moved toward an empty stool at the counter.

"How's Miss Ronnie doin'?" Hambone moved along with her.

"Fine," Celeste said curtly, then caught herself. "Well, not fine exactly, but she's doing really well. Improving every day!" It sounded phony even to her, but she couldn't find middle ground this morning.

"And your mama?"

"Couldn't be better. I'd like some coffee, Hambone. If it isn't too much trouble?"

Hambone felt the shift in gears. "Comin' right up." Still carrying the melon, he spoke to the girl behind the counter, who immediately picked up the carafe and headed in her direction.

After making a lengthy show of examining the menu, Celeste finally ordered a stack of buttermilk pancakes with eggs over easy, bacon, orange juice, and coffee. She knew she'd never eat it all, but it was a lot of food, which gave her a lot of time.

Celeste cut tiny wedges from the big golden circles on her plate, chipped away at the ends of the extra crispy bacon until it looked like the pseudobits you shake from a jar. When she pierced the egg yolk with her fork and watched the gooey liquid run into the rim of her plate, she felt inexplicably sad and had to fight to keep the tears at bay. She'd played with her food for half an hour when Lucille, dressed in her turquoise smock, popped through the door. Celeste managed to give the same answers to the questions Hambone had asked. She felt self-conscious with her shades on inside, like Lucille knew she was hiding something.

"Well, you tell 'em both I said hey!" Lucille's hand rested on Celeste's shoulder, and the warm touch felt comforting. Without warning, a tear slipped from the corner of Celeste's eye and splashed on her cheek before she had a chance to catch it. *What is the matter with me?!*

Lucille smoothed it away with her thumb and kept talking. "And soon as Ronnie's able, we'll have that dinner that never happened 'fore y'all go back." She started away, then turned back around. "When you're done here, stop on over. Let me work you in for a shampoo. I bet that'll feel good."

"You know, I haven't gone this long without getting my hair done in twenty-five years." Celeste smiled. "Thanks."

"All right, then. See you when you finish up." She patted Celeste, then headed toward Hambone at the cash register.

With her shades for cover, Celeste watched Hambone and Lucille reenact the loving morning ritual she'd seen on her first day in Prosper. Her small hand on his meaty arm. His big, round head bobbed and nodded as they laughed. Opposite in every way but so in sync, an easy give-and-take passed between them like current.

And like a shot Celeste felt the ache in her heart, the hole in her life. *I miss Everett so much!* She gasped aloud, then cleared her throat and drank some juice as explanation to the young man to her right, with a sun tattoo on his forearm, who turned to see if anything was wrong.

Hambone rested his pudgy paw on Lucille's narrow waist and leaned over. She stood on tiptoes, kissed him bye, and this time when he squeezed her butt, she pinched him. Celeste thought about the time she pushed Everett away because he was sticky or wet, or somehow it didn't seem proper. *Proper to who?*

Panic propelled Celeste out of her seat. *What the hell have I done?* She fumbled for her wallet, left money by her place, and headed toward the phone in the back. It was still in a wood and glass booth, and she sat on the perch, left the accordion door ajar so the light wouldn't come on. She dialed her home phone number, prayed for Everett to pick up. *One ring. Two rings*—"*You've reached the residence of*—" She hung up slowly, remembering he wasn't due back from Portugal for another few days. Then she heard his words, the finality in his voice. "*Always is over.*" *And what could I say on the phone to make that any different?* She stared at the keypad, adding the numbers in horizontal rows. *Six, fifteen, twenty-four.* Feeling all the time she'd let slide by and all the distance she'd put between them. Celeste added the numbers in columns. *Twelve, fifteen . . .* A tap on the glass brought her around.

"Ma'am? Are you okay?" Mary the hostess stood outside.

"Yes—Fine—The number was busy—I guess I can try again." Celeste waved and began pressing keys. Her fingers found another familiar pattern.

"*This is me. You know what to do.*"

Not again. She wanted to scream but steadied her voice enough to leave a message. "This is your—This is Mom. I haven't spoken to you since—Uh—In a while—"

"Just a second."

The male voice was unfamiliar, but Celeste knew who it was. She could still see his picture. And she winced as she heard Niki's loud whisper. "Don't pick it—Aw shit—"

"Hello—Uh-oh—Hold on—"

Celeste shielded her ear from the shrill whistle of feedback. It stopped when he turned off the machine. "Hello, Brian—This is Brian, isn't it?"

"Yes, ma'am. Brian Cadieux."

Celeste could also see that box of condoms. "I'd like to speak to my daughter."

"Sure. Hold on."

"Brian? I look forward to meeting you," Celeste added quickly, hoping that when the time came she'd have found a way to mean it, since he meant so much to Niki.

"Thanks. I look forward to that too."

Somehow Celeste was surprised by how manly he sounded. How confident. *Nicole's ol' man.* It almost made her laugh. *I wonder if Mother went through that with me and Everett.*

"What a surprise, Ma. It's not Tuesday."

Celeste ignored the sarcasm. "I don't really want anything." *Except that you not completely despise me.* "I was just checking on you . . . to see how you're doing."

"You just caught me. I'm unplugging the phone in a minute. The car's packed. We're on our way outta here."

"You're leaving? Atlanta? Already?" *How could she be prepared for a move? Without any help?*

"I told you we were going in early July. Or did you forget?"

She's got help. It's just not from me. "The time got away from me." Celeste could feel Niki's force field, hear her impatience to be done with this call. "I'm still in Prosper. Your aunt is too. She's been in the hospital. . . ."

"What happened?!"

"She'll be fine." Celeste filled Niki in on the recent events. "How long are you planning to take for the drive?"

"Couple a days. No big rush."

"I know it might be out of your way—" Celeste took a deep breath. "I'd really love to see you, Niki—You and Brian." For once, an idea went from her head to her lips and she said it before she had the chance to reason her way out of it.

"I don't know."

"No lectures, no advice, I promise. I just want to see you before you start your—before you start school. Besides, it'll lighten things up around here. And I know it would make Ronnie feel better."

"Any blood yet?"

"No more than usual—" *Who am I kidding?* "Maybe a little more. We've had our moments." Celeste felt like she could hear Niki thinking.

"I won't promise, but give me the address and stuff and I'll see."

As soon as she hung up, Celeste got out her agenda book and dialed before she lost the momentum. "Doug Pryce, please."

* * *

After Celeste's escape, Ronnie retreated to the living room and spent the rest of the morning agonizing over the pieces to her puzzle, moving them around in hopes of finding a solution that didn't involve a complete loss of face and loss of faith in herself. And unilateral surrender to her mother. *I'm not that out of it.* So, for the first time in years, Ronnie attempted to write a résumé. Not the kind that accompanied her head shot and listed her acting credits; she updated that regularly. The balled-up pages at her feet were her attempts to arrange her patchwork of temp jobs and part-time work to showcase her marketable skills.

What is anybody gonna hire me to do? Ronnie scratched jagged lines through her latest effort, ripped the page off the pad, and folded it into a paper airplane. After launch it took a nosedive and disappeared under the table. *Crash and burn, the story of my life.* She looked at the next blank page. *All right. Cut the drama and think.* Trying to put down in black and white what she knew how to do made her edgy. A little of this and a little of that is how she generally thought about it, but that was too vague. Ronnie could do basic word processing. She could talk to anybody, although she couldn't figure out a category for that. *Gets along with people? Sounds like a beagle.* She could do makeup, and she'd been pretty successful at selling Sable Shades, which should have been the highlight of her career to date. Ronnie figured Marilyn Ellis would have given her a good recommendation if she hadn't fired her first. None of it looked substantial enough to account for so many years of her life. *Did I accomplish anything?*

By the time Della called her for lunch, Ronnie felt the net tightening around her. She picked the bologna out of her sandwich, rolled it up, and popped it into her mouth, glad Della didn't seem ready to pick up where they had left off. Ronnie downed her iced tea and wished she felt strong enough to walk down to the pond. Maybe she could think clearer sitting on the stump, tossing stones in the water.

"Ma, you ever go fishin' in the lake?"

"Not much. I used to like goin' there 'cause couldn't no-body see you unless they knew you were there. Your daddy used to fish sometimes. He and—a friend. They'd catch a few sunnies, but nothin' you could make a steady diet on." Della rinsed a plate and placed it in the drainboard. "Why? You plannin' on a new hobby since that young man brought you that fishin' pole?"

"Nooo! I was just askin'." She felt silly. Ronnie wasn't expecting to get snagged. "I like it there too. It's peaceful."

"Is that so? Humph." She dried her hands on a dish towel. "You know he's sweet on you, that Doug."

"Ma, please. He's a real estate agent who happens to be a nice guy." Nice had always meant boring as soggy cornflakes in Ronnie's lexicon, but that's not how she meant it this time. *Everett's a nice guy. . . .*

"I know. You sent me to talk to him the other day."

"What did you say to him?"

"Wasn't your conversation." Della dried her hands on a paper towel. "And I don't know when your sister is planning to show herself around here. She can't keep runnin'."

Ronnie had been so busy in her own problems she hadn't thought about how upset she was with Celeste. *I open up like a can of soup, spill my guts. But she didn't think enough of me to say boo about her and Everett splitting up. Like I'm the only one whose life is a wreck.* Everett was good people. Ronnie used to think if she could find a guy like that she'd really have something. *If they can't keep it together, I don't have a prayer.*

Ronnie left Della in front of the TV and, glass of iced tea in hand, went to sit on the porch, hoping the small change of scenery would stimulate her thoughts. She tried to go back to her résumé writing but ended up with a page full of doodled curlicues. Based on her steady improvement she estimated she'd be able to start her job search in another week, and she braced herself to look for a full-time, for-real job, one with medical coverage. Then there was the matter of what she was going to be, now that she had to grow up, or at least stop chasing a dream she couldn't quite catch, and concentrate on building a more stable foundation. Ronnie had gone through the classifieds to see what jobs she might qualify for. She had circled ads for administrative assistants, airlines, banks, customer service reps, sales, discouraged by the number of places that listed a college degree as a minimum requirement. Then she got a lump in her throat when she thought about doing the same thing five days, forty hours a week, month after year, ad infinitum.

But all the "what if's" Ronnie explored fell apart when she had to explain where she was going to live and what she was going to live on to start out. In desperation she even considered taking Kayla up on her offer to stay in Brooklyn with the witches, at least long enough to convince her friend it was time to leave the coven so they could get a place together. Then Ronnie went back inside to the living room and called Kayla, who had a week's worth of stories about getting over, getting by, getting seen, getting laid, and getting paid in the city. Midway through the conversation, Ronnie felt like she'd heard this tune too many times, like a song that repeats and repeats in your head until you're sick of it and you don't want to hear it again for a long time. When Kayla asked when she was coming back, Ronnie said, "I don't know if I even *wanna* come back." It was the truth, and it surprised her as much as it did Kayla. Ronnie hung up, more confused than before. *What the hell am I gonna do?*

When she heard car tires, she figured it was Celeste. *'Bout time.* Ronnie had plenty to say to her, like how trust works both ways, but she was surprised to hear men's voices drifting in through the open windows.

"You seem pretty familiar with the property. Any thoughts on how you'd like your acreage to run?"

Ronnie tucked her tank top in her shorts. *What is Doug doin' here?!*

"Nothin' hard-and-fast. If we start at the northern boundary of the land and go twenty acres in, that would encompass the house. And both parcels would have lakefront."

She smoothed a hand over her head. *Who's that with him? His voice sounds so familiar.*

"You expectin' somebody?" Della appeared at the living

room door, looking perturbed, but she already knew who it was.

"Sounds like Doug brought the buyer here, but I don't know what for. Celeste hasn't agreed to anything." Ronnie heard their footsteps approaching.

"Yes, sir, this place brings back a whole lotta memories."

A whole lotta memories?! That's him! Ronnie finally placed the silky baritone as she headed to the door. "Ma, I think he's a local DJ named Johnny DuPree."

But Della, hands on hips, was already standing in the doorway. "What in the devil are you doin' here?"

"I wasn't sure you were still in Prosper, Della." Lester smiled sheepishly at her. "I'm lookin' to buy me a piece of this place since your girls wanna sell it."

"Wait a minute. I'm confused." Ronnie saw the man she had met as Lester. He looked long and cool in royal blue linen pants, the matching shirt worn loosely over them. His red Corvette was parked by the road in front of Doug's car. "You sound just like this radio guy—Johnny DuPree, your morning MC." Ronnie mimicked his delivery.

"Guilty as charged." Lester answered Ronnie, but he looked at Della, who looked away.

That explains the earring. "If you and Ma are old friends, how come you didn't tell us you wanted to buy this place?" Ronnie put her hands on her hips until she realized her mother was doing the same thing. Then she dropped her arms to her sides.

"I've had the word out for years that I was interested in this property. Edna, Doug here's mama, is an old friend from my Charlotte days. I asked her to keep an eye open and if it ever came on the market to let me know. When I found out y'all were comin' down, I said make the offer, but use DW Enterprises, one of my company names. I didn't want to put pressure on anybody, and I didn't want to be in the middle of your family business."

Della avoided Lester's glance and edged toward the steps. Doug spoke up. "I just found out myself. Mother never mentioned the buyer by name, and we've communicated mostly through an assistant in his office. Can we come inside and continue this?"

"This isn't my business—If you'll excuse me." Della headed down the stairs.

"You can stay, Ma." Ronnie wanted company for whatever talk they were about to have, but Della headed for the path and never looked back.

Ronnie showed the two men inside. Lester peered in the rooms off the hall. "It was the biggest house in town, back then. When I was growing up, I always wanted a place like this."

"It's still pretty big, but don't go by me. I've been livin' in apartments with rooms the size of closets for too long. And you're certainly welcome, Lester, but I'm not sure why Doug brought you out. Celeste hasn't budged, and since we own it fifty-fifty—"

"You don't know she called me?" Doug asked.

"When?"

"This morning—said you-all were prepared to sell the house and we should move forward."

"She did?" Ronnie's heart skipped a beat, but it wasn't from joy. This was the news she'd been waiting for, but she had the same sick feeling that came over her when she stepped in her ransacked apartment, like she'd lost something she couldn't replace.

"In fact I spoke with her a few times. She suggested we come out today if we could swing it, so we can talk about how the land would be divided while you're both here. She said she'd be back this afternoon. Is something wrong?"

"No. I—uh—haven't heard from her—I'm not even sure where she is." There was so much noise in Ronnie's head she struggled to string the words together. "Uh, let's sit in here." She led the way to the living room.

Doug and Lester took turns discussing surveyors, boundary lines, and lake access. They drew maps on the pad in Doug's folder, and Ronnie nodded, but all she heard was the voice that started small and grew steadily louder. *I want to stay here!* Definitely not the words she was expecting, but they were the only ones she could hear. *This doesn't make sense.* But Ronnie felt right in this house, which she couldn't admit even to herself until now. She hadn't felt right in so long it was hard to recognize.

"So what do you think?—Ronnie?"

It took a moment before she realized Doug had said her name. "I'm sorry. You're both gonna think I'm crazy." Ronnie took a deep breath, huffed it out. "I can't do this."

"Okay. What's your suggestion?" Doug scooted up to the edge of the chintz armchair. "There are lots of possible ways to divide the acreage."

"The house—I mean, I can't sell the house." *I can't believe that just came out of my mouth.*

Lester looked confounded. "I thought we were all in agreement here."

"So did I." Doug looked pissed.

"This is my fault." Ronnie moved next to Lester on the sofa. "My whole reason for coming here was to hound my sister into selling this place. But in the time we've been staying here I've kinda gotten to like it. And I'm at this point in my life where I need to switch up. Do something completely different, and Prosper is about as different from Manhattan as it gets."

"Can't argue with that." Lester cracked a wry smile.

"I apologize for this misunderstanding." Doug glanced over at Ronnie like he was waiting for an explanation.

"Ain't nothin' but a thang." Lester unfolded his long legs and stood up. "So you're gonna stay with us awhile."

"If I can work it out."

"Let me get this straight. Are you keeping all the acreage, or can we do some business here?" Doug clasped his hands together and leaned forward.

At first Ronnie thought she should leave well enough alone, but she knew that to stay she'd need some money, at least to get a car. She got a gleam in her eye, stood up next to Lester. "Can I interest you in some lovely lakefront property that's ripe for development? It would make an excellent site for a home. A compound, really. I mean, main house, guest house, garage, stables." She made a wide sweep with her hand to encompass the grand estate she described. "Something befitting a radio personality like yourself."

"You're a handful, aren't you?" Lester grinned.

"At least. Sometimes two."

"Why don't you and Doug here have a talk about it and let me know what you come up with? I'm gonna take a little walk, if that's all right with you."

"Of course. I don't know where Ma went."

"I bet I can find her. And Doug, my man, I'll talk to you before I leave."

"Sure thing." Doug gathered his papers, shoved them in his folio, and he and Ronnie accompanied Lester to the porch and watched him walk toward the path to the lake.

Doug sat on the top step. "So, have you developed a sudden attachment to the family estate, or is this some kind of twisted way to get back at your sister? Or to make me look bad?"

"Look, I'm sorry. I didn't know I was gonna say that before it came out of my mouth. I swear." She eased down next to him, looked around her. Everything, the trees, the grass, the air, buzzed and hummed with life. This place had survived neglect, maybe it needed the same second chance she did. "I also didn't expect Celeste to do a flip-flop like that. She can be like a pit bull with a pork chop." She started laughing. "The one time I get her to come around, I go and change my mind. Oh, man, is she gonna give me mucho hell. Ma too." She held her stomach, but was pleasantly surprised to find it didn't hurt to laugh anymore. "I'm not a nut job, Doug. Honest." She rested a hand on his knee for a hot second and was startled by the tingle. *What's that about?* "You ever do something that seemed crazy, but it turned out to be right?"

"I'd say quitting my job and moving back to Charlotte falls in that category." He shrugged. "Sometimes you gotta do what you gotta do, even if nobody understands but you."

"It needs to make *some* sense. Ma and Celeste had to kinda bail me out, and I need to show 'em I can take it from here."

Ronnie looked over at Doug. "At this point I need to prove it to myself. I got diddly to go back to in the Apple." *Why am I telling him this?* "It's a long story, but selling this place meant I could afford another go-round in New York, or L.A. for that matter, except I'm not up for any more of the city shuffle. At least not now. I guess I had to fall on my butt to realize it's okay to say 'when.' " Ronnie held her head in her hands for a moment, and Doug waited until she looked up again. "I didn't mean to start rambling."

Doug had been a reporter long enough to know when somebody needed to tell a story, but he wasn't obliging her for professional reasons. "You'll know if I'm bored. I snore."

Ronnie grinned. "Fair enough." And as she told her story, Doug did one of the things he did best: listen.

Before long they were interrupted by the chirping of Doug's cell phone. "Celeste? Yes, we're both here—It's not a problem, really—I've heard it always takes longer than you expect at the hairdresser." He grinned and raised an eyebrow at Ronnie. "No need to rush. Uh—no—not exactly—I think you should talk with your sister." He handed the phone to Ronnie.

21

". . . what could have been, what would have been, and what was."

"What are you doin' down here?" Della groused. "Your business is up at that house." *'Cause I got enough mess stirred up without addin' you to it.* She sat on the old hickory stump, half looking at the murky water, not daring to turn around and look at him. Whatever wrangling Ronnie and Lester had to do about Little Pond was between them. Della wanted no part in it.

"My business, huh? If I didn't know better, I'd swear you were tryin' to run me off." Lester strolled into the clearing from the woods. "You still knew I was here. Always wondered how you did that."

A tingle traced the back of Della's neck when he stopped behind her. *Same as I knew you were at the hospital before I saw you.* Only now the vibration was stronger because they were alone. "I don't know, Lester!" She shrugged. "I could always tell, that's all."

He bent down, scooped up a handful of pebbles. "It's pretty overgrown down here."

"What in the world do you want with it, then?! Of all the places you have been in your life, why would you come back to Prosper?" Della asked her questions to the lake because she didn't dare face him yet.

"You really wanna know?" Lester selected a flat, gray stone from the cluster in his hand. "It's home." He rubbed the rock between his thumb and forefinger. "If you wanna be technical, I was born in Charlotte, but Prosper's true home for me. And I've dragged my rusty dusty within fifty miles of anywhere you point to on a map, pitched my tent in a few of 'em, at least long enough to keep my son from feeling like a gypsy."

He has a son? In all these years she'd never imagined Lester with a family. Not one that didn't include her. A sigh slipped through Della's lips.

"Truth is, I had a good life here, once. I do again. And as for this particular place—" He hurled the stone so far over the water that they barely heard it splash. "—When we were kids, back before I had two quarters to rub together, I wanted to own all this land. It was the biggest spread around, but nobody in it was happy. I was fool enough to think that if it was mine—ours—we'da been happy here."

"Why are you tellin' me this?"

"'Cause you asked—'Cause I shoulda said it a long time ago when it counted."

The velvet of Lester's voice wrapped itself around Della the way it used to when they were young and she used to feel like her heart wouldn't beat without him. *This don't make no kinda sense.* "That was two lifetimes ago, yours and mine."

"Doesn't mean it's not worth sayin'. I was always sorry I wasn't here when Henry killed your father. Maybe I could have . . ."

"Wasn't nothin' you coulda done. Nobody could. Took me a while to believe that myself, but it's true. Henry was one a them people that got evil where the good should be."

"He didn't start out that way, but the older he got, the more rotten he got. Me and Will, we knew it. It got him killed in the end." Lester spoke over the top of Della's head.

A breeze rustled the leaves and blew ripples across the water. "I guess Will heard he was dead when he was down here in 'sixty-nine, but I wouldn't let him tell me nothin' about it." Henry had been her personal boogeyman for so long that it was almost comforting to have him around to hate. But everybody she ever knew seemed determined to jump up in her face and make her take a second look, and it looked like Henry was no exception. "What happened to him?"

Lester shook the stones in his hands like dice. "Was in

'sixty-seven I was in New Orleans. Heard he was missing more'n a week before they found him in the woods, just south of here, near where the church picnics used to be."

Della nodded. She hadn't thought about the place in years, but she knew exactly where he meant.

"Somebody stabbed him. Never found out who, or why, but I bet he finally mouthed off to the wrong person."

"Humph." Della stared at the pond. "I used to think hearin' he got his would make me feel good. I guess bad don't make you feel better."

"It was bound to happen. I used to think he'd outgrow the nasty streak."

"No. That works for some. But bad like that? It grows with you—and if the world is lucky it kills you before you kill somebody else." Della kicked the heel of her sneaker against the tree. They stayed that way for a while, both thinking, neither speaking.

Lester cleared his throat. "Della, whatever made you think I wasn't comin' back for you?" He looked at the pebbles in his hand, then lifted his gaze to her.

Della finally turned and looked at him, but the hurt in his eyes, the pain in his voice made her quickly turn away. *I shoulda trusted you, but I was so scared.*

TUESDAY, SEPTEMBER 17, 1957
PROSPER, NORTH CAROLINA

"Whatchu gon' do, Odella?" Will rared back on a Coca-Cola crate, his back propped against the wood plank walls of Pal's storeroom. "You can't stay here but so long." His hat was cocked down over his eyes, but its stingy brim didn't offer much shade from the glare of the naked lightbulb hanging from the ceiling.

"I don't know yet, Will. I still can't think straight." Odella stood next to the shelves lined with cans of shortening, sacks of beans, and other restaurant supplies. There had been too much crazy stuff this past week. She was numb, had been since she came to at the foot of the stairs, her father's body still splayed on the floor next to her. When Will found her the next day, sitting by the lake, at first she wouldn't talk to him. She stared straight ahead, but Will knew something was wrong, something big. She looked disheveled, hair standing all over her head, but more than that, her eyes looked stone-cold.

"You sure you got all your stuff?" Will looked at the suitcase in the corner. "We can go to the house. Henry ain't gon' try nothin' while I'm watchin' him. He knows I'll whup his ass. He'd wait till my back was turned, and I ain't about to do that."

Odella remembered her composition books in the piano bench. "Everythin' I need. I ain't never goin' in that place again. Not while I'm livin'." She cupped her left hand around her right. The bandages were gone, but her bare fingertips were still tender where she'd torn off the nails, trying to hold on to her father.

"I know you upset 'cause a your daddy, but that's still your house."

"I don't want nothin' else from there!"

"Aw right. Don't get upset." Will stuffed his hands in the pockets of his plaid sport jacket. He pulled out a sheet of white tablet paper, folded it into smaller and smaller squares.

It felt strange to Odella, being in Pal's after midnight, without plates clattering or Hambone mouthing off. But the air still smelled like onions and grease. She didn't know what she would have done if they hadn't let her stay, because after the funeral she couldn't bear to be in that house. Before the burial she'd lie awake at night, a chair barricading her door. Once the show was over, she had to get out. "I wish I'd gone with Lester. He begged me to come. Maybe none a this woulda happened." Lester had been gone three weeks now, scouting new places for them to sing, making connections, he called it. He wanted to take her, but she said she needed more time to get ready. Last time he called he was in Baltimore, on his way to Cleveland. It was the first long-distance call she ever got.

They only spoke a minute. Long enough for him to tell her he might go as far as Chicago or even New York because they cut records there. And to say he missed her.

Will refolded his paper. "I talked to Lester last night—"

"When were you gon' tell me!?" Odella put her hands on her hips.

Will shoved his hat back on his head. "I didn't know how to put it."

"Put what?" She held her breath.

"He called your house. Henry started blessin' him out, so he hung up and called me—I told him what happened."

"What did he say? When is he comin' back?"

Will jammed the paper in his pocket. "He ain't."

"What?!" Odella's pulse throbbed in her neck.

"He's goin' to Chicago. Said there's a record company there wants to sign him."

"When's he comin' for me?" She barely had breath to speak.

"He ain't comin', Odella. Said he had to strike while the iron was hot—I'm sorry."

It was like somebody threw all the pieces of her life in the air, and none of them had landed in the same place. "What do you mean he ain't?" She sank to the cot, too dizzy to stand.

Will came and sat beside her. "I can't make this no better than it is, or you know I would."

"You told him everythin' that happened? About Henry, what he did to Papa—about me livin' here?"

"Yep."

Right then Odella felt alone and as hollow and abandoned as a dry well.

Will moved closer, put his arm around her. "Odella—I'm leavin' Prosper too."

"What?"

"I can't stay here no more. Ain't no reason." He took off his hat, sat it on his knee. "I been sayin' I was goin' to Buffalo to get me a job at the steel plant. My cousin says they're hirin' now, so I gotta make a move." Will took her hand. Odella looked startled. "Come with me."

"What?"

"I know Lester had you all goosed up about this singin' thing, but that wasn't gon' be no kinda life for you. Hangin' 'round honky-tonks. Wishin' on stars." He squeezed her tighter. "Marry me, Odella. I'll take care a you, like a man's supposed to."

Odella stared in Will's direction. She knew his lips were moving, but she couldn't hear him because she was still trying to make sense of what had been said. She pressed her hand to her chest, trying to keep her heart from pounding through her skin. Lester had dropped her the first chance he got. She wouldn't believe it if anybody but Will had told her. And now he was talking about getting married. *Will Frazier?*

"Are you all right?"

Odella returned to the room when she felt him shake her. "I don't know, Will."

"You don't have to promise nothin' now. Come with me to Buffalo. You'll be gone from here." Will squeezed her hand. "I sure hope you give me a chance."

Odella looked at him, mouth open, not knowing what to say.

"Think on it. I'm leavin' in a couple of weeks. I know that means you'll be missin' out on your last year of school."

"I ain't hardly thinkin' about that right now."

"Well, let me know whatchu wanna do."

Odella looked over at him. She trusted Will more than blood. He looked out for her like a real brother would. *I just never thought about marryin' him.* She was so confused. "I don't know, Will. Give me some time."

"Sure thing." He kissed her hand, put on his hat, and left.

Odella turned out the light and lay on her cot. She could see the crescent moon through the small window in the back door. And she didn't know what in the world she was gonna do.

"Odee?" Lester walked around and stood next to her.

She lifted her head, looked up at him, and her heart skipped a beat. *After all this time? I'm too old for this foolishness.* It took a few seconds to compose herself enough to an-

swer. "Long story. It doesn't even matter anymore. I know
Will lied on you, and I guess part of me knows why." She
turned back to the pond. "I let it go long time ago."

"Forgiveness is a mighty big thing, Odee."

"Oh, it ain't up to me to forgive. That work's a little too
important for us down here." She raised her eyes skyward a
moment.

"Never thought about it like that." Lester opened his palm
flat and examined the stones. "Will was always sweet on you,
Odee. I knew that too. When he saw his chance, he took it. I
blamed him for a long time. Blamed you awhile too. But none
of it did any good." Lester looked out over the lake. "He
treated you good?"

Della looked back at him, puzzled by the question. "Will?
Of course. Couldn't have asked for a better father or husband." She saw Lester bow his head, then look off into the
woods. "I mean—"

"No need to explain." Lester hurled another stone into the
pond. "Will Frazier was a good man. And you deserved that."

"What about you?" It was time for her to turn the tide of
this conversation.

"Let's see. Been married. Been divorced. Been around."
He punctuated each phrase with the toss of a pebble, then
chuckled. "More of the last than anything else. Truth is, I'm
not sure how good I woulda been to you back then. I got a little full of myself. And I'm back to drinkin' RC again."

"Does flingin' them stones make it easier for you to speak
your mind?"

"What?"

"You used to do that whenever you had somethin' big to
say." The banter felt familiar to Della. All that was missing
was her history book.

"I did? Guess some things don't change—and some things
do." He bent down for another handful and would have stolen
a look at her legs except she was wearing pants. So he squatted, resting his butt on his heels. "My son runs my station in
Wilmington."

"Wilmington? I heard you once or twice since I been down here. Made Ronnie turn that mess off." Della smirked. "How many do you have?"

"Six. Four in North Cakalackee. Two in South. My first one and my favorite is the one here, though. WDLA."

"WDLA?" At first she didn't get it, then the lightbulb came on. "You don't mean?"

He nodded. "Seemed right I name it after you."

She looked at him and shook her head. "Still makin' up names, huh?" Despite the white fuzz at the temples and the furrows in his brow, he looked good, still full of energy. And he was still a snazzy dresser. She felt frumpy by comparison.

"I think I'm still pretty good at it too." He reached for a twig. "Anyways, I been thinking about buyin' another group that just came up for sale, but at my age, I don't know if I still want to work that hard."

"Seems like a long way from that summer I saw you in Buffalo to owning a bunch of radio stations."

"Not so long. Matter of fact, it was pretty direct. The sixties and rock and roll, it changed the music business." Lester drew circles in the dirt. "I was old-timey and work dried up faster than a Texas creek bed. Couldn't get more'n a few gigs here and there, couldn't get air play on the radio no more. I was mad at the whole world, but after I figured out nobody cared, I looked for some other way to use my voice."

"I still got your records. Ain't played 'em in years." Della peeked at him out of the corner of her eye.

"Well, do tell." He stopped drawing and cocked his head to look at her sideways. "You still sing, Odee? Church and stuff like that?"

"No." She crossed and uncrossed her feet at the ankles. "I stopped long time ago. Didn't feel it anymore."

"That's a shame. I still ain't heard nobody could match you." His voice trailed off for a moment. He scuffed out the circles he had made with the toe of his shoe. "Anyway, about three years after I started DJing, there was a government program around to give minority folks a shot at owning and operating radio stations, and I got the chance to buy into one. Later, my partner sold out to me, and the rest is, as they say, history."

"So you did become a rich man." Della stood up. "And now you want to buy this place." She brushed dust and bits of dead leaves from the seat of her trousers. She stopped when she realized he was watching.

Caught, he grinned, shoved his hands in his pockets, and looked at her face. "I wouldn't exactly say rich, but I've done all right. I think I could have enjoyed it more, though. Which is kinda how I feel about Little Pond. It's about time somebody enjoyed it. I'd like to clean up the sludge here around the shore, clear out some of this old dead wood. You should see what they've done with the waterfront over in Jessup."

"You're crazy as you always were, Lester Wilson!" She turned to go.

"Odee?" He reached out and touched her arm as she passed him.

Della stopped. The same electricity that had always passed between them coursed through her when his fingers touched her skin.

"I don't know what your girls are gon' do about this place, since they can't seem to make up their minds." Lester glanced down at his shoes, then back at Della. He didn't expect her to still shake him up, but he felt it when he first saw her at the hospital. When his parents shipped him out to the country after an "almost" brush with the law, Lester developed a swagger and bravado meant to let everybody know he was a little bit ahead of their game. After all, he was from Charlotte. Henry Womack was the first boy he met, followed by Will and then nearly everyone else in Prosper, and they were duly impressed with his shiny, city ways. Then Odella showed up, and he knew from the beginning he wasn't fooling her. Most people he came in contact with were still impressed, but right now that didn't matter. "I know you got to be gettin' back—but—I—"

"Spit it out, Lester. I hope you don't fumble around like that on the radio!" She laughed. "If you wanna know what my

daughters are gonna do, I'm out of it. Woulda let the land and
everything on it rot 'cause I wasn't ever comin' back. Except
Will talked me into signin' it over to him. They got it when he
passed. I never could get Celeste and Ronnie to agree on anythin', so if that's what you're askin'—"

"Uh—No—It's not that." He knew Della didn't buy his
hotshot act then, and he liked that about her. And he could not
believe, standing here forty-odd years later, that she still made
him feel like a bumbling schoolboy. "I—Can I take you to
dinner?"

Her arm still felt hot where his hand had been, and she
fought the urge to rub the spot. This felt so strange. "Lester,
you don't have to do that. I'm sure you got plenty of company."

"Do you see my arm twisted behind my back? Huh?" He
took both of her hands.

"Uh—Well—No."

"Then let me take you out. I believe in taking second
chances."

Della thought for a moment, about what could have been,
what would have been, and what was. And for the first time in
years, she didn't know what was to come. "I'd like that,
Lester." She shocked herself. "Tomorrow?"

He crooked his arm, she slipped hers through it, and they
headed back to the house.

"I think you're grabbing at straws." Celeste, who had finally
shown up after her unintended full day of beauty, sat next to
her sister on the step. "It seems like a good idea now, but
that's because you haven't tried it. What on earth would you
do here?"

"I can start a whole new life down here. Doug was telling
me how good the job market is." Ronnie felt more hopeful after their talk.

Doug stood by the porch railing, observing the back-and-
forth volleys. The tone seemed less hostile than the earlier encounters he'd seen. Celeste wasn't even too upset about
Ronnie's change of heart. The employment issue seemed to

be the sticking point. "If it doesn't work out, she can always leave."

"Yes, I've read there's a lot going on in the corporate sector of Charlotte, but you—"

"I'm sure I can find something. I even thought of talking to Lucille about offering makeup lessons and applications at the salon, kinda my own little freelance business. And I won't have to worry about a place to live. I've got one." Ronnie looked back at the house. "I know it sounds nuts, but I kind a like it."

"You don't even have a—what in the name of—" Celeste elbowed Ronnie in the side.

"Ouch!" A little too hard. Ronnie winced.

"Psst!" Celeste hissed in Ronnie's ear and nodded toward the path.

"That hurt." Ronnie frowned at Celeste. "Did you forget I just had an operation?!"

"Be quiet and look!" Celeste's eyes had locked on a target.

Ronnie followed Celeste's pointed gaze and saw her mother coming through the trees, having a spirited talk with Lester. But Ronnie knew Celeste was fixated on Della's arm looped through his. "Who'd a thunk it?" Ronnie grinned.

"Is that all you have to say?!" Celeste stood up and threw her hand in the air. "Fine! Everybody *has* taken leave of their senses! What does she think she's doing?" Celeste demanded.

"Looks to me like she's taken a walk with an old friend. And from where I sit, looks like a pretty good one!" Ronnie was still smiling when Della, suddenly aware of the viewers, withdrew her arm from Lester's as they neared the house.

"So," Lester spoke before he reached them. "Have we come to an agreement yet?"

"Lester?" Ronnie felt the now or never moment and jumped in. "If you're still interested in buying twenty acres from the south boundary, with lakefront, no house, we have a deal." She turned to Celeste. "Okay?"

Celeste hesitated.

"Trust me this once, Celeste."

Celeste looked at her sister, then at Lester. "Deal."

"What are you gon' do with the house?" Della interrupted.

"Live in it." Ronnie smiled at her mother.

"Have you even thought about a job, Ronnie?" Della persisted. "And you can't live out here without a car! Do you even still have a driver's license?" Della launched her questions.

"You work for the DMV, Ma! Last time I checked, New York City was still part of New York State! Of course I have a license! And since we're obviously going to talk about this now—" Ronnie looked at her family, then at Doug and Lester. "I'll get a job. Doing something. It can't be any harder than where I've been! At least I'll have a roof over my head."

Doug interjected, "I don't think she'll have a big problem finding work."

"Who asked you!?" Della snapped.

"I did," Ronnie said defiantly. "And I'll ask everybody I know, everybody I meet. Isn't that what you always say?" She turned to Celeste, who sank back down on the step. " 'It's not what you know, it's who you know'? Well for once I'm gonna take your advice! Speaking of who you know—Lester? I've heard the announcements for jobs at the station almost every day on the radio. You work there. Who should I see about putting in an application?"

"What in the world do you know about a radio station?" Celeste couldn't believe what she was hearing.

"Don't need to know much about radio for some of them," Lester said. "If you're really interested we can talk about it. I know someone who has an in with the boss!" He winked at Della.

"Thank you." Ronnie bowed her head. "See!" she said to her mother and sister.

"Good. I'll have Doug here draw up the new paperwork, and we'll be cookin' with gas!"

Ronnie shook Lester's hand, then gave Della and Celeste a big, silly grin.

"Just like your mama." Lester smiled at Della. "When she thought she'd said somethin' smart. Isn't that right, Odee?"

"I did no such thing, Lester Wilson!" Della almost giggled.

"Odee?" Ronnie looked at them over imaginary glasses.

"I'll pick you up tomorrow about six?" Lester pecked Della on the cheek.

"Fine."

"I'm outta here too." Doug got out his car keys. "I'll get the ball rolling and be in touch with everybody ASAP. Ronnie, any questions about Charlotte, give me a ring. I'll be happy to give you a tour if you like."

"Sounds like a plan." Ronnie smiled.

Lester nodded to Celeste and Ronnie, then he and Doug headed toward their cars. Before Lester got in his, he turned and waved. Della grinned and waved back.

Ronnie smirked, watching her mother act like a schoolgirl.

And Celeste simmered. "What was all that about?"

"Wasn't about nothin'." Della's eyes followed Lester's car as he drove off.

"That's not how it looked to me-ee," Ronnie sang and sidled up next to Della.

"And do you think he offers that tour to *all* his clients?" Della joked.

"How can you carry on like that?!" Celeste's face had clouded. "Daddy's been gone less than a year and I . . ."

"Celeste, it's not what you . . ."

"I don't understand you, Mother! I just don't!" Celeste trotted into the house.

"... just let it all hang out."

The next morning Della was the first one stirring. She shuffled through the rooms downstairs in the half light, letting her hands glide over lampshades and books, rest on chairbacks and desktops, finally embracing how familiar she felt here in spite of decades spent denying the memory. Walking the hall toward the front of the house she traced her finger along the oak wainscoting the way she used to when she was a girl and nobody was looking. A tragedy had first brought her to Prosper, and another one chased her away. This trip could have been tragic too, but mercifully it wasn't. Ronnie was fine, Della was grateful, and now she was ready to make her peace with this house, this town. *It wasn't all good, but it wasn't all bad, either.*

Della stood for a long time at the living room doorway in her yellow nightgown, envisioning the room the way it used to be, full of sober furniture, covered with knickknacks and antimacassars. She remembered how stuffy it seemed, how gingerly she used to walk through the room so she wouldn't break anything. Then her father bought the piano, and it was the only thing in there that mattered to her.

Cautiously, Della approached the piano, sat on the bench. Her piano. She reached out her hand, lightly touching the shiny black surface. When she got to the safety latch, her hand froze, anticipating Henry's oppressive presence hovering over her, still sworn to keep her from playing what her heart called for. But in that instant she realized there was nothing left of Henry but dust and a ghost she'd been dragging around too long. A breath of relief replaced the too familiar dread as she lifted the lid, positioned her hands over the keys. She didn't know what she was going to play, but her fingers would know.

So she began, softly at first, with a melody she hadn't even hummed to herself in years, one that first came to her on an evening full of June bugs, down by the pond, and she'd later written it in her blue composition book. It felt good as the notes swirled around her, traveled through her. Last night all she heard was static between herself and her daughters, over secrets kept and misunderstandings. If anything was going to change, she knew it had to start with her. Maybe it was time for music. Music and the truth.

After a while Della had heard Ronnie's footsteps upstairs, then water running in the bathroom, heard Ronnie pause, trying to make out the sounds from downstairs. She heard Celeste's door open and their whispers. Just as she had heard them cough in their sleep when they were little, or toss and turn, fitful and restless on a hot night. She would go into their rooms, give them a sip of water or turn their pillow to the cool side, and they never knew she'd been there, because they never really woke up. They weren't supposed to know. She was. She was the mother.

So Della played louder as they tiptoed downstairs, like kids on Christmas Eve trying to catch Santa leaving goodies under the tree. And now she heard their breath as they stood in the doorway behind her.

But she kept playing, because yesterday, after Lester had gone, she realized Lucille was right. She was a mystery to her daughters. She had eased her own mind by locking away the pieces of her life she couldn't make fit, but she finally saw that it had left Celeste and Ronnie with an incomplete picture of who their mother was and how she got that way. Della went to sleep thinking about Lucille's advice and knowing it was time to add color and shading to her self-portrait.

Celeste and Ronnie stood on the threshold, wondering what this change was all about, waiting to see who would make the first move.

Roots was on Ronnie's tenth-grade reading list the last time she'd questioned Della about what it was like when she was a girl. "All that old-timey stuff don't matter. What happens now is what counts." Later Celeste, pregnant with Niki, broached the subject and inquired about the family medical history, reasoning that since her grandparents hadn't made it to old age, there might be some things she needed to know. Della shot down Celeste's questions as she had Ronnie's. "Ain't no point worryin' 'bout what you can't change no way."

When Della started to hum, resonant and rich, Ronnie could no longer resist. She entered the room, sat on the couch. Celeste looked on from the doorway.

Della finished her song and stared at her hands. The hands that used to play this piano didn't have ridges in the fingernails, slack skin, or knobby joints. She finally looked up at Ronnie. "I gave this up an awful long time ago."

Celeste, who had been braced for the worst, relaxed her stance, let herself be drawn closer.

"But why, Ma?" Ronnie asked. "You sound so good."

"Oh, it's all rusty now. I *used* to be good. Least that's what folks said. And I guess I was." Della looked from one daughter to the other. "But it caused way more trouble than it was worth." She saw the questions written on their faces and knew the answers were written on her heart. "Lord—" She let her fingers walk a C scale. CDEFGABC. "There's just so much y'all don't know." She shook her head. "I guess this is as good a place as any to start."

Celeste eased down on the piano bench next to her mother. Both she and Ronnie, still not sure they weren't dreaming, tried not to look too eager, for fear it might stop Della. They needn't have worried. She had held it all long enough. There wasn't any more room. There wasn't any more strength. She was tired.

"Me, your father, and Lester were all friends," Della began, but then stopped. She looked off, beyond Ronnie and Celeste and into a past that was so full of shadow even she wasn't sure she knew her way around. Finally she gathered herself, at least enough to spare the bits and pieces she needed to leave a trail behind her. She would have to find her way back. "It didn't start out that way, and it didn't end up that way either, thanks to Henry. But for a while . . ."

Della began in the middle, her arrival at Little Pond, alone, afraid with her whole world turned inside out. By the time she paused for a breath on her way back to Cadysville and Annie, Celeste was hard at work trying to find a place for the notion of her mother as—*illegitimate?* Ronnie, on the other hand, was drawn into the unfolding tale, captivated by the depth of love Della described between Odell and Annie and sorry they didn't get to live it together. *Ma was a love child?*

Della had become Scheherazade, and there were a thousand more stories to go, so she zigzagged through time and place, letting it come out as it came up. She knew if she stopped to organize it, like Celeste would prefer, she might not make it all the way through. Her story kept getting blown off course by questions and comments, and Della had to struggle to get back on track, to keep her train of thought.

When she finally arrived at that afternoon in the chicken coop when Henry tried to rape her and Will saved her, Della's tale stalled. She looked at Celeste and Ronnie a long moment, grateful they never had to go through what she did.

Della built up enough steam and lurched forward again. In halting words, she minced through her recollection, searching for a way to tell what she had never spoken before.

Celeste felt the floor drop out from under her. She had barely thought of her mother as a *woman*, certainly not as a vulnerable teenage girl. For once in her life she didn't know what to say so she scooted closer to her mother. Close enough for their shoulders to touch. Close enough to feel the weight that had been there so long.

Ronnie got up and dragged one of the straight-backed chairs up to the piano. She gripped the seat to control her trembling hands, and her breath came in short, shallow wisps. Light-headed and nauseated, she forced herself to swallow hard against the bile rising in her throat. She knew how terrified, trapped, and violated she had felt in that photographer's studio. She never dreamed of telling her mother or anyone what happened to her; it would be too embarrassing. Besides,

Della would have no way to understand. Now Ronnie realized she had never given her mother credit for having lived a life that wasn't totally safe and predictable.

Della's voice still quivered as she moved on to why she and Will left Prosper for Buffalo and recounted the night Henry killed her father. As she spoke, she could feel him plunging too hard and fast for her to catch him, see the rail posts splinter as they broke his fall. She picked up the composition book from the music stand, rolled it into a tube. "It was the awfulest thing I ever saw." Della rocked side to side to keep herself together.

Celeste rocked with her, put an arm around her, tried to help her carry the load. Celeste felt awkward at first, cradling her mother, but soon settled into the rhythm of the embrace.

Ronnie was outraged. "Your stepmother watched and didn't try to help you?!" As far as she knew her grandparents were dead. Had been since their mother was little. That was the party line. She always thought of her mother as a loner, without people. That's how Della came, relatives not included. She'd never given Ronnie any reason to think about the void those losses left or the sadness that remained. "Why didn't they put him in jail!? Under the jail!? Even if you didn't tell, how come they didn't find out during the investigation?"

"What investigation?" Della chuckled. "Way out here in the woods didn't nobody see or hear nothin' but us. So a Black man who owned his own business, drove new cars, and had more money than half the White folks fell down the stairs and broke his neck in his own house. Didn't nobody *investigate* things like that." Della rolled the music book into a slender tube. "Accident or on purpose, some thought it was good riddance to—anyway, that's why Will wanted to get away from down here. At least one of the reasons."

Ronnie reached over and rubbed her mother's soft fleshy arm. "Ma, I'm so sorry I made you come back here."

"I was too, at first." Della eyed them both, patted Celeste's knee. "I'm not anymore."

They each let her words sink in for a moment, but not too long. There was more to talk about.

"So what happened to him? Henry?" Ronnie asked.

"I just found out myself. I always expected this place would be his." Della shook her head. "Lester told me somebody stabbed him to death. Years ago."

"Good for him!" Ronnie had to restrain herself from clapping. If she despised this man so intensely just from hearing about him, she couldn't imagine what her mother must have felt.

"I spent too many years hatin' him for what he did—and myself for lettin' him threaten me into not doin' anything about it—I gotta let it go now. Took a while for me to learn that punishment and forgiveness don't always seem equal, but it works out, if you give it time."

Della uncurled the book and smoothed it out across her lap while she told them how she thought Lester had dropped her as soon as he got a whiff of success, and then how Will finally stepped forward to let her know how he felt and asked her to marry him. It was hard talking to them about Will. What they knew about him as their father was a little different from things she knew about him as a man. "If I don't move now, my knees won't never work again." Della stood up and peeled her damp nightgown from the backs of her thighs. She needed a break.

It was afternoon and the air in the living room had grown close. The three of them, in their nightgowns, were unaware that they had too.

Della fanned herself as she headed toward the kitchen. "And I don't know about y'all, but I'm hot and my stomach thinks my throat is cut."

Ronnie got up, stretched, and followed after her. "Why didn't you keep singing, or at least playing? We had a piano sitting in the living room all those years and you never used it."

Celeste, dabbing sweat from her neck with a tissue, joined the procession. "Well—" She almost didn't bring it up, but it had always bothered her. "—Never, except for that time I caught you and you told me . . ."

"I know what I told you that day—" Della took three glasses from the cabinet, then an ice tray from the freezer

"—and I'm sorry. I just couldn't explain it then. I couldn't."
She spoke to Celeste while she popped a handful of cubes into
each glass. "Besides, things aren't always what they seem."
She turned on the tap, pulled back the curtain, and looked out
the window while she let the water run cool. "I found that out
the summer your father bought that piano." Distracted by
what she knew was to come, Della filled her own glass, took a
long drink over the sink, refilled it, and went to the table.

Celeste watched her mother sit, then went over to the sink,
filled the other two glasses, and handed one to Ronnie. "That
was the summer of the first moon walk."

"That was the summer we got the color TV," Ronnie said.

"It was the year before that summer that I saw Lester
again. Hadn't seen him since we left here and didn't expect I
ever would, but I guess I'd been mad all that time. One day the
three of us were out—Where had I taken you critters? I don't
remember where we'd—yes I do—We all went to the dentist.
Y'all remember Dr. Howard? Boy, you hated that trip." Della
smiled faintly at the memory.

"It was hot that day, hot for Buffalo. But after that first
winter when we moved up there and it was cold as the devil, I
swore I'd never complain about hot again." Della took a sip
and wiped her cool, damp hand over the back of her neck.

"Doc had an office full, as usual, so it was late afternoon
when we got out. You didn't have no cavities, Ronnie, so you
went skippin' ahead down Jefferson, playin' hopscotch with
the street cracks. Celeste, you walked with your hand covering your mouth where it was still crooked from the novocaine.
I tried to tell you it didn't look that bad, and if you'd put your
hand down nobody would notice, but as usual, you didn't listen."

Ronnie elbowed Celeste. "Some people never change."

"Look who's talking." Celeste swatted Ronnie.

"Anyway, we passed in front of the Pine Grill, and who did
I see on a poster but Mr. Johnny DuPree."

"The Pine Grill?" Celeste had a hard time visualizing her
mother jammed in the crowded, noisy club. She could almost
smell the Hai Karate, taste the Harvey Wallbangers, hear the

Ohio Players. *The Pine Grill?* She and her friends had used fake IDs to get in when she was a teenager. Imagining her mother hanging out in the same place was a challenge.

"Hasn't that been closed about a million years?" Ronnie asked.

Della nodded. "But it used to be the place to go, at least one of 'em. There were quite a few spots around town. And Will and I used to go out from time to time." She looked at Celeste. "Didn't see no need to tell you where we were goin', Miss Busybody." Della picked up her deck of cards and turned the box around and around in her hand. "For the rest of the walk home I told myself I should let bygones be bygones. Lester had once been a real good friend." She opened the flap and ran her thumbnail along the top of the deck. "I was kinda surprised he was still singin' in clubs since he hadn't had a hit in a few years, but he'd done all right for himself. Me and your father were doin' okay." She shook the cards into her left hand. "But I guess what I really wanted was to cuss him out. So I went."

Celeste's jaw dropped. "You sneaked off to see this man without telling Daddy!?" She sputtered, appalled that her mother could have done such a thing. "How could you?" Before the question was out of her mouth, she saw herself sneaking around on Everett. *Is that what this is all about!? She had an affair with this man?* "Are you trying to tell us that . . ."

"Maybe if you shut up long enough you'll find out what she's trying to tell us!" Ronnie interrupted.

"Both of you can hush." Della started shuffling the deck in a slow-motion cascade. "Anyhow, I remembered Lester liked to feel a place out before a performance, so I went early, way before show time. When I got there, he was right where I thought he'd be. Walkin' back and forth across the stage, blocking out his moves. I got a little dressed up that day. Went to the Sample Shop and bought a new dress—pale blue with a white portrait collar." She didn't tell them that Will had been trying to get her to do some shopping for herself for a while and that this finally seemed like a good enough reason. "Got shoes too. Navy leather with a strap across the arch that fastened with a white button."

"I remember those," Celeste said.

"Thought I looked pretty good, if I do say so myself. He recognized me the second I walked in the door."

"You got done up to go see this man?! An old boyfriend?" Celeste interrupted again. The notion of her mother primping for any reason was foreign enough, but to go see another man?

Della looked from one daughter to the other. "I know neither one of you thinks I ever cared about that kind of stuff—I used to—but that was before . . ." Then she resumed her tale. "Anyway, he hopped right off the stage. He always liked to do that." She paused, remembered the heat of his hands around her waist when he used to help her down.

"And?" Ronnie snatched Della back to the story. "Did you cuss him out?"

"Oh, yes I did. Laid him low." Della shook her head. "He tried telling me that Will had promised to bring me to meet him in Cleveland on his way to Buffalo. He swore he waited two weeks. Even told me the name of the place where Will was supposed to be bringin' me. He said after we didn't show up that he went back to Prosper lookin' for me, and folks told him I'd gone off to marry Will. Had the nerve to stand up there with his conked hair and say he thought I was comin' to tell him what happened and apologize. I called him a liar and everything but his name. I didn't even know I could say all that." Della smiled, tickled by the memory of her vitriol. "It made me feel good to see him squirming and still tryin' to lie. I finished my say-so and walked out. Left him and his shiny shoes sittin' at the bar holding a can of Carling Black Label."

"So why would you even speak to him now, much less walk arm in arm?" Celeste waved away the offending image of Della strolling up the hill with Lester. "Maybe we shouldn't even sell this place to him."

"Hold on a minute, now." Ronnie jumped in before Celeste got carried away. "What does all that have to do with the piano, Ma?"

Della's ice had melted, and her glass of water sat in a puddle of sweat. She picked it up, drained the last swallow. "Wish I never saw that blasted piano."

"I know Daddy bought it and a bunch of other stuff after he took a trip down here."

"So I wouldn't kill him." She put the cards down, avoiding the wet spot on the table. "This may be the hardest part for me to tell you, and it won't be easy for you to hear neither. And you need to know that we got past all that more'n twenty years ago."

"What?!" Ronnie fidgeted in her seat. It was getting harder for her to be comfortable on the hard chair, but she was too curious about her mother's story to move.

Celeste was growing more uncomfortable too, but it had nothing to do with her seat. She was afraid to know where Della's tale was leading. Afraid it would reveal more than she could handle.

"Lester was tellin' the truth."

"He couldn't have been!" Celeste jumped to her father's defense. "Daddy said . . ."

"I was there. You weren't. I know what your father said." Della got up and went to the refrigerator. She needed some help to get through this part of her story, and making sandwiches was about the only distraction she could think of on such short notice. "Will was workin', and you two were helpin' me clean out the closets and pack up old clothes to send to the Salvation Army. It was July, and I was already thinkin' about back to school, but I knew not to say that to the two of you or there'd a been nothin' but long faces." Della took out a package of deli ham and the jar of mustard. "We spent the mornin' fillin' up big green garbage bags with stuff y'all had outgrown or wouldn't wear 'cause it wasn't in style. Your job was to check the pockets before I folded them up." Della opened the breadbox. "Make sure we weren't givin' away more'n we thought we were." She spread mustard on six slices of whole wheat bread. "We had the bags sittin' by the back door waitin' for the truck to come pick 'em up." She turned to Celeste. "Then you dragged out a box of stuff that we must've put in the basement when we first moved from

Chester Street and just forgot about. You found this old red and green plaid sport jacket of your father's. Humph. He had that coat on when he asked me to marry him."

"The one still hangin' in the hall closet?" Celeste asked.

"Yep. I left it there so he wouldn't ever forget." Della laid slices of ham on the bread, then nodded toward Ronnie. "And you just about fell out laughing. That jacket *was* pretty ugly." Della got a flash of Will sitting on that crate in Pal's storeroom. *Lester called it backwoods country.* "But you put it on and started actin' real silly, talkin' funny like one of your cartoon characters or somethin'. The sleeves were practically down to your ankles, and you were flappin' your arms. We were all crackin' up then." Della grabbed three plates from the cabinet and put a sandwich on each one. "When you finally took it off, Celeste went diggin' in the pockets." *And I wished you hadn't been so determined at your job.* "I don't know how you managed to fish that little folded up scrap of paper out through the hole in the pocket where it fell down in the linin'. And then you asked if we knew anybody in Cleveland."

Ronnie's hand shot up over her gaping mouth.

Della got a knife out of the cutlery drawer and sliced the sandwiches in half the square way. "It was the address where he was supposed to bring me to meet Lester."

Celeste looked like her world had crashed down around her ears. "How could Daddy lie to you like that?"

"I know he didn't do it to hurt me. If anythin', he was tryin' to protect me. I guess he was doin' what he thought was best. But right then, it was all I could do not to throw somethin' before I could send you all out to play." Della leaned against the counter, bracing the weight of the memory. "Anyway, the night you found that paper, your daddy called to tell me he'd be late. Some tenants he had to evict had helped themselves to the bathroom sink and toilet and left a mess that he and Shorty had to clean up. I said fine. Never let on. I put y'all to bed early, and you pitched a fit 'cause it was still light out and there was no school to get up for. But there were some things your little ears didn't need to hear."

That night, when Will walked in the back door and sat

down on the steps to take off his work boots, he didn't know
what she knew. Unaware of what awaited him, he climbed the
stairs, footsteps tired and heavy, his sweaty, smelly socks
sticking slightly to the linoleum. He grabbed his favorite
glass, a quart Mason jar, filled it to the top with ice cubes and
grape soda. Then he joined Della who sat in front of a game of
solitaire at the kitchen table. But when she looked up from her
cards and into his face, he saw a Della he'd never seen before.
She reached in the pocket of her housecoat and put the note,
still folded, in front of him.

   "He knew what it was without openin' it. Before I could
say two words he started talkin' real fast. He admitted what he
did, told me Lester had called my house lookin' for me. It was
after Papa's funeral, but Lester didn't know what had happened. By then I was stayin' at the back room at Pal's with
Lucille and Hambone 'cause I couldn't sleep here. When
Henry cussed him and hung up, he called Will to find out
what the hell was goin' on. Lester was all excited 'cause some
producer, or whatever you call it, from a record company
wanted him to come to Chicago and make a record. He was
plannin' to drive home to get me, 'cause he was sure they'd
want me too as soon as they heard me. When Will told him
what had happened, Lester was gonna leave right then for me.
That's when I guess your daddy's feelin' got the best of him.
He told Lester he had me stayin' with his sister and she didn't
have no phone. Then he said he was leavin' for Buffalo, and
Cleveland was right on the way, so he'd drop me off. Maybe
he really intended to right then. I don't know, but by the time
I heard it, Will told me Lester was through with me. Asked me
to marry him. And from that day to this, I ain't never been to
Cleveland."

   The hum of the refrigerator was the only sound while Celeste and Ronnie absorbed the meaning of the story.

   "Why did he keep the note all those years?" Ronnie asked.

   Even now, Della didn't know why he hadn't thrown it
away. It would have been so easy. A toss in the trash, a flutter
out the window of the car as they snaked along the Sca-
jaquada Expressway.

"That I'll never know. After a while I guess he just forgot it." Della, still holding the knife, shrugged her shoulders as she answered. "We tried to keep it away from you two, but it was a bad summer after that. Boy, every time I laid eyes on your father I'd get mad all over again, and Will couldn't say nothin' 'cause—he couldn't. Anyway, he decided to go away for a while. Give me a chance to cool down."

"That's why he came here." Celeste didn't mean to say it out loud. "Hambone told us he was in Prosper that summer."

Della nodded and continued her purge. "When he got back, I was still hot. Next thing I knew he'd gone out and bought that piano. He was tryin' to make it up to me. I know he was. But I just couldn't play. Even when I got around to not bein' mad anymore, I didn't want anythin' to do with that piano. Seemed everywhere I turned, no good never came from it." She put the knife in the sink. "I know he lied because he loved me. Your father was a good man. From day one I knew that. And after a while I realized that it took a powerful lot of love to make a man honest as him live with a lie that big for so long. I believe he thought if I went to Cleveland I'd be followin' Lester's dream, not mine. And of course he thought he would do better by me than Lester. And maybe he was right—about both things." She carried the sandwiches to the table. "Anyhow, I'll never know."

"Did you love Daddy? At all?" Celeste asked. And she realized that as much as she didn't want to know what was behind that door, she had to. Maybe there were some answers for the questions she hadn't dared to ask herself. *Do I love Everett? Did I?*

Della sat down and took a deep breath. "I did. Still do and always will. Forty-five years is a long time to stay with one man just 'cause you promised you would." Della pushed her sandwich aside and picked up the cards again. "What we had was good—strong—comfortable. With your father, I felt safe and at home for the first time since my mother died. He protected me against Henry. Maybe that's why it was so hard when I found out he'd lied to me. I trusted him so much." She shuffled. "It just wasn't the same as—I never felt that—"

"Mother!?" Celeste never thought of Della having feelings like that. She was the mother.

"Spark? Fire? Passion?" Ronnie, on the other hand, had no doubts about wanting to know what was on the other side of the door. She wanted to yank it open and rummage around, find stuff to try on, see how it fit, like she'd done in the closets upstairs. "Come on, Ma?! Don't stop there," she teased.

"Well—I guess. All of that. It's a special feelin'—there's somethin' about the way it gets you all stirred up, hatchin' crazy plans. It warms you up, cools you down, makes you dizzy. Once you know that, you always know what it is—and *isn't*.

Celeste played with the crust on her sandwich, pinching it off in tiny bits.

"So it wasn't that I didn't love your father. It just wasn't—like that."

Ronnie lifted the bread off her sandwich, picked out a slice of ham, started to take a bite, then put it back on the plate.

"I know this has been more than a mouthful to swallow. But it took me too long to get started, and now I need to finish. This won't take but another minute or so." Della paused, collected herself. "You're more like me than you'd like to admit, both of you. I used to pretend it wasn't so, but ain't no point to it." She turned to Ronnie. "Missy, you need to hold on to somethin', make it yours. I guess I pushed what you thought were your dreams, because they once were the same ones I thought I had. Problem is I can't live mine through you. Your father might have been right, and I didn't even know if I really wanted all that, but you have to find out for yourself what *you* really want. Maybe your decidin' to stay down here a while is for the best. You been chasin' your tail too long, and at least you finally figured out you'll never catch it."

Now she spoke to Celeste. "And you got to let go of all that petty, picayune stuff you hold onto like it's so important. One day, I hope before it's too late, you'll find out it ain't worth squat. You're all closed up, shut off from the people who care about you, Everett and Niki. Shut off from yourself even. And I know exactly where you got it from. I didn't mean to put that on you, but you picked it up anyway. Let that mess go before that's all that you have left. Don't waste your todays."

"I didn't mean for it to be like this." Celeste wasn't paying attention when she reached for her glass. She tipped it over and water spilled onto the table and into her lap. She covered her face but couldn't hold back the tears. "I'm sorry."

"I know this ain't about that spilt water." Della got up and grabbed a dish towel. "And it probably wouldn't hurt you to get yourself some hormones. They sure did me a world of good when I was your age. But if these tears are for Everett, shouldn't he see 'em?" Della mopped up the water on the table and the floor.

"I loved him like that—like you were talking about—I really did. I don't know what happened," Celeste blubbered.

"You do so know what happened! You kept workin' on it, pickin' at it, tryin' to fix it, till you finally broke it. I don't know if you can do anythin' about it now, but try. Don't let this be like that speakin' contest you entered in eighth grade. You didn't win. You wouldn't talk about it and you never tried again." Della tossed the wet towel in the sink.

"You remember that?" Celeste blew her nose on the napkin Ronnie handed her.

"Of course I remember. You were so grown up that day, up on that stage soundin' so intelligent. I was proud of you."

"You were?"

"I never told you. I know." Della looked at Ronnie now. "And I never told you, either. Your daddy wasn't the only one braggin' about what you were doin'. I was always proud of both of you. I shoulda told you that—I thought you knew." Della picked up her glass and uneaten sandwich from the table and put them on the counter. "Call him. Go home. Hidin' down here won't solve nothin' back there. I gotta go to the bathroom."

The segue was abrupt, direct, welcome, and so like Della. It was the first thing Celeste and Ronnie had heard in hours that actually sounded like the mother they knew.

Having dug her way from beneath the load she had buried herself under years ago, Della left the kitchen feeling years

lighter. But Celeste and Ronnie sat, poised on the edge of the
excavation, surrounded by all that had been unearthed and
afraid that any sudden movement might damage the artifacts
that had been discovered or, worse, cause the hole to cave in
on itself.

"Wow." Ronnie fiddled with the abandoned deck of cards.

"Yeah, I know," Celeste replied, staring off into space.

They stayed that way awhile, looking stunned. Their
mother had excused herself from the awkward nakedness of
the morning's revelations and left them trying to figure out
whether to avert their eyes, cover up, or just let it all hang out.

"Let's go for a walk," Ronnie said after a while.

"You feel up to it?" With her middle finger Celeste mashed
the sandwich crumbs that had fallen on the table and sprinkled them on her plate.

"Today I need it."

"We can go up and change. . . ."

"How many acres we got here? Forty-five? I think this
great big nightshirt will do just fine. Already got my sneaks
on." Ronnie wiggled her feet.

Celeste started to object, then laughed and hitched up her
blue and white striped pajama bottoms. "Ready when you
are."

Outside, the sun hung directly overhead. Ronnie's steps
were slow and deliberate. Celeste fanned her PJ top to create a
breeze and shortened her stride to stay by her sister's side.

"I've been itchin' to go to the pond for a week. You haven't
been yet, have you?"

Celeste shook her head.

"Not scared, are you?" Ronnie remembered Celeste's hesitation the day they arrived. "I can hold your hand."

Celeste swatted at Ronnie. "I'm ignoring you." As they
marched around the side of the house, her eyes were drawn to
the chicken coop. "Ma went through so much—I mean her
mother dying so suddenly—Coming here to live, basically
with strangers, even if they were family—And Henry—What
he tried to do to her—" She shuddered, then looked at Ronnie.
"How could she keep *that* to herself?"

Ronnie walked on a few yards, looking at the ground in front of her, hands clenched at her sides before she answered. "She was hurt and ashamed, afraid people would blame her. At least Daddy knew, so she wasn't totally alone—Like I was."

"Huh?" Celeste couldn't imagine Ronnie meant what she thought she heard.

"It was right after I moved to New York." Her tongue primed by her mother's candor, Ronnie struggled to give voice to a memory that had lived its whole life as a whisper. "The photographer who shot that cigarette ad—It was a nightmare."

Celeste took hold of one of Ronnie's balled-up fists, smoothed it open, and gripped her sweaty hand.

"Those damn billboards were everywhere. And I hated every one of them. But Ma, Daddy, everybody was so proud. Even you were—a little bit. I couldn't screw all that up, so I kept my mouth shut."

"I am so sorry." Celeste pulled her closer, slid her arm around Ronnie's waist.

"You didn't know." Ronnie draped an arm over Celeste's shoulder.

"That's not the point. You should have been able to tell me, but I never gave you a reason to think you could confide in me." She tilted her head, rested it on Ronnie's shoulder. "I'm sorry for that too."

Ronnie squeezed Celeste's shoulder. "It's okay. We'll make up for it now."

They continued in silence until they reached the clearing. "This is it. The pond in Little Pond. Doesn't look like paradise, but I like it here, looking at the water, listening to the birds." Ronnie took a seat on the hickory stump. "Doug says we can clear up the crap, maybe have a place for a rowboat or somethin'. That would be kinda hip." She positioned her oars in the air. "Row, row, row your boat, gently down the . . ."

"Do you really want to do this? Stay here by yourself?" Celeste stood in a patch of dappled sun at the water's edge. "You don't have to, you know. We can work something else out."

"It's what I want. Honest. I'm really gonna find a job and make this fly. At least for now." Ronnie peeled a strip of bark off the stump. "And I don't know how long she's gonna stay, but looks like Ma has some unfinished business here too."

"Mother with some man who's not Daddy is still too weird for me to process right now." Celeste pulled up a blade of grass and twirled it between her fingers.

"Guess you have homework to do."

"It's not my biggest assignment, though." Celeste walked over and sat next to Ronnie. "What am I gonna do about me and Everett? I don't want to lose him."

"Humph! I'm probably the last one on the planet you wanna ask for advice." Ronnie looked Celeste in the eye. "But just be straight with him and see how it goes. If you want an ear, you know my digits."

"Thanks." One fat teardrop fell from Celeste's eye, landed on Ronnie's knee. "And in case you haven't been too sure lately, I love you."

"Back atcha, sis." Ronnie smiled. "I just wish I had a picture of you out here in your jammies. I bet there are people who'd pay good money for it!"

23

". . . steps in a new direction."

Celeste had been in the shower more than half an hour, ever since she forced herself to come in from the pond and get moving. She felt too raw and exposed for her usual steaming water, and now she was having a hard time bringing herself to get out of the soothing, tepid spray. *I can't stay in here for-ever.* There were new players in her family drama, and the old ones, including herself, had new wrinkles; the heroes were tarnished, the villains not so guilty, and her own lofty place above it all cut down to size.

Reluctantly she turned off the water, stepped onto the bath-mat, and snatched her towel from the rack next to the tub. *All of this came out of nowhere. What am I supposed to do now?* Celeste patted dry, trying to figure out her next move. She was used to discounting her mother's advice, but it was time to lis-ten. *Because she's right.*

I love Everett. Always have. Always will. There was noth-ing Celeste could do to change the past, but seconds of the present were ticking away, and she knew she didn't have any to waste.

Still wrapped in her towel, Celeste grabbed her robe off the hook behind the door, but before she put it on she caught her reflection in the full-length mirror, square in the eyes. *You're all closed up . . . Shut off from yourself even.* Her mother's words came back to her as she pulled off the shower cap and continued the exploration. *What am I hiding?* She let the robe drop to the floor, then abandoned the towel beside it and forced her eyes to drop down and examine her body. She ac-knowledged the dark rings around her neck that didn't used to be there when she was younger. They reminded her of the rings inside a tree trunk that told its age. For years she'd been covering them with necklaces and high-necked shirts and not admitting how much they bugged her.

Celeste moved on to her breasts, which didn't point front and center anymore without Lycra and underwires. *These definitely don't belong to a young chippy—but they're healthy, and they look pretty good for a chippy in her middle years.* Her belly, stretch marks and all, had a little pooch to it, right below the navel. She turned to the side and considered her butt, which was wider than it used to be but still round and firm. She wasn't young and high and tight all over anymore. *But this is me and I look all right.* Celeste touched her arms, chest, rubbed the flat of her hand against her stomach. Her skin was still soft and smooth. *Why haven't I been able to—?* She shook her head. *If I haven't even seen myself, then I sure haven't seen Everett or Niki either. Not the way they are.* Celeste thought of the "just so" polish she'd smeared on the people and things in her life of her "just so" friend Lydia and what a phony she really was. *I've wasted so much time trying to be what I'm not.* She swung open the door and marched down the hall to her room, naked as the day she came into the world.

And without stopping to cover up, she hopped up on her bed, ripped the to-do list off her pad, and tossed it in the wastebasket. She stared at the blank page, searching for a place to begin.

> *Dear Everett,*
> *I can only hope you'll read this, because if I were you, I'm not sure I would. I've been stubborn and stupid and just plain wrong. . . .*

Celeste went on for twelve pages, no holding back. She apologized for being rigid and insensitive, pleaded for the chance to make a change, told Everett how much she admired him, loved him, didn't want to lose him. The words came in a rush, almost faster than she could write them down. And before she could reread, edit, or correct, Celeste jumped into the first thing she pulled from the closet, ran a comb through her hair, and dashed downstairs.

"Hey! Where are you goin'?" Ronnie called from over the upstairs railing.

"To the post office. I'll be right back!"

"I'll ride with . . ." But Celeste was already gone, so Ronnie, who was washed, brushed, and dressed, made her way downstairs, wondering what prompted the postal emergency since there was no hint of it when they came in from the pond.

Ronnie found Della in the kitchen playing solitaire. "You're mighty dressed up for a kitchen table card game, Queen Bee!" She eyed Della's short-sleeved yellow suit, black scoop-neck shell, and black patent pumps. Ronnie even detected a smidgen of lipstick. "Oh—that's right. Somebody's got a hot date tonight," she teased.

"I've got no such thing!" Della snatched up the cards and shuffled again.

"Dinner? A man? No. Not just a man. An old boyfriend. Spells D-A-T-E to me."

Della rolled her eyes. "You never did good in spellin'. And before I forget, Doug Pryce called. Said he'd be out this evenin' with papers for y'all to sign."

"So soon? I'm surprised."

"Humph! Seems to me that man is either desperate to make this sale or he has an interest in all this that's not just about real estate."

"If you think that I—that he—That's crazy, Ma."

"So you're sayin' it only *looks* like somethin' it's not? Now where have I heard that?" Della cocked her head at Ronnie and waited.

"You win, but you look kinda cute for your—appointment."

"Never mind all that." Della smirked, and even though she wasn't about to admit it, she was glad to hear she looked nice. She arched the two piles of cards into a bridge and they fell neatly into a single stack.

"Remember how I used to try to do that?"

"And have cards flyin' all over the room?!" Della shuffled the deck again.

"Wanna play rummy?"

"Humph. Haven't played that since—Humph." Five hundred rummy used to be a game for a snowy Saturday, a rainy summer Tuesday, or to take Ronnie's mind off a scraped knee. Della taught Celeste first, but she didn't have much interest in card games. When Ronnie was old enough to learn, Della thought Celeste might enjoy it more, since three players made the game more interesting, but Celeste still didn't see the point. So it became Ronnie and Della's game. When Della won, Ronnie would complain that she could catch up if they played another hand, then another. After a while, they upped the winning score to a thousand, then two, until it finally became ten thousand rummy. Della was sure there was still the score sheet for an unfinished game, wrapped around a deck of cards in the back of a kitchen drawer at home.

Della looked at the woman across from her and still saw her baby girl. She smiled to herself and dealt two hands, seven cards each.

"What?" Ronnie caught the smile.

"Nothin'." Della put the remaining stack in the center of the table, turned the top card faceup. "Nothin' at all. It's your turn, or have you forgotten how to play?"

"I'll keep score." Ronnie grabbed one of Celeste's notepads, drew a T down the middle of a blank page, and printed "MA" on the left and "ME" on the right.

"Your addin' wasn't much better than your spellin'. Hope you've improved with age."

"I can manage." Ronnie fanned her cards, arranged them according to suit, then scrutinized her hand.

Della watched her, amused. She used to be able to finish cooking dinner during Ronnie's turns. She would consider all her options and the possible results of every move before she made it. Somewhere along the line, all that deliberation gave way to whim and desperation in the potluck that had become Ronnie's life. *Yes. Maybe this'll be good for her. She can take her time down here. Examine her hand.*

In the middle of their third hand Ronnie laid down three eights, threw away the deuce of hearts. "As soon as I get some money from selling the land, I'll pay you back for the hospital and all."

Della retrieved the deuce. "Don't worry about that right now. I'm thankful I got it to spare." She laid down the ace and the three to go with it. "Now don't think I won't take your money, 'cause I sho 'nuff will. But you concentrate on straightenin' yourself out. There's time later." Della winked. "You add on my score?"

"What else am I doin' with this pen?" After she reached the new total she looked up. "Thanks, Ma." Ronnie winked too. "I'm a little scared."

"Anybody with good sense would be." She patted Ronnie's hand.

Ronnie smiled. "Are you plannin' to discard anytime soon?"

"Don't rush me!"

It was 647 to 514 in Della's favor when Celeste came into the kitchen. "Who's winning?" She pulled up a chair and slipped off her shoes.

"Ma. But I'm about to catch up. You went out in that?" Ronnie pointed to Celeste's blouse. "You're missing a button."

"I was in a hurry. Had to send a letter overnight mail. Even us mules get the point if you hit us hard enough." She grinned and gave Della a knowing glance. "When can you deal me in?"

"You?" Ronnie sputtered.

Celeste crossed her arms and leaned toward Ronnie. "Afraid I'll kick your butt?"

"Hardly! And to show you what kind of a sister I am, I'll concede to Ma in this first game, so I can get right to whippin' you!" Ronnie gathered the cards, shuffled them badly.

"Humph. If Celeste's gon' play, maybe we should make it a penny a point. You could get started on a down payment for that car you gon' be needin'!"

"Very funny, Mother."

They had played three trash-talking hands and were in the

middle of the fourth when they heard the knock on the front door.

Della looked at the clock on the stove. "It's too early to be Lester."

"Doug's bringing the new contracts," Ronnie said to Celeste. "Must be him."

"Anybody here? Ma? Grandma?" Niki called through the screen.

Celeste dropped her cards and jumped up. "I asked her, but I didn't say anything because I didn't think she'd come."

"Somebody must be home. The door's open."

"This is the country, Brian. People leave their doors open."

"She brought a man with her? Brave!" Ronnie whispered to Della as Celeste trotted out of the room.

Brian leaned his long, wiry body against the door jamb. "And when did you get to be an expert on country ways? After you had me carry you across that stream because you were afraid of snakes?" He stood a head taller than Niki.

"I just wanted you to carry me!" Niki tilted her head up to kiss him.

Just as Celeste threw open the screen door. "I can't believe you came!"

"Ma!" Niki quickly retracted her lips. "Don't worry, we're not gonna stay, I . . ."

"You just got here! You can't start talking about leaving!" Celeste hugged Niki tight and kissed her on the cheek, leaving Niki puzzled by the joyous reception. "And you must be Brian." Celeste took his hand in both of hers. "Come in! And welcome to Little Pond! Mother! Ronnie!"

"I'm right here." Della came into the hall and threw her arms open wide when she saw Niki. "You're not too grown to gimme some sugar, are you?"

"Nope!" Niki folded herself into her grandmother. "How's Aunt Ronnie? Ma said . . ."

"Aunt Ronnie's doin' fine." Ronnie joined them. "What did she tell you? I was on my last legs?"

"No." Niki laughed, extricated herself from her grandmother, and hugged Ronnie. "Just that you'd had a pretty rough time, and if I was a good and dutiful niece, I'd stop and see you on the way to Hyde Park." She saluted. "Good and dutiful reporting."

"So are you gon' let your young man just stand there?" Della prompted.

"Oh! Yeah." She pulled him in the door. "Everybody, this is Brian Cadieux."

"Nice to meet you, Brian." Ronnie stepped forward and offered her hand. "She did warn you about us?"

"Well, we can't keep standing here in the hall. The living room is right—or maybe it's cooler on the porch?" Della suggested.

"First I have to check out this place!" Niki craned her neck to look into the living room. "Wow! It really looks like somebody lives here."

"Seems somebody's going to do just that." Celeste eyed Ronnie, then followed Niki who was headed for the dining room. "Are you going to tell her, or shall I?"

"Tell me what?" Niki ran her hand over the maple sideboard, her finger along the embroidered hem of a napkin. "Nice," she said, almost to herself.

"I'm sure your version will be much more interesting than mine, so be my guest." Ronnie bowed slightly and joined the tour.

"You're welcome to join them," Della said to Brian.

"We've been in the car for hours. I'd really like the bathroom and a glass of water. In that order."

Della showed him the way and continued to the kitchen where she met up with the chatter and laughter of mother, daughter, and auntie.

"Wow! That's kinda cool!" Niki said when Celeste finished filling her in on Ronnie's decision to stay in Prosper. "It'll be an adventure! I'm just finding out that I like being able to start new, in a different place. I mean, I loved Atlanta, and after Ithaca it was just what I needed. But I'm ready to move on. I'm looking forward to the next stop!"

"Cooking is a very portable career!" Brian added as he joined them. "I've lived all over the world since I left New Orleans. And I expect this opportunity to teach at the CIA will open even more doors." He accepted the glass Della handed him. "Thanks." He brushed his locks behind his ears, tilted his head back, and took a long swallow.

"Yep. This is just the next stop. Who knows where we'll go after I finish my training?"

Who knows where we'll go? It was a mouthful, but Celeste kept it down. "I guess change keeps you fresh." *What did Everett say? You need to shake up your life or the good stuff settles on the bottom.*

"And I've learned goo gobs about people and food from moving around," Brian added. "Niki, I've gotta run out to the car. Be right back." He squeezed her shoulders.

"Not bad, Niki girl. Not bad at all!" Ronnie watched Brian stride down the walk.

Niki grinned. "I think he's pretty special!"

Celeste watched Niki watch Brian and fought to control a wave of sadness. *Just like I used to think your father was special.*

"Speaking of change—What's up with y'all?" Niki folded her arms across her chest and looked at her family. "Ronnie's got a buzz cut, Ma's barefoot, and Grandma, I haven't seen you so dressed up since my graduation. Is it something in the water? Should we go buy some bottled?" Niki dropped her voice and did her best horror movie announcer imitation. "Or will the strange force lurking in the old family manse overtake the unsuspecting newcomers?"

"Not much to tell about my hair. The weave got raggedy. Lucille took it out for me," Ronnie said.

"Who's Lucille?"

"That's a whole 'nother story. Let's save it for later. When we can really dish!" Ronnie laughed.

"And you, Ma. No slippers? Shoes thrown under the kitchen table. I don't know."

Celeste sucked her teeth. "I was just sitting around . . ."

"Since when does that matter?" Niki asked.

Celeste smiled. "Since now."

"The real news here is Miss Della!" Ronnie teased. "Isn't that right, Ma?"

"Hush up that foolishness. Ain't no news. I was plannin' to go out, that's all."

"With?" Ronnie prompted.

"With an old friend," Della answered.

"He's not just an old . . ."

"He?!" Niki sputtered. "You have a date?!"

"I don't have no such thing! Don't get Niki started on this mess too. Besides, now that you're here, I think I'll see if we can do it another time. How long you gon' stay?"

"We're heading out this evening. We can get a couple of hours up the road before we stop. My first class starts in four days. All I really wanted to do was check on Aunt Ronnie and make sure there was no mayhem going on here. You know how the three of you can be!"

"Well, I've told you I'm fine, and as you can see there are no serious wounds," Ronnie said. "But why don't you stay the night? Get a fresh start tomorrow? While your grandma is out carousing, maybe we can all go to Pal's. That'll be a hoot! And I'm dying to have something besides sandwiches and broiled chicken. No offense," she said to Della and Celeste, "but that stuff's starting to make hospital food a fond memory!"

"Humph!" Della said and went to call Lester.

"What's Pal's?" Niki asked.

"Boy do we have an earful for you," Ronnie said.

"I don't know if we should put all that on her." Celeste gathered up the three ghost hands of rummy from the kitchen table.

"Well, wasn't that the point? This is stuff we all need to know, Niki included." Ronnie settled in the chair and put her hand on her belly. "Whew! I really needed to do that."

Della came back from the phone. "They said he's gone already. I hate for him to drive out here for nothin'."

"I wouldn't call it nothing! I've seen him lookin' at you, and I think he'll take a look-see if that's all he can get. For now." Ronnie grinned at her mother.

Della looked as close to a blush as any of them had ever seen. They burst out laughing just as Brian and Lester walked in.

"Did we miss something?" Lester asked.

"No!" The four women shouted all at once.

"Of course, you're Odee's granddaughter!" Lester smiled at Niki. "Lester Wilson. You remind me of her." He looked at Della. "It doesn't even seem that long ago."

"I do?" Niki, tall and strong, always thought she got that from her father. No one had ever compared her to her grandmother. But she could see that Lester was genuinely taken with the resemblance and realized she liked the comparison, the connection. "Thanks."

"You're crazy, Lester. But then you always were." Della smiled at him. "Listen. I'm sorry to do this, but could we go to dinner another night? Niki and her friend are leavin' tomorrow and I . . ."

"Not a problem. I'm disappointed, but I understand."

Brian whispered to Niki, and she nodded. "What if we cook?" She looked at Ronnie. "You'll get a meal that's a whole lot better than hospital food." Then turned to Lester and Della, who stood side by side. "You two can still have dinner and—" She winked at Lester. "—No one will go home disappointed."

"And I'll get to ask all the questions I want about that car of yours," Brian added.

Lester turned to Della. "As long as I can get a rain check on our date."

Della smirked and looked beyond Ronnie, who had definitely made note of the *d* word. "I think that might work out. If you play your cards right." She turned to Brian. "But makin' dinner is too much trouble."

"I know how you feel about a stove, Grandma, but we like to cook!"

"Then it sounds like a plan to me!" Ronnie said.

"There's not much to choose from here." Celeste opened the refrigerator.

"Celeste, you know you about bought out the store," Della reminded her.

"Well, you couldn't prove it by the way we've been eatin' around here." Ronnie laughed.

"I'm sure we'll be okay with whatever we find." Niki moved her mother aside and rummaged through the shelves.

"You sure you're a chef?" Della looked Brian up and down. "Friend of mine's had a restaurant more than forty years and he says, 'Never trust a skinny cook.'"

"Yes ma'am. Not only do I cook, I love to eat too."

"Puh-lease! Spare me the 'I'm naturally skinny' routine!" Ronnie joked. "It's too painful."

"Thank you." Niki popped up from her exploration of the fridge with a handful of tomatoes and a plastic bag of string beans. "I run six or seven miles a day and still have to watch what I eat. But this one. Eats seconds and dessert and looks like this." She patted his flat belly.

Celeste was taken by how radiant Niki looked. *She's really happy.* "Nik? Could I talk to you? Alone?"

Niki looked up warily. "Uh—sure."

"It'll only take a minute." Celeste walked out the back door.

"Fine." Niki braced herself for whatever tidal wave of complaints her mother had built up. "Here. See what else you can scare up." Niki handed Brian the vegetables and followed her mother out the door and down the steps.

Celeste hadn't gone far down the path that led to the woods. She heard Niki, stopped, and waited for her to catch up. When Niki was at her side, Celeste took her hand, and they walked down the path Ronnie had shown her. Down by the pond. She perched on the edge of the hickory stump and patted it for Niki to take a seat too.

"As you have probably gathered, this trip has turned out to be quite different from what I expected. And today I can say I'm glad. If you'd asked me yesterday or the day before, I'm not sure my answer would have been the same." Celeste stopped and took a good look at Niki. "What I'm trying to say is I'm sorry. I've been wrong about so many things, but one of the worst has been that I was wrong about you—thinking I knew what you should be doing with your life. I'm your mother, and sometimes I still think of you as my little girl. It's hard for me to accept you're a grown woman and that you have the right to make your own choices, good ones and bad ones, and I have to respect them. I don't have to agree with you or even be consulted." She smiled. "Unless *you* want to, of course." Celeste laughed, wrapped an arm around Niki's shoulder. "You're bright, Nicole. And kind and beautiful and responsible. Everything a mother could want for her child. Any woman would be proud to have you as her daughter— and I'm no exception." Now she cradled Niki's face. "I love you. I want you to be happy."

Niki was all prepared to do battle again, so she was caught off guard. "Ma—I mean Mother—I don't know what . . ."

"Shh." Celeste held her index finger up to her lips. "Ma is fine. And you don't have to say anything. This was my little speech, and you were my intended audience. All you have to do is go on being who you are, doing what you've been doing." Celeste saw the tears pooling in Niki's eyes. "This isn't about tears. This is about laughing at what an idiot I've been. Come on. Let's go back before they send a search party!" She got up and tugged Niki in the direction of the house. "There's so much more I want to tell you. Things I just found out myself, but now isn't the time. After you get settled maybe we'll do a girls' weekend in the city and I'll fill you in." Niki fell in step beside her mother. "And I like Brian, at least from what I've seen. I don't know him, mind you, but I can tell he really cares about you. You two remind me of your father and me— a long time ago—I've written him—said some of the things I just said to you and then some more. He's due back from Portugal today. My letter should arrive tomorrow. I'll go home and face the music, whatever it is, the day after that. I may be too late, but I want you to know I'm going to try. We're a family. I really want it to stay that way."

"Me too, Ma." Niki's voice cracked unexpectedly, so she cleared her throat in a feeble attempt to mask the emotion trapped there. Then, almost as an afterthought, she quickly pecked her mother on the cheek and pulled open the kitchen door.

While Niki and Brian worked their magic with the loot from their refrigerator raid, Ronnie took a much-needed nap, and out on the porch Della and Lester talked and laughed about whatever subject blew their way. Lester did his best smooth talking, trying to convince Della that Ronnie could probably use help a little while longer and maybe Della shouldn't plan on going back yet. She pooh-poohed him, but she'd already decided on staying a few weeks more to see after Ronnie. And to get reacquainted with old friends like Lucille and Hambone—and Lester.

Celeste decided this was the perfect occasion to christen the dining room. She hummed and smiled to herself as she set the table with the china from the breakfront and folded each napkin into a perfect triangle, not because it was proper, but purely because right now she was happy and she wanted to celebrate with her family. She didn't try, even once, to supervise the cooking. It was actually a relief not to have to play overseer. She felt it as clearly as Ronnie had felt her lungs fill with air she could breathe when the smoke machine she'd been running overtime finally self-destructed, as distinctly as Della had felt the dead weight of her secrets lifted from her soul. Celeste knew she still had a long way to go, but like her mother and her sister, she'd taken enough steps in a new direction to believe she was on the right path.

When the savory smells emanating from the kitchen made it obvious there was a feast simmering, Della called Hambone and Lucille, who said they'd make it for dessert.

"If I had known there was a party going on, I'd have come another time," Doug said when he arrived and saw all the activity. Celeste had just finished with the table and offered to set another place, but he begged off until Ronnie came down. She got herself together in a hurry when she heard his voice and jokingly threatened not to sign the contracts if he didn't stay for dinner. Doug laughed and quickly gave up trying to make an exit.

"After all the trouble we've been, it's the least we can do!" Ronnie was glad to see him, and she really wanted a chance to talk to him when there was no crisis and she wasn't performing, just being herself.

The meal started with a salmon mousse that they all thought was out of this world. Then came a huge salad with freshly made croutons, and the tomatoes, onions, garlic, and Celeste's leftover wine became a sauce for the sautéed chicken Niki and Brian served over linguine Celeste had picked up by mistake, thinking it was a box of spaghetti.

"It's hard to believe this came from the same groceries we been eatin' all along!" Della announced. And just as amazing, they got through an entire family meal without a cross word from anyone. She wasn't sure that had happened in the history of the Frazier family, but it felt good. *I could get used to this.*

"Nothin' beats a little know-how," Lester said as he pushed back from the table. "Especially in the kitchen."

"You haven't eaten Della's cooking, have you?" Ronnie teased, then turned to Brian. "Are there any more at home like you? A brother, maybe?"

"He didn't do it by himself!" Niki elbowed Brian.

Brian put his arm around Niki's shoulders. "Sorry, no brothers. I do have two sisters!"

"Thanks anyway! The one I have is more than enough," Ronnie cracked. She wasn't fooling herself. She didn't expect they would ever become a warm, fuzzy, huggy, kissy kind of family, but the gap had narrowed considerably.

Just as the last forkful was eaten and they all swore they were about to burst, Lucille and Hambone arrived with a huge peach cobbler.

"It's my specialty," Hambone said as he put it down on the table.

Lucille took a seat next to Della. "Everythin' is your specialty, let you tell it."

After dessert, coffee, and conversation, Niki and Brian started gathering the dishes.

"Cooks don't do KP!" Lester said. "Your grandmother and

I will take care of cleanup. You-all officially have the rest of the night off. You've earned it."

"I'll help you," Celeste chimed in, but Ronnie kicked her under the table before Celeste could get up.

"Go enjoy your daughter's company. We can handle it, can't we, Odee?" Lester took the plates from Niki.

"I expect we'll do just fine," Della replied and reached for the empty pasta platter.

It was Lucille's turn to nudge Della under the table.

"I don't think I'm gonna be much company, Ma. I'm beat and we need to get on the road early." Niki plopped back down.

"Why don't you take the bedroom upstairs that nobody's using? Brian can sleep down here in the study," Celeste suggested.

"Are they plannin' on separate rooms when they get where they're goin'?" Della stood up, hands on her hips and waited, but no one ventured an answer. "Just what I thought." She picked up her stack of dishes. "Then why don't they just go on upstairs and go to bed?"

"Mother!" Celeste looked at Ronnie, who shrugged.

"Listen." Della grabbed two glasses with her empty hand. "Haven't we all had enough pretendin'? I know I have. That's how we got in this mess in the first place." She headed to the kitchen but stopped in the doorway. "Sleep tight. Both of you."

"Thanks, Grandma." Niki smiled and hugged Della, whose hands were too full to hug Niki back.

"It's about time for me to get going. I've got a long one tomorrow." Doug got up.

"I'll walk you out." Ronnie couldn't keep a straight face, and Doug's departure was a great cue for an escape.

"I can't believe my mother said that," Ronnie announced to Doug when they got outside.

Doug chuckled. "My theory is this 'understanding' thing skips a generation. My mother was a one-woman hit squad with me, but she's Granny Sweetness with my kids. I kinda like it, though. Helps make 'em closer."

"Hmm, the Pryce theory of family relations. You got any other theories in your pocket?" Ronnie brushed against his arm and felt the jitters all of a sudden, as she finally let it sink in that she'd like to get to know this man as more than her broker.

"Nothing but these babies." He patted the contracts in the jacket pocket of his khaki suit. "I don't see any reason why we can't close pretty soon."

"Sounds good to me." Ronnie clasped her hands behind her back, searching for something to say, but her tongue was tied. "Nice night. It's good the nights are cool. Good for sleeping." *Is that the best I can do?*

"Yep. I'd say so." He smoothed his mustache with his fingertips. "Hey look, I enjoyed the company. I'll ah—give a call."

"Bet." Ronnie watched him start down the steps, not wanting him to go yet.

Three steps down the path he turned around. "Ronnie— I've got a proposition for you that has nothing to do with property."

"Yeah?" She leaned against the porch rail.

"Since I'm not on the meter right now—And you'll let me know if I'm outta line—"

"Yeah?"

"How 'bout I take you out next week? Show you 'round since you're planning to stay."

A big grin came over Ronnie's face. "How 'bout let's go fishin'?" *Did I just say that?* "I could try out that pole you gave me." Her smile felt lopsided, a little goofy, like she hadn't flirted with a man in a hundred years. *Maybe I haven't meant it in a while.*

"Well—uh—"

"My father would say, 'Don't dig it here!' Ronnie laughed. "The well, I mean."

"That's almost as bad as my real estate jokes." He cocked his foot up on the bottom step, his eyes shining a warm smile. "But it would be my pleasure. One morning next week."

"I figure I should start learning the local customs if I'm

gonna become a Prosperite. Prosperian? Prosperer?!" Ronnie laughed. "I've got a lot to learn."

"I bet you're a quick study." Doug swatted at a moth flying around him. "But we gotta start early. Are you a morning person?" he asked.

"Crack a dawn these days."

"Great! I'll call you." Doug smiled at her. "From my home phone." He headed toward his car, then turned to look at her. "And whether we catch anything or not, I'm a pretty good cook."

Ronnie smiled back and waved. *I guess I'm goin' fishin'.* She watched until his taillights disappeared.

The next morning Celeste got up at first light to see Niki and Brian off. At the car she threw her arms around Brian. "Take care of her."

"You know it," he replied and loaded their bags into the trunk.

Celeste wasn't sure what to say to Niki, but her daughter cut through the words and swooped in for a hug. "Love you, Ma."

Celeste barely got out, "Me too," then hustled them on their way.

She put on a pot of coffee, carried a cup upstairs, and sipped while she started to gather her things to go home tomorrow and worried what Everett would do after he read his letter. When she heard signs of life from her mother's room, she went down the hall.

Della sat at the foot of her bed, still waking up. "Niki and Brian get off okay?"

"Uh-huh." Celeste sat down next to her.

"Humph. They look right cute together." Della smiled to herself, then looked over at Celeste's long face. "Ain't no point in my tellin' you not to worry, Mother. You're gon' do it anyhow, but I think Niki will do just fine—with Brian or with whichever somebody she chooses. I think the girl's got more sense than any of us."

"Y'all didn't start the party without me, did you?" Ronnie came in and took her place in the bedside lineup. "Who's this?" She picked up the brown-skinned rag doll with the black woolly hair that lay near Della's pillow. "I didn't see her when I cleaned up this room." She laid the doll across her lap.

"That's Susie. She's the very first doll my mama gave me." Della smoothed the doll's lacy white dress.

"You mean Miz Ethiopia?" Celeste asked.

"No. No. My mama—Her name was Annie." Della looked at Celeste. "And the older you get, the more you favor her."

"I do?" Celeste never thought she looked like anybody in her family, so this was a surprise.

"Do you have any pictures?" Ronnie asked.

"Not a one. Only what I remember—I sure do miss her."

It was the first time Celeste or Ronnie had heard Della talk about her mother.

"Anyhow, let me get this old body cranked up before I want to get back in the bed." Della stood up.

"Mom, I called the airline yesterday. I'm going home tomorrow."

Celeste hadn't called her "Mom" since she got too grown to be that familiar. "Well—that's good." Della nodded her head, propped her hand on the doorknob. *I guess there's one more thing we got left to do.* "Then there's someplace we need to go today," she said.

Della hurried them through breakfast, showers, and dressing without telling them the destination. They were in the car, ready to pull off, when Celeste heard the phone ring. She yanked off her seat belt and raced inside like her life depended on it, leaving Della and Ronnie scratching their heads.

A few minutes later Celeste returned. She'd obviously been crying, but she smiled wide when she slid behind the driver's seat. "That was Everett. He's picking me up at the airport." Celeste cleared her throat, grabbed the wheel with both hands. "So? Where am I heading?"

"Go left on Albemarle." Della folded her hands in her lap and looked straight ahead. She took a deep breath before she spoke again. "It wouldn't be right if y'all didn't see Cadysville, where I was born—Visit my mama's grave."

"Ma?" Ronnie was hesitant. "When's the last time you went there?"

"Come Christmastime it'll be fifty-one years."

"Do you still remember the way?" Celeste asked as they passed Pal's on their way through Prosper.

"It's all comin' back to me." Della leaned forward in the backseat, a hand resting on each daughter's shoulder and gazed through the windshield.

They didn't go far before they saw the bright green sign. "Cadysville 102 miles," Ronnie read aloud.

Della relaxed back into her seat. "Humph. It always seemed further away than that."

Authors' Note to the Readers

Dear Reader,

When we were tossing ideas around for this book, we weren't sure what road we were taking, or where it would end up. It's tempting to walk a familiar path—it's safe, and you know where it goes. But we wanted more of an adventure, so after several months of discussion we decided to take off in a different direction.

Some journeys, like the one we took you on in *Tryin' to Sleep in the Bed You Made*, span decades. With *Far from the Tree* we were looking for one of those unexpected trips that turns your life upside down in an instant and barely leaves you time to pack. And whatever the circumstances that caused you to leave so suddenly—hopefully you return home with a new experience, a new friend, a new vision, a new you.

As we talked, we kept coming back to the strained relationship between Patricia Reid and her mother, Verna, two of the characters we wrote about in *Tryin'*. Despite the years of hurt and misunderstanding between them, most folks who wrote us wanted them to work it out.

Mothers and daughters—is there a more basic, and more complicated relationship on the planet? Especially once everybody is grown. The idea of venturing into this territory was both scary and exciting.

So, through Della, Celeste, Ronnie, and Niki, we decided to explore what would happen if mothers and daughters were forced to rediscover one another outside of their accustomed roles. What's it like for the daughters to realize that before she was your mother, she was a woman, just like you? How do the mothers feel when they finally recognize the women their daughters have become? So often we forget that we walk on common ground.

And the truth is that whether we like it or not, whether it skips a generation or even two, none of us ever truly falls *Far from the Tree*.

We welcome hearing from you, so if you'd like to let us know how you feel about *Tree*, please drop us a line or an e-mail, or visit our new Web site. We have to say that we were blown away by your response to *Tryin'*. We had no idea whether we'd hear from a soul, but now, more than 15,000 letters later, we're still amazed and honored by the time so many folks took to write us back. You shared not only your reactions to the book, but you told us how *Tryin'* related to your own personal experiences, some of them funny, some difficult and painful. And we were particularly happy to hear that so many people read the book and were moved to try to mend friendships that had unraveled, to reach out to find friends who have slipped out of touch, or to make the time to tell a friend how much they really mean.

Although it may have taken us a while, we tried to answer every letter we received. If somehow we neglected to respond to you, please accept our apologies and know that we'll try to do better this time!

Don't let the good stuff settle on the bottom,

Virginia DeBerry   Donna Grant

DeBerry and Grant
P.O. Box 5224
Kendall Park, NJ 08824
E-mail: Farfromthetree@aol.com
www.deberryandgrant.com

". . . an invisible crack in the world."

I gotta pee . . . bad," Gayle whispered to Pat. Fat snowflakes had settled on Gayle's rabbit fur hat and on her bangs, framing her small almond face like a halo.

"You went before we left school!" Pat knew Gayle was stalling to keep from facing her parents with dismal grades. Pat pulled at her green knit cap, trying to keep her hair dry. Her straight-A report card was tucked inside the folded newspaper cover of her math book, but she'd have hell to pay if Aunt Verna had to get out the pressing comb before Saturday.

First thrown together in kindergarten by the random selection of alphabetical order, Patricia Reid and Gayle Saunders were as different and as inseparable as day and night.

Pat had been raised by MaRay, a cake-baking, opinionated woman with immense bosoms and fat, hugging arms, in Swan City, a hiccup near Raleigh Bay on the North Carolina coast. Lil' Daddy had passed, soon after Pat's hello holler to the world, "But MaRay's here for you, Sugar." Then, when Pat was six, MaRay passed, too. Pat went north to live with her aunt Verna, a hard knot of a woman with no space in her heart or her life for a little girl.

Her first week in the small dark second-floor flat, Pat learned not to mention MaRay and to be very quiet, especially

after her aunt's late nights on her job at the Easy Street Bar &
Grill. Luckily fall came soon. Since Pat was from the South,
which to teachers up North meant she was at least borderline
backwards, she was put back a grade, but starting school
meant that for at least half a day she didn't have to be quiet,
and she wasn't alone.

Pat was chubby and chocolate brown with a wise, wide-
eyed face she would "grow into" and hair that resisted the
taming of heat and grease. Her classmates called her "Aunt
Jemima on the pancake box" and made fun of her accent,
which was thick and slow as the molasses MaRay had laced in
her infant bottles. The madder they made her, the more determined she became not to show it. Gifted with keen intelli-
gence nurtured by the strong mother wit of MaRay, Pat
quickly proved she was smarter than she looked. In class she
always had the answer, which impressed the teacher, but not
the students, except for Gayle.

Dainty and honey-colored, with long, wavy "good" hair,
Gayle was the answered prayer of Joseph and Loretta Saunders. They married late, past the point when anyone at the
venerable Mt. Moriah Baptist Church thought they'd bother.
To make up for lost time, they worked hard, saved money for
a house, and soon moved from Harlem to St. Albans, Queens,
the home of Count Basie, James Brown, and other important
people Loretta was happy to tell you. It was a two-bedroom
frame house, with a brick front, pale green siding, a bay window, and, best of all it was detached, a fine thing to all their
apartment-living friends. The lot was even big enough for a
carport and a brick barbecue pit in the backyard.

Joseph and Loretta were all set for a family, yet after twelve
years and three cruel miscarriages folks said they were too old
and ought to stop. Goodness, most of their friends' children
were nearly grown. But ever since she was little, Loretta, the
ninth of ten in a family where nothing seemed new or enough,
had dreamed of being grown and having a daughter. Only one,
so she could dress her in pretty clothes bought just for her.
She'd have a pink room with dainty white furniture, a room
like Shirley Temple must have had, a room of her own.

Just when Loretta and Joseph were beginning to think their friends were right, praise the Lord, their prayers were answered and Gayle Denise Saunders arrived, crying and hollering and demanding to be noticed. Although Loretta was thrilled, she worried that Joseph might be disappointed since she knew men wanted sons, but Gayle landed like an arrow, smack in the bull's-eye of her daddy's heart. He worked for two days with no sleep, laying carpet, hanging Peter Rabbit wallpaper in the nursery, and putting the finishing touches on the new dresser and canopied cradle.

Gayle was their pretty, pampered prize, loved and spoiled by her parents every day, so kindergarten was a rude awakening. She was unhappy to find herself surrounded by dozens of children clamoring for the teacher's attention. Gayle's long hair—worn loose, not braided—her clothes—Sunday-best for other children—and her standoffishness marked her as someone who thought she was too cute, and she was isolated accordingly.

Gayle was so miserable that her good Baptist parents considered enrolling her in Catholic school. But on a day the class had to choose partners for an outing to the park, Gayle decided not to be left alone again. She chose Patty, the other girl nobody ever picked, and a friendship began. To Gayle, Pat seemed like she knew things, and she never seemed lonely or worried, even when she was by herself. And Gayle let Pat into her fantasy world, where anything was possible and it was okay to be a child. They shared finger paints and animal crackers and the hand clap-slap of "Miss Mary Mack, Mack, Mack, All Dressed In Black, Black, Black." They played dolls and blocks, but they always played together, and by first grade, each declared the other her best friend.

Loretta, however, did not approve of Pat, or "her people," meaning she didn't like Verna Reid's job as a barmaid. She kept trying to convince Gayle she could find a nicer girl to be her best friend. Gayle didn't care what Loretta thought on the subject and persisted in inviting Pat over. Lips pursed and nose out of joint, Loretta would complain to Joseph that Verna and her ilk were exactly what they left Harlem to avoid.

"Patty's only a child, 'Etta," Joseph had said over the sports page. "Smart one at that. Gayle can learn a thing or two from *her*." Loretta was so put out with Joseph, she put him out of her bed for a week.

Verna thought Gayle's family was uppity, for no good reason. "Her daddy's a damn janitor and her momma does day work!" Pat sat in silence, playing with a bowl of Trix and pretending to watch *Soul Train* while Verna ranted. "They treat that silly-ass girl like she somethin' special, always tossin' her hair like she White." Verna couldn't figure out why the hell Pat, with her flat face and eyes like a walleyed pike, wanted to be around somebody who made her look even more homely, but if Pat wanted to be a fool, that was on her.

Now in fifth grade, the unlikely twosome was inseparable. The very children who had disliked Gayle because she was so pretty were eventually drawn to her for the same reason. Pat had all but lost her Carolina drawl, but brains didn't make you popular. She was quiet and a little too bookish, but she could be funny sometimes, she always had the right answers to math homework, and her inexplicable closeness to Gayle sealed her acceptance.

And the girls' walk home was ritual. By three-forty they would reach Pat's street. She had orders from her aunt not to let "any little bastards in my house." Verna called most days at four o'clock to make sure Pat was home alone, so rain or shine, the girls talked outside until three-fifty-five. They discussed schoolwork, sang songs from the radio, and sometimes said things they didn't want anyone else to hear, like how Pat wanted to be a doctor or lawyer, somebody important so she didn't have to work at night like Aunt Verna or wear those clothes that made men click their tongues and talk to her out the side of their mouths. Gayle couldn't wait to be old enough to wear makeup, date, and get married, probably to a prince, because her daddy always had dirt under his nails and her momma's hands were so rough they snagged her stockings. Besides, they worked all the time and didn't seem like they had any fun. Pat inevitably asked the last time she saw a Black prince. "That doesn't mean there isn't one, and I plan to marry him! I'll find a prince for you, too, and we'll have a double wedding!" Gayle would announce, then stroll home daydreaming about gowns and weddings, which she would draw until her mother made her get her homework.

The snow was falling double-time, and car tires whined, spinning for traction. Gayle stomped the caked snow off her boots. "Just went doesn't help when I gotta go now, Patty!" To show the urgency of the situation, Gayle passed up their daily stop at J&T Candy Corner, where she would check for new hairstyle magazines and Archie comics because she loved that Veronica Lodge. Pat would buy a chocolate chip cookie the size of a 45 record to knock the edge off until she warmed the dinner plate Aunt Verna always left her.

"You are the peeingest girl in the world. If there was a peeing contest, you'd win." Pat giggled, and Gayle held her stomach and tried not to laugh, but she did anyway.

"Shh!" Gayle chided Pat, as she glanced back and saw Marcus Carter climbing to the top of an icy gray mound, piled high by a snowplow. "Going to the bathroom is girl stuff. Don't let him hear."

Last year, Marcus had moved around the corner from Gayle and appeared in their class and on their walk home. At first they ignored him. He was, after all, a boy, but when Gayle developed a crush on Marcus's eighth grade brother, Freddy, Marcus became the first male member of this very exclusive club.

Marcus leapt off the bank with a whoop and grinned like a fool as he landed on his butt in the fresh snow. "Everybody pees!" He got up, galloped past them, and snatched Gayle's hat. Trotting backwards he added, "I can pee and write my name in the snow at the same time!" Freddy had just taught him this miraculous feat.

"That's nasty, and gimme back my hat!" Gayle squealed and ran after him.

They arrived in front of Pat's house, and, hat in hand, Gayle shifted her weight from foot to foot, looking pitiful. She knew Pat wasn't allowed company, but three C's, two D's, and an F in geography meant she'd have to listen to a lecture on how important education was so she could take care of herself and not have to scrub other people's floors and toilets.

"Come on, Pat-ty, I can't hold it. I gotta go . . . *now!* I can't walk another step." Gayle crossed her heart and her legs.

"You mean if I tickle you, you'll pee all over yourself," Marcus said, his fingers wiggling in anticipation.

"Marcus Garvey Carter, I'll scream if you touch me," Gayle threatened.

Pat hemmed and hawed, yanking at a drooping kneesock. A resounding "whap" interrupted her debate as the frozen sparks of a well-aimed snowball exploded off Marcus's head. His books fell and skittered across the snow as he spun to face his attacker.

"*Steeerrrriiike!* Right in yo' bean head," shouted Freddy, bounding up to the trio. At thirteen Freddy, a cocoa brown length of budding muscle and energy, viewed tormenting Marcus as his brotherly right, secure that he was big enough to call the shots. "Freddy 'Fastball' Carter wins the World Series! Roberto Clemente eat that! Tell me I ain't bad."

"Baseball is lame!" Marcus yelled, then barreled into Freddy, knocking him to the powdery pavement.

Ignoring the melee, Pat continued, "You only live four more blocks, Gayle. You could make it if you stop talkin' and start walkin'."

"*Pleazzzz!* It's too cold, and I can't wait!" Gayle looked near tears.

"All right! . . . But you gotta hurry up." Pat swung open the chain-link gate and felt under her scarf for her keys, which dangled from the braided orange lanyard Gayle had made for her last summer in vacation Bible school.

Gayle followed, but a howl stopped them before Pat unlocked the door.

"Aw, Freddy man, you busted my lip. Look, I'm bleedin'." Marcus triumphantly pulled his lower lip down to display the blood collecting around his teeth. "Wait 'til I show Daddy. He's gon' whip yo butt. He tol' you to quit messin' wit me."

"Eeeyew!" Gayle groaned, as Marcus spit out a mouthful of blood that dotted the snow like Redhots.

"Don't be no sissy, man. You ain't even hurt." Freddy lifted his drawstring gym bag and gingerly dusted off the snow. "Besides, I got somethin' in here I was gonna show you, but I can't be showin' no sissy," Freddy said, baiting his hook.

"You ain't got nothing in that stupid bag but s'more a them stupid motorcycle magazines," Marcus said, trying to resist the enticing lure.

"That's what you say. Not what I know." Freddy dangled the bait in front of Marcus.

"What's he got in there?" Gayle whispered to Pat.

Marcus, unable to ignore temptation, bit. "Okay, okay, I won't tell." He prepared to spit again.

"Don't you spit no more blood out in front of my house," Pat yelled, knowing that somehow she'd be blamed for it.

"What I'm s'pposed to do?" Marcus tried not to swallow.

"You could come up to wash your mouth out, and Freddy could come, too . . . so you act right," Gayle offered.

"Gaa-yle." Pat shot her friend a scalding glance, which was answered by Gayle's "Oh come on, just this once" smile. Pat sighed and reluctantly opened the door. "But y'all have to be outta here by four. No kidding." Everybody could do their business by then.

They rumbled up the steps and into the apartment. Pat hurried Gayle into the bathroom and tried to confine the others to the narrow hall, except that meant they were right outside the bathroom and Gayle wouldn't pee until they moved. The boys were remanded to the living room.

"Dag, you sleep on the couch?" Marcus poked the pile of clumsily folded sheets and blankets.

"None a your business and keep your ole nasty hands offa my stuff." Pat emerged from the kitchen and handed Marcus a napkin for his mouth. She missed her bed in Swan City. It was near a window, and she would lie at night counting the stars beyond a clutch of scruffy pine trees except when there was thunder and lightning. Then she would take her covers and hide with MaRay in the pantry, where there were no windows and nothing electric. Ma would tell stories about when she was little while they waited out the storm. The sofa was comfortable, though, and she could watch TV in her pajamas with all the lights out when she was by herself at night.

"What'cha gon' show me?" Marcus zeroed in on Freddy, forgetting his injured mouth.

Freddy knelt on the parquet linoleum and carefully loosened the drawstring of his bag. The hood of his jacket fell forward, obscuring most of his face. "You gotta swear not to tell. You hear me . . . never . . . nobody." Freddy hunched over like a wizard fiercely protecting the secret magic hidden in his pouch. Pat's curiosity drew her closer. "You too. You have to swear." Caution, fear, and excitement tinged his solemn voice. Good sense told Pat that Freddy should take his bag, its contents, and his brother and get out because Aunt Verna was going to call any minute, but her eleven-year-old need to know made her slowly nod yes as she crossed her heart and swore not to tell.

Freddy milked the anticipation. "I shouldn't be showing you this. Y'all just kids, but . . ." He reached inside and slowly, reverently, withdrew his secret by its black, plastic handle.

Patricia's mouth dropped open as she backed away. "You gotta get outta here. Now . . . you gotta leave . . ."

Marcus swelled with an excited intake of air. "Where'd you get it? That's a toy, man. That ain't no real gun." Marcus looked skeptically at the Saturday night special.

"This ain't no toy, chump. I found it. On the way to school . . . next to a garbage can in Baisley Park."

"You lie . . . Lemme hold it." Marcus sprang toward Freddy.

Time oozed in thick oily seconds. Pat wanted to be outside again, waving good-bye to Gayle, but she couldn't alter the past or grab hold of the present enough to change it.

"Naw, man . . . it's dangerous." Freddy moved to tuck the gun away.

Dense and slippery, the time slick spread.

"I bet you never saw lips like these." Gayle sashayed from the bathroom, her mouth painted with Verna's lipstick in a plum so deep it looked like crude. She stopped cold when she saw the melee.

"Come on . . . lemme hold it." Marcus reached around Freddy, grabbing at the pistol.

"Stop, Marcus!"

But he couldn't, and the boys locked, struggling over the weapon.

"Marcus, cut it . . ." A crackle, no louder than a finger snap, stopped them all. Pat saw Freddy fall through Marcus's arms and land on the floor in slow motion. Then the shrill ring of the phone cut the thick silence. Pat knew it was her aunt, and she couldn't answer.

"Get up," Marcus commanded, standing over his brother. "Quit playin'." He took hold of Freddy's shoulder and turned him faceup. Gayle screeched. Freddy's mouth opened and closed, opened and closed, but no words escaped. Marcus pleaded, "Come on, get up," but then the scarlet trickled from the corner of Freddy's lips. Pat knelt and unzipped his parka, revealing the small hole and the big wet spot on the front of his striped velour shirt.

Stumbling clear of hearing and the sick, greasy knot in her throat, Pat found the phone and called for help.

Time blurred and focused. In the lucid moments Pat said just tell the truth, you didn't do it on purpose, but Gayle ranted they would all rot in jail if they told that Marcus and Freddy had fought over the gun. "Freddy tripped over his books. It was an accident," she insisted. Marcus paced, not uttering a sound, like something wild that was cornered.

Sirens blared. Paramedics worked feverishly on Freddy as a cop ushered the children outside past the crowd that had gathered and bundled them into a patrol car. A quiet man in a brown tweed coat squatted next to the open door and asked what happened. Without hesitation Marcus told about coming upstairs to wash his bloody mouth, what Freddy said about finding the gun, and heaping the lie on the pile of truth, about how Freddy stumbled over his books and fell on the gun and it went off. Pat and Gayle nodded their agreement. After a few more questions Tweed Coat left them alone.

They knew it wasn't snowing anymore. They knew there were no handles on the inside of the police car doors. They knew they were scared. And they knew they would keep Marcus's secret.

"But what happens when Freddy wakes up? He'll tell the truth," Pat asked.

Gayle and Marcus looked startled by this thought, but before they could answer a cop got in the car and started the engine.

"Freddy's okay, right?" Gayle asked.

The cop sighed, tossed his cap on top of a clipboard in the front seat, and ran a hand through his hair. "I'm sorry, kids."

And then they knew that Freddy was dead. Gayle wailed like a banshee. Pat tried to comfort her. Marcus clutched his arms around himself like a straitjacket and stared out the window, clenching and releasing his jaw, the salty taste of blood still in his mouth.

Gayle's parents arrived at the precinct house first, and as soon as Gayle saw them she dissolved in tears. Loretta gathered her daughter into her lap. She wiped Gayle's eyes, cleaned the lipstick smeared around her mouth, and rocked her. Joseph watched, looking pained and sucking so deeply on a cigarette, he barely exhaled any smoke. Eventually Gayle calmed down enough to answer questions for the detective. When she explained what she was doing at Pat's, Joseph said, "But you know to come straight home after school."

"Hush, Joseph. The child's been punished enough," Loretta said.

When Tweed Coat finished with Gayle, Joseph and Loretta tried to take her home, but she got hysterical, refusing to abandon Pat and Marcus, so they stayed.

Booker Carter appeared, still wearing his blue-gray postal uniform and thick-soled black shoes. Ethel, his wife, was too upset to come, so he had a neighbor stay with her. Booker's shoulders always listed to the left to mark the place where his mailbag hung, but now they both slumped, the weight of his sons a heavier burden than he could bear.

Marcus sat, head bowed, silent, wedged in the corner of a wooden bench. He saw the black shoes, polished to shine like patent despite the snow, and raised his eyes to meet his father's, but the pain he saw in a split second was blinding, and he lowered them again.

Booker T. Washington Carter, Jr., had a government job. That meant he had done better in life than his father, but he felt that the prophecy of his great name had not been fulfilled. When his sons were born, he decided to give them each their own great name legacy, and with it their own chance at something more. But now that hope, that wish for better lives for his sons, leaked like tears from the corners of his heart.

Tweed Coat escorted Booker to an office and spoke to him in sympathetic official tones. It was terrible about his son. The police had reason to believe the gun was ditched after a liquor store robbery, and by the way, where was Freddy last night?

"My son ain't robbed no liquor store," Booker said with finality.

After more questions and paperwork Tweed Coat told Booker he'd have to go to the morgue and identify the body, then he brought Marcus in. The boy told his story, showing his bloody lip and telling the tale of Freddy's fall. When they were done father took son lightly by the arm. Booker walked like his legs wouldn't carry him much farther, and when they got to the door he gave way, slumped against the frame, and sobbed open and unashamed. His shoulders heaved, his face glistened with tears. "Oh Lawd, why did you take my boy?" The hustle bustle of the room quieted to an embarrassed, nervous murmur. And Marcus, who had never seen his father cry, wished with all his heart he was dead, too.

In a minute Booker collected himself, mopped his face with his handkerchief, and took Marcus home to his mother.

Verna came in the door, black leather coat flapping, cussing, the sour malt smell of Johnny Walker Red punctuating every word. "Where the shit is she?" A Salem dangled from her lips and wagged as she spoke. Pat, who sat staring at her fat knees, still shiny from this morning's greasing, flinched when she heard the gritty voice. She steeled for the harangue.

"Goddam police draggin' me down here 'cause this little bitch decides she's gon' have a party while I'm out workin' my ass off. Knew from the git-go you wasn't never gon' be nothin' but trouble."

Gayle tuned up to cry again. Pat tried to explain, but went silent when Verna raised the back of her hand. The blow landed with a resounding whack on Pat's cheek. Joseph rose from his seat, but Tweed Coat intervened and led Pat and Verna, still fussing, to his office.

Pat answered questions the best she could with Verna's commentary in the background. Tweed Coat seemed nice, and Pat wanted to tell him she was a good girl and show him her report card as proof, but she just told him what he needed to know and told it the way they all promised they would. When he was done with her he asked her to wait outside on the bench. He wanted to talk to Verna alone.

Verna's outbursts periodically interrupted the hum of the station house. "None a your damn business what time I get home," or "Ain't nobody give me nothin' 'cept her, and I *didn't* want that." With each outburst Gayle and Pat huddled closer, Loretta cringed and gave Joseph her "I told you about that woman" look. Pat stiffened when she heard the furious tap-tapping of Verna's high-heeled boots against the green-and-gray tiled floor. Hand jammed into waist and disappearing into a roll of flesh, Verna posed in front of her niece. Pat stood automatically.

"Don't be too hard on the girl," Joseph said, gathering his family to leave.

Verna cut her eyes. "Maybe you ought to stop mindin' my business and ask your child what she and them boys was doin' in my house." She pinched the shoulder of Pat's coat, snapped, "Come on," and propelled her into the night.

The day of the funeral Pat and Gayle clutched hands in their pew of the storefront Temple of the Lord, trying to be brave. Loretta and Joseph sat beside them, looking weary.

Pat listened to "Just As I Am," played low on the organ, and tried to ignore her stinging legs, a reminder of the extension-cord whipping she got the night of the shooting. In Swan City, church was part of every week, but Verna didn't hold much with religion, so Pat hadn't been to church since MaRay's funeral. Now, Pat heard Ma's alto singing, ". . . Without one plea, But that thy blood was shed for me." That's when she saw Freddy in his blood-soaked shirt and closed her eyes to stay the tears.

Frightened, but unable to look away, Gayle stared at the array of flowers guarding the white casket. She thought the ruffly lining looked like Reddi Whip. Then she saw the arm of Freddy's white suit, and a vision of Marcus and Freddy, caked in snow, flashed in her mind. She shuddered and faced Pat, whose lids fluttered open. Silently Gayle asked, "This all happened, didn't it? Freddy's really dead?" Pat's eyes answered back, "Yes."

Just then the Carter family entered the church. Booker supported Ethel, who moaned helplessly, "My baby . . . oh my baby . . ." Marcus followed solemnly, wearing a baggy blue suit. He looked vacant. Holding-back tears hung at the corners of Pat's eyes when she saw him. As he passed their pew, Gayle began to sob, and Marcus paused long enough to give her his handkerchief. Gayle peered at it, then timidly looked at him. *He doesn't hate me.* She clutched the starched square as he continued up the aisle.

The preacher worked the congregation until he dripped sweat, and their misery flowed in anguished sobs and shouts. Freddy's baseball coach spoke movingly of the wasted potential and promise. As the soloist sang "His Eye Is on the Sparrow," ushers signaled each pew to file by the casket and say good-bye to Freddy. By the time their row was called Gayle was crying so hard that Joseph stayed behind and cradled her as she clutched the now sodden handkerchief. Pat followed Loretta to the front of the church. On either side of Freddy's head were white satin pillows, lettered in gold, one "Son," one "Brother." His skin looked chalky to Pat. *Just like MaRay did.* When she stood opposite Marcus, she didn't know what to say. There was nothing *to* say. He reached out and took her hand in a dry-cold grip, and she leaned in and kissed him on the cheek, then moved on.

When it was time for the family's farewells, Ethel Carter tried to climb into the coffin. "Leave him be. He's just restin'," she wailed, and had to be restrained until Marcus spoke. "It's okay, Mom. It'll be okay," he said, but in her mind it was Freddy talking, and she calmed down, saying, "See, I told you he was just sleep."

Gayle's folks decided not to go to the cemetery, afraid the scene would be too hard on the girls. After a lunch they all picked over, they left Pat at her door as Verna had instructed, looking small and frightened despite her valiant front.

Pat dragged upstairs, wishing she could have gone home with Gayle, but grateful her aunt was already gone. She just wanted to lie down and wait for the pounding in her head to stop. Her breath rose in puffy clouds, which meant the landlord had let the oil tank run dry again, so she tried to light the oven. Holding the match over the hole and turning the knob at the same time proved a greater challenge than Pat was up to, and each time she bent over, her head throbbed harder, so she gave up. Still wearing her coat and hat, she lay on the sofa, swaddled in her blanket, and wished for MaRay. Then, she bolted up and rummaged through the plaid fabric suitcase that still held everything she had brought with her from Swan City until she found it.

After MaRay was buried in the old cemetery behind the church, everybody had come back to the house. They ate and drank, and people started taking things, knickknacks or the silver cream pitcher, "something to remember her by." Pat wanted something, too, so she sneaked into MaRay's bedroom while the others were busy reminiscing. It was strange being in the dark, crowded room. It still smelled like her, like lavender soap and sassafras tea. Pat reached way in the back corner of the mahogany chifforobe, behind the shoes, avoiding the mousetrap, and found the bergamot tin where MaRay kept her good jewelry, the jet cluster earrings, the Sunday strand of just-like-real pearls she bought at the Belks in Raleigh, a cuff link with fancy letters Pat liked to trace with her finger, and the one lacy gold hoop earring. Ma had laughed 'til she cried when Pat asked if her daddy was a pirate.

Holding the tin made it seem that Ma was with her, and Pat settled back into the blanket and closed her eyes, clutching the box in the hand she shoved in her pocket.

That siren sounds like it's right outside. Pat thought only minutes had passed, that the clanking she heard was still her headache. *But at least it's a little warmer.* Good, I won't have to hear Aunt Verna cuss the landlord when she gets home.

". . . a few more blocks." ". . . not gonna make it . . ." *Who's talking?* But the voices were jumbled and unfamiliar . . . *I musta left the TV on.* Pat tried to open her eyes, but her lids felt leaden. *Ma, I dreamed about her . . . back in Swan City . . . I was following her down the dirt road and she turned around.* "Go on back chile, you can't come with me. Not now . . ."

"Hey, I think she's comin' 'round!" Pat felt like she was hurtling through space, but when she tried to move she was stunned to find herself firmly strapped in place. Forcing her eyes to open a sliver, she saw a plastic bag of clear liquid suspended in the air and swinging like a manic pendulum. Fear gripped her, but she tried to speak and found her mouth was covered. "That's right, just keep breathin' . . . Pat . . . that's your name, right? We're pulling in right now, you're gonna be okey-dokey, Patty."

The rest was a banging of doors, a blur of doctors, nurses, needles, questions. "What?" "How?" "When?" "Who?" And answers; "I don't know." "Yes." "No." "I don't know." *What did I do wrong?* Voices hovered nearby. ". . . gas on . . ." ". . . so thick your eyes watered . . ." ". . . could be a suicide, but she's so young" ". . . thank God for the neighbors . . ." "Where are her parents?"

Pat heard her name. Slowly, the fog lifted. Pat still didn't understand what had happened, but she knew it was bad. Then a woman who smelled vaguely of mothballs started asking questions again. Before Pat could answer, she heard it. Tap-click. Tap-click. Tap-click.

"What the fuck she do now?" Verna never did get those raggedy boots fixed. The steel shank had worn through the rubber lift and sidewalk-shredded leather curled around the heel. "First she let some boy get offed in my house . . ." The rings holding the pale yellow curtain around Pat's cubicle trembled noisily against the rod as the drape flew open. The

Ambush Verna had generously dabbed behind her ears and poured down her cleavage mixed with Johnny Red, cigarettes, and her own musk, creating a heady, unique perfume.

"Mrs. Reid?" The woman who'd been questioning Pat stepped forward into the scented smoky air that surrounded Verna.

Verna stepped back. "The only Mrs. Reid's my momma, and she's dead." Her head and shoulders rocked and rolled, an indignant choreography for each word.

Pat watched helplessly from her bed.

"Who the hell are you? You a cop like him?" She nodded toward the policeman who stood by the doorway. "Bein' stupid ain't no crime, las' time I checked!" Chuckling at her own humor, she looked at Pat. Then, momentarily distracted, dug feverishly in her purse.

Pat wished she could melt right into the covers. She didn't know how any of this had happened, but Aunt Verna, who finally found her pack of Salems, was definitely drunk.

"I'm not a policewoman, I'm with the Department of Social Services."

"That's the Welfare. I ain't on no Welfare!" Verna huffed drunkenly, and put a cigarette to her lips.

"It's better if you don't smoke in here," the officer said.

"Better for who?" Verna retorted, and struck a match. "Fuck you, naw come to think of it, a cop's a lousy lay. The only thing they shoot off is they mouth and they gun!"

Pat closed her eyes and silently inched down until the sheet covered her mouth.

"Please put that out. There's oxygen in use." He indicated the sign.

Verna touched the match to the end of her cigarette. "It's a free country." She took a drag. "They can take that sign and shove it up they . . ."

The policeman snatched Verna by the sleeve. The rip under the arm of her black leather coat sputtered farther along the seam as Verna drew back her arm and landed a punch on the cop's nose. Pat wanted to explain that her aunt didn't mean it, she just got mad sometimes. But a swarm of guards pulled Verna away in a cloud of cussin'.

The next day, Pat was surprised when the social worker arrived and helped her dress. Undershirt and socks accompanied questions about Pat's home life, which she answered as best she could. Yes, she was alone sometimes, but she didn't mind. Aunt Verna was nice enough to take her in, and she promised not to be any more trouble.

"Why do you call your mother Aunt Verna?"

Pat looked puzzled. "My momma's dead." She wasn't sure of much right now, but she was sure of that. She reached for her coat, pulled MaRay's bergamot tin from her pocket, and pried open the lid. "See. This stuff was hers." *If MaRay was here now, she'd fix everything.*

Then, the woman sat her on the bed and slowly, like she was talking to a three-year-old, proceeded to rewrite the story of Pat's life. Verna went from the aunt who rescued her to the mother who threw her away. *MaRay was my grandmother?* Pat lost her grip on the bergamot tin and it clattered to the floor. She couldn't make her arms move to get it. Putting those things back in the box wasn't going to help. She wanted to stomp the beads and earrings into dust, but the woman got down on all fours and continued talking while she picked them up.

". . . only assault" ". . . But the cocaine possession . . ." "jail." ". . . custody." "Hearing . . ." ". . . group home." "Foster parents . . ." ". . . court order."

Finally the social worker placed the small metal box in Pat's palm, folded her fingers around it, and asked if she understood everything. Pat nodded yes mechanically, but she hadn't heard much above the roar of her own thoughts. *They wouldn't all lie to me? She must be wrong. Aunt Verna can't be my mother.* Pat put on her coat and sat in the wheelchair. *And where am I going now?* She felt her throat constrict against the bitter taste biting at the back of her tongue. *I won't throw up.*

Outside an icy gust whipped candy wrappers and newspaper scraps into a motley whirlwind on the snow-clogged street, but Pat didn't feel the cold. She climbed into the battered green Dodge and rested her head against the frosty car window. The last thing that made sense was waving good-bye to Gayle as the Saunderses drove off. *I won't cry. I won't.*

Pat felt like she'd entered the Twilight Zone, and from the moment she'd crossed her heart and promised Freddy she wouldn't tell she'd slipped through an invisible crack in the world and landed in another dimension.